THE SHERBROOKE BRIDE

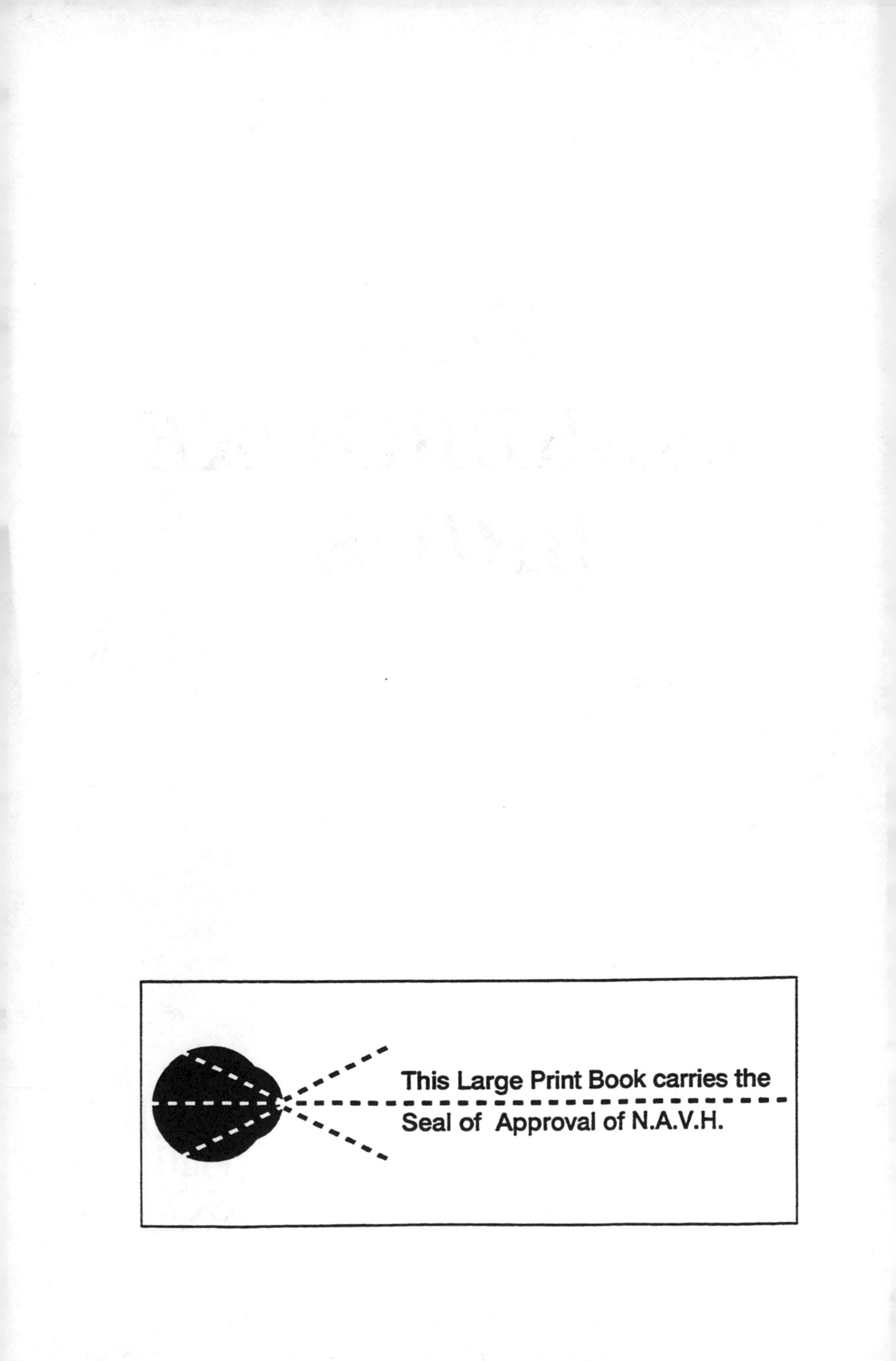
This Large Print Book carries the
Seal of Approval of N.A.V.H.

THE SHERBROOKE BRIDE

Catherine Coulter

G.K. Hall & Co.
Thorndike, Maine

Published in 1995 by arrangement with
The Berkley Publishing Group.

G.K. Hall Large Print Romance Collection.

The text of this Large Print edition is unabridged.
Other aspects of this book may vary from the original edition.

Set in 16 pt. News Plantin by Juanita Macdonald.

Printed in the United States on permanent paper.

Library of Congress Cataloging in Publication Data

Coulter, Catherine.
The Sherbrooke bride / Catherine Coulter.
p. cm.
ISBN 0-7838-1293-0 (lg. print : hc)
1. Large type books. I. Title.
[PS3553.O843S54 1995]
813'.54—dc20 95-9761

To David,

The Good, the Sexy, the Humorist, the Competent. I hope you laugh as much reading this novel as I did writing it. Do try it out on beautiful Lori.

CHAPTER 1

Northcliffe Hall
Near New Romney, England
May 1803

"I saw her last night — the Virgin Bride!"

"Oh no, not really? Truly, Sinjun? You swear you saw the ghost?"

There were two shuddering gasps and fluttery cries of mingled fear and excitement.

"Yes, it had to be the Virgin Bride."

"Did she tell you she was a virgin? Did she tell you anything? Weren't you terrified? Was she all white? Did she moan? Did she look more dead than alive?"

Their voices grew fainter, but he still heard the gasps and giggles as they moved away from the estate room door.

Douglas Sherbrooke, Earl of Northcliffe, closed the door firmly and walked to his desk. That damned ghost! He wondered if the Sherbrookes were fated to endure unlikely tales of this miserable young lady throughout eternity. He glanced down at the neat piles of papers, sighed, then sat himself down and looked ahead at nothing at all.

The earl frowned. He was frowning a lot these days for they were keeping after him, not letting up for a day, not for a single hour. He was bombarded by gentle yet insistent reminders day in and day out with only slight variations on the same dull theme. He must needs marry and provide an heir for the earldom. He was getting older, every minute another minute ticked away his virility, and that virility was being squandered, according to them, for from his seed sprang future Sherbrookes, and this wondrous seed of his must be used legitimately and not spread haphazardly about, as warned of in the Bible.

He would be thirty on Michaelmas, they would say, all those uncles and aunts and cousins and elderly retainers who'd known him since he'd come squalling from his mother's womb, all those sniggering rotten friends of his, who, once they'd caught onto the theme, were enthusiastic in singing their own impertinent verses. He would frown at all of them, as he was frowning now, and he would say that he wasn't thirty on *this* Michaelmas, he was going to be twenty-nine on *this* Michaelmas, therefore on this day, at this minute, he was twenty-eight, and for God's sake, it was only May now, not September. He was barely settled into his twenty-eighth year. He was just now accustoming himself to saying he was twenty-eight and no longer twenty-seven. Surely his wasn't a great age, just ample.

The earl looked over at the gilded ormolu clock on the mantel. Where was Ryder? Damn his brother, he knew their meetings were always held on the first Tuesday of every quarter, here in the estate room of Northcliffe Hall at precisely three o'clock. Of course, the fact that the earl had only initiated these quarterly meetings upon his selling out of the army some nine months before, just after the signing of the Peace of Amiens, didn't excuse Ryder for being late for this, their third meeting. No, his brother should be censured despite the fact that Douglas's steward, Leslie Danvers, a young man of industrious habits and annoying memory, had reminded the earl just an hour before of the meeting with his brother.

It was the sudden sight of Ryder bursting into the estate room, windblown, smelling of leather and horse and the sea, alive as the wind, showing lots of white teeth, very nearly on time — it was only five minutes past the hour — that made the earl forget his ire. After all, Ryder was nearing an ample age himself. He was very nearly twenty-six.

The two of them should stick together.

"Lord, but it's a beautiful day, Douglas! I was riding with Dorothy on the cliffs, nothing like it, I tell you, nothing!" Ryder sat down, crossed his buckskin legs, and provided his brother more of his white-toothed smile.

Douglas swung a brooding leg. "Did you manage to stay on your horse?"

Ryder smiled more widely. His eyes, upon closer inspection, appeared somewhat vague. He had the look of a sated man, a look the earl was becoming quite familiar with, and so he sighed.

"Well," Ryder said after another moment of silence, "if you insist upon these quarterly meetings, Douglas, I must do something to keep them going."

"But Dorothy Blalock?"

"The widow Blalock is quite soft and sweet-smelling, brother, and she knows how to please a man. Ah, does she ever do it well. Also, she'll not get caught. She's much too smart for that, my Dorothy."

"She sits a horse well," Douglas said. "I'll admit that."

"Aye, and that's not all she sits well."

Only through intense resolve did Douglas keep his grin to himself. He was the earl; he was the head of the far-flung Sherbrooke family. Even now there might be another Sherbrooke growing despite Dorothy's intelligence.

"Let's get on with it," Douglas said, but Ryder wasn't fooled. He saw the twitch of his brother's lip and laughed.

"Yes, let's," he agreed, rose, and poured himself a brandy. He raised the decanter toward Douglas.

"No, thank you. Now," Douglas continued, reading the top sheet of paper in front of him, "as of this quarter you have four quite healthy sons, four quite healthy daughters. Poor little Daniel died during the winter. Amy's fall doesn't appear to have had lasting injury to her leg. Is this up-to-date?"

"I will have another baby making his appearance in August. The mother appears hardy and healthy."

Douglas sighed. "Very well. Her name?" As Ryder replied, he wrote. He raised his head. "Is this now correct?"

Ryder lost his smile and downed the rest of his brandy. "No. Benny died of the ague last week."

"You didn't tell me."

Ryder shrugged. "He wasn't even a year old, but so bright, Douglas. I knew you were busy, what with the trip to London to the war office, and the funeral was small. That's the way his mother wanted it."

"I'm sorry," Douglas said again. Then he frowned, a habit Ryder had noticed and didn't like one bit, and said, "If the babe is due in August, why didn't you tell me at our last quarterly meeting?"

Ryder said simply, "The mother didn't tell me because she feared I wouldn't wish to bed her anymore." He paused, looking at the east lawn through the wide bay windows. "Silly wench. I wouldn't have guessed she was with child although I suppose I might have suspected. She's already quite great with child. She may well give me twins."

Ryder turned from the window and swigged more brandy. "I forgot, Douglas. There's also Nancy."

Douglas dropped the paper. "Nancy who?"

"Nancy Arbuckle, the draper's daughter on High Street in Rye. She's with child, my child. She will have it in November, best guess. She was all tears and woes until I told her she needn't worry, that the Sherbrookes always took care of their own. It's possible she might even wed a sea captain for he isn't concerned that she's carrying another man's child."

"Well, that's something." Douglas did a new tally then looked up. "You're currently supporting seven children and their mothers. You have impregnated two more women and all their children are due this year."

"I think that's right. Don't forget the possibility of the twins or the possibility of Nancy marrying her sea captain."

"Can't you keep your damned rod in your pants?"

"No more than you can, Douglas."

"Fair enough, but why can't you remove yourself from the woman before you fill her with your seed?"

Ryder flushed, a rather remarkable occurrence, and said, his voice defensive, "I can't seem to keep my wits together. I know it isn't much of an excuse, but I just can't seem to withdraw once I'm there, so to speak." He stared hard at his brother then. "I'm not a damned cold fish like you, Douglas. You could withdraw from an angel herself. Doesn't your mind ever run off its track, doesn't it ever turn into vapor? Don't you ever want to just keep pounding and pounding and the consequences simply don't come into it?"

"No."

Ryder sighed. "Well, I'm not so well disciplined as you. Do you still have only the two children?"

"No, the babe died whilst I was in London. There is only Cynthia left now, a sweet child, four years old."

"I'm sorry."

"It was expected and just a matter of time so the doctors kept telling his mother. I went to London not just to see Lord Avery in the War Office but also to see Elizabeth. She'd written me about the babe's condition. His lungs never really properly developed." Douglas drew out a clean sheet of foolscap and adjusted last quarter's numbers.

"Your lust becomes more costly," he said after a moment. "Damned costly."

"Stop your frowns, Douglas. You're bloody wealthy, as am I. Great-uncle Brandon would be pleased that his inheritance to me is being put to such excellent use. He was a lusty old fellow until his eightieth year, as least that's what he told me. Bragged like a bat he did.

"You're always saying that our bastards are our responsibility and so I agree with you. I also agree with this plan of yours, for it ensures we don't miss any. What a general you would have made! A pity you had to sell out when you were only a major."

Ryder was chuckling when the estate room door

opened. He looked up to see his youngest brother come somewhat diffidently into the room. "Ah, if it isn't Tysen. Come in, brother, our meeting is nearly done. Douglas has already told me my lust must soon poke holes in my pocketbook. Now he is completing his mathematics, truly a meager number, particularly when one considers what one could do with more available fields to plow and sow and tend."

"What meeting?" asked Tysen Sherbrooke, coming into the estate room. "What numbers? What fields?"

Ryder shot a look at Douglas, who just shrugged and sat back in his chair, his arms folded across his chest. He looked ironic, and if Ryder hadn't known him so well, he would have thought him annoyed rather than obliquely amused.

Ryder said to Douglas, "Look, brother, Tysen wants to be a vicar. It's important that he understand male frailties and that, without mincing matters, is basic lust. Attend me, Tysen, this is our quarterly meeting to determine the current number of Sherbrooke bastards."

Tysen stared, then turned an agonized eye toward Douglas. "Your *what?*"

"You heard me," Ryder said. "Now, you're nearly twenty-one, Tysen. It's time you come to our meetings. Isn't it time we included him, Douglas? After all, we don't want him sneaking in a bastard all unknown to us, do we? Think of our reputation. All right, my lad, have you gotten any of the local girls with child?"

Tysen looked apoplectic. "Of course not! I wouldn't ever do anything so despicable! I will be a man of God, a vicar, a shepherd who will lead a righteous and devout flock and —"

Ryder rolled his eyes. "Please, stop! It boggles the mind that a Sherbrooke could speak thusly and believe it. It makes one want to puke. Ah well, it's too bad that you are what you appear to be, Tysen, but one always hopes, particularly if one is of an optimistic nature."

"Does optimism go hand in rod with lust?" Douglas said to the room at large.

Ryder laughed and Tysen looked stunned. He knew his brothers were men of the world, that they understood many things that he'd scarce thought about, but this humor? A meeting to count up their bastards? Sweat broke out on his forehead. He began to inch toward the door.

"At least smile, Tysen," Douglas said. "A vicar can have a sense of humor, you know."

"Oh no," Tysen said. "It's just that — of course I can smile, it's just that —"

"You're not finishing any of your sentences, Tysen," Ryder said, his tone utterly irreverent. "You're repeating yourself."

"Well, a man of God can also share his boundless love with a specific sort of love. You know, I can also love a lady, and, well, I do!"

"Oh Jesus," Ryder said, turning away in amused disgust. "Do you want some brandy now, Douglas?"

"That's nauseating," Douglas said, "and I probably couldn't keep the brandy down, so no, Ryder." Then he took some pity on Tysen, whose lean cheeks were alarmingly red. "Who is the chit, Tysen? Surely as you're a future vicar, she's no actress or shop girl?"

"No," Tysen said, his voice strengthening, now bordering on very unvicarlike worship. "Her name is Melinda Beatrice and she's Sir Thomas Hardesty's daughter."

Ryder cursed. "I know the wench. She's silly, Douglas, and she simpers, for God's sake, and she acts as if she's better than everyone else, and she's got no breasts to speak of. Her eyes look watery, her elbows are bony, and she's got two names and her parents use both of them. It's beyond too much. Two names!"

"She will make a fine wife for a man of God!" Tysen would have further defended his goddess, but he stopped abruptly as Douglas slowly rose from his chair, staring at him. Ryder's insults were forgotten under Douglas's look, an expression that was alarmingly identical to their now-dead father's. Tysen began to step back, slowly, slowly, until he was hard against the closed door. Douglas said ever so softly, "You mean to tell me that at twenty years of age you've decided to fancy yourself in love with a girl who is your equal in birth and fortune? We are speaking of the Hardestys of Blaston Manor?"

"Yes," Tysen said. "I'm nearly twenty-one."

"Young fool," Ryder said dispassionately, flicking a dust mote off his sleeve. "He'll get over it within the month, Douglas. Remember how you thought you wanted that duke's daughter? When was that — yes, some three years ago, you fancied yourself tip over arse in love. You were home with that shoulder wound. Now, what was her name? Melissande — yes, that was it."

Douglas sliced his hand through the air, silencing Ryder. "You haven't spoken to Sir Thomas, have you?"

"Of course not," Tysen said. "You're the head of the family, Douglas."

"Don't forget it, no one else allows me to. Now, just promise me you'll not declare yourself when the chit smiles at you, or gives you a glimpse of her ankle. I've determined that girls must be born knowing all sorts of tricks to entice the unwary male, so you must be on your guard, all right?"

Tysen nodded, then said quickly, "But not Melinda Beatrice, Douglas. She's kind and honest. She has a sweetness about her, a goodness, that will make her a wonderful shepherdess to my flock, a helpmeet to cherish. She would never —" He saw that both brothers were on the verge of incredulous laughter. His jaw tightened, his brows lowered, his back stiffened, and he said, "That's not why I came in, Douglas. Aunt Mildred and Uncle Albert are here and want to speak with you."

"Ha! Preach to me is more like it. I suppose you told the servants to bag it and volunteered yourself to come find me so as to escape their eagle eyes?"

"Well, yes." Tysen paused when Douglas groaned, then went on in an apologetic voice, "Yes, you're right about their visit. I heard them speaking about the Marquess of Dacre's eldest daughter, Juliette, a diamond of the first order, Aunt Mildred was saying, and just perfect for you."

Douglas looked sardonic and remained silent as a stone.

"God grant you long life, Douglas," Ryder said with fervor. "I respect you and am grateful to my toes that you are the eldest son and thus the Fourth Earl of Northcliffe, the Sixth Viscount Hammersmith, the Ninth Baron Sanderleigh, and therefore the target of all their cannon."

"I respect you too, Douglas," Tysen said. "You make a fine earl, viscount, and baron, and I'm certain Uncle Albert and Aunt Mildred think so too. All the family agree if only you'd marry and —"

"Oh God, not you too, Tysen! Well, there's no hope for it," Douglas added as he rose from his chair. "Ah, Tysen, your gratitude will make me endure, no doubt. Pray for me, little brother. Our meeting for this quarter is adjourned, Ryder. I believe I'll speak to your valet, Tinker, and see if he can't sew your randy sex into your breeches."

"Poor Tinker would be appalled to be assigned such a service."

"Well, I can't ask one of the maids. That surely would defeat the purpose. I vow you would break our pact if one of the younger ones did the task."

"Poor Douglas," Ryder said as his brother left the room.

"What did Douglas mean about your pact?" Ryder asked.

"Oh, we have both vowed that any female in our employ is not to be touched. When you are safely out of love, and thus your wits are yours again, we will gain your assurances as well."

Tysen decided not to argue with his brother. He was above that. He would be a vicar; his thoughts and deeds would be spiritual. Also, to the best of his memory, he'd never won an argument with either brother, and thus said, "This girl they're going to batter at him about is supposedly quite wonderful."

"They're all wonderful with pillow sheets over their heads," Ryder said and walked out of the estate room.

Leaning against a dark mahogany Spanish table was Sinjun, her arms crossed, looking as negligent and indifferent as a potato, and whistling. She stopped when she saw that Ryder saw her, and said with a wonderfully bland voice, "So, how went the meeting?"

"Keep your tongue behind your teeth, brat."

"Now, Ryder, I'm young, true, but I'm not stupid."

"Forget it, Sinjun."

"How are all your Beloved Ones?"

"They all do very well, thank you."

"I'm silent as a soap dish," she said, grinned at him, blew him a kiss, and walked toward the kitchen, whistling again, like a boy.

CHAPTER 2

The earl wasn't frowning. He was anxious and he felt in his innards that something was going to happen, something he wasn't going to like. He hated such feelings because they made him feel helpless and vulnerable; on the other hand he knew it would be stupid to ignore them. Because the government was in disarray, and that damned fool Addington was dithering about like a headless cock, he thought that this anxiety in his innards must spring from his fear of Napoleon.

Like all Englishmen who lived on the southern coast of England, he worried about an invasion. It didn't seem likely, since the English ruled the Channel, but then again, only a fool would disregard a man of Napoleon's military genius and his commitment to the destruction of the English.

Douglas dismounted from his stallion, Garth, and strode to the cliff edge. Surf pounded at the rocks at the base of the cliff, spewing plumes of white-foamed water thirty feet into the air. He sucked the salt air into his lungs, felt it gritty and wet against his face. The wind was strong and sharp, blowing his hair about his head, making his eyes water. The day was cloudy and gray. He couldn't see France today, but when the sky was clear, he could see Boulogne from this vantage and the bleak coastline to the northeast toward Calais. He shaded his eyes and stared into the grayness. The clouds roiled and overlapped, but didn't part, rather they thickened and seemed to press fatly together. He didn't turn when he heard the horse approach and halt near him.

"I thought you would be here, Douglas. This is your favorite place to think."

He smiled even as he was turning to greet his young sister seated astride her mare, Fanny. "I see I shouldn't be so predictable. I didn't see you at breakfast, Sinjun, or at lunch. Was Mother punishing you for some infraction?"

"Oh no, I forgot the time. I was studying my —" She broke off, lightly slipped out of the saddle and strode toward him, a tall, thin girl, with long legs and wild pale hair that swirled thick and curly around her face, hair once held at the nape of her neck with a ribbon, no doubt, a ribbon now long lost. Her eyes were a vivid sky blue, clear as the day was gray and filled with humor and intelligence. All of his siblings had the Sherbrooke blue eyes and the thick light hair, though Sinjun's was lighter and filled with sunlight. All except him.

Douglas was the changeling, his eyes as dark as sin, his old nanny had happily told him many years before, aye, and he looked like a heathen

Celt, all dark and swarthy, his black hair making him look like the master of the cloven hoof himself.

When he was very young, he'd overheard his father accusing his mother of cuckolding him, for his son looked like no Sherbrooke in either their painted or recorded history. His mother, Douglas recalled, had apologized profusely for what she accepted as her error in the production of this, the implausible Sherbrooke heir. Ryder was fond of telling Douglas that it was this un-Sherbrooke appearance that made everyone obey him instantly, for it made him appear so austere and forbidding.

But as Douglas looked at his sister, his expression wasn't at all severe. She was wearing buckskins, as was he, a loose white shirt, and a light brown leather vest. Their mother, he knew, would shriek like a banshee when and if she saw her young daughter thusly attired. Of course, their mother was always shrieking about something.

"What were you studying?"

"It isn't important. You're worrying again, aren't you?"

"Someone must since our government doesn't seem to want to concern itself with our protection. Napoleon has the best trained and the most seasoned soldiers in all of Europe, and they want to defeat us badly."

"Is it true that Fox will return and rout Addington?"

"He is ill, I hear, and the time isn't yet ripe

enough for him to oust Addington. He is as misguided and as liberal as Addington, but at least he is a leader and not indecisive. I fancy you know as much as I do about the situation." He was well used to his sister's precociousness — not that precisely, but her erudition, the interest in issues and subjects that should have been years beyond her, things that would leave most gentlemen and ladies blank-faced with disinterest. And she seemed to understand him better than either of his brothers or his mother or the myriad of Sherbrooke relatives. He loved her very much.

"No, you're wrong," she said now. "You must have seen a lot when you went to London last week and spoke to all those men. You haven't yet told me the latest mood in the war ministry. Another thing, Douglas, you've armed all the men on our farms and some in the villages as well. You've drilled them over and over again." On the heels of her very adult appraisal, she giggled like the young girl she was, saying, "It was so funny watching Mr. Dalton pretending to beat away the Frogs with that gnarly stick!"

"He was best at retreating and hiding. I'd rather have trained his wife. Now she would be the kind of mean-boned soldier the French would fear."

Sinjun said abruptly, her light blue eyes taking on a gray hue, "I saw the Virgin Bride last night."

"I overheard you telling your friends. Your audience was most appreciative, albeit so gullible it was embarrassing. But, my dear girl, it is all nonsense, and you know it. You must have eaten turnips for dinner and it turned your dreams to phantoms."

"Actually I was reading in the library."

"Oh? I pray you won't tell your mother if you chance to peruse my Greek plays. Her reaction staggers the brain."

She smiled, distracted. "I read them all two years ago, Douglas."

He smacked his palm to his forehead. "I should have known."

"I think the most interesting one was called *Lysistrata*, but I didn't understand how the ladies could expect their husbands to just stop fighting just because they threatened to —"

"Yes, I know what the ladies did," he said quickly, both appalled and amused. He eyed her, wondering if he should attempt some sort of brotherly sermon, or at least a caveat on her reading habits. Before he could think of anything relevant to say, Sinjun continued thoughtfully, "When I went upstairs around midnight, I saw this light beneath the door to the countess's chamber, next to yours. I opened the door as quietly as I could and there she was, standing by the bed, all dressed in white, and she was crying very softly. She looked just like all the stories have described. She was very beautiful, her hair long and straight to her waist and so blond it was almost white. She turned and looked at me, and then she simply vanished. Before she vanished, I swear that she wanted to say something."

"It was turnips," Douglas said. "You forgot you ate them. I cannot credit the ghost. No intelligent person would credit a spiritual phenomenon."

"That is because you haven't seen her and you don't trust a female to report the unvarnished truth. You prefer vegetables for an explanation."

"Turnips, Sinjun, turnips."

"Very well, but I did see her, Douglas."

"Why is it that only women see her?"

Sinjun shrugged. "I don't know if it is only women she's appeared to. All past earls who have written about her have claimed it to be only women, but who really knows? In my experience, gentlemen aren't inclined to admit to anything out of the ordinary. They won't take the risk of looking foolish, I suppose."

Douglas continued, as sardonic as could be. "Your experience, hm? So you think our Virgin Bride was standing over the bed, bemoaning the intactness of her maidenhead, knowing that her bridegroom would never come? Thus she was doomed never to become a wife and a mother?"

"Perhaps."

"More likely the chit remarried within a year, bore sixteen children like every good sixteenth-century woman did, and died of old age, hair straggly and gray, and no teeth in her mouth."

"You're not at all romantic, Douglas." Sinjun turned to watch a hawk fly close overhead, its wings wide and smooth, a beautiful sight. She then gave Douglas a smile that was dazzling in its pleasure. It shocked him. She was a little girl, only fifteen, and this wondrous natural smile gave promise of the woman she would become. Actually, he realized, it scared the hell out of him.

"But I did see her, Douglas, and others have as well. You know there was a young lady whose husband of three hours was murdered and she killed herself when she heard the news. She was only eighteen. She loved him so very much she couldn't bear to live without him. It was tragic. It was written down in full detail by Audley Sherbrooke, the First Earl of Northcliffe. Even Father wrote of her once."

"I know, but you can be certain I shan't write a word about that nonexistent phantom. It is drivel and all reported by hysterical females. You can be certain that your Virgin Bride will end her ceaseless meanderings with me. Doubtless all our ancestors did their recounting during long winters, when they were bored and sought to amuse themselves and their families."

Sinjun merely shook her head at him, touching her fingers to his coat sleeve. "There is no reasoning with you. Did I tell you? My friends — Eleanor and Lucy Wiggins — they're both in love with you. They whisper and giggle and say in the most nauseating way imaginable that they would swoon if only you would smile at them." Then, after that girlish confidence, she added, "You are a natural leader, Douglas, and you made a difference in the army just as you're making a difference here. And I did see the Virgin Bride."

"I hope that may be true. As for you, too many turnips and lewd Greek plays. Oh, and give Eleanor and Lucy another couple of years and it will be Ryder who will draw their female swoons and sighs."

"Oh dear," Sinjun said, her brow furrowing. "You must make Ryder promise not to seduce them for he'll find it an easy task because they're so silly." Sinjun fell silent for Douglas was obviously distracted again.

He was thinking that he would protect what was his just as had his long-ago ancestor, Baron Sanderleigh, who had saved Northcliffe from the Roundhead armies and managed through his superior guile to convince Cromwell of his family's support, and after him, Charles II. Throughout the succeeding generations, the Sherbrookes had continued to refine the fine art of guile to keep themselves and their lands intact. They had provided mistresses of great mental aptitude and physical endowment to kings and ministers, they had excelled in diplomacy, and they had served in the army. It was rumored that Queen Anne had been in love with a Sherbrooke general, a younger son. All in all, they had enriched themselves and kept Northcliffe safe.

He shook his head, backing farther away from the cliff edge. There'd been a recent storm and the ground wasn't all that solid beneath his feet. He warned Sinjun, then fell into abstraction again as he sat on an outcropping of rocks.

"They won't leave you alone, Douglas."

"I know," he said, not bothering to pretend ignorance. "Damn, but they're right and I've been a stubborn bas— fool. I have to marry and I have to impregnate my wife. One thing I learned in the army is that life is more fragile than the wings of a butterfly."

"Yes, and it is your child who must be the future Earl of Northcliffe. I love Ryder dearly, as do you, but he doesn't want the title. He wants to laugh and love his way through life, not spend it with a bailiff poring over account books or hearing the farmers complain about the leaks in their roofs. He doesn't care about all the pomp and dignities and the knee-bending. His is not a serious nature." She grinned and shook her head, scuffing the toe of her riding boot against a rock. "That is, his is not a serious nature about earl sorts of things. Other things are different, of course."

"What the devil does that mean?"

Sinjun just smiled and shrugged.

Douglas realized in that instant that he'd made his mind up; more than that, he also knew whom he would marry. Ryder had himself brought her up during their meeting. The girl he'd fancied three years before, the beautiful and glorious Lady Melissande, daughter of the Duke of Beresford, who had wanted him and had cried when he'd left and hurled names at his head for what she'd seen as his betrayal. But three years before, he'd been committed to the army, committed to destroying Napoleon, committed to saving England.

Now, he was only committed to saving Northcliffe and the Sherbrooke line.

Aloud, he said, "Her name is Melissande and she is twenty-one, the daughter of Edouard Chambers, the Duke of Beresford. I met her when she was eighteen, but I left her because I had no wish to wed then. The devil, I was only home because of that bullet wound in my shoulder. It is likely she is long wed now and a mother. Ah, Sinjun, she was so beautiful, so dashing and carefree and spirited, and behind her was the Chambers name, old and honored, become dissolute only in her grandfather's day. There was little money for her dowry three years ago, but I didn't care if she came with naught but her shift on her back. Aye, her brother is another rotter, and even now he brings new odor to London with his profligacy. He is dissolute and a wastrel, gaming away any guinea he can get his hands on. It is likely that he will finish off the Chambers line."

"I think it noble of you not to be concerned with a dowry, Douglas. Mother says again and again that it is the only basis for marriage. Perhaps your Melissande has waited for you. I would. Perhaps no one wed her because there was no money, despite the fact she's a duke's daughter and beautiful. Or, what if she did wed another but is now a widow? It's possible her husband would have been obliging and died, and it would solve all your problems."

Douglas smiled at that, but nodded, again, com-

won't hear more of that *Sinjun* nonsense. Your name is Joan Elaine Winthrop Sherbrooke."

"But I like Sinjun, Mother," she said, feeling her mother's fingers tighten painfully on her shirtsleeve. "Ryder named me that when I was ten years old."

"Hush," said the unknowing soon-to-be Dowager Countess of Northcliffe. "You aren't Saint John nor are you Saint Joan — Sinjun is a man's nickname. Dear me, you have that preposterous name all because Tysen decided you were Joan of Arc —"

"And then," Douglas continued, "he decided to martyr her and thus she became Saint Joan or Sinjun."

"In any case, I won't have it!"

Douglas said nothing. Since he could scarce even remember his sister's name was really Joan, he doubted not that their mother would have to hear Sinjun for many years to come.

Douglas took himself to the library to write and send off his letter to the Duke of Beresford. He wouldn't say anything about his plans until the duke had shown his approval of the scheme. And Melissande too, of course. He knew he could trust Sinjun to keep quiet about it. He realized he trusted his little sister more than his own brothers. After all, she never got drunk. He also liked the name Sinjun, but he hesitated to go against his mother's wishes. She was tied to many notions that appalled him, was occasionally mean and spiteful with both servants and her children and

fortable with speaking aloud his thoughts and his plans to Sinjun. Yes, he had liked Melissande, found her careless ways fascinating, her clever manipulations intriguing. He'd also wanted to bed her very badly, had wanted to see her tousled and whispering endearments to him, adoration in her eyes for him.

Sinjun said quietly, "If Melissande is still available then you won't have to worry about spending time in London to find another appropriate girl."

"You're right," he said, rising and dusting off his breeches. "I will write immediately to the Duke of Beresford. If Melissande is still available — Lord, it makes her sound like a prize mare! — why then, I could leave immediately for Harrogate and marry her on the spot. I think you would like her, Sinjun."

"I'll like her if you do, Douglas. Mother won't, but that doesn't matter."

Douglas could only shake his head at her. "You're right. Do you know she's the only one who's never carped at me about marrying and providing the Sherbrooke heir?"

"That's because she doesn't want to give up her power as chatelaine of Northcliffe. The Sherbrooke dower house is charming but she disdains it."

"You sometimes terrify me, my girl, you truly do." He touched his fingers to her wind-tangled hair, then cupped her chin in his large hand. "You're a good sort."

She accepted this token of affection calmly, then

said, "You know, Douglas, I wondered why the Virgin Bride would come at this particular time, but now it makes sense. I think she appeared because she knew you were planning to marry. Perhaps her coming is a portent; perhaps she is trying to warn you or your Melissande about something that will befall you if you aren't careful."

"Nonsense," said the Earl of Northcliffe. "However, you are still a good sort, even if you are overly fanciful upon occasion."

" 'There are more things in heaven and earth, Horatio, Than are dreamt of in your philosophy.' "

"Ah, Sinjun, and I shall say back to you, " 'Rest, rest, perturbed spirit.' "

"You are sometimes a difficult man, Douglas."

"You sulk because I out-Shakespeared you?"

She poked him in the arm in high good humor. "You are too earthbound, Douglas, but perhaps that won't continue after you are wedded."

Douglas thought of the immense passion he fully planned to enjoy when he bedded Melissande. "Sometimes, my girl," he said, giving her a fatuous grin, "you are also delightfully perceptive."

The earl wasn't frowning when he returned to Northcliffe Hall. Everything would work out. He had the unaccountable Sherbrooke luck as did the first son of the Sherbrookes for the past untold generations. It would continue, for the Sherbrooke luck had never yet deserted him, and he would have no more worries.

He paused, standing next to his sister in the front hall, listening to the Northcliffe butler, Hollis, when their mother, Lady Lydia, swooped down on them, demanding that Joan come upstairs *immediately* and change her highly repugnant clothing and *try,* at least try, to *appear* the young lady, despite all the blocks and obstacles Douglas and his brothers — who positively encouraged the silly chit — put in her path.

"I gather we are expecting guests, Mother?" Douglas asked, after sending Sinjun a commiserating wink.

"Yes, and if the Algernons — Almeria is such a high stickler, you know! — if she saw this child in her breeches and her hair like —" She faltered and Sinjun said quickly, "Like Medusa, Mother?"

"A revolting witch from one of your dusty tomes, I dare say! Come along, Joan. Oh, Douglas, please refrain from calling your sister that absurd name in front of the Algernons!"

"Did you know that Algernon means 'the whiskered ones'? It was the nickname of William de Percy, who was bearded when every other gentleman was clean shaven, and he —"

"Enough!" said the Dowager Countess of Northcliffe, clearly harassed. "No more of your smartness, young lady. I have told you repeatedly that gentlemen do not like smartness in females. It irritates them and depresses their own mental faculties. It makes them seek out their brandy bottles. It sends them to gaming wells. Also, I

her neighbors. She was blessed with an intellect as bland as cook's turtle soup, was plump and pink-cheeked with sausage curls tight around her face, and carried at least three chins. She spoke constantly of her duty, of the rigors of bearing four children. He wasn't certain he loved her for she was vastly annoying at times. He knew that his father had endured her for he had told Douglas so before he'd died.

Was Sinjun right? Had his mother remained quiet in the eye of the marriage storm because she didn't want the wife to wrest the reins of control over the household from her? He tried to picture Melissande wanting to oversee Northcliffe, demanding that his mother hand over the chatelaine keys, but such an image wouldn't form in his mind. He shrugged; it didn't matter.

And what was wrong with a simple nickname like Sinjun?

CHAPTER 3

Claybourn Hall, Wetherby
Near Harrogate, England

"This is difficult to believe, Papa," Alexandra said finally, her voice strained and paper-thin. She couldn't seem to take her eyes off that single sheet of paper her father calmly replaced on his desktop. "Are you certain it is the Earl of Northcliffe who wants to marry Melissande? Douglas Sherbrooke?"

"Yes, no doubt about it," said Lord Edouard, Duke of Beresford. "Poor fool." He smoothed his long fingers over the letter surface, then read it aloud again to his youngest daughter. When he finished and looked over at her, he thought for a moment that she was somehow distressed. She seemed pale, but it was probably only the bright sunlight coming through the wide library windows. He said, "Your sister will probably be ecstatic, particularly after Oglethorpe didn't come up to scratch four months ago. This should be a great balm to her wounded pride. As for me, why, I should like to throw my arms about Northcliffe and cry on his shoulder. Good Gad, the money he offers will save me, not to mention the handsome settlement he'll provide."

Alexandra looked down at the roughened nail on her thumb. "Melissande told me she refused Douglas Sherbrooke three years ago. He begged and begged to have her, she said, but she felt his future was too uncertain, that even though he was the earl's heir, it wasn't enough since his father was, after all, still alive, and that since he insisted on remaining in the army and fighting, he could be killed and then she wouldn't have anything, for his brother would become earl after his father's death. She said being a poor wife was very different from being a beautiful but poor daughter."

The duke grunted, a dark eyebrow raised. "That's what she told you, Alex?"

Alexandra nodded, then turned away from her father. She walked to the wide bow windows, their draperies held back in every season, regardless of the weather, because the duke refused ever to close them over the magnificent vista outside. His wife complained endlessly about it, claiming the harsh sun faded out the Aubusson carpet and the good Lord knew there was no money to replace it, for that was what he was always telling her, wasn't it, but the duke paid her no heed. Alex said slowly, "Now Douglas Sherbrooke is the Earl of Northcliffe and he wishes to come here to wed her."

"Yes, I give him permission and we will come to agreement over the settlement in short order.

Thank God he's a wealthy man. The Sherbrookes have always used their money wisely, never depleting the estates through excesses, not forming alliances that wouldn't add to their coffers and their consequence. Of course his marrying Melissande won't bring him a single groat, indeed, he will have to pay me well for her, very well indeed. He must really care for her since the chances would have been excellent that she would have already been wed to another man. I must say too, in your sister's defense, that her consequence displays itself in equal measure to her pride."

"I suppose so. I remember that he was a very nice man. Kind and, well, nice."

"Hotheaded young fool, that's what he was," the duke said. "He was the Northcliffe heir and he refused to sell out. Not that it matters now. He survived and now he's the earl and that makes things quite different. All the Sherbrookes have been Tories, back to the Flood I dare say, and this earl is very probably no different. Staid and well set in his ways, I'll wager, just like his father, Justin Sherbrooke, was. Well, none of that has any bearing now. I suppose I should speak to your sister." He paused a moment, looking toward his daughter's profile. Pure and innocent, he thought, yet there was strength there, in the tilt of her head, in the clear light in her gray eyes. Her nose was straight and thin, her cheekbones high, and her chin gently rounded, giving the impression of submissiveness and malleability, which wasn't at all the case, at least in his experience with his daughter. But, strangely enough, she didn't appear to know she had steel in her, even when she argued with him. Her rich titian hair was pulled back from her face, showing her small ears, and he found both her ears and her lovely. She wasn't an exquisite creation like her older sister, Melissande, but she was quite to his taste, for here was little vanity or pettiness in her and there was a good deal of kindness and wit. Ah, she was the responsible one, the child who wouldn't gainsay her papa ever, the one who would do her duty to her family. Again, he had the inescapable feeling that she was distressed and he wondered at it. He said slowly, "I told you of this first, Alex, because I wanted your opinion. Even though your mother believes you to be much like the wallpaper — quiet and in Melissande's shadow — I know differently, and thus I would like to know what you think of this proposed match."

He thought she trembled slightly at his words and frowned, wondering if her mother had perhaps tried to flatten her spirit again with her constant comparisons to her sister. He watched her closely. "Are you ailing with something, my dear?"

"Oh no, Papa. It's just that —"

"That what?"

She shrugged then. "I suppose I wonder if Melissande would have him now. She wants to enjoy another Season, you know, and we are to leave next week. Perhaps she would wish to wait to see what other gentlemen are available to her. She much savors the chase, she told me. Oglethorpe, she said, was a spineless toad and she was vastly relieved when his mama made him cry off before he cried on, so to speak."

The duke sighed. "Yes, your sister was right about him, but that isn't the point now. You know, Alex, that money must play a big part in any decision. Our family hasn't been in overly plump current for many years now, and the expense of London during the Season, the cost of staffing the Carlyon Street house, the price of her gowns and gowns for her mother, all of it together is exorbitant. I was willing to do it again as an investment, for I could see no alternative. Now with the Earl of Northcliffe proposing to her, I will get a settlement without having to endure London and all its costs." The duke realized, of course, that by canceling out another Season for Melissande, he was also preventing Alexandra from having her first Season. But the cost of it — he ran his hand through his dark red hair. What to do? He continued, saying more to himself, than to his daughter, "And there's Reginald, my twenty-five-year-old heir, gambling in every hell London can boast, raising huge debts to Weston his tailor, and to Hoby his bootmaker, even to Rundle and Bridge for 'trinkets' as he calls these supposed insubstantial baubles for his mistresses. My God, you wouldn't believe the ruby bracelet he bought for one of those opera dancers!" He shook his head again. "Ah, Alex, I've felt trapped for so long now, but no longer is my life falling down on my shoulders. You know well the economies I've tried to initiate, but explaining the necessity to your mother, well, an impossible task, that. She has no concept, telling me in a bewildered way that one must have at least three removes at dinner. Nor does Melissande. You, of course, understand something of our situation, but anything you do is insignificant. And Reginald — a wastrel, Alex, and in all truth I have little hope that his character will improve."

He fell silent again, a small smile on his mouth now. He was saved. He felt hope and he wasn't about to allow Melissande to toss her beautiful head and tell him she wasn't interested. Bread and water in a locked room would be fitting were she to go against him.

"What do you think, Alex? You do not mind about a Season? You are such a sensible girl and you understand there is no money and —"

Alex just smiled. "It's all right, Papa. Melissande is so beautiful, so sparkling and gay, so natural in her gaiety. If we went to London, no one would have paid me much attention in any case so I don't mind not going. I am not lying to you. It terrified me, the thought of meeting all those ferocious ladies — if their eyebrows twitch, you're forever beyond the pale — that's what Mama says. So, you needn't worry. I go along fine here. There are other things besides parties and routs and Venetian breakfasts and dancing holes in one's slippers." There were other things, but that list was woefully short.

"Once Melissande is wed to the earl, she will do her duty by you. As the Countess of Northcliffe, she will take you about so that you may meet appropriate young gentlemen. That is what is right and she will do it. And you will comply because that is the way one normally secures a husband worthy of one."

"Young gentlemen don't appear to be remarkably attracted to me, Papa."

"Nonsense. There are very few young gentlemen here about to see you, and those who are, look upon your sister and lose what few wits they possess. It is of no matter. You are a dear girl, and you are bright and your mind is filled with more than ribbons and beaux and —"

"When one isn't a diamond, Papa, one must cultivate other gardens."

"Is that your attempt to rephrase Monsieur Voltaire?"

Alexandra smiled. "I suppose so, but it's the truth. There is no reason to quibble about it."

"You are also very pretty, Alex. You surely don't wish to insult your glorious hair — why 'tis the same shade as mine!"

She smiled at that, and the duke thought, pleased, everything would work out all right now. The Earl of Northcliffe had just offered to save him from inevitable financial disaster and rid him of his eldest daughter at the same time, a set of circumstances to gladden any father's heart and purse.

"I trust Melissande will decide to take Douglas Sherbrooke this time," Alexandra said. "As I said, he is a very nice man and deserves to have what he wants." Her fingers pleated the folds of her pale yellow muslin gown, and her eyes remained downcast as she added quietly, "He deserves happiness. Perhaps Melissande will care for him and make him happy."

That was the sticking point, the duke thought, grimacing. He could imagine Melissande making a gentleman's life a series of delightful encounters until the gentleman chanced to disagree with her or refuse her something. Then . . . it made him shudder to think of it. He wouldn't worry overly about it. It wouldn't be his problem. However, he would pray for the Earl of Northcliffe once the knot was tied.

"I'll go fetch Melissande for you, Papa."

The duke watched his daughter walk from the library. Something strange was going on here. He knew her well, for she was his favorite, the child of his heart and of his mind. He remembered her sudden rigidity, the trembling of her hands. And he thought blankly, as a crazed notion bulleted through his brain — does she want the Earl of Northcliffe? He shook his head even as he tried to remember three years before when Alexandra was only fifteen, painfully shy, her beautiful auburn hair in tight braids around her head, and still plump with childhood fat. No, no, she'd been much too young. If she'd felt anything for Douglas Sherbrooke, why it had to have been only a girlish infatuation, nothing more.

He wondered if what he was doing was wise, then he knew that there was no choice. The gods had offered him a gift horse and he wasn't about to have it race away from him toward another stable, one doubtless less worthy and less in need than his. If Alexandra did feel something for the earl, he was sorry for it, but he couldn't, he wouldn't, change the plan. If the earl wanted Melissande, he would have her. The duke sat down to await the arrival of his eldest daughter.

The interview between the Duke of Beresford and his eldest daughter proceeded exactly as the duke expected.

Melissande was in a towering passion within two minutes of her father's announcement. She looked incredibly beautiful in a towering passion, as she did in most moods. Her cheeks were flushed, her eyes — blue as the lake at Patley Bridge in the late summer — sparkled and glinted. Her thick black hair, darker than a starless midnight sky, shone vividly even in the dim light of his library, and the artless array of curls that clustered around her face bounced as her passion grew. She drew a deep breath, tossed her curls another time, and nearly shouted, "Ridiculous! He thinks he can simply *crook* his finger after three years — *three years* — and I will not gainsay him at all, that I will come rushing to him and allow him to do whatever he pleases with me!"

The duke understood her fury. Her pride was hurt, and the Chambers pride was renowned for its depth and breadth and endurance. He also knew how to deal with his daughter, and thus spoke slowly, empathy and understanding for her feelings filling his voice. "I am sorry that he hurt you three years ago, Melissande. No, don't try to rewrite the past, my dear, for I know the truth, and it is a different recipe from the one you fed your credulous sister. But that isn't important now, save that you must keep in mind what really happened then. The earl spoke to me before he left, you know, explaining himself quite nicely I thought at the time. But as you can see, it is you who have the last word here, it is you and no other who caught his fancy and kept it, and now he admits that his fancy and his hand are eager to be reeled in by none other than you."

Melissande was doubtless the most beautiful creature the duke had ever seen. He found himself marveling even now that she had sprung from his loins. She was exquisite and she'd been spoiled and pampered since her birth. And why shouldn't she be petted and given whatever she wished, his wife would ask? She was so beautiful, so absolutely perfect, she deserved it. Judith would also say, doubtless, that Melissande deserved a duke, at least, not a paltry earl, even though he was one of the richest in all the land. But dukes weren't all that plentiful, any duke, one teetering on the edge of the grave or a young, almost presentable one. The father looked at his daughter now, watching her sort through his words, bringing a sense to them that would please her vanity and salve her wounded sensibilities.

"Still," she said after several moments of silence, "still he expects too much. I won't have him, Father! You must write back and inform His arrogant Lordship that I now find him repellent, yes, that's it, utterly repellent, just as Oglethorpe was repellent and a toad. I won't have him; I will wed another." She stopped, spun about, her white hands pressed to her cheeks.

"Oh dear, what if he feels that he broke my heart three years ago and that is why I haven't wed! What if he believes that I've pined for him? I can't bear that, Father, I just can't! What shall I do?"

The duke made soothing noises. Pride, he thought, damnable pride. Well, he'd infused her with all the pride that was in his lineage. Inspiration struck and he smiled to himself. "The poor fellow," he said in a mournful voice, shaking his head.

Melissande whirled about to face her father, blinking in confusion. "What poor fellow?"

"Why, the Earl of Northcliffe, of course. The man has wanted you for three years, has doubtless suffered more than you and I could possibly imagine. He wanted you, Melissande, but he felt great dedication for England, felt honor bound by what he believed to be his sacred duty. He did not dismiss his honor, despite his ardent desire for you. Surely you cannot fault him for that. And now he tries to make restitution. He pines for you. And now he bows himself before you, my dear, begging that you forgive his lamentable integrity, that you please consider that you will have him now." The duke wasn't about to tell his daughter that the earl had sold out some nine or ten months before. Even Melissande would wonder at the earl's depth of passion were she to know that he hadn't pushed to have her for nearly a year after he was free to do so.

"He was very distraught," Melissande said slowly. "Even as I took him to task for his devotion to his absurd duty, he did appear genuinely distraught."

"He is the Earl of Northcliffe, and his home is one of the premier estates in England."

"Yes, that is true."

"He has wealth and standing. He is still a man to be reckoned with in the government. I hear he still consults with the War Ministry, even with Addington." The duke paused, then added smoothly, "A man in such a position desperately needs a wife of grace and consequence to oversee his social obligations. He is also a handsome man as I recall. I hear he is much in demand in London drawing rooms."

"He is very dark, too dark. He is probably hairy. I do not like men so dark, but he is an earl."

"You liked him well enough three years ago."

"Perhaps, but I was very young. He was severe then; he is probably more so now. He did not laugh very much; he was far too serious. No, even his smiles were rare."

"He was suffering from a rather serious wound."

"Still, he rarely showed a glimmer of humor when I was amusing. It was a fault I saw but ignored then."

"But my dear, how could he be so very severe when he admired you? His admiration, as I recall, was quite remarkable in its scope." That was true, but he'd known that the earl, had he remained longer in his daughter's orbit, would have removed the blinders from his eyes. He fully intended to have them wed as quickly as possible.

"Not as remarkable as his devotion to his country!"

"Now his devotion would be to you, his wife, no longer to his country. You are an intelligent girl, Melissande. Surely with such a devoted husband, you would arrange matters quite to your liking. Ah, how you would shine when you took your rightful place as the Countess of Northcliffe in London society."

The duke stopped, knowing the seeds were all well planted, watered, and fertilized. Perhaps even a bit too much fertilizer. He must wait now and see if her mental powers were sufficient to bring the seeds to fruition. He hesitated to threaten her but he would do so should she refuse what he wanted her to do.

She was looking thoughtful, a circumstance that normally would have made him very wary, for her perfect brow was furrowed, a condition that she wouldn't have allowed had she been aware of it, for it diminished her beauty. It made her look remarkably human. Soon, thank God, another man would have to worry about her tantrums, her passions, her sulks, the inevitable scenes that gave him indigestion. Ah, but then again, the man who would be her husband would also have one of the most beautiful women in England in his possession.

The duke wondered if that would be enough. He liked the Earl of Northcliffe, believed him a fine young man. Since he was fit again, he probably did smile and laugh from time to time. The duke hadn't remembered him as being overly serious and severe. And now he would give him a prize that would gratify any man's soul.

He would give himself desperately needed funds to keep the ducal ship afloat.

CHAPTER 4

"But what do you think, Alex? Should I agree to marry Douglas Sherbrooke?"

Why, Alexandra wondered yet again as she looked at her sister, did people go through the pretense of asking for another's opinion? It was as if Alexandra, more than most, gave an impression that encouraged people to speak to her of their innermost thoughts, to ask her view, but of course, she wasn't to expect that they would ever heed anything she had to say.

Slowly she raised her chin and said clearly, "I think Douglas Sherbrooke deserves to marry the most beautiful woman in the world."

That drew up Melissande, for she'd been pacing her bedchamber like a healthy young colt, clearly involved in her own thoughts. "What did you say?"

"I think Douglas Sherbrooke —"

"Oh, all right, I heard you! Well, if I decide to wed him, you will have your wish, won't you?"

Alexandra eyed her sister thoughtfully, then said slowly, "I hope that Douglas Sherbrooke will believe so."

Melissande had very nearly convinced herself

that becoming the Countess of Northcliffe would be quite the thing for her to do when their mother, Her Grace, Lady Judith, came into the bedchamber like a small whirlwind, spots of angry color on her thin cheeks, her hands fluttering, saying, "Your father says you will marry the earl soon — next week if it can be arranged! He says we won't go to London, there won't be the need to go! Ah, the man is impossible! What are we to do?"

Alexandra said mildly, "You know there isn't much money, Mama. London would cost Papa a fortune he can ill afford to spend."

"Stuff and nonsense! It is ever his plaint. I want to go to London. As for you, my girl, you must find a husband, and you'll not find one hanging over the garden wall watching you as you weed your infernal plants! After your sister chooses the gentleman she wishes, why then, the others will realize that you are to come next. They will put their feelings for your sister behind them and turn to you. As I said, your father has always complained that there is no money for anything, but there always is, except for your poor brother, who is quite unable to pry sufficient funds from your father to live like a young gentleman should live in London. It is disgraceful, and so I told His Grace."

Lady Judith stopped to catch her breath. "What did Papa say?" Alexandra asked quickly during this brief respite.

"He said I should mind to my own affairs, if

it is any of your concern, my girl."

Alexandra wondered why her father had told his wife about the marriage plans, but decided he'd probably been forced into it somehow. She sat back and watched with a good deal of detachment as her mother and Melissande whipped themselves into a state of advanced outrage. It was ever so when one or the other didn't get her way. Eventually Alexandra rose and walked from her sister's peach and cream bedchamber, her departure unregarded.

Alexandra knew that Melissande would agree to marry the earl. She also knew that on that day, she would wish to be on another continent so she wouldn't have to see it, wouldn't have to live through it. She didn't want to face up to it, but she had to. She also knew there was no hope for it; she would be here, aloofness and silence her only defense, and she would be forced to smile and to greet the earl as a future sister-in-law should and she would have to watch him look at Melissande as he spoke the words that would make her his wife.

Alexandra had come to realize in her eighteen years that life could concoct many lavishly inedible dishes to serve on one's plate.

Northcliffe Hall

Douglas couldn't believe it, couldn't at first take it all in. He stared from the Duke of Beresford's letter to the other short, urgent scrawl dispatched by Lord Avery himself just that morning, brought to him by a messenger who awaited his reply in the kitchen, doubtless downing ale.

He picked up the duke's letter again. It was jovial to the eyebrows, filled with jubilation and relief and congratulations. Douglas was to marry Melissande next week at Claybourn Hall in the ancient Norman church in the village of Wetherby. The duke would become his proud papa-in-law in seven days. His new papa-in-law would also shove quite a few guineas into the needy ducal pocket once the marriage had taken place.

He picked up Lord Avery's letter. He was also to go to Etaples, France, as soon as possible, disguised as a bloody French soldier. He was to await Georges Cadoudal's instructions, then follow them. He was to rescue a French girl who was being held against her will by one of Napoleon's generals. There was nothing more, absolutely no detail, no names, no specifics. If Douglas didn't do this, England would lose its best chance at eliminating Napoleon, for Georges Cadoudal was the brain behind the entire operation. Lord Avery was counting on Douglas. England was counting on Douglas. To hammer the final nail in the coffin, Lord Avery wrote in closing, "If you do not rescue this wretched girl, Cadoudal says he won't continue with the plan. He insists upon you, Douglas, but he refuses to say why. Perhaps you know the answer. I know you have met him in the past. You must do this and succeed,

Northcliffe, you must. England's fate lies in your hands."

Douglas sat back in his chair and laughed. "I must wed and I must go to France." He laughed louder.

Would he sail to France to rescue Cadoudal's lover, as doubtless this female was, or travel to Claybourn Hall as a bridegroom?

Douglas stopped laughing. The frown returned to his forehead. Why couldn't life be simple, just once? He was responsible for England's fate? Well, hell.

He thought about Georges Cadoudal, the radical leader of the Royalist Chouans. His last attempt to eliminate Napoleon had been in December 1800, his followers using explosives in Paris that had killed twenty-two people and wounded well over fifty, but not harming any of Napoleon's entourage. Georges Cadoudal was a dangerous man, a passionate man who despised Napoleon to the depths of his soul, a man who sought the return of the Bourbons to the French throne; he counted no cost, be it lives or money. But evidently this girl's life he counted high, so high that he would renege on his plans with England if she weren't rescued.

Cadoudal knew Douglas, that was true, had seen him play the Frenchman several years before and succeed in a mission, but why he would insist upon Douglas and no other to rescue his lover would remain a mystery until and unless Douglas went to Etaples, France. And now the English government was backing Cadoudal in another plot. And the plot was in jeopardy because Georges's lover was being held prisoner.

When Hollis, the Sherbrooke butler for thirty years, who looked remarkably like a quite respectable peer of the realm himself, walked soundlessly into the library, Douglas at first paid him no heed. Once, many years before, when Douglas was young and prideful as a cock and equally jealous of his own worth, a friend had joked that Douglas resembled the Sherbrooke butler more than he did his own father. Douglas had flattened him.

Hollis cleared his throat gently.

Douglas looked up, and a black eyebrow went up as well in silent question.

"Your cousin, Lord Rathmore, has just arrived, my lord. He said I wasn't to disturb you but one simply doesn't disregard His Lordship's presence, you know."

"That is certainly true. To ask Tony to remain in a quiet corner to await someone's pleasure would never do. I'll come directly. I wonder what His Lordship wants? Surely not to press me about marriage."

"Probably not, my lord. If I may speak plainly, His Lordship looks a bit downpin, a bit tight about the mouth. Perhaps ill, although not of the body, you understand, but of the spirit. Were I to hazard a guess, knowing His Lordship's penchants, I dare say it would involve the fair sex." He looked off into the distance, adding, "It usually does, regardless of penchants."

"Damnation," said Douglas, rising from his desk. "I'll see him." He stared down again at the two letters. The messenger could wait a bit longer. He had to think, had to weigh all the alternatives open to him, he had to have more time. Besides, Anthony Colin St. John Parrish, Viscount Rathmore, was the son of his mother's first cousin, and a favorite of his. It had been six months since they'd been in each other's company.

His first view of his cousin did not gladden his heart. He looked depressed as the devil, just as Hollis had said. Douglas strode into the small estate room, closed the door firmly behind him, and locked it. "All right, Tony," he said without preamble, "out with it. What is wrong?"

Tony Parrish, Viscount Rathmore, turned about from his perusal of nothing in particular outside the window to look at his cousin. He straightened his shoulders automatically and tried for a smile. It wasn't much of a smile, but Douglas appreciated the effort, and repeated mildly, "Tell me, Tony. What's happened?"

"Hollis, I gather?"

"Yes. Tell me."

"That man should have been a bloody priest."

"Oh no, it's just that he isn't blind. Also he's rather fond of you. Now, talk to me, Tony."

"All right, curse you, if you must know, I am no longer engaged. I am now without a fiancée. I have been betrayed. I am alone and adrift. I am here."

Was Hollis never wrong? Still, Douglas was incredulous. "You mean to say that Teresa Carleton broke it off?"

"Of course she didn't. Don't be a simpleton. No, I did. I found out she was sleeping with one of my friends. Friend, ha! The bloody sod! Can you believe it, Douglas? The woman was to marry me — *me!* — she was to be my bloody wife. I had selected her with great care, I had nurtured her as I would the most precious of blossoms, treated her with consideration and respect, never doing much of anything except kissing her and not even with my mouth open, mind you, and all along she was actually one of my friend's mistresses. It is impossible to believe, Douglas, it is intolerable."

"It isn't as if she were a virgin to begin with, Tony," Douglas said mildly. "She's a widow, after all. I dare say you've continued sleeping with your lovers and I doubt not that some of them are friends of Teresa's."

"That's not the point, and you know it, damn you!"

"Perhaps not to you, but —" Douglas broke off. "It is over then? You're a free man now? Have you really broken the engagement or are you here to lick your wounds and consider your unanchored state?"

"Yes, I've broken it off, and I would like to kill the woman for her perfidy! Cuckolding me! *Me,* Douglas!"

"You weren't yet wed to the lady, Tony."

"The principle remains the same. I cannot take it in, Douglas, I can scarce convince my mind that it has really happened. How could a woman do such a thing to me?"

His cousin, Douglas thought, held a very good opinion of himself, and truth be told, so did most other people. No woman, so far as Douglas knew, had ever played Tony false. Indeed, it was always Tony who had stepped away, laughing, as carefree as Ryder when it came to the fair sex, until he met Teresa Carleton, a young widow who had, for some obscure and unfathomed reason, charmed Viscount Rathmore to his Hessian-covered toes and marriage had popped into his mind and out of his mouth within a week. Then she had proceeded to play the game by the same rules Tony employed. The blow to his esteem must be shattering. No wonder he was reeling from it.

"I can't go back to London now for I would see her and my temper is uncertain, Douglas, you know that. I must rusticate until I regain my balance, until I am once more in control — cold and hard in my brain once again — and in no danger of cursing that scheming slut and slapping her silly. Do you mind if I stay here for a while?"

The solution to his problem came to Douglas in a blinding flash, fully fleshed and brilliant, and he grinned. "Tony, you may stay here for the remainder of the century. You may drink all my fine French brandy; you may even sleep in my earl's bed. You may do anything you wish."

Douglas strode to his cousin, grabbed his hand and pumped it, all the while grinning like a fool. "In addition, you, Tony, are about to save my life. Heaven will welcome you for what you will do for me."

Tony Parrish looked at his cousin, then smiled, a real smile, one filled with curiosity and humor. "I expect you will tell your expectations of my future bravery," he said slowly.

"Oh yes, indeed. Let's go riding and I will tell you all about it."

Tony's smile remained intact, his interest level high for about five minutes into Douglas's recital, then he looked astounded, aghast, then once again, he smiled, shrugged, and said, "Why not?"

Claybourn Hall

Why not indeed, Tony Parrish thought five days later, his eyes a bit glazed from the vision that stood not five feet from him. She was the most exquisite creature he had ever seen. Every feature complemented the other, and each was arguably well nigh perfect. None of his former or present mistresses, nor his former fiancée, Teresa Carleton, came near to her in the flawlessness of her features. He'd always believed fair-haired women were the most beautiful, the most delicate and alluring. By all the saints, not so. Her hair was black and thick with no hint of red, her eyes an incredible dark blue, slightly slanted upward and sinfully long-lashed. Her skin was white and soft and smooth, her nose thin, her mouth full and tempting. Her body was so precisely perfect in its wondrous curves that it made him break into an immediate sweat.

He felt his belly cramp. He felt himself pale. He just looked at her, unable not to, and watched a slow smile touch her mouth. She spoke, saying softly, "Viscount Rathmore? You are the earl's cousin, I believe?"

He nodded like a dimwitted fool and took her hand, turning it slowly, and kissing the soft palm. She knew her effect on him, he thought, her warm hand still held in his. She knew that he was stunned; and she would attempt to manipulate him, but he didn't mind. Odd, but it was so. Suddenly he felt her fingers tighten slightly in his grasp as he returned her smile. Was she also a bit stunned as well? He would soon see. He knew he had to regain his confidence, sorely diminished by Teresa Carleton. He had to regain his mastery. He could, if he wished, make this glorious creature bend to him. He could and he would . . .

His thinking stopped cold in its tracks. Her name was Melissande and he was here to marry her by proxy to his cousin, Douglas Sherbrooke.

Etaples, France

Douglas was in the middle of Napoleon's naval invasion stronghold, although anywhere from Boulogne to Dunkirk to Ostend and all points in between could be considered part of his "immense project." It was, actually, one of the safest places to be in France, particularly if one were an English spy, for there was no security at all and people came and went and looked and talked and listened and even drew sketches of all the ongoing work. Douglas marveled at the thousands upon thousands of men who labored around the clock in the basins and harbors and on the beaches, building hundreds of transports of all kinds. Alongside the score upon score of workers were soldiers, and they did little as far as Douglas could tell. There was constant activity everywhere.

Douglas wore a private's uniform, new and shining but three days before, and now appropriately soiled and wrinkled. He'd been scouting about as he'd waited for Cadoudal to contact him, gleaning information from the loose-mouthed officers and enlisted soldiers in the neighboring taprooms. All he could do was wait. His French was flawless, his manners just as they should be — commiserating with the enlisted men, joining in their complaints and grievances — and listening to the officers from a discreet distance, exhibiting due deference. All the talk was of an impending invasion simply because Napoleon had visited the many encampments along the coast two weeks before, assuring the men that soon, very soon now, they would cross that dismal little ditch and teach those English bankers and merchants that it was the French who ruled the land

and the sea. Fine words, Douglas thought. Did Napoleon really believe that the English peasantry would rise up and welcome him as their liberator when and if he managed to cross the Channel, smash through the English navy, and land at Dover?

Two days passed. Douglas was bored and restless. As it turned out, he got Georges Cadoudal's instructions from a one-legged beggar who sidled up to him, stinking like rotted cabbage, and poked a thick packet into his coat pocket. The blighted specimen managed to get away before Douglas could question him. He read the letter twice, memorizing the precise instructions, then carefully studied each of the enclosed papers and documents. He sat back, thinking now of what Cadoudal expected him to do. He shook his head at the complexity of it all, the sheer heedless arrogance of it. Georges Cadoudal was imprudent at all times, outrageous upon occasion; he was at once brilliant and feckless; failure chaffed him and as of late, he'd known few successes, as far as Douglas knew.

It was obvious he'd spent hours formulating a plan to rescue this damned girl, this Janine Daudet. However, since Cadoudal was the brain behind the plot to kidnap Napoleon and create insurrection in Paris, setting the Comte d'Artois, the younger brother of Louis XVI, promptly on the throne, and since he held more than a million francs from the English government, Lord Avery was inclined to meet his demands. Obviously

Georges couldn't take the risk of attempting a rescue himself. Obviously he knew that Douglas was an expert on General Honoré Belesain and that was why he'd asked for him specifically. Obviously, he believed Douglas would succeed. Douglas wondered if Georges knew of Belesain's scaly reputation with women. Damnation.

The following morning Douglas was fastening the buttons of his unfamiliar britches and straightening his stark black coat. Once he reached Boulogne, he would become an official functionary from Paris, sent by Bonaparte himself, to oversee the preparations for the English invasion. He devoutly prayed that Cadoudal's papers were in good order. With all the English money he'd gotten, Georges could afford the best forgers. Douglas didn't want to be discovered and shot as a spy.

At precisely twelve o'clock, looking every inch the officious functionary, whose authority in all likelihood exceeded his brains and his manners and his breeding, he made his way to Boulogne to the residence of General Honoré Belesain, not a difficult house to locate since it belonged to the mayor and was the largest mansion in the entire city. The general was the good mayor's guest. The good mayor, upon further inquiry, hadn't been seen in over three months.

Douglas did know just about everything about General Belesain. Nothing the general did could surprise Douglas. He was a brilliant tactician, a competent administrator, though most details were attended to by aides. He was vicious to both his prisoners and his own men, and he was more than passing fond of young girls. He fancied himself both the epitome of a military man and of a lover. Douglas knew that his wife, evidently long-suffering, was well ensconced in faraway Lyon with their four children. The general was on the portly side but believed himself a god amongst men. He lacked control and lost his temper quickly and with deadly results, as his men and the young girls he fancied discovered to their own detriment. In sexual matters, he wasn't known for his gallantry, even when in the best of moods. He many times drank himself into insensibility after he'd had sex.

The mayor's house was three stories, a soft yellow brick that had mellowed with age, large and rectangular, and covered with thick ivy. It was set back from the road, its long drive lined with full-branched oak trees, green and abundant in early summer. The mayor was obviously a man of substance. Or had been. There were at least a dozen soldiers patrolling the perimeter or simply standing guard outside the several doors to the house.

He looked up, wondering which of those third-floor rooms held Janine Daudet. He wondered if the general had raped her yet and then he knew that of course he had. Who would have stopped him? He prayed the general hadn't played his perverted games with her. He wondered if the general had any idea who he was holding. There was no way knowing because the general was more arrogant, more perverse, than any leader Douglas knew about.

An aide, Grillon by name, Douglas knew, came to greet him in the large entrance hall. He swaggered in his importance and in his fine scarlet uniform with all its braid, yet there was also an air of wariness about him. He was uncertain face to face with this unknown man; he was also a bully when he knew the rules and the players. Douglas gave nothing away; he was enjoying the fellow's unease. He counted four more soldiers in the entrance hall.

"I am Monsieur Lapalisse. You, of course, know who I am. I will see the general now." Douglas then looked about the house, quite aware that the lieutenant was studying him closely. He tried for a supercilious expression, but it was difficult, for Douglas had never been good at sneers. He saw a cobweb in the corner and that helped his lip curl.

"Monsieur Lapalisse," Grillon said at last, "if you will wait but a moment, I will inform the general of your presence and see if he wishes —"

"I am not in the habit of waiting," Douglas said, looking the young man up and down and finding him lacking. "I suggest that you announce me immediately. Indeed, let us go now, together."

Grillon fidgeted, then quickly turned on his heel. The general was suffering from a headache. He'd overindulged the previous night and was paying the price today, the fool. He'd not known exactly when this damned bureaucrat was to arrive, but he should have realized it would be exactly when he didn't wish to see him. The general was also nervous about this man's visit because no one higher in the government had notified him of it. Well, to hell with him.

General Belesain was standing behind his cluttered desk, eyes cold, body stiff, his forehead furrowed. When Douglas entered beside Grillon, he straightened to his full height, but Douglas wasn't fooled. His attitude was both wary and defensive. Excellent, Douglas thought as he strolled into the large salon as if he owned it. He gave the general a slight nod, saying in his perfect French, "It is a pleasant day."

"Yes, it is," General Belesain said, taken off balance. "Er, I am informed you are from Napoleon's war committee, although I do not understand. He was here not long ago and expressed his pleasure at how his invasion plans are progressing."

"A committee is such an amorphous sort of entity," Douglas said, striving yet again for a supercilious smile and a Gaelic shrug. "I am not a representative of any committee. I am here as Napoleon's personal, er, investigator."

The general stiffened even as his jaw slackened and his brain quickened. "Investigator?"

Had Napoleon somehow heard of the death of the two soldiers he'd ordered flogged the previous week? Perhaps he'd heard of the girl's beating, a girl whose relatives had a bit of clout? Damn the foolish girl. She'd protested, but he'd known she wanted him, the little tease, and thus he'd taken her, perhaps a bit roughly, but it wasn't as if she wouldn't recover to enjoy him again. She hadn't succumbed to his logic and his charms as had the woman he held upstairs in the small room next to his bedchamber.

Belesain believed Napoleon invincible on the battlefield, but he loathed him for his hypocritical bourgeois attitudes. He must tread warily. This man standing before him was nothing but a bureaucrat, a nonentity, obviously a lackey with few brains. But he did have power, curse him, which meant he, Belesain, would deal with him. If he couldn't deal with him, he would have him killed. After all, robbers and scoundrels of all sorts abounded on the roads.

"Yes," Douglas said. "As you doubtless know, Napoleon has always believed it imperative that plans and those carrying out the plans must be overseen. An endless task, no?"

"You have papers, of course."

"Naturally."

At three o'clock that afternoon, Douglas walked beside General Belesain through the encampment on the beach at Boulogne. The general hated this — this forced graciousness to a damned bureaucrat, this air of cooperation with a man he both feared and despised. He tried to intimidate Douglas, then ignored him, acting as though he knew everything and could control everything, and that made Douglas smile. Dinner that evening was with a dozen of Belesain's top officers in the mayor's dining room. By the time the lengthy meal was done, most of the officers were drunk. By midnight, three of them had been carried back to their billets by their fellow officers. By one o'clock in the morning, Douglas was more alert than he'd ever been in his life, waiting for his chance.

He prayed no one would discover he was really an English spy. He had no wish to die. After all, when he returned to England, it would be to his new wife, to Melissande — ah, how sweet her name sounded on his tongue — and she would be in his bed and he would keep her there until she conceived the Sherbrooke heir.

When the general challenged him to a game of piquet, Douglas gave him a bland smile, and his heartbeat quickened. "The wager?" he inquired, flicking a speck of dust off his black coat.

The general suggested francs.

Douglas showed mild irritation with such banality. Surely such a brilliant and sophisticated man as the general could come up with a more interesting . . . ah, a more enticing wager?

The general thought this over, then smiled, off center, for he was drunk. He rubbed his hands together and his eyes gleamed as he said, "Ah, yes, certainly. The winner of our little game, monsieur, will enjoy a succulent little morsel who currently lives with me here. Her name is Janine and she is very talented at pleasuring a man."

Douglas agreed with remarkable indifference.

CHAPTER 5

Claybourn Hall

Alexandra can't believe it. She stood still as a stone by Melissande's Italian writing desk, whose surface for once held something other than a myriad of perfume bottles. She still wore her dressing gown, and her hair hung in a thick braid over her shoulder. She stared down at the single sheet of paper. She closed her eyes a moment, closed them against the knowledge . . .

You hoped this would happen.

Perhaps, perhaps not. Regardless, she'd kept silent. She'd watched. And it had happened. Melissande and Anthony Parrish, Viscount Rathmore, had eloped to Gretna Green the previous night. Slowly Alexandra picked up the paper upon which Melissande had scrawled her few sentences, words that had changed all their lives, words that were mispelled because Melissande disdained any attempt at scholarship. Alexandra was calm; she felt strangely suspended, as if something more were going to happen. She would have to take the note to her father. She would have to confess that she guessed what was happening between the two of them.

She hated herself at that moment, knew herself to be a jealous creature, petty and mean-spirited, who deserved no consideration from anyone.

After the duke had read the letter, he laid it carefully on his desktop, walked over to the wide windows and stared out onto the east lawn. There were four peacocks strolling the perimeter, three geese, and a goat tethered to a yew bush. After a near decade had passed, at least in Alexandra's mind, he turned to look thoughtfully at his younger daughter. He smiled at her then, actually smiled. To her astonishment, he said mildly, "Well, it's done, wouldn't you say, my dear? No big surprise, no startling revelations. No, I'm not taken aback by this, Alex, because Tony left me a rather fulsome letter, much more articulate than Melissande's, much more apologetic. His honor abuses him. We will see."

"Oh Papa, I knew, I knew, but I wanted . . ." Her father chuckled and shook his finger at her. "You too realized what Lord Rathmore would do, my dear?"

"Not that they would go to Gretna Green, but perhaps that they would refuse to go along with the wedding . . . I can't lie to you, Papa. But I hadn't realized that you also —"

Alexandra stood there, wringing her hands, her distress enough to make any fond parent soften. Her guilt was strong, not subsiding. The duke watched her for a moment, then said, "Yes, I knew Tony wanted Melissande and that she wanted him.

I have never before seen two people more enraptured with each other so quickly. Tony is a fine young man — intelligent, witty, and blessed with good looks, an important ingredient to females. Further, he is nearly as rich as the Earl of Northcliffe. Doubtless he will offer a settlement to rival his cousin's; indeed in his letter he gives me his assurances. I imagine his guilt must prick him sorely, as I said — much greater than yours, Alex! — for did he not betray his cousin and take the woman the earl had chosen away from him? Ah yes, he despises himself for what he has done, now, of course, that he has done it, and there is no going back. Conscience, I've found, is all the more potent once the deed is done and irreversible. But despite this lapse, this quite unfortunate behavior, the viscount appears an honorable man. He will bring Melissande back here, and very soon. She, the minx, won't want to see us because she knows she's disaccommodated your mother and fears a great scold, but her husband will force her to come." The duke smiled into the distance. "Tony Parrish isn't a man to be wound around a woman's finger even though the woman is so beautiful it makes your teeth ache just to look at her. Aye, he will bring her back regardless of her pleas and her tears and her sulks."

"But I did guess, Papa, I truly did." There, it was out, all of it. She stood stiff and miserable, waiting for the parental tongue to flay her.

The duke took his daughter's hand and raised it to his lips. "All I regret is the immense bother occasioned by this irresponsible act. It is never a father's wish to have any of his offspring wed across the anvil in Scotland. A duke's daughter, in particular, isn't supposed to behave with such a lack of propriety." The duke paused then, and a myriad of expressions crossed his face. He said abruptly to Alexandra, "You want the earl so much, then?"

"You guessed that as well? Oh dear. It is revolting. I am as transparent as the fish pond."

"You are my daughter. I know you and I am rather fond of you."

"It's true. I have loved him, Papa, for three years, but now . . . now, I will not even have him as a brother-in-law."

She looked up at her father, desolation and pain in her fine eyes.

The duke said abruptly, "I just received a letter from your brother. I will tell you the truth, Alex. Even the settlement Tony will doubtless provide won't save this family. Your brother has left England in disgrace, on his way to America, he writes. He leaves immense debts behind him that will bankrupt me utterly. Even Tony's settlement, generous though I know it will be, won't settle the debts. I've been wondering what to do, thinking, worrying, struggling, but now . . . ah, now perhaps there is a ray of light." He turned on his heel and left the library, leaving Alexandra to stare speechlessly after him.

In approximately one hour Tony Parrish and

his new viscountess would arrive at Claybourn Hall. She was sulking, enjoying a truly royal snit, he knew, and it made him smile. He'd informed her in no uncertain terms that they had to return to her father's home, that he had to make things right again. She'd pleaded and begged; she hated her guilt and didn't want her nose rubbed in it. She'd even cried on his shoulder, immensely beautiful crocodile tears, he'd observed aloud to his new wife, who had then promptly flown into a passion. He'd laughed. Outraged, Melissande had thrown one of her hairbrushes at him but he'd simply thrown it back at her. She was so stunned at his retaliation, she was dumbstruck. He left the room, telling her to be downstairs in ten minutes. Another hairbrush had struck the closing door. She'd come down in eleven minutes and he'd looked at his watch and frowned at her. He said nothing. She had obeyed him. She would accustom herself, in time, to obeying him without scenes and tantrums and without using any extra minutes.

They rode in a private carriage Tony had rented from a stable in Harrogate to take them to Gretna Green. This was the second day of his marriage and in an hour he would have to face his new papa-in-law, who would doubtless want to strangle him. But he had to return. It was the right thing to do. There was no choice. Besides he'd written to the duke that he would return to discuss the marriage settlement and to make amends as best he could.

He smiled at his bride's altogether lovely profile and didn't question that he wanted her very much, right this instant. He had but to touch her hand and he wanted her. He had but to hear her voice from another room and he wanted her. He had but to see her flushed with anger and yelling at him and he wanted her. Having her so close to him was more than he could bear.

He turned and said, "Take off your pelisse."

Melissande was in the throes of guilt, embarrassment, fury with her new husband for treating her with no consideration at all — he'd actually thrown the hairbrush back at her! "What did you say?"

"I said to take off your pelisse."

"I'm not at all too warm."

"Good."

She frowned at him, then unbuttoned the pelisse. He helped her remove it, tossing it to the other seat. He lightly touched his fingertips to her chin, caressing her, holding her head steady. He kissed her, lightly, not parting his own lips on hers.

"Tony!"

"Hush. Now, dear one, remove your bonnet. I can't kiss you properly with that nonsense on your head. Also it flattens your beautiful hair. Black as the most sinful night, your hair. I want to feel it cascading through my fingers."

Since his order also contained a very nice compliment, Melissande, mollified, removed her bonnet, tossing it atop her pelisse.

"Now," Tony said. His long fingers began on the long line of buttons that marched up the front of her gown. She gasped and slapped at his hand. "We're in a carriage, Tony! It is in the middle of the day! Goodness, you must stop, you can't do that, you —"

He kissed her again, pulling her onto his lap. His right hand was beneath the hem of her gown, moving up her leg, higher and higher until he touched the bare soft flesh of her inner thighs. She was squirming on his lap, and he knew it was from embarrassment, not coyness. It didn't matter. He wanted her and he fully intended to take her, right here, in the carriage, with her sitting on his lap, facing him, and he would come deep inside her. He nearly moaned aloud with the thought.

She continued to struggle and he said into her mouth, "You will be quiet now. You are my wife, Melissande, and you will learn, very soon now, that you will obey me. I want you and I intend to have you. I haven't taken you since last night because you were a virgin and thus sore from that plowing. But you have had time to recover. I will go easily with you. I want to see your breasts, to fondle them, to taste them with my tongue. You will leave your gown on and I will come into you after you've lifted your skirts."

She stared at him in disbelief, so adrift in uncharted seas that she could find nothing to say. The previous evening, she'd felt wicked, truth be told, because of what they'd done. She had shown the damned Earl of Northcliffe that she wouldn't be ordered about by either him or her father. Tony was lovely; he was gallant; he teased her mercilessly, making her want more. He fascinated her. He was like quicksilver. She'd quickly recognized the strength in him, the male stubbornness, the arrogance that was bred in him, but she'd never doubted that she could handle him. After all, she'd handled every other gentleman who'd chanced to swim into her ken.

He'd introduced her to sex in a very polished way. She recognized, vaguely, that he was immensely experienced but she was unable to appreciate his finesse. She found the entire procedure horribly embarrassing, and the darkness she'd begged for hadn't slowed him down a bit. He hadn't hurt her overly much. As for any pleasure from coupling, she sincerely doubted that such a thing existed. She knew that all she enjoyed was compliments and kissing and his wicked smiles, and perhaps the tip of his tongue lightly touching her ear.

And now he wanted to stick that man-thing of his up into her whilst she sat on his lap, fully gowned yet naked whilst he had his way with her, and all in a moving carriage!

"No," she said very firmly. "I shan't do that."

Tony merely smiled, and thrust his fingers upward until they were pressed against her woman's flesh. She paled then yowled. His right hand busily worked on the buttons over her breasts. She slapped at him, until finally he said in his sternest voice, "You are my wife. How many times must I remind you, Melissande? I know you received little or no pleasure last night. You were a virgin and that is why. You bled and that pleased me. However, I intend to rectify that now. You will accept pleasure from me. You will hold still and stop playing the outraged maiden."

But she didn't stop struggling, even when she felt one of his long fingers slide upward into her. She yelled, and he kissed her, hoping the carriage driver hadn't heard her.

"A delightful virgin, a beauty, and a spoiled handful," he said, his breath warm on her mouth. "That's what I married. I'm not complaining, don't misunderstand me. I had an excellent idea of your character before I ever nibbled that sweet spot just behind your left ear. But I will beat you, you know."

"You wouldn't! No, I shan't allow such a thing! Stop, damn you! Stop doing that!"

"Oh yes, I will beat you," he said as his thumb found her flesh and he began to fondle her. "And I have no intention of stopping. You will see that I shall do whatever I wish to with you." She was undoubtedly beautiful, absolutely exquisite, even with her eyes near to crossing in rage, and truth be told, glazed in utter incomprehension, for she'd never encountered his like before. She tried to jerk away from him. He merely removed his hand, pulled up her gown, her petticoats, and her shift, then bent her back so that she was lying across his lap against his arm. She was wearing her black leather slippers and stockings that were just above her knees, held there with black garters. From there on, she was naked to her waist, and he looked down at her and smiled.

"Very nice," he said only and splayed his fingers over her white belly. "Very nice indeed. I fancy I'll keep you. Were you a trout I wouldn't toss you back into the water. No, indeed."

"You cannot do this, Tony! My father will challenge you to a duel, he will cut your ears off, he will — I'm not a damned fish!"

"Dearest wife, your father wouldn't dream of telling me, your legal husband, master, owner, and lord, not to give you pleasure. And that is what I will do if you would simply close your quite lovely mouth and attend my fingers."

She opened her mouth to yell again at him, then realized the driver would probably hear her. She felt sunk with embarrassment, so mortified she held herself quiet until his fingers began to caress her in that very private place he'd touched the previous night. She hadn't protested much then for she'd still been feeling wicked, and it was dark in the bedchamber, and truth be told, she'd felt very powerful — ah, she'd eloped to Gretna Green! — so she hadn't fully realized . . . simply hadn't known that he would want . . . but now, now it was different. It wasn't black as pitch. It was daylight. They were in a carriage. He had actually looked at her, spoken easily as he'd looked, and she'd been naked and he'd touched her belly and other lower parts. It wasn't to be borne. Suddenly, she felt a deep piercing sensation that made her hips jerk upward against his fingers.

She stared up at him, not understanding, and saw that the damned sod was smiling at her, a knowing smile, a master's smile, so smug and satisfied that it was more than she could stand. She threw back her head and screamed at the top of her lungs.

The carriage jerked to a sudden halt.

Tony's smile didn't slip. He eased her up, helped her straighten her clothes, and waited for their coachman to appear at the window, which he did almost immediately. His eyes went at once to Melissande, and she realized that he must know what her husband had been attempting to do to her.

"Go away!" she yelled at the hapless man. "Ah, just go away!"

"Yes," Tony said easily, sitting back against the squabs, his arms folded over his chest. "Forgive my wife for disturbing you. Sometimes ladies, well, they forget themselves . . . you understand."

The coachman was very afraid he did understand, and, flushing, hurried to climb back to his perch. The carriage jerked forward.

Tony was quiet.

Melissande arranged herself with quick clumsy movements, so furious and embarrassed and disconcerted she wanted to shriek at him until she was hoarse. But it was difficult with him just sitting there, looking out the windows, saying nothing, looking bored. *Bored!*

She smashed her bonnet back onto her head, not caring that her lovely coiffure would suffer irreparable damage from her show of rage. She pulled on her pelisse and refastened the buttons, putting the wrong ones in the wrong holes and not caring.

He looked at her then and the smile was still on his lips. "You know, Mellie —"

"Mellie! What a horrid nickname! I hate it, it is perfectly dreadful and I —"

"Shut up, my dear."

"But, I —" She saw something in his eyes that she'd never encountered before in her twenty-one years. She closed her mouth and turned away, momentarily routed.

"As I was saying, Mellie, for you I betrayed my cousin. However, it isn't the sort of betrayal that destroys the soul. You don't really know Douglas nor does he know you. Lord, were he to have seen your games during the past few days, he would have been utterly disillusioned. He probably would have snuck out in the dark of night to escape you. He wouldn't have taken you to Gretna Green. Indeed, three years ago, I doubt you even saw him beyond a handsome man who praised your immense beauty. He left you because of his honor, because he felt he had to place his duty above matters of the heart. I will tell you truthfully, my dear, he doesn't love you. He remembered that he had desired you, had admired you, had laughed and been entranced by your carelessness, your seeming guilelessness. He remembered your beauty, nothing more.

"But he doesn't love you nor did he then. His family has been ruthless in their attempts to get him wedded so that there will be a Sherbrooke heir within the year. He saw you as a way to batten down his family, to wed himself to a beautiful creature, and save himself from having to travel to London to see the crop of available debutantes.

"Even as I knew I would have you, I was thinking of all the pros and cons of what I was doing. One thing I'm quite certain of though, Douglas will come to realize what a favor I did for him by removing you from the scene. One day he will thank me. You would have driven him mad, utterly mad." Tony now turned to his wife. He was looking very serious. "He is much more the gentleman than I am, you know. He would never have beaten you, no matter the provocation. He would have withdrawn from you, not at all what would bring you into line."

She said slowly, "I don't believe you. Douglas Sherbrooke does love me. He loved me then, he loved me for three years, and he still loves me. He will mourn me the rest of his life. I will be his lost love. Aye, I have broken his heart by wedding you. He will hate you forever for what you have done. He will never forgive you."

Tony said quietly, "I hope it will not be so. I believe that only Douglas's pride will be a bit bruised. Then he will recover with alacrity when he sees what I must do to keep you under control. He will pump my hand in his gratitude. He will blubber all over me with thankfulness."

Melissande looked down at her gloved hands. "You speak as though you do not hold me in esteem. You speak as though I am not a person to be admired or loved. You speak as though you took me away only to save your cousin. I thought you adored me, wanted me desperately."

"Ah, that is true enough. Understand, just because I adore and want you doesn't mean that I am blind to your character. However, it isn't at all to the point. You see, what I have done demands retribution. I owe Douglas payment, of sorts, so that he won't have to start again at the beginning in his quest for a wife. Indeed, in my letter to your father I hinted as much."

"What do you mean?"

"I don't believe I will tell you, Mellie, not yet, because I have yet to be certain whether my notions are accurate." He gave her a crooked smile. "You see, I was thinking too much about you, about having you naked beneath me, to keep an excellent mental accounting of what I hoped would be true. Well, hopefully your father will have determined the accuracy by the time we return to Claybourn. Now, my dear, your bonnet looks quite dowdy. I suggest you endeavor to make yourself look a bit more charming, for we are nearing Claybourn."

He'd silenced her questions for the moment by appealing to her vanity. He watched her pull a small mirror from her reticule. She was efficient in her efforts, from long practice. She was so beautiful it made him shake. Her body was undoubtedly lovely — at least the parts he'd just managed to uncover and see and touch. He'd wanted to see her face when he took her virginity the previous night, but she'd been so frightened, so embarrassed, that he hadn't the heart to insist upon the lamp being lit. But what really shook him and surprised him as well was that no woman had ever affected him as she had. He had also known instantly that she was utterly impossible, spoiled, vain, as arrogant as he was, but it hadn't mattered. He'd wanted her. Despite Douglas, despite everything, he'd wanted her and he'd taken her.

Now the trick would be to live with her.

Another trick would be to bring her pleasure. The thought of a frigid wife was intolerable. It was nauseating.

The most important trick would be to pay Douglas back.

Odd, Tony thought, as the carriage bowled onto the long narrow drive of Claybourn Hall, but he hadn't given Teresa, his perfidious former betrothed, a thought since he'd met Melissande. He looked at his wife, saw that she was pale and that she was wringing her hands.

He rather hoped her father would yell at her.

Then he, Tony, would step in. He was her protector, her master, her husband. Then, he prayed, he and the duke would come to another agreement.

Boulogne, France

Douglas won the piquet match. He hadn't even had to cheat. Belesain had been so drunk by the end of it, Douglas doubted he'd minded losing very much because as the winner he would have had to perform sexually, a feat he probably couldn't have managed. He'd given Douglas a key and told him to explain to the lovely wench he found in the small room that he was here to be pleasured. He said the wench loved threats and a bit of pain. Then, the bloody drunk fool had decided to accompany him. "Because," he said as they climbed the stairs to the third floor, "she isn't exactly trained fully as yet." Douglas watched him unlock the door and stride inside.

He followed, saying nothing. It was a spare room, with only a bed and dresser and a single circular rug in the middle. There was only one occupant, a single woman standing in the middle of the room. Was this Janine Daudet? The general grinned drunkenly at her and said with a flip of his hand, "Strip off those clothes."

The woman hesitated, then complied. He'd expected someone younger, though why he should have he didn't know. No, she wasn't really a girl, Douglas thought, looking at her more closely, but rather a woman in her mid-twenties. She was obviously scared and she was lovely, despite her pallor, the shadows beneath her very dark eyes, and her thinness.

Belesain waited silently until she'd stripped to her shift. Then he lurched to her, grabbed her chin painfully in his fingers and kissed her, fondling her breasts with his other hand through the thin lawn. Then, suddenly, he grabbed the front of her shift and ripped it off her. He laughed, saying over his shoulder to Douglas, "I wanted to see if you approved of her. Nice, eh? A bit thin for my taste, but her tits are nice." He pushed her back onto the bed, leaned over her, and said low, "You see this man, my girl? You do everything he wants you to do or . . . you know the punishment, don't you? I would like to remain and watch, but I am sorely tired." He straightened and turned to Douglas. "You are quiet. Don't you think she is lovely? Not a virgin, but not overused either. She belongs to me, and now, because she isn't stupid, she obeys my every command. Now you may enjoy her, but just for tonight."

He lurched out of the room. Douglas moved after him and listened as his footsteps receded down the corridor and then down the stairs. He listened to another door open and close on the second floor. Then he turned back to face the woman.

She was standing now by the bed, trying to cover herself with her hands. Douglas couldn't believe his good fortune but he wasn't about to doubt it, not for a moment.

His voice was urgent as he strode to her. "Is your name Janine Daudet?"

She was small, very fair, her hair falling straight down her back nearly to her waist. She had light blue eyes, very blond brows and lashes, and she was lovely.

"Are you?"

She nodded, taking a step back.

"Don't be afraid of me. I'm here on behalf of Georges Cadoudal."

Douglas wasn't able to keep his eyes on her face. He hadn't had a woman in a while. His body was responding with deplorable enthusiasm. "Do you know Georges Cadoudal?"

She nodded, still obviously afraid of him, not believing him for a moment, despite the flare of hope he'd seen.

"I wish you to dress, quickly. I am here to take you away, to Georges. We must hurry."

"I don't have any gowns."

Douglas looked around. "A cloak, anything. Come, we must hurry."

"I don't believe you." So there was some spirit left in her after all. She was nearly strangling on her fear but she still kept on. "I know that he gave me to you, he said so, and I know why he did it."

"It's because I won a wager."

"Oh no." She became even paler. Her rouged lips parted, then closed. She shook her head, then said in a rush, "He wants me to find out what you will tell Bonaparte when you return to Paris. He worries also that you are really a spy. I think he would prefer a spy to you being from Bonaparte because he fears Bonaparte will discover the wicked things he's done. He told me I must discover the truth or he will kill my grandmother."

"Ah." Douglas smiled down at her and gently began to run his hands up and down her thin arms. So, the general hadn't been drunk at all. The piquet, the wager, his loss, it had all been Belesain's plan to trap him. Not bad.

"Easy now," he said absently, trying to calm her, all the while thinking furiously.

"Where is your grandmother?"

Janine started. "She's at the farm, two miles from Etaples to the south. He says that he has a man there watching her and that the man will kill her if I don't do as he orders."

"If I know Georges, he's already taken care of any guards at your grandmother's farmhouse. I am really here to save you. Now, let's get you dressed in something. I am taking you and your grandmother to England."

"England," she said slowly, her dark eyes wide with surprise. "But we only speak French."

"It doesn't matter. Many people speak French in England and you will learn. Georges lives there much of the time and he can teach both of you English."

"But —"

"No, I can say no more. Georges wishes me to take you to London. You will be safe there until he returns to fetch you. There are chores he must attend to here first. Will you trust me?"

She looked up at him, worship and trust shining from her face and said simply, "Yes."

"Good. Now, listen to me. Here's what we will do." Douglas wondered, as he stared down into that pale tense face that held such radiant trust for him, why people in general and females in particular believed him to be some sort of Saint George. He hated it but at the same time he found it amusing. He thought of Georges Cadoudal, and fervently hoped she would remember him. After all, Douglas was probably a married man by now and he wanted no moonstruck female on his arm on his return to England.

CHAPTER 6

Northcliffe Hall
Five Days Later

Douglas opened the door of the library, saw a lone candle burning on the small table beside his cousin, and strode into the room, a tired smile lighting his face.

"Tony! Lord, it's good to see you and good to be home again." Douglas rubbed his hands together. "Ah, it's wonderful to be home and I fancy you know well my reasons."

"Douglas," Tony said, rising. He strode to his cousin and shook his hand. "I gather you were successful in whatever mission you undertook?"

Douglas gave him a fat smile and continued to rub his hands together. "Very successful, thank a benevolent God and a very stupid general who thought he could outsmart me. All, that dressing gown of yours is very elegant, but if you're not careful, your hairy legs stick out." He walked over to the sideboard. "You want some nice French brandy? I did promise you all you could drink until the next century."

"No, I think not."

Douglas poured the brandy, took a deep drink, felt it snake a warm trail all the way to his belly. "Hollis said you had to speak to me, that it was quite important, that it couldn't possibly wait until morning. I thought for a moment he was going to cry, but of course that's nonsense. Hollis never cries or yells or shows any unsuitable emotion. But it is nearly midnight, Tony, and I'm babbling because I'm about to collapse at your feet. Of course, once I see my beautiful bride, I imagine I'll forget all my fatigue. Still, I was surprised to see Hollis still up. What do you want?"

"I tried to tell Hollis to take himself off to bed, that I would await you in the entrance hall, but being Hollis, he refused."

Douglas took another long drink of his brandy, then sat himself in a deep wing chair next to his cousin's. "What's wrong?" There was dark silence, and Douglas suddenly knew that something he wasn't going to like at all was very near now, and Tony was the messenger. "You did marry Melissande, did you not?"

Tony looked at him full-face. "Yes," he said, "I did marry her." He drew a deep breath, knowing there was no hope for it, and blurted out, "I also married her younger sister."

Douglas had just taken another sip of brandy. He spit it out and choked on a cough. "You *what?*"

"I said I married two women." Anthony Parrish turned to stare into the fireplace, at the glowing embers. So much for his rehearsed explanation.

He felt as tired as his cousin. In addition, he carried a burden of guilt that was well-nigh dragging him underground. "You may select to challenge me to a duel, Douglas. It will be your right. I will not fire against you, that I swear."

"What the hell are you talking about?" But Douglas didn't want to know what his cousin was talking about. He wanted to leave, right this minute, and go up to the huge master suite, to the huge master bed where Melissande awaited him. He didn't want to hear any more about Tony marrying two women.

"I didn't marry Melissande by proxy for you. I married her first over the anvil in Gretna Green, then once again later at her father's house. I then married Alexandra, her younger sister, by proxy, to you."

"I see," Douglas said. He rose, set his brandy snifter down carefully on the side table, nodded to his cousin, picked up a candle, and strode from the library.

"Douglas! Wait! You don't understand. For God's sake, come back here!"

But Douglas wasn't about to stop. He heard Tony coming after him and quickened his pace. A mistake, that's what all this was, no, it was a wicked joke, a joke worthy of Ryder . . . no . . . something else. He heard his cousin on the stairs behind him as he turned into the eastern corridor. He ran down the long hall to the master suite at the end. He pulled open the double doors, dashed inside, then slammed them closed behind him, and quickly turned the key.

He looked toward his bed, holding his candle high. The covers were as smooth as when he'd left Northcliffe Hall two weeks before. The bed was empty.

He walked to the dais and stood there staring down at that damned empty bed. He'd dreamed of this bed. Not empty like it was now. No, he'd dreamed of Melissande lying on her back in the middle, her arms open, inviting him to come to her.

He turned, furious, nearly beyond understanding anything. He looked toward the adjoining door and realized he was being a fool. Naturally she wouldn't be in his bed, she would be in the countess's bedchamber next to his. He was a stranger to her, somewhat, and it wouldn't be proper for her to be in his bed, at least not yet. Not until he had, as her husband, formally fetched her into his bed.

He flung open the door to the adjoining bedchamber. This room was smaller, its furnishings soft and very female; this was the room visited by the resident ghost who didn't exist and never had existed except in bored or fevered female minds. He saw that the bed covers were rumpled. But this bed was also empty. It was then he saw her. It was a girl and she was standing in the shadows, wearing a long white gown that covered her from her chin to her toes. He couldn't see her all that clearly, but he knew that she was very pale, and clearly startled. And was it fear he saw as well? Fear of him?

Hell, she should be afraid, he thought, and took two steps forward. She wasn't Melissande. She was a bloody stranger and she had the gall to be here in his wife's bedchamber, standing there as if she belonged, staring at him as if he were an intruder at the least, perhaps even a murderer. He stopped dead in his tracks. "Who the devil are you?"

He sounded very calm, which surprised him no end. He was shaking on the outside, his gut cramping on the inside, and he quickly set down the candle on the stand beside the bed.

"I asked you who you are. What the hell are you doing in here? Where is Melissande?"

"Melissande is down the hall, in the west wing. The bedchamber is called the Green Cube, I believe."

Her voice was scared — high, thin, and reedy. "I don't know you. Why are you here?"

The girl stepped forward, and he saw her square her shoulders. In the dim candlelight he saw that she was small, slight of build, and her hair was a rich dark red, long and waving down her back and over her shoulders.

"I was sleeping here."

"You aren't Melissande."

"No," she said. "I'm Alexandra. I'm actually your wife."

He laughed then, and it was an ugly raw sound, holding disbelief and utter incredulity. "You can't be my wife, sweetheart, for I've never seen you in my life. I believe you must be one of Tony's wives or perhaps one of his many mistresses."

"You have seen me before, my lord, it's just that you don't remember me. I was only fifteen at the time and you saw only my sister."

"Yes, and I married your sister."

There was loud pounding on the door in Douglas's bedchamber. He could hear Tony working the doorknob frantically. Douglas looked up, hearing Tony shout, "Douglas, open this damned door! Alexandra, are you all right?"

"I'm all right, Tony," she called out. She turned back to Douglas and said in a voice calm as a nun's, "Shall I let him in, my lord?"

"Why not? He appears to be married to everyone, thus it is his right to visit any number of female beds."

When the strange girl walked past him into his bedchamber, Douglas moved quickly to the hall door of this adjoining chamber, and was out the door just as Tony burst into his bedchamber. Tony saw him take off on a dead run toward the west wing.

"Douglas, damn you, stop! Where the hell are you going now? Oh, no! Stop!"

But Douglas didn't stop until he flung open the door of the Green Cube bedchamber. There, in the canopied bed, lay his wife, his bride, Melissande. She was sitting up now, looking dazed, then alarmed, framed in the candlelight. She met his gaze and blinked, pulling the sheet up to her chin.

"Douglas Sherbrooke?"

"Why are you in this room? What are you doing in his bed?"

"Because she's married to me, dammit! Douglas, please, come away, and let me explain what happened."

"No, I want to take my wife back to my bedchamber. I want her in my bed. You can't marry every woman, Tony. It's not legal except in Turkey. Truly, you must be a Muslim. So, I'll take this one."

"She's not your wife! I married her for myself, not for you. I've slept with her, Douglas! I took her virginity. She is my wife." Tony had begun on a roar but he managed to end on a lower, much calmer octave.

Douglas, very pale now, stared at Melissande. God, she was the loveliest creature he'd ever seen. Her black hair was tousled about her white face, her startling dark blue eyes large and deep and so seductive he could feel himself getting hard despite what was happening, despite the fact she was apparently married to Tony, despite . . . Douglas shook his head. He was tired, exhausted actually, but he'd ridden like the devil's own disciple to get home tonight, to his bride. He thought briefly of Janine and wondered how she would do here as a third wife. He shook his head and looked again toward his bride.

But there was no bride.

No, that wasn't right. There was a bride and her name was Alexandra and he'd never seen her before in his life even though she claimed he had.

He turned slowly to look at his cousin. "I want you to tell me this is one of your benighted jests."

"It's not. Please, Douglas, come with me back downstairs and I will explain everything."

"You can explain *this?*"

"Yes, if you'll just give me a ch—."

"You bloody bastard!" Douglas bared his teeth and lunged at his cousin. He slammed his fist into Tony's jaw, sending him sprawling. Tony rolled over and came up again, shaking his head. Douglas hit him again. This time, Tony grabbed Douglas's lapels and pulled him down with him. They fell with a loud thud, struggling, arms and legs flailing and thrashing.

Melissande screamed.

Alexandra stood in the open doorway, her candle held high. She saw Tony roll over on top of Douglas and smash his fist into his jaw. Douglas grunted in pain, brought up his knees and slammed them in Tony's back, lurching up. Tony hit Douglas again, harder now, making his head snap back.

Alexandra howled. She quickly dropped the candle to a tabletop and leapt upon Tony's back, pounding at his head with her fists, then jerking his hair. "Stop it, you brute! Let him alone!"

She pounded and pounded and jerked and jerked. Tony, so surprised by this unexpected onslaught that he froze, was quickly upended by Douglas. Both Alexandra and Tony went sprawling. Douglas grabbed Tony by his shirt and dragged him upright. He slammed his fist into his belly. Tony grunted, bending over, hugging his arms around himself. Suddenly, Melissande came flying through the air to leap upon Douglas's back, wrapping her legs around his waist. She pounded her fists at his head, screaming right into his ear, "Leave him alone!"

Douglas felt his entire brain begin to vibrate. His ears were ringing. She was pulling his hair out, still screaming at him, right into his ear. Then, the other wife, the small one, was tugging madly at Melissande, jerking her off Douglas's back. Both women went down together in a twist of white nightgowns and flying masses of hair.

Tony was still bent over, trying to regain his breath. Douglas felt as though he should be bald. His scalp throbbed from Melissande's attack. He stood there, surveying the disaster. He watched as the small girl untangled herself from Melissande, rose, and rushed to him. Her face was white, her eyes dilated. She was trembling and panting.

He stood silent as a stone as her hands went from his shoulders to his chest, then to the length of his arms. He still didn't move, didn't say a word. "Are you all right? Did he hurt you? Please, tell me if you have pain." Her fingertips skimmed lightly over his jaw and he jerked back just a bit. "Oh, forgive me, it's tender, isn't it? I'm sorry. It's not broken, no, but he hit you very hard."

Douglas shook his head, but otherwise he still didn't move. For the life of him he couldn't come up with one reason why he should move or say anything, for that matter. Her hands continued their journey over his body, feeling, lightly prodding. Finally, when she was about to drop to her knees and feel his legs, Douglas grabbed her wrists and pulled them together in front of her. He shook her to get her attention. He said very slowly, "I'm just fine. Leave me alone. Go feel him — your other husband." He looked beyond her to Melissande, who was standing beside Tony, her long black hair an incredibly soft curtain that hid her face from him. Her soft hands were on Tony's body.

Douglas stepped back from the second wife and looked toward the open doorway. He said quite calmly, "Hollis, please come in here."

Hollis, not one ounce of dignity lighter, stepped into the den of chaos. He said very gently, "My lord, should you care to accompany me, the others may then attire themselves in more suitable garb. I will serve brandy in the drawing room and they may join us when they wish. Come now, my lord. That's right. Come with me. All will be well."

Douglas allowed himself to be led away. He felt oddly numb now, even though his scalp still throbbed and his ears were still ringing. Melissande had strong fingers and even stronger lungs. He felt he should be someone else; he didn't want to be Douglas Sherbrooke because that poor fellow was an absurdity. He was a fool, a dunce, an ass, who'd nearly had all his hair pulled from his head and lost his bride. He heard himself say in a voice that didn't resemble his at all, "But Hollis, that girl jumped on Tony. Why would she do that? He said he'd married her. I've never seen her before. Why would that little twit seek to rescue me?"

"Don't concern yourself just now, my lord," came Hollis's soothing voice. "You must be pleased that she would try to protect you."

"Protect me! Damnation, she looked ready to fight to the death."

"Yes, my lord. It is fitting for her to do so. She is your wife, my lord, and your countess. Indeed, she has lived here for two days now and has gone along very well."

Douglas said very firmly, "No, she isn't my wife. That is quite impossible. I told you I'd never seen her before. Melissande is my wife. Her, I recognized. I will kill Tony for this." Douglas paused in his tracks, looking back over his shoulder. "Do you think if I leave that girl here she will kill Tony for me?"

"Probably not, my lord. Her violence was only brought on by his attack on you. Lord Rathmore is now subdued and thus she has achieved her aims. Come along now. Everything will look a bit differently in the morning."

"I can't sleep in the same bed with that strange girl, Hollis. I'm a gentleman. Since you allowed her to come into my house, I can assume, can

I not, that she isn't a possible mistress? You say she's been here two days? No, I cannot like it or accept it. Even though she tried to kill Tony, I can't sleep with her."

"No, my lord. I understand your reasoning perfectly. Your sentiments are most commendable. Her Ladyship will appreciate your motives. Come along now. You need to rest and allow your mental parts to reassemble themselves."

With silence and coffee, not brandy, Douglas's mental parts quickly came together again, but that coming together built such rage in him that he choked on the coffee.

"I will have to kill him, Hollis."

"Perhaps not, my lord. You must listen to Lord Rathmore first. You were — are — quite fond of him, you know."

"Ah! There you are, you damned scoundrel!"

Douglas rose half out of his chair, only to feel Hollis's hand firmly on his shoulder. He subsided.

But he didn't want to. He wanted to go to bed and sleep for twelve hours, awaken and find that everything was as it should be. No, he wanted to kill his cousin.

Instead, Douglas, the man of normally fine-working mental parts and skilled strategies, said very calmly, "Tell me why you betrayed me."

Tony's hair still stood on end, the result of that other female's attack. He was still wearing his dressing gown, now ripped beneath the right arm and hanging longer on one side than on the other. He kept his distance. "Will you listen to me without trying to kill me again?"

"I'll listen. As for killing you, I dare say that will happen some morning soon at dawn."

"God, Douglas, don't talk like that! Damn, I didn't mean it to happen, but it did."

Hollis cleared his throat, saying gently, "Enough *mea culpas,* my lord. His Lordship is in need of facts. All this emotion is wearisome and not at all to the point."

"I fell in love with Melissande the moment I saw her and she fell in love with me. I know all her faults, Douglas, faults you can't begin to imagine, but I didn't care. I understood her and I knew that I could handle her. We eloped. Upon our return to Claybourn Hall, the duke and I decided that I would wed Alexandra by proxy to you. She was willing and the duke was more than willing. Indeed, he had just heard his wastrel son had not only left England in the dark of night, he had also bequeathed his father a mountain of debts. The duke was frantic and thus agreed, for your settlement in addition to the one I made him would rescue him and his family from disgrace. Still, I wasn't certain, Douglas, you must believe that, but there were so many good reasons for doing it, least of which Alexandra is lovely, she's a lady, she's not stupid, and you won't have to go to London and start all over again to find another wife. You have one and she's quite all right and here and you will get to know her and everything will be fine.

"Perhaps this angers you, perhaps you believe I did it just to try to placate you, perhaps everything I'm saying rings false to you, but I swear to you that I gave it great thought. I studied Alexandra thoroughly, and I swear she is worthy of you. She's a good sort. She isn't arrogant or vain. She's kind and steady and loyal —"

"You make her sound like a damned horse, Tony. Or a panting hound. She isn't Melissande!"

"No, lucky for you. Come, you saw how she defended you, her husband, nearly killing me! Truly, Douglas, you wouldn't be pleased for long with Melissande for your wife."

"Ha! You slippery sod, you make it sound as though you saved me from a fate worse than death. You want me to believe that you removed the plague from me and took it onto yourself, that you martyred yourself for me. You stole my wife, Tony! Damn you, it is too much, I have listened to your lame excuses and I —"

"My lord," Hollis said softly, his hand once more on Douglas's shoulder, "we must remain for the moment with the facts. Emotion is enervating and leads, evidently, to violence. I cannot allow more violence in Northcliffe."

"Where is my sister? Where are Ryder and Tysen and my mother?"

"Master Ryder insisted they all leave Northcliffe until everything was sorted out. He is an intelligent young man. Once he understood what had happened, he had the family gone from here within two hours. They, ah, are staying presently in London, at the Sherbrooke town house."

Lord, he'd very nearly taken Janine to the town house, but in the end, Lord Avery had seen to her lodgings. Douglas twisted about to look up at Hollis. "So, I'm alone in the house with this bloody wife thief?" Douglas rubbed his hands together and he smiled. "Excellent! That means I can kill him with no one the wiser, without Tysen preaching to me from his future pulpit, without Ryder laughing at me, without my sister and mother falling into a swoon. No, that's not true, is it, Hollis? It wasn't all Ryder's idea, was it? No, you were afraid there would be disagreements and so you convinced Ryder to remove them all. Ah, I don't mind, indeed I don't. Thank God, you sent them away. Now, I am going to kill this damned bastard cousin of mine!" Douglas roared to his feet.

"Please, no more, my lord."

Douglas stopped cold and stared at the same slight female who'd been upstairs in the midst of the fray. She was now standing in the open doorway, that same female who'd tried to protect him. The same one who was supposedly his cursed wife. He shuddered with the strangeness of it; it was absurd; it wasn't real; he couldn't, wouldn't, accept it.

"Tell me your name, at least," he said, his voice harsh, his fury boiling near the surface.

"My name is Alexandra Gabrielle Chambers. I am the Duke of Beresford's youngest child, but I am not a child, I am eighteen years old and a woman." She paused and he saw the strain on her face, really a quite pretty face, with rather luminous gray eyes that weren't stupid. She'd pulled her hair back and tied it with a ribbon at the nape of her neck. She had nice bones, a nice mouth, pleasantly arched brows and quite pretty small ears. It didn't move him one bit, none of it. She fretted with the sash on her pale blue dressing gown, then looked up to face him again. "Don't you remember me at all, my lord?"

"No."

"I suppose I have changed a bit. I was plump then and even shorter. I even wore spectacles sometimes to read, my hair was always in tight childish braids, so it was likely that you disregarded me entirely, but now —"

"I really don't care if you were bald and obese. Go away. Go back to bed. You can be certain that I won't come to ravish you tonight. I am not in the habit of bedding women who are strangers to me."

She paused a moment, drawing up, straightening just a bit more. She looked briefly at Tony, then nodded. "As you wish, my lord. I will sleep in the adjoining bedchamber if that is all right with you."

"Sleep in the corridor! Sleep with Tony for all I care. After all, he appears to have married you too."

"Really, Douglas —"

Alexandra turned without another word and left. She picked up a candle from a huge Spanish table in the entrance hall. She walked slowly up the wide staircase. What had she expected? That he would look at her and fall into raptures at the gift Tony had bestowed upon him? That he would compare her to Melissande and decide straightaway in her favor? That he would fall instantly and madly in love with her? That he would sing hallelujahs and donate his wealth to charities for what Tony had brought about? Or rather what her father had convinced her to do? Ah, her father . . . She remembered exactly what he'd said, how he'd begged her, pleaded with her, used her own feelings against her, how . . . Alexandra shook her head. No, it was on her head, no one else's, all of it. If she had wanted to toe the line, had really wanted to refuse, her father wouldn't have forced her to wed Douglas by proxy. But the money, he'd needed it so desperately, and he actually believed that the addition of both Douglas Sherbrooke and Anthony Parrish to the family would force his fatuous heir, Reginald, once he returned to England, to curb his wild, spendthrift ways.

Ha! She was doing it again, trying to find reasons to convince herself that what she'd done was right and just and really marvelous. When, in fact, there were no good reasons at all. Douglas had been betrayed by his cousin and by Melissande and by her father. And by her. She'd been hoping, desperately hoping that his reaction when he learned about her would be different, but now Douglas had come home and reality had presented a furious face. *It will be all right. You mustn't give up. It will be all right.* Her silly litany, Alexandra thought, climbing the stairs. Stupid and immature and . . .

Melissande was waiting at the top of the stairs, clutching her hands spasmodically to her bosom.

"Well?" she said without preamble. "Have they started fighting again? Have they drawn guns or their swords? Will they fight for me?"

"Are you palpitating?"

"No, don't be silly. What does that mean?"

Alexandra only shook her head. Nastiness toward the bone of contention between the two men was unworthy. "He told me to go to bed," she said, forcing all emotion from her voice.

"You knew this would happen, Alex. I warned you; I warned Father, but he talked you into going along with him. I warned Tony. All of you knew that Douglas wanted me desperately, not you. How could he ever want you or any other lady once he'd seen me? He doesn't even remember you, does he?"

Alexandra shook her head.

"It isn't that I mind you being a countess, Alex, though you certainly won't be happy being one. If your husband hates you, if he can't bear to look at you, if he leaves the room when you enter, how then can you be happy? No, I'm the one who should be a duchess or a countess, but here I am only a viscountess. But it is what I chose, isn't it? I chose Tony and he had no choice once I'd chosen him. Poor Alex! Poor Douglas!

Are you certain Douglas isn't trying to kill Tony again?"

"Hollis will control both of them."

"A butler giving the orders," Melissande said. "I wouldn't stand for it were I mistress here. It is beyond strange."

"Yes," Alexandra said as she passed by her sister. She said over her shoulder, very quietly, "He wants you, of course, you're quite right about that. He probably will always want you."

Melissande smiled. "I told Tony the earl wouldn't forgive him. I told him, yet he chose to disbelieve me. I have found that men do not always accept the truth even when it is presented to them with sincerity and candor. They always believe they can rearrange things to suit themselves." Melissande paused a moment, then marred her lovely forehead with a deep frown. "I begin to think now that perhaps I made a mistake. Tony isn't the man I married. He wants to order me about, to treat me like a possession. He even told me he wasn't the gentleman Douglas was. He actually wanted to take liberties with my person in a carriage, Alex, in broad daylight, and not an hour from Claybourn Hall! Can you believe that? I couldn't allow such a monstrous sort of man-behavior. Perhaps Douglas isn't so indelicate, so uncaring, about a lady's sensibilities. Yes, I probably made a mistake. Why, do you know that he threatened to —" Melissande closed her mouth over further illuminations.

Alex stared in dismay at her sister. Melissande

was now regretting marrying Tony? But how could that be? Tony certainly teased her, mocking her, but Melissande appeared to find this to her liking. Oh Lord. There were already too many untold ingredients in the pot. "Then why did you attack Douglas?"

"Because you had attacked Tony," Melissande said matter-of-factly. "It seemed the thing to do. Before Tony went downstairs to speak again with Douglas, he hugged me and told me next he would send me a dragon to slay. It pleased him that I acted the hoyden, that I yelled and nearly pulled out Douglas's hair. It's all very strange. He is quite unaccountable. Men are quite unaccountable."

Alexandra could only stare at her sister. "Tony will make things right with Douglas. The two of them are very close. Hollis said so."

Melissande shrugged. "I think Tony should suffer for what he did."

"But you did it right along with him!"

"Tony is a man; it is his responsibility."

"That's drivel," Alexandra said, and left her sister at the top of the stairs, peeking over the railing. She walked quickly down the long eastern corridor whose walls were lined with portraits of past Sherbrookes, many of whose faces and costumes sorely needed restoration. She went into the adjoining bedchamber and stood in the middle of the room, shivering. The bed was much smaller and shorter than the one in the master bedchamber. Alexandra supposed that since she was small and short, it didn't matter.

She remembered when Hollis had shown her through the master suite and she'd stood there and just stared at that huge bed, realizing for the first time that husbands and wives sometimes slept together if they wished to have children, that this was the bed where a child would be conceived. She didn't understand the process, but the thought of not wearing her clothing in front of a man made her brain clog and close down. Hollis, bless his astute soul, had said calmly, "I believe it wise to allow some time for His Lordship to accustom himself. You must be recognized as a wife, my lady, before you can be recognized as the Sherbrooke bride."

It was just that this room was so very cold and empty, much more empty than before Douglas had come home.

She snuffed out the candle and climbed into the bed, shivering violently between the cold sheets. She wondered if she would remain in this room for the rest of her years. For the moment, she had lost a goodly portion of her optimism about this marriage. Was Melissande right? Would Douglas ignore her or treat her badly?

She wasn't even a marriage of convenience, for Douglas Sherbrooke had paid dearly for her. Actually, he had paid dearly for Melissande and he had gotten her instead. And she hadn't brought him anything at all.

Tony had spent hours telling her about Douglas, reassuring her, reeling off anecdotes at a fine rate.

She knew all his questions to her were to judge whether or not she was worthy of his esteemed cousin. At least she'd passed Tony's tests. He wanted her for a cousin-in-law, he said, and when she said she was already a sister-in-law, he'd gotten that gleam in his eyes that Melissande seemed to adore, and said, "Ah, then I shall have you so deep in my family that you'll never escape." Again and again he'd said Douglas didn't love Melissande, that she was merely a quite beautiful convenience for him, that he didn't know her at all, and would have been horrified to have found himself married to her, then hastened to add that he, Tony, most certainly did know her, but it didn't matter because he was him and not Douglas. All quite confusing, really.

So Douglas Sherbrooke didn't love Melissande. Ha! So now he was wedded to an unbeautiful convenience and he didn't love her either.

Alexandra burrowed deeper into the sheets, seeing her husband bursting into the bedchamber. She hadn't seen him for three long years. During the last two days she'd wondered if he'd changed, grown fat, perhaps, or lost his hair or his teeth, and then he'd appeared and she'd only been able to stand there gaping at him, utterly witless. He looked older, she'd thought, staring at him, a hard-faced man with dark hair and eyes even darker and high-bridged nose that made him look utterly superior, utterly arrogant. As if to ruin the image of centuries of noblesse oblige, nature had added a cleft in the middle of his chin. Ah, but he was beautiful, this man who was now her husband, his body as lean and hard as his expression was severe, the most exquisite man she'd ever imagined.

Oddly enough though, Alexandra hadn't realized she loved him completely and utterly, with every ounce of feeling within her, until he'd thrown his head back, yowled like a madman, and flung himself at his cousin.

He was the man she wanted. Her natural optimism surfaced a bit. It will be all right, she repeated to herself yet again. She was still awake many hours later when she heard him moving about in the bedchamber next to hers.

And what, she wondered, would happen on the morrow?

CHAPTER 7

"What the hell are you doing here?"

It was seven in the morning, surely too early an hour for him to be here, in this precise spot, in the vast Sherbrooke stable. It was foggy, damp, and cloudy — all in all a dismal morning, a morning to match her mood and his too, evidently. The light was dim inside the stable and none of the half-dozen stable lads were about. The smells were comforting — hay, linseed, leather, and horse. Douglas was wearing buckskins, a dark brown coat, and Hessians that sorely needed polish. He looked tired, unshaved, tousled, and vastly irritated. To an objective person he would perhaps appear an ill-tempered dirty-looking brute. To her jaundiced eye, however, he looked immensely wonderful.

"I was going to ride, my lord."

"Oh? Perhaps my vision has become suddenly deficient for I don't believe I've seen any unknown horses in my stables. Where is this horse you were going to ride? I assume it is a horse. Even though I am apparently the ass in this drama, you cannot ride me."

Alex was silent a moment, then said calmly

enough, "Mr. McCallum has given me Fanny to ride since I've been here."

"Fanny belongs to my sister."

"I know. She is a spirited mare with a sweet mouth and nice manners. I know how to ride, my lord, truly. You don't have to worry that I cannot handle her properly. Or would you prefer that I ride another horse?"

He was frowning ferociously at her. "So you brought no horse of your own?"

"No." Actually, her father had sold many of the ducal horses some two months earlier, clearing out the once glorious Chambers stables before he'd known about Douglas and his offered bounty, before he'd known he'd need more than Douglas's bounty to save Claybourn.

"You're wearing a riding costume, though it is not new nor is it even in last year's style. I may assume then that your esteemed blackguard thief of a father sent you away with at least enough clothes to cover you until you could wheedle some more out of me?"

As a verbal blow, it showed promise.

"I don't know. I had not thought about it."

He actually snorted and she heard an answering snort from one of the closed stalls. "That's Garth," Douglas said absently. "So you don't think about furbelows and ribbons and flounces —"

"Certainly, when it is necessary to do so."

"I cannot imagine Melissande not wanting lovely clothes and furbelows and all those other things you females clothe yourselves in to attract males and make fools of them. Why would you be any different?"

"Melissande is beautiful. She needs beautiful things and admires them and —"

"Ha! She doesn't need anything. She would look glorious in naught but her white skin."

As a verbal blow, it exceeded the last one.

"Yes, that is also true. What do you wish me to do, my lord?"

"I wish you to leave and turn all this damnable debacle into a nightmare from which I'll awaken."

It was difficult, but Alex remained standing straight, remained with a fixed pleasant expression on her face, forced herself not to scream at him or make fists or fall to her knees and wail. "I meant, do you wish me to ride Fanny or ride another mare or not ride at all?"

Douglas shoveled his fingers through his hair. He stared at the small female who everyone had informed him was indeed his wife. She looked pale in the shadowy light but that back of hers was as straight as if she had a broom handle bound tightly against her backbone. Her hair was tucked firmly up under a rather dowdy riding hat. One long tendril had come loose and was in a loose curl on her shoulder. The hair was a nice color, rather an odd dark red color, but it didn't matter one bit. It could be blue for all he cared.

She was a complete and utter stranger, this female.

He cursed, long and luridly.

Alex didn't move an inch.

"Oh, the devil! Come along, you may ride Fanny and I will judge if you ride well enough to continue mounting her."

Mr. McCallum, fifty, wiry, strong as a man of twenty, baked brown from decades in the sun, and married to a young widow of twenty-two, was standing outside the stable giving orders to a stable lad when the earl and Alex led their mounts outside.

"Good morning, my lord."

Douglas only nodded at him. As far as he was concerned, McCallum had betrayed him, giving this cursed female Sinjun's mare. As had that accursed bounder cousin of his, that damnable Tony who deserved to be shot, and his own butler, Hollis, as well.

"Her Ladyship has a nice seat and light hands," McCallum said, unknowingly stoking the embers of Douglas's fury as he stroked the horse's soft nose. "Ye needn't worry that Fanny will suffer from any bad handling."

Douglas grunted. Who cared if she were cowhanded? He didn't. Indeed, who had bothered to care about him? No one, not one single bloody person.

He gave Alex a leg up, then turned to mount Garth. The huge stallion, left in his stall to eat his head off for two weeks, snorted, flung back his head, and danced to the side, all in all, giving a fine performance.

Douglas laughed aloud with the pleasure of it. He spoke to his stallion, patted his neck, then without a backward glance, he urged him into a gallop.

Alex watched the stallion and the man for a moment, then said, "Well, Fanny, perhaps we should show him we're made of firm stuff and not to be left to choke on his dust."

She gave a jaunty wave to McCallum and followed her husband down the long drive bordered with thick lime and beech trees, now full-branched and thick and riotously green.

Douglas was waiting for her just beyond the old stone gatehouse. He watched her ride toward him. His expression didn't change. McCallum was right. She rode very well. It pleased him only to the extent that she wouldn't hurt Fanny's soft mouth. He merely nodded at her, and click-clicked Garth into a gallop. He took a fence into the northern fields of Northcliffe, watching from the corner of his eye as Alex gave Fanny her head and easily took the fence after him. He pulled up finally at the edge of the winding narrow stream that had been one of his favorite haunts as a boy.

When she pulled in Fanny beside Garth, Alex looked about her, and said with pleasure, "What a lovely spot. There is a stream much like this one on the Chambers land. When I was a little girl I spent many happy hours there fishing, swimming — though the water was usually too low for anything other than just thrashing about and getting thoroughly wet — all in all, having a wonderful time."

As a conversation effort it didn't succeed.

Douglas looked off into the distance toward the Smitherstone weald, and said without preamble, "Tell me why you did it."

Alex felt her heart begin to pound, low, dull thuds. The good Lord knew that there were many truths at work here. She would give him one of them and hope it would satisfy him, one that Tony had doubtless already pressed upon him the previous night. It was a good one, actually, the primary one, if one spoke from her sire's point of view. "My father desperately needed funds, for my brother has just fled England leaving mountains of debt on his shoulders, and any settlement Tony made wouldn't be nearly enough and — Don't you see, my lord? Time was of the essence else we would have lost our home and —"

Douglas slashed his hand through the air. Garth took exception to his master's peculiar behavior, twisted his head around and took a nip of Fanny's neck. Fanny shrieked, rearing back onto her hind legs. Alex, taken off guard, cried out in surprise, flailed her arms to find balance, failed, then slid off Fanny's rump, landing on the narrow path on her bottom.

She sat there, feeling as if her bones had been jarred into dust. She was afraid to move. She looked up at Douglas, who was calming his horse. He looked down at her, his eyes darkening to a near black, then quickly dismounted. Fanny, curse her hide, kicked up her back legs once more and wheeled about, galloping back toward the Sherbrooke stables.

"Are you all right?"

"I don't know."

"Luckily you appear well padded, what with all those petticoats and the like. Can you stand?"

Alex nodded. She came up onto her knees, felt a strange shock of dizziness, and shook her head to clear it.

Douglas clasped her beneath her arms and drew her upright. She didn't weigh much, he thought, as he continued to support her. She did, however, feel very female. Finally, he felt that damned broom handle stiffen all the way from the back of her neck to her waist.

He released her. She weaved about, then straightened. "I'm all right." She looked back toward the hall, obscured by two miles of trees and fields. "Fanny left me."

And it was his fault, Douglas thought, wanting to howl because it meant that now he would have to hold — actually *hold* — this girl in front of him. He didn't even want to look at her, much less be in her company, much less hold her.

He'd even have to talk to her, since it was all his bloody fault that she'd been thrown.

"You're obviously not as proficient a horsewoman as you claimed, else you would have been more alert."

As a verbal blow, it was the very best thus

far, for it struck a killing blow to a pride inborn in her. She was not just a competent horsewoman; she was the best. She had ridden since before she could walk. She was beyond the best and above the best as well.

Her voice was as cold as the gaping shred in her pride. "Since your stallion is so ill-mannered as to take exception just because you fling yourself about on his back, yes, you are doubtless right." She turned away from him and began the long walk back to the hall.

Douglas watched her go.

He should apologize.

He should take her up on Garth.

Well, hell.

Her riding costume was dusty and he saw a rip beneath her right arm. A good length of the hem had come unstitched and dragged behind her in the dirt. Her riding hat lay in the middle of the road and her hair was falling down her back. She was limping just a bit.

He cursed, quickly mounted Garth, and went after her.

Alex heard him coming. She kept walking. At this moment, she hoped he would rot, every beautiful inch of him. Suddenly he swooped down, catching her around her waist, and lifted her up to sit sideways on the saddle in front of him.

"I'm sorry, damn you."

"That was most romantically done. Mrs. Radcliffe couldn't have penned a more dashing performance."

"Just because I didn't wish to argue with you or dismount again . . . What damnable drivel!"

"I could have walked," she said mildly. "It isn't all that far."

"You look like a ragamuffin. You look like a serving wench who's enjoyed half a dozen men but didn't please them sufficiently and got no coin for her labors."

She said nothing, merely sat with that straight back of hers, looking off toward the side of the road.

"I suppose I'll have to buy you a new riding habit now."

"It would appear that I didn't have to wheedle even a tiny bit."

"Since it was somewhat my fault — your fall, that is — I shall make reparations. Still, you should have been more alert, more prepared for the unexpected."

Alex was mild-tempered. She was patient and long-suffering; she knew how to endure; she knew how to hold her tongue to avoid distasteful scenes. She was never reckless. Even when her mother was at her pickiest, Melissande at her most demanding, she'd merely smiled and gone about her business. But with Douglas, her husband . . . how dare he continue to insult her riding ability? She simply couldn't help herself. She twisted against his arm, pushing at him with her entire weight. Caught unawares, Douglas went over the other side. He would have saved himself had Garth not decided that the extra weight on his back demanded that he make his master realize he wasn't to be treated like a common hack. Garth reared and twisted in the air. Alex managed to retain her balance, clutching wildly at Garth's mane. Douglas lost everything. He hit the road with a loud thunk, landing on his back, winding himself. The reins were dragging the ground and Garth immediately sidestepped away from his master.

Like Alex, Douglas just lay there, waiting to see if anything was broken, if anything had shaken itself loose.

He opened his eyes, still not moving, and said, "I will beat you for that."

"Tony said that you were a gentleman. Gentlemen do not beat ladies nor do they make such bullying threats."

"Being a gentleman pales when one is confronted with a wife one doesn't know, doesn't want, never did want, never even knew existed, a wife who is violent, heedless, without control." He drew breath to continue on this fine monologue when the ground shook and he watched, speechless, dust flying into his open mouth, as the female rode Garth — his stallion — away from him.

He nearly forgot to whistle.

Garth, thank heavens, heard him, stopped dead in his tracks, whipped about and trotted back to his prone master.

Alex was grinding her teeth. She stared down at Douglas, who was now sitting up in the middle of the road.

"I believe," she said clearly, "that you, my lord, are also in need of new riding clothes."

"These aren't really riding clothes. They're morning garb. Are you ignorant as well as a sham?"

"Sham? I am not!"

"Then why did you do it?"

Both Alex and Garth were motionless. She opened her mouth, then closed it. It was obvious that Tony had failed utterly to bring the earl around. She could not repeat that her father had been in horrible financial difficulties, repeat that all the Chambers holdings would have been lost, that the heir had fled to America, that her father would have been disgraced, perhaps had to blow his brains out with the shame of it. She shuddered with the thought of how those offerings would be received. Then there was the other truth, but she couldn't, wouldn't, tell him that.

"No answer, hm? Well, I'm not surprised, particularly after all the drivel Tony was feeding me last night." Douglas got to his feet, queried his body, was satisfied with the response, and walked to his stallion. He picked up the reins, stroked the stallion's nose, and said slowly, "I am to believe that you were willing to sacrifice yourself on the marital altar because your beloved father was going to lose everything if you didn't? That you and your father convinced dear Tony — that traitorous sod — that it would save me having to find myself a proper female amongst the current batch of debutantes in London? That all of this was done for *my* benefit? But then you, honorable to your female toes, told your father you couldn't do it? Because of your nobility of spirit? Then he forced you?"

How could Tony have said that? It was ludicrous! Certainly she'd refused, at least at first she had. Before she could say anything, Douglas snorted, just like his horse. "Sorry, but I don't believe that. In this day and age, fathers cannot coerce their children to do anything against their will." Even as he spoke the words, they rang false and he knew it. Actually Tony had said nothing of the like but Douglas was probing, and the chit wasn't telling him anything that sounded reasonable.

Alex said quietly, "No, Papa didn't force me. He loves me, but I had to —"

"Yes, I know. You had to save him and sacrifice yourself. I hope you're pleased with my purchase, since I have paid dearly to have a stranger for a wife."

Alex straightened as tall as she could in the saddle. "I would that you would give me a chance, my lord, that you not despise me out of hand. I will make you a good wife."

He looked up at the disheveled female atop Garth. She was pale now and he wondered momentarily if she had been hurt in her fall, but then she added, "Tony said you would rather have a tooth extracted than spend a Season in London. He said the last thing you wanted to do was be forced to attend all the routs and balls and parties and sniff out available young ladies for your consideration. He said you felt like a plump partridge in the midst of well-armed hunters. He said you hated it."

"He did? And you believed him? I don't suppose it occurred to you during your spate of nobility that Tony would have said anything to try to find excuses for himself? To justify what he did to me?"

"I am sure that he still feels immense guilt. He is very fond of you."

"But more fond of your sister!"

"Yes, he loves her."

"He's a Judas and I should blow his brains out."

"He did not intend for it to happen. Surely you don't believe he married Melissande to thwart you? To somehow spite you? No, even in your foulest mood, you wouldn't believe that. Did he lie about your feelings toward going to London?"

Douglas looked down at his scuffed Hessians. Finkle would have a fit when he saw it. "No, but it wasn't up to him to make that decision for me. It is all a part of his justification, nothing more."

"I'm sorry."

Like hell she was! "You know, don't you, that I can have this farce of a marriage annulled and demand the settlement back from your black-hearted father?"

"Don't you dare speak of my father like that!" She waved a credible fist at him.

Douglas didn't move. He merely stared up at her, no expression on his face. "What am I to believe?"

Alex felt an awful wave of guilt for what she'd done to him. "I'm sorry, my lord, truly, but don't you think that perhaps you could allow me to be your wife for a while? By annulment, you mean you would send me home and the marriage wouldn't still be a marriage?"

"That's right. Our temporary union would be dissolved."

"Please, you must reconsider. I don't want to be annulled or dissolved. Perhaps in a very short time you won't mind my being here at Northcliffe, for I will keep out of your way. I will try to make things comfortable for you —"

"Women! Don't you think a man can be perfectly content without one of you hanging about his neck, handing him brandy and cigars?"

"What I meant was that I wouldn't be obtrusive and that I would make certain your house runs smoothly."

"It runs smoothly right now, or have you forgotten that I have a mother and more servants than I can count?"

She had momentarily forgotten the mother. He also had two brothers and a younger sister. Hollis had told her they were all visiting friends in London. But they would return soon to Northcliffe. Oh dear. Would they hate her, despise her as much as Douglas did? Would they follow his lead and scorn her? She drew a deep breath and said,

"I had forgotten. I'm sorry." She leaned unconsciously toward him. "Please, my lord, perhaps you won't mind that I am in your home after some time has passed. Perhaps you won't even notice me after a while. I beg you not to annul me just yet."

"Annul you? You make it sound like a violent act." Douglas suddenly frowned; there was contempt in his eyes. "Ah, I begin to see the direction of your thinking or perhaps your sire's thinking. You hope to climb into my bed, don't you? You know that I cannot annul you — damnation — obtain an annulment — if I take your virginity. That's what you want, isn't it? Once I take your precious virginity, then your precious father will be safe and all my money will remain with him. Did your father counsel you to try to seduce me?"

Alex could only stare down at him. She slowly shook her head. "No, I hadn't thought any of that and no, no one counseled me about anything."

He was silent, staring up at her.

"Truly, my lord, I know nothing of seduction. Surely seduction isn't something done between husband and wife. My mother told me that seduction was only done by wild young men who wanted to ruin innocent young ladies."

"Really? Did this motherly Delphi warn you of anything more specific?"

"That if a man ever flattered me or stepped too close to me or held my hand too long after kissing it, that I was to leave the vicinity immediately. He was up to no good, she said."

Douglas laughed, he couldn't help himself.

Alex brightened. She'd amused him, that or he was laughing at her. She waited, then said, "I will do my best to please you, to make you a comfortable wife. My temper is usually rather placid and —"

"Ha! You were beyond vicious, a shrew, a fishwife, and a less comfortable female I've yet to encounter. You knocked me off my damned horse!"

Alex frowned. "Yes," she said, surprise in her eyes and in her voice, "yes, it appears that I did, which is very strange. It is very unlike me."

Douglas saw that the top two buttons of her riding habit had come unfastened. He saw a patch of white flesh. Very soft-looking white flesh. He thought of her virginity and he thought of taking it, of pushing through her maidenhead. "Perhaps," he said, continuing to stare at her breasts, "perhaps I could be proved wrong. It is possible that you could be the one to demand an annulment. Perhaps you will want to leave Northcliffe as fast as your carriage wheels can roll away with you."

"Oh no, I want to be your wife —"

"Let's see, shall we? Unfasten the rest of the buttons. I can only see the curve of your breasts. I would like to see the rest of you. You're quiet? Is that a touch of pallor I see? You're shocked at my bluntness? I've assaulted your precious virgin sensibilities? Well, so there are ways to shut you up."

He was right about that, she thought, stunned.

"How old are you?"

"You know I am eighteen. I told you last night."

"Old enough to be a woman and a wife. You said that too. Oh, hell. Just be quiet, all right?"

"But I didn't say —"

"Damnation, be quiet or I shall demand that you take off that riding jacket and let me see your breasts and your nipples and your ribs. All your upper parts I've paid so dearly for."

Alex was silent as a stone.

Douglas eyed her, waiting, but she remained silent and still, that broomstick firmly in place down her back. He shrugged. "I will lead Garth. A good walk is balm to a weary soul."

She wondered why he'd gotten that bit of errant treacle, but was wise enough to keep her curiosity to herself. She watched him walk ahead of her; there was a jagged rip in his buckskins. She could see a patch of hairy thigh. Black hair. It looked rather nice to her. She looked down at herself then, jerked her chemise about, covering any hint of skin. She straightened again, and kept her eyes on the back of her husband all the way back to the stables.

This annulment business was still somewhat a mystery. She would have to ask Tony about it. She knew too little about marriage sorts of things. All she knew about virginity and virgins was that she was one. She would have to be in her husband's bed before she wasn't one anymore.

She should ask her husband, but she doubted

he would take any question of that sort in a proper frame of mind.

He stopped suddenly in the middle of the road and turned back to face her. "I'm tired. Garth is tired. Get down and come here. We will rest a moment beneath that oak tree."

Alex slid from the saddle, saying not a word.

Douglas didn't bother to tether Garth, just left his reins loose. "Sit down," Douglas said, pointing to a grassy spot.

Alex sat.

Douglas sat also, a good three feet away from her. He leaned back against the thick oak trunk and crossed his legs at his ankles. He sighed, folded his arms over his belly, and closed his eyes.

"I am sorry you're so tired," Alex said. "Tony said you were on some sort of mission and that was why he'd come to us rather than you."

"Yes. I certainly made the wrong choice, didn't I? I certainly chose the wrong man to trust. Jesus, my entire life ruined because —"

"Was your mission successful?"

"Yes." He opened his eyes then and looked at her. Perverseness sang through his veins. "Actually, I would have preferred the lovely lady I rescued in France to be here rather than you. Her name is Janine and she's a woman, not a girl playing at being a woman, and she was more than interested in me as a man. She offered herself to me, without guile, without playing the coquette. However, since I believed I was a married man, believed that Melissande was awaiting me here, I didn't take her. Indeed, I pushed her away." He closed his eyes again.

"You are a married man."

"You, however, are not Melissande."

"This woman you rescued, she is French?"

"Yes, and a very important man's mistress."

"Surely you wouldn't want a mistress for your wife."

"Why not?"

"That's beyond foolish! You're only saying that to hurt me, to make me feel horrible. No man wants a woman who isn't all that is proper. It's all a matter of heirs. I heard my father saying that to a neighbor."

"There speaks eighteen-year-old wisdom and eavesdropping."

"Will you annul me?"

He was silent.

"Won't you at least give me a chance?"

"Be quiet. I wish to rest now."

Alex eyed Garth, who was placidly chewing thick grass at the side of the road. If she coshed Douglas, then he couldn't whistle for his horse and then the horse would take her back to the Sherbrooke stables. She sighed, closing her own eyes. The morning was warming and becoming clear. Soon the sun would shine fully.

Alex said then, "I had the oddest dream the first night I was here in your home, sleeping in the countess's bedchamber. I dreamed there was a young lady in the room and she was standing next to the bed, just looking down at me. I thought she wanted to say something, but she remained silent. She looked so sad and beautiful. When I awoke fully, she was gone, of course. A dream, yet it seemed so real."

Douglas opened his eyes. He stared at her. He said very slowly, "The devil, you say."

"Dreams are strange, aren't they? They seem so real, so tangible, but of course —"

"A dream, nothing more, nothing less. Forget it. Do you understand?"

Why would he behave so strangely about a silly dream? She nodded. "I understand."

CHAPTER 8

"Yes, Hollis, it's indeed the one Sherbrooke you neither expected nor wanted to see. Yes, I know, you would probably like to see me at Jericho, but I'm back. The suspense was more than I could bear. I told Mother, Tysen, and Sinjun that I was going to the Newmarket races. They all believed me except Sinjun, no surprise there, she's a smart little chit, sometimes too smart, damn her eyes. But forget that. I had to see Douglas's new wife."

Hollis was dismayed. He stared at the wind-blown young man he'd known and loved all his life, a young man almost too vital and handsome for his own good, a young man who was far too young to be so very cynical. Now, facing him, Hollis was forced to smile. "No, not at all, Master Ryder, do come in, though I do understand that Jericho is quite nice this time of year. Yes, do come in. Give me your cloak. You will see that the new countess is a charming young lady. However, just so you will be properly advised, it may take His Lordship a bit more time to adjust himself to his good fortune. The new countess was, as you know, somewhat unexpected."

"Yes, and you decided Douglas should be left here alone to sort things out without family interference. I'll tell you, Hollis, Mother is fair chomping at the bit to chew the chit to bits. Poor little twit, I don't envy her when Mother returns. So Douglas didn't particularly approve the female Tony attached him to? Odd, I've never known Tony not to have exquisite taste in females, all except for that Carleton woman who somehow wrung a proposal out of him, which will remain a mystery in the annals of malehood into the misty future. Ah, well, Douglas is fickle and he is demanding as the devil."

"I don't believe fickleness is a particularly noble quality, Master Ryder, thus it doesn't fit well with His Lordship's character. No, it is all a matter of change, I believe. Abrupt change is difficult even for the best of men. The new countess, as I said, is all that a gentleman would wish for in a wife."

"Ah ha! I begin to understand. The chit isn't all that toothsome. She's nothing compared to the succulent Melissande, isn't that right, Hollis? Is that what you're trying to tell me in that wonderfully understated way of yours?"

Melissande, who'd immediately spotted this dashing young man with his fair good looks and his even fairer speech from the breakfast room door, thought a moment about being succulent, wasn't actually certain of its meaning, but decided the intent was obvious enough, and thus she cleared her throat and sang out, "Hello, I'm Lady

Melissande. Who are you, sir?"

Ryder turned toward the unfamiliar voice and looked at the female standing there. To Melissande's utter amazement, this gentleman, unlike all the other male specimens of her acquaintance, did not turn to mesmerized stone at the sight of her; he did not metaphorically fall at her feet and lie there inert as a dead dog. She knew the sight she presented was enough to smite down the most jaded of gentlemen. Whatever was wrong? Was her hair not perfect? Was her figure not just as perfect, and the lavender of her silk morning gown beyond glorious against her white skin? Was his vision defective?

Of course nothing was wrong with her. Nothing was ever wrong. Still, he merely stood there, his head cocked to one side. For the life of her, Melissande couldn't see any incipient signs of besottedness about him, no sudden pallor or stiffening, no hint of soulful reverence in those lovely blue eyes of his. Ah, but maybe he was tongue-tied, and that was his afflicted reaction in the presence of her succulent self. Then he smiled and said, his voice lazy and smooth as warm honey, "I'm Ryder Sherbrooke, Douglas's brother. Where is the new countess? And what are you doing here?"

"She's with me, Ryder."

"Hello, Tony," Ryder grinned at his cousin, who'd come around his wife from the breakfast room. Ryder stepped forward and gripped his hand. "I am rather pleased you are still alive or is it still in question? Is Douglas still at your throat or have you convinced him that he is all the better off for this good deed you performed for him?"

"Look, Ryder, I —"

"No, cousin, Hollis didn't tell me any secrets, it's just that I had to come and see for myself. It's dashed good to see you in one healthy piece, Tony."

"I'm Melissande."

"Yes, I know. My pleasure."

Ryder immediately turned back to his cousin. "Is that a swollen lip I see, Tony? Perhaps that's a bruise on your cheek? So you did tangle with Douglas, did you? I trust you gave as good as you got."

"I'm Tony's wife."

"Yes, I know. My pleasure."

Ryder continued to his cousin, "Well, did you?"

"Did I what?"

"Punch Douglas in his pretty face."

"I got in a few good blows, but not enough. His wife attacked me."

"I'm Melissande. I attacked Douglas."

Ryder knew the glorious creature was miffed, and he was amused by it. Obviously Tony was meant to be an Atlas among men; he would need to be in order to control this delightful package of vanity that was his wife. If he didn't manage her well, he would probably wish rather to carry the world on his shoulders. It wasn't Ryder's problem, thankfully, so he said, "Come along,

Tony, I want to hear all the details. Is Douglas here?"

"No, he and Alex are riding, I believe."

"Alex?"

"Alexandra."

"I'm Melissande. I'm Alexandra's sister."

"I know. My pleasure, ma'am. Come along, Tony."

Melissande was left standing in the entrance hall, staring after her husband and the unobservant clod of an oblivious cousin-in-law. Hollis gently cleared his throat. "Should you like anything, my lady?"

"No," Melissande said, her voice absent, for she was still suffering minor shock. "I must go upstairs and see what is wrong."

Hollis smiled after her, knowing that her mirror would soon enjoy her image and her puzzlement.

Five minutes later he wasn't smiling. His Lordship and his wife came into the hall, both looking as if they'd been dragged through a ditch. "My lord! Goodness! My lady, are you —"

"No, don't fret, Hollis." Douglas turned to Alexandra. "Go upstairs and do something about yourself."

As a dismissal, it was clear and to the point. Even though he looked very probably as bad as she did, Alex kept quiet. She went upstairs.

Douglas said to Hollis, "We both fell from our horses, but no harm done."

"Her Ladyship is limping a bit."

"It serves her . . . well, perhaps a bit, but

she'll be just fine, don't fret, Hollis."

When told that his brother had come to grace the Northcliffe portals, Douglas cursed, cursed some more, stomped past Hollis, and stomped into the library. Three maids were peeking around the Golden Salon doors and two footmen were stationed unobtrusively beneath the stairs, staring out. Hollis, as was his wont, very gently sent them back to their duties.

"Ah," Ryder said upon Douglas's entrance. "Let me see your face. Tony claimed that you nearly beat him to a bloody pulp and you escaped without a mark. He said, of course, that he let you, that he only tried to defend himself."

"It was his wife who nearly killed me," Tony said. "She was first my sister-in-law, but now she shows me no loyalty. It isn't right of her. I feel flayed with treachery."

"Treachery! You damned cur! I'll —"

Douglas stopped. There was nothing more to say. What he had to decide now was whether or not to annul the marriage. And now Ryder was here. He looked with some dislike upon his brother. "All right, why are you here, Ryder? Is Mother all right? Tysen and Sinjun?"

"Mother is carping about you at full steam. Sinjun is reading voraciously, as usual, and Tysen was prosing on and on until Sinjun threw a novel at him. In short, everyone is just the same, Douglas. They all think me at Newmarket. I was curious, that's all. Where's the chit Tony married you to? Does she have a squint? Is she fat with several chins? Missing teeth? Flat-breasted?"

"Don't be an ass, Ryder," Tony nearly shouted. "Alex is lovely and sweet-natured and —"

"Sweet-natured! Ha! You would say so, certainly, since you married her to me! She's not Melissande."

"I saw Melissande, Douglas," Ryder said slowly, staring at his brother. "Tony was standing near her. I believe he's afraid that every man who lays eyes on her will lose his head."

"You saw her. He's justified."

"But you didn't appear to," Tony said thoughtfully to Ryder. "Why not?"

Ryder merely shrugged. "One woman's much the same as another. So long as they're warm and loving in bed, why then, who cares? Sorry, but I don't mean to insult your wife, Tony, it's just that . . . I will try to make her a fine cousin-in-law, all right?"

Tony chewed this over. He liked Ryder but he didn't understand him. This cynicism of his, this utter bland indifference toward women in general, hadn't led him to monkish tastes but rather to a satyr's appetites. No, he didn't like women particularly, yet he supported his bastards and their mothers. He never blamed a woman for becoming pregnant. It was perplexing. Women were sport to Ryder, nothing more, and he was quite willing to pay for it and accept the consequences. It was also a relief that Melissande was safe from his ogling. But Douglas . . . Tony turned to his cousin and said, "I understand you and Alex were riding. She's a superior horsewoman."

Douglas grunted.

"You are a bit disheveled, Douglas," Tony persevered. "What happened?"

"I fell off Garth; rather, that cursed woman you married pushed me off my horse. She fell off first and now I will have to buy her a new riding habit. Did you see the one she was wearing? Old and dowdy, doubtless all her other clothes are equally distasteful, and I'll wager it was all planned by her fond parent so I would be forced to buy her a new wardrobe. She looks a fright, Tony, damn you to hell."

Tony frowned. "That's odd. Melissande has beautiful gowns and the softest silk, er, feminine things."

Ryder said quickly, "There's a faint bruise by your left eye and over your right ear, Douglas. Any other battle marks?"

Douglas said nothing whilst he poured himself a brandy. He sipped it, then waved his snifter at Tony. "I am going to kill this miserable sot. Would you like to second me, Ryder?"

"You've a tear in your britches. And no, I truly cannot second you. I like Tony. I always have. Look, Douglas, it seems to me that you must allow a relative some latitude, particularly a relative of Tony's closeness. We spent much of our boyhood together. He has never before done you in, has he? No, you will be forced to say, and I must agree. Thus, it's just this one time that he has fallen off the cousinly straight and narrow. Only one time. Thus, forgiveness is —"

Douglas threw his brandy snifter at Ryder, who promptly ducked. The glass shattered against the brick hearth.

There was a knock on the library door.

"Come in," Tony shouted.

Hollis entered, carrying a massive silver tray with the Northcliffe crest emblazoned upon it — a lion with his front paws on a shield, looking both noble and vicious. "I brought some refreshments, my lord."

"Which lord?" Douglas said.

"You, my lord."

"Ha! You came because you feared I was trying to murder Tony again."

"It's wise to be vigilant, my lord. Here are also some rather tasty scones from Mrs. Tanner's kitchen, your favorite, my lord. And Master Ryder, here is your favorite strawberry jam. Come, my lord."

"What about me, Hollis?" Tony said.

"For you, my lord, there are thick slices of shortbread."

"Ah, you are a prince among butlers, Hollis."

"Yes, my lord."

Douglas cursed under his breath, Tony reached for a slice of shortbread, and Ryder had his hand around the jam pot.

Hollis stood back, feeling a modicum of relief. When he heard the footsteps from outside the library door, however, he felt himself pale. Oh dear, now wasn't the time for the two wives to make appearances. But there was naught he could do.

Both ladies came into the library. Lady Melissande glided forward on graceful feet; Lady Alexandra made solid thuds until she reached the thick Aubusson carpet. Lady Melissande's glorious black hair was in soft waves and ringlets about her face; Lady Alexandra's hair was a lovely color, true, but it straggled out of the crooked bun at the nape of her neck. She needed more time in front of her mirror. Lady Melissande's gown was a soft peach silk that draped over her womanly shape with subtle invitation — she'd changed from the lavender. Lady Alexandra wore a pale blue gown with nothing more memorable than a deplorably high neck.

With the two females standing side by side, Ryder understood his brother's sense of betrayal. He had a mouth full of scone and strawberry jam. He swallowed too quickly and choked and continued to choke. Alex calmly walked to him, and hit him as hard as she could with her fist between his shoulder blades.

She nearly knocked him over with the force of her blow. He stopped choking, however. Still red-faced, Ryder looked up at the young lady and quickly got to his feet. He studied her in silence for several moments, then nodded slowly.

He took her hand and kissed the wrist. "I'm Ryder, your brother-in-law. You're Alexandra."

"Yes. Are you all right?"

"You nearly sent my back through my chest, but yes, I am quite fine now. The bit of scone found its proper way down. Welcome to the Sherbrooke family. Did you really knock Douglas off his horse?"

Alex shook her head even as she said, "I didn't really mean to do it at the time."

"Ha! I recall making an observation about something quite bland and you coshed me onto the ground!"

"She is quite large and brawny, isn't she?" Ryder said. He lightly closed his fingers around her upper arm. "Ah, strong as an Amazon and as muscled as Squire Maynard's bull. She is terrifying, Douglas, she certainly is."

"You weren't at all bland," Alexandra said to Douglas.

"Neither am I," Melissande said.

Tony laughed. "No one in his right mind would ever call you bland, sweetheart."

"Would you call me succulent?"

Tony's face tightened ever so slightly. "I would but no one else would dare to."

"Ah," Melissande said and gave Tony a look so provocative it would sizzle any male's toes.

Douglas stared at her.

Ryder said to Alexandra, his voice easy, and oddly gentle, "Won't you sit down and join us?"

"I shall join you too," Melissande announced. She eyed her sister with grave perplexity. This was beyond strange, she thought, staring at Ryder, who was looking closely at Alex. Mirrors didn't lie. Perhaps poor Ryder was excessively myopic as she'd first thought. She turned back to her husband, saw that mocking gleam in his dark eyes, frowned, then turned to Douglas. Her soul found instant balm. His heart was in his eyes and both looked wonderfully bruised to her.

She gave him a sweet smile and nodded. "Please forgive me if I caused you discomfort last night."

Douglas shook his head.

"Come and serve me tea, Mellie," Tony said.

"I told you I don't like that horrible name!"

Douglas's right eye twitched.

"Come, Mellie," Tony said again.

"It's a lovely nickname," Ryder said, eyeing the heart-stopping creature, who looked ready to spit at her husband of two weeks. When she didn't react, he stoked the fire a bit. "I rather like the feel of 'Mellie.' It sounds rather mussed, comfortable, like a pair of old house slippers a man can slip his feet into and point them toward the fire."

Alexandra laughed. " 'Tis better than Alex. I would rather sound comfortable than like I was a man."

"No one would ever make that mistake," Ryder said.

Both Douglas and Melissande frowned together.

"Your gown is deplorable," Douglas said to his wife. "It is so out of fashion I doubt it was ever in fashion at all."

Her chin went up and the broom handle straightened alarmingly up her back. "It is blue, and blue is a very nice color."

"You look like a schoolgirl."

"Then perhaps you would like to buy me a new one? Or perhaps a dozen? Is my tone wheedling enough, my lord?"

Douglas realized this wasn't the time to show his ill-humor. He drew himself in and sought control, a commodity of which he'd been plentifully endowed until but twenty-four hours before. The chit had stripped it off him. He felt raw and exposed.

He picked up a scone and bit into it.

"Did you ride Fanny?" Ryder asked.

"Yes, she is a wonderful mare. However, I am uncertain if His Lordship is convinced that I ride well enough."

"You did fall," Melissande said. "That wasn't well done of you, Alex."

To Douglas's surprise, Alexandra said only, her voice quite apologetic, "It was unfortunate but I shall be far more careful in the future."

Douglas wondered if there would be a future. He had to get out of here and do some serious thinking. Annulment seemed the best answer. It seemed the only logical thing to do. He looked over at Alexandra. She was looking directly at him and he saw such wariness in her eyes that he winced. And there was fear also. Fear of him? Because of what she'd done to him, doubtless. The twit should be afraid of him, curse her.

Douglas rose quickly and nodded to the assembled company. "I have work to do with Danvers. The mail is doubtless here by now."

He left. As he closed the door behind him, he heard Ryder's laughter.

The mail, however, didn't cheer him at all.

It rained in the early afternoon, a light soft drizzle that soon cleared away, leaving a very blue sky and very fresh air. Alexandra found Ryder Sherbrooke in the overrun garden at the west of the house, leaning against an oak tree, staring at nothing in particular, seemingly content to bask under the warm sun that filtered through the branches.

"Ryder?"

"Ah, my little sister. Am I an accident or did you search me out on purpose?"

She'd never met his like before, but oddly enough, she trusted him. "I asked Hollis where you were. He always knows everyone's whereabouts."

"True. Come sit here next to this fat nymph. What do you think of all these statues? Brought by my grandfather from Florence during his Bacchanal phase, so wrote one of his friends, Lord Whitehaven, an old roué who bounced me on his knee."

"I've never seen them before," Alex said, staring at the line of naked females, each in a startling pose. "This is my first visit to the gardens."

"In the depths of the gardens are all the naked

male statues and the assorted couples. Grandfather evidently had some qualms about childish eyes and curiosity. The statues are nicely hidden. Do you like Northcliffe?"

"I don't know."

"Why do you bind your breasts?"

Alex nearly swallowed her tongue. She stared at him, mute as a snail.

"Sorry. I didn't mean to offend you. I am known for speaking my mind, what there is of it."

"How did you know?"

"I know women. There is nothing a woman can do that would fool me. The fairer sex is really rather obvious. Take your lovely sister, for example. Melissande will learn that life has a way of dishing out prunes along with the strawberries. She will play her games with Tony and he will allow them and doubtless enjoy them, within reason, of course. Already he controls her well despite his besottedness with her."

"You don't like ladies?"

Ryder gave her a surprised look. "Good Lord, I couldn't live without them. I doubt there is anything else in life to compare to the pleasure a man derives from a woman's body."

Alex gasped, she couldn't help it.

"Sorry, I did it again, didn't I? You're young, Alexandra, but you're not fluff. You've got steel in you and I dare say you will have to use it, very soon. Now, what do you want of me?"

"I came to ask you if you believed Douglas

would annul our marriage and how I can make Douglas wait and just give me a chance before he does it."

"Ah, I thought that was the direction of his thoughts." Ryder looked at her closely. "I will tell you what I think, since you ask me. Douglas is very likely seriously considering an annulment. He has been clipped hard in the chin, so to speak. He is angry, feels betrayed, and wants to strike out. He is also stubborn and hard and untractable. After seeing your sister today, after seeing Douglas seeing your sister, I believe time is short. If you want to keep him for your husband, I suggest that you climb into his bed and seduce him. Continue until you're with child. Then there will be no question of annulment."

Alex stood very slowly, staring in mute fascination at her brother-in-law.

"I doubt Douglas has had a woman for a good while now. It's likely he will be amenable to your approach. Do it, Alex. Patience isn't a virtue in this case. Don't be Penelope."

Her hands were shaking. She thrust them into the folds of her gown. "I don't know anything about seduction."

Ryder laughed. "All females are born knowing about seduction, my dear. Just take off your clothes in front of him. An excellent start. You do understand about sex, don't you? About conception?"

There came a shout. It was Douglas. "Ryder! Come here, now!"

"Ah, the lord and master wishes my presence. He probably wants to send me back to London." He paused, looking down at his new sister-in-law. "I think you're a good sort, Alex. Now isn't the time to be patient with Douglas; you must act quickly. Also, if you're wise, you'll insist that Tony and Melissande remain here for a while. Comparisons are wonderfully enlightening sometimes, and my brother isn't stupid. Seduce him tonight; don't think about it, just do it. A man's brain can be diverted." Ryder wasn't so certain about Douglas's brain, but he didn't wish to discourage Alex.

Ryder left her then to stare after him in bemusement and to bemoan the poor condition of the garden and of her marriage. Her fingers itched to dig in the rich black soil. Why were the gardens so neglected? Rosebushes begged for pruning. She realized with a small smile that Douglas needed pruning too.

At dinner that evening, Douglas announced, "There was a letter from our plantation manager in Jamaica. There is trouble at Kimberly Hall. Ryder will leave on the morrow to deal with it."

"What sort of trouble?" Alexandra asked.

"Grayson wrote of strange doings, of black magic and visions from hell itself, murders and the like, of slave uprisings. You undoubtedly get the idea."

"Grayson excels in exaggeration," Ryder said. "If a fly flew past his head, he would call it a gigantic wasp and claim it was bedeviling him.

This talk of perversions sounds interesting, but knowing Grayson, it involves nothing more than two noisy cats."

"Ah, but he is a good man and an excellent manager," Douglas said.

Ryder thought about his children and frowned. He'd dealt with all that needed to be done in his absence, but still, he would miss the little devils. He said aloud, realizing he'd been silent overlong, "I'll leave for Southampton early tomorrow. Thus tonight is my last chance to ingratiate myself with my sister-in-law. I like the pink gown, Alexandra. I have always said that deep red titian hair is complemented by certain shades of pink."

"Yes, it is," Tony said, frowning at Alex, as if he'd never really seen her before.

"The gown is old and is cut like a nun's habit," Douglas said. "It is as dowdy as the blue gown you were wearing earlier this afternoon."

The broom handle stiffened. Douglas raised his hand. "No, I didn't say I would replace any of your gowns, so I don't need more of your comments about wheedling. I was merely noting that your feminine display is sorely lacking."

"It's true a lady should attempt to display well," Melissande said.

Douglas looked over at Melissande. She looked so utterly feminine and unspeakably delicious that for a moment he was mute.

"Your display, Mellie," Tony said, caressing her bare upper arm, "would make our randy

Prince George slip down in a puddle of his own drool."

Alex laughed. "I should like to see that. Will you take Melissande to London, Tony, so that the prince may see her and slip?"

"In good time," Tony said. "In good time."

"I should like to go now," Melissande said. "You have a town house I have never seen. I should like to give a ball and invite everyone important."

"In good time," Tony said. "First you must see Strawberry Hill, my family estate in the Cotswolds."

"A wonderful place to raise children," Ryder said. "Do you remember, Douglas, how we used to swing off that old maple branch into the spring, screaming at the top of our lungs?"

"Yes, and the time Tony broke the branch and nearly drowned because it struck him on the head when he hit the water."

"I should prefer London," Melissande said.

"You will prefer what I wish you to prefer, Mellie," Tony said very matter-of-factly.

Ryder said quickly, his voice limpid as that same spring in summer, "I agree that Melissande would enjoy London, but only if Tony was enjoying it with her. Since he prefers Strawberry Hill, why then, she will prefer it also. Melissande understands that it is a wife's duty and pleasure to obey her husband, to honor him by her every word and deed and soft caress. Don't you agree, Alexandra?"

Alex said with a smile, "I should like to see

the branch that coshed Tony on the head and nearly drowned him."

"I should also," Melissande said, beautiful eyes wary, "but after I have enjoyed London, with my husband, naturally."

Douglas took a sip of the rich claret. He looked at Ryder over the edge of the crystal goblet.

"As I was saying," Ryder continued, "Strawberry Hill is a wonderful place to raise children. I have heard Tony say that he would like a good half-dozen children attaching themselves to his coattails."

Tony, who had never uttered such a longing in his entire life, smiled like an already besotted parent.

He looked at Ryder from the corner of his eyes, then directly at his wife. She looked remarkably flushed, and frankly appalled. He cleared his throat and whispered in a voice that carried to every corner of the dining room, "Should we continue trying to begin our brood after dinner, Mellie?"

"Don't call me that!"

"But the other names I call you really aren't appropriate for the dining room. But if you would prefer, if you feel so very comfortable with all those here at the table, why then, who am I to quibble? How about honey-po—"

Melissande slapped her palm over her husband's mouth. He took her slender wrist between his long fingers and pulled it away. "Now, where was I?"

"Please, Tony."

He looked at her closely. "Did I truly hear a 'please'?"

She nodded.

He looked at her another long moment, then said calmly, "You have pleased me. Eat your stewed green beans, Mellie. They're quite delicious."

Alexandra, who'd been a fascinated observer, now looked toward her own husband. He was staring at Melissande and Tony and there was a deep frown on his forehead. As for Ryder, he was smiling at his turtle soup.

Two hours later, alone in her bedchamber, Alexandra stood irresolute, staring at the adjoining door. Ryder had said to seduce Douglas. Ryder said that all women were born knowing how. She wondered if Douglas would laugh at her if she tried. Ryder had said time was of the essence, that she must act quickly, that she mustn't wait patiently, like the faithful Penelope did for Ulysses. Very well then. She would do it and she would do it now. Before she lost her resolve.

Alex doused her candle and walked to the adjoining door. Slowly, she opened it.

CHAPTER 9

Alex walked slowly into the large master bedroom. Her eyes went immediately to the bed and she stilled. It was empty, the covers unruffled. She saw him then and walked quietly toward him. A branch of candles burned on a table beside the wing chair in front of the fireplace. There were only embers still burning, dull orange, throwing off little light and warmth.

Douglas sat in the chair, his long legs stretched out in front of him, crossed at the ankles. He was wearing a dark blue brocade dressing gown. It was parted over his legs. She stared at his legs, hairy, thick, strong. His feet were bare. They were long and narrow and quite beautiful to her. His chin was balanced on his fist.

She was scared silly; but she was determined, she had to be. It was very possible that her future with this man depended on what she did and how well she did it in the next few minutes. "My lord?"

"Yes," Douglas said, not moving, not looking at her. "I heard you come into my room. I never thought I should lock my door against a woman. What do you want?"

"I wanted . . . you're thinking about what to do with me, aren't you?"

"Yes, that and other things. I am also worried about Ryder voyaging to the West Indies. It is never a safe sailing. But he insisted that he be the one to go." Douglas turned then to look up at her. "Ryder said I should remain here and come to grips with myself and my marriage to you. He believes you a perfectly fine sort."

She said nothing.

Douglas looked over at her then. He brooded, stroking his fingers over his chin now. "Your nightgown is a little girl's, all white and long and high-necked."

"I don't have any others."

"The brass I will have to spend on clothing you begins to boggle the mind."

"There is nothing wrong with my nightgown. It keeps me warm and it is soft against the skin."

"It is a virgin's nightgown."

"Well," she said reasonably, "that is what I am."

"No self-respecting woman would wear such a garment."

Alex sighed.

"What do you want? Ah, I see. You wish to plead with me some more. You wish to further detail how indispensable you can be to me. You wish to bray on about your housewifely accomplishments. I beg you not to tell me you will also sing in the evenings to me and perhaps accompany yourself on the pianoforte. Why the devil do you have your hair braided? It looks absurd. I don't like it."

Alex never stopped looking at him. She hadn't thought about her braid; she should have, for a braid couldn't be considered remotely seductive. Melissande never braided her hair. Alex would learn. She set her single candle down on the table by his chair. She raised her arms and slowly began to unbraid her hair. As the plaits came loose, she tugged her fingers through the deep ripples, smoothing them out. He merely sat there, watching her, saying nothing.

When she finished, her hair was loose to the middle of her back.

"Bring some hair over your shoulder."

She did.

"There. Your hair is a nice color and it is of a nice thickness. At least the hair hides some of the hideous nightgown. Now, what do you want?"

There was really no hope for it. Either she opened her mouth and told him, or she left. He appeared impatient with her and saw her as naught but an unwelcome intrusion. It was daunting.

"Well? Get on with it. I can take anything except whining and wheedling."

She said without preamble, chin up, back straight, "I've come to seduce you."

"Ah, the female's final weapon," Douglas said. "I really shouldn't be surprised, should I? If naught else, I put it in your mind this morning.

I should have known, should have guessed. When all else fails, bring out the female body and parade it about in front of the randy man's nose."

"My only problem is that I'm not certain how to go about doing it."

"That's twaddle."

"Perhaps if you could help me just a little bit, I could figure it out."

"Let me make something clear to you, something it's obvious you haven't considered in this plan of yours. I can still have this farce of a marriage annulled even if I take your virginity. Do you understand me? Who would know, after all? Would you or anyone in your family announce to the world that you were damaged goods?"

"You make me sound as if I would be a mangled parcel. Surely that is absurd."

"Oh no, a virgin who has lost her maidenhead is much worse off than a mangled parcel. Imagine your father's reaction. He would be appalled but would remain silent, for he would know that if he opened his mouth and announced what I had done, you would be utterly ruined and he would be a laughingstock. As for me, why, no one in our great land would regard me with one less whit of consideration."

"But why? That seems absurd. It seems hardly fair."

"Fair rarely has a meaningful place in anything. The fact is that men of our class aren't anxious to afflict themselves with wives who don't arrive in the marriage bed pure and untouched. Thus, if a female slips, it is kept quiet so the poor fool who does marry her is well and truly trapped. So, you see, no one would know what I did or didn't do to you. If I chose, I imagine I can take you with impunity for as long as I wished to."

"I cannot believe that gentlemen are so callous, so uncaring about the women they love."

"Ah, yes, there is the question of love, isn't there? But that doesn't come into this marriage, does it? You are a stranger, nothing more, just a stranger and —"

"In addition to seducing you, I must keep it up until I am with child. Then you couldn't annul me. But, you see, that is my problem."

Douglas's attention was fairly caught now. He'd used up most of his words, and he'd spoken truthfully to her but with no visible effect. Still, he couldn't believe the chit was standing beside him, dressed only in her virginal nightgown, her feet bare, her toes curled from cold, looking like some sort of pathetic sacrifice. But she was here and she appeared quite resolute. She wasn't a coward, he'd give her that. The question was, what was she? Would she do anything for her father, then? "Who told you to keep it up?"

"Ryder."

"Ah, my dear doting brother. Curse him to hell, but he must always meddle, it's his nature."

"But he didn't have time to tell me how to go about it, this seduction business, I mean. I am your wife, my lord. I am willing to become your wife and sleep in that bed. I am willing to sleep in that bed until I am with child. Do you not want an heir? Isn't that your primary reason for wishing to wed?"

"It was, but you are the wrong wife, as you well know, as I am tired of saying because repetition is beyond boring."

"I will give you your heir. I am young and healthy and I will give you a half-dozen heirs."

"I have never in my male adult life heard a woman offer to become a man's brood mare. Why, Alexandra? Another agreement with your villain of a father? Hell and damnation, just go to bed. You're a little girl, a virgin, and I haven't the inclination to show you anything or take your virginity or hear you whimper. I am tired. Go away."

Alex bent down, clutched the hem of her gown, and lifted it over her head. She tossed the gown to the floor. She stood there, arms at her sides, stark naked. She raised her head and looked directly at her husband.

Douglas froze. He opened his mouth. He closed it. He stared at his wife. He hadn't had any idea that she was built so very nicely. Her breasts . . . good Lord, he hadn't imagined, hadn't realized that . . .

"You bind your breasts. Why?"

"My nanny said they were too big. She said that the boys were staring at me and saying things that weren't nice. Because I had big breasts they assumed that I wasn't a proper young lady. My nanny taught me how to bind them."

"Your nanny was a stupid old prig. Your breasts are an asset, a fine one at that. Don't bind them any more. Now that I know what you've got, I want to see them."

"You are."

"This morning, when we were riding, I couldn't tell that you were so finely endowed."

"No."

Douglas fell silent. He was still staring at her breasts. They were high and very full, as white as her belly. They would fill his hands to overflowing. His fingers itched, his palms were hot.

She hadn't known how Douglas would react, but this conversation about her breasts, as bland as discussions about the weather, was unnerving. She saw him raise his hand, then lower it. He was still looking at her, oh yes, he was looking and his gaze was intent and, of all things, his eyes looked even darker. She forced herself to keep perfectly still.

"Pink goes nicely with red. I can see a pink nipple showing through your red hair."

Alex wanted to quite simply fold her body into a very small ball and roll away. But she didn't move. Her entire future was in this room, contained in this very minute. This man was her husband; she belonged to him more than she'd ever belonged to anyone else in her life.

Douglas tried to be blasé. He was an experienced man, a man who'd enjoyed many women, a man who was selective, a cold fish, Ryder had called him, because he could always control his passion. But, truth be told, he was stunned. Aside from the most beautiful breasts he'd ever seen in his life, breasts nearly too big for her slender torso, her waist was narrow, her belly flat, the curls covering her woman's mound, a soft dark red. Her legs were long and nicely curved. There was a mole on her belly, just below her navel. She looked very nice. She didn't look at all like a little girl. She stood straight and tall even though she was small. That damned broom handle against her backbone. He wanted to tell her to turn around so he could see her back and her buttocks.

Good Lord. What was he to do?

"Come here," he said before his brain could countermand the order, and parted his legs.

She came to stand between his legs, still and silent, her arms still at her sides. Still he didn't touch her, merely looked and looked some more, now at her belly, and she knew it. It was almost beyond what she could bear, this intense study of her body by this man. Even she herself had never looked at her body as he was looking now.

Finally, after an eternity of minutes, Douglas raised his head and looked her in the face. "You do not displease me. Your female endowments are adequate. Should you like to part your legs so I may see the rest of you? No? That isn't part of your seduction plan? How far do you plan to go if I do nothing?" He looked away from her then, into the fire. "You say nothing.

I have already brought you to stand between my legs. Cannot you think of anything to do yourself?"

Alex brought her hand up to cover her breasts, the other hand to cover her woman's mound. It was an absurd gesture, but she simply couldn't bear standing there any longer, exposed and open to him. His disinterest was obvious and it was so painful she couldn't bear it.

"You know, Alex," he said, looking back at her now, "not only can I take you again and again, I can prevent you conceiving a child. I can easily withdraw my sex from you before spilling my seed inside your body. I am not a boy; I am a man with a man's control. Don't look so damnably blank! You cannot conceive a child if my seed doesn't reach your womb. Thus I can freely take what is offered and still annul this farce of a marriage." He waved a hand at her. "However, tonight, this very minute with you standing here before me with only your white hide covering you, I find I have no interest. You are not Melissande. You are not the wife I wanted. Go away."

Alexandra felt beyond humiliation. She could scarce think for the pain roiling through her, the pain, the failure, the emptiness his words had carved out inside her. She stood there in front of him, not twelve inches away from him, because she was incapable of moving. She wasn't as embarrassed as she was devastated. He had rejected her, completely. He'd not been particularly cruel about it, just utterly matter-of-fact. He had made his feelings quite plain. Even though he had seemed to find her acceptable, he still didn't want her enough to take her and then discard her. He didn't want her for anything. Ryder hadn't judged his brother's feelings correctly this time. Ryder had been wrong. There was nothing more she could do.

She stepped away from him then, her blood pounding wildly through her, then ran from his bedchamber.

Douglas saw the flash of white skin. He heard the adjoining door close very quietly. He didn't move for a very long time. Then he rose and picked up her discarded nightgown. He looked toward her chamber. Then, very deliberately, he tossed the nightgown into his chair.

He knew what he'd done. He knew he'd kicked her and then kicked her again. But, damn her, he refused to be cornered, to be bribed and blackmailed with sex. He would never allow a woman to dictate to him, to try to make him lose his logic and his brain by flaunting her body. But the look on her face as he'd spoken. He cursed as he flung off his dressing gown. It landed beside her nightgown on the chair. He cursed as he climbed into his big empty bed and burrowed under the blanket. He felt disgusted with himself, but he wouldn't back down. He would do what he wished to do, and he wouldn't be coerced, certainly not by an eighteen-year-old chit with the most beautiful breasts he'd ever seen in his life.

In the dead of night Douglas awoke with sweat thick and clammy on his forehead. He held himself perfectly still. He'd heard a sound. He waited, completely awake and alert. He heard the strange noise again. It sounded like a woman. She was crying, low and soft, yet he heard her distinctly. No, it wasn't crying, rather deep moaning, hurt and raw. He knew that she was moaning because of a great pain. He didn't know how he knew this, but he did. He frowned into the darkness toward the adjoining room. This was absurd.

It was Alexandra, crying because he'd put her properly in her place. She was sulking; she had failed to get her way, and she was trying to draw pity from him. Crocodile tears, nothing more. That was it. He was a man, but he wouldn't be swayed by a girl's tears, sham tears because she hadn't managed to make him lose his head. But it wasn't crying . . . it was moaning, it was a deep, deep pain. He cursed and flung back the bed covers.

He walked naked to the adjoining door and quietly opened it. He knew it had to be Alexandra. It had to be, but still he was quiet, and the door made no noise as it opened.

He walked into the bedchamber. There was a narrow beam of moonlight coming through the window, slicing over the center of the bed. The bed was empty. No, wait, there she was, standing on the other side of the bed, staring down at it, and she was moaning softly, very softly, only he would swear that her mouth didn't move, that she was making no sound at all. But he heard the crying, the moaning, he heard it clearly in his head. It was so quiet he couldn't imagine how he had heard her in his bedchamber. She was hugging her arms around her, and then she looked up and saw him.

She was still now. He opened his mouth, but nothing came out. In the next instant, she was gone, fading slowly like a soft white shadow into that thin beam of moonlight.

"No," Douglas said, loudly and firmly. "No, dammit! I will not accept this!"

He ran to the other side of the bed. Alexandra wasn't there. Damnation, he'd dreamed it, all of it. He felt guilty and he was having strange visions because of his guilt.

Where was Alexandra? She was fast in hiding herself, he'd give her that, the damned twit. There weren't many places to search. He looked in her armoire. He even got on his knees and looked under the bed.

She wasn't here. She wasn't anywhere. It was the middle of the night.

Where the hell was she?

He saw her face then, clear in his mind. He saw her pallor, the humiliation in her eyes as his words had struck her, hard and remorseless, words that wounded deeply. And he'd even thrown her sister at her while she'd stood there standing still and solitary between his parted legs, naked and vulnerable and terribly, terribly alone. And she'd run from him, stripped of every shred of dignity, deeply wounded, but still he'd let her go.

Well, hell.

It wasn't, thank God, as late as he'd first thought. It was just past midnight. Not many minutes after he'd fallen asleep then awakened so abruptly. He dressed quickly and made his way quietly downstairs. He didn't light a lamp, he didn't need one. He knew every foot of Northcliffe. She didn't. There were a million places to hide but she didn't know of them. No, she wouldn't want to remain here.

He didn't question how he knew this. He unlocked the massive front doors and slipped into the cold dark night. The sliver of moonlight was gone, covered now with dense gray clouds. It would rain soon, a thick cold rain. The air was damp and heavy.

He hadn't thought of the cold and now he shivered from his thoughtlessness. He was wearing only a shirt, tight buckskin breeches, and boots. The wind was rising, the storm was coming closer.

"Alexandra!"

The wind rustled through the leaves. A shutter banged against an upper-story window. He felt sudden urgency. He ran toward the stables. They appeared deserted, naturally, all the stable lads in bed. He walked more quietly as he neared Fanny's stall. Then he stopped completely. Quietly, efficiently, he lit a lamp near the stable door. He lifted it and just looked.

Alex dropped the saddle, whirling around when the light struck her. She couldn't see anything because the light was in her eyes, blinding her.

"Who's there?"

She sounded scared. Good, she deserved it. He was furious now with her; she'd roused him from a deep sleep — well, it had obviously been some sort of nightmare — but still, it was her fault. She'd forced him to come looking for her. She'd made him worry; she'd made him suffer needlessly; she'd made him feel guilty.

"Please, who is there?"

He set the lamp down.

"You move an inch and I will beat you," he said and walked to where she was standing. Garth, recognizing his master, whinnied. Fanny twitched her head around and whinnied in response.

"Take off the bridle."

It was time to take a stand. "No," Alex said. She wanted to drop the saddle for it was very heavy, but she clung to it, holding it against her chest.

"You were planning to steal my sister's mare?"

"No. Well, just for a while. I'm not a thief. I would have returned her."

"Drop the damned saddle before your arms fall off."

Instead, Alex hefted the saddle onto Fanny's back. The mare twitched her tail and leaned around to take a nip of Alex's shoulder. It was close, but Alex managed to draw back in time.

"May I ask where you intended going?"

"Home. Now will you leave me alone? I'm leaving; annul the marriage, I don't care! Do you hear me, I don't care! Just leave!"

Douglas leaned against Garth's stable door and crossed his arms over his chest. "I had believed you many things, but not stupid. However, with the proof of your stupidity before me, I must bow to the obvious facts. You are incredibly stupid. You are a blockhead. Were you planning to ride Fanny all the way back to Harrogate?"

"Yes, but very slowly, and only at night. I also took some money from your strongbox in your desk."

"Dishonest and stupid."

"I have to eat. I would have returned it."

"Ah yes, your father who has all the guineas in the world would have paid me back. I think I shall beat you."

Alex knew a man's anger when she saw it. He hadn't been content to humiliate her. Now he wanted to beat her. Until she was bleeding and senseless? She wondered if he would use a riding crop. "Why did you wake up? I was very quiet."

He frowned. "I just did, that's all. I was in the army. I am a light sleeper." It was a lie but it would serve. He always slept like the dead and had very nearly died because of his habits two times in Italy. Thank the Lord for his valet cum batman, Finkle. "I'm a very light sleeper and I heard your every movement."

She didn't know how that was possible for she'd

been so quiet she'd barely heard herself. But he obviously had heard her and followed, why, she couldn't begin to guess. "Why do you care if I leave? You don't want me here. I'm a stranger and I betrayed you as much as Tony did. So I am leaving and I will never return to bother you. Isn't it what you want?"

"I will tell you what I want when I want to tell you. You will take no action until I tell you to."

"That is absurd! You wish me to wait around like some sort of slave until you decide to boot me out? Damn you, my lord, it is you who deserve to be beaten!"

It all happened very quickly. Douglas was more amused than concerned when she grabbed a rake that was leaning against Fanny's stall and ran toward him carrying the rake in both hands over her head. Then, at the last minute, she lowered it, like a knight brandishing a lance in a tourney, and sent it into his belly with such force that he reeled to the side, then landed on his back. Then she struck the lamp and it promptly went out, plunging the stable into darkness.

He jumped to his feet, his belly feeling like it had a hole poked through it, only to have Fanny snort in his face and nearly run him down. He leapt out of the mare's way. He twisted about to see that damned girl riding bareback, her hair flying out behind her head, hugging herself low to Fanny's neck. The saddle lay on its side in the straw. She was riding like the devil was after her.

The devil would very soon be after her. Douglas was so furious, so disbelieving of what she'd done to him, that for an instant, he was overwhelmed with the force of his rage. He drew a deep breath, removed Garth from his stall, put a bridle on him and swung up onto his bare back.

He would, quite simply, kill her once he caught up to her.

Alex continued to ride like the devil. She was an excellent horsewoman and the feel of the horse against her thighs and bottom gave her a feeling of great control, much more so than the decorous sidesaddles society had forced upon females.

She pressed her face against Fanny's neck, holding her legs close against the mare's sides and whispering encouragement. The mare quickened her pace. Her neck felt warm against Alexandra's cheek, warm and alive and the mare was giving all she had. She was smooth-paced and fast as the wind and Alex simply gave her her head.

It was a good five minutes before it occurred to her to question what she was going to do. Fury, humiliation, and a profound acceptance of having lost, with no more recourse available, had doused her like a flood of cold water, and she'd acted without thought. It took only another minute to hear the thudding hooves of Garth coming after her.

The stallion was fast, no doubt about that, strong and fast, but not brutal, not like his master would be if he caught her. But why was he coming after her? Was it his male pride? His arrogance that no one should act without his precious Lordship's permission?

Alex shook her head against Fanny's neck. She wouldn't think about him, about his motives. It was true, she didn't want to do this; she didn't want to run away by herself, a female alone and thus vulnerable to every villain on the English roads. But she wasn't stupid. She fully intended to ride only at night and hide during the three and a half days it would take her to get back home. She had ten pounds of Douglas's money, surely enough to feed herself. No, she wasn't stupid. She would be very careful. Perhaps that was why Douglas was riding after her. Men gave women no measure of credit for accomplishing anything on their own. He probably saw her riding into the midst of thieves, heedless, reckless, unthinking. He probably thought his reputation would be damaged if something happened to his wife — she still was his wife. Ah yes, if something happened to his runaway wife. Such an eventuality would harm his pride, make his gentlemen friends raise their brows.

The rain came down quite suddenly, in thick cold sheets, washing away her body warmth and her thoughts in an instant. She gasped aloud. She hadn't counted on rain in her plans. She hadn't even thought about the possibility of rain. Perhaps Douglas was right; perhaps she was stupid.

Alexandra shook her head. What was a little rain? She wasn't a bolt of silk to fade and unravel. No, she would be fine. In all her eighteen years she'd never known a day's illness. Yes, she would be just fine if she managed to elude Douglas.

He was closer. She sensed him, she heard Garth's hooves. She turned to see him coming around a curve in the road, just as she went around a blind curve herself. It was her chance, perhaps her only chance. She quickly turned Fanny off the road into a copse of maple trees. She slid off Fanny's back and quickly pressed her nostrils together with her fingers to prevent her from whinnying to Garth. She held her breath.

Douglas passed by. He was riding hard. He looked magnificent on Garth's broad back, strong and determined even under the bowing rain, a man to trust and admire. And she would have admired him if she hadn't wanted to massacre him so badly.

Good, she'd fooled him. The rain was not quite so dense because the thickly splayed maple leaves slowed it. Alex patted Fanny's neck.

"We'll be all right, my girl. I'm not stupid and I won't abuse you. I am self-reliant and even though I haven't seen all that much of the world, I still know how to go on. We will be safe. You will like the stables at Claybourn, for they're very nearly empty and you'll have no stupid stallions to bother you."

Alex remounted, swinging herself up easily with the help of Fanny's thick mane. She headed the mare back onto the road. She had to be watchful. Douglas could turn back and she could run right into him. She kept the mare close to the edge of the road, ready to turn her off into the trees in an instant.

The rain continued, relentless and colder by the minute.

Fanny tired and Alex slowed her to a walk.

She would have missed him if she weren't being so vigilant.

CHAPTER 10

He came out of the trees like a black shadow, yelling like a madman, Garth rearing up on his hind legs, Douglas big and frightening on the stallion's back. He got the stallion under control in a few moments, hauling him sideways, effectively blocking the road.

He smiled at her, an evil smile. "Got you," he said, satisfaction and rage mixed in his voice.

Alexandra pulled Fanny to a halt and simply sat on the mare's back, looking at him. "I tried," she said quietly. "I truly did, but you know, I couldn't bear to remain in the trees, hiding and growing colder by the moment. I was listening for you, that's why we were going so slowly, I was listening for I feared you would turn back and I would run into you. But you are very smart, aren't you, my lord? Very cagey. You simply lay in wait for me."

He remained silent, just looking at her. She thrust her chin into the air.

"I am not going back, Douglas."

"You will do precisely what I tell you to do, madam."

"You make no sense. You don't want me. Is

it your plan to humiliate me further? Do you wish to accompany me back to Claybourn Hall, a rope around my neck, perhaps, and hand me back to my father? To announce that I am worthless, that I am not deserving of your consideration? I had not guessed you to be so cruel."

Douglas frowned. His rage was justified, certainly it was. And she was putting him on the defensive, making him sound a veritable monster. He was a man, educated, fluent, well stocked in his brain, and yet, she was doing him in. No female had ever before managed it, but she was doing it quite nicely. He wouldn't stand for it. He would stop it now.

"Come along," he said. "We're going back to Northcliffe Hall."

"No."

"How do you intend to prevent me from dragging you back? Perhaps you're making ready to come after my guts with a rake again? Well, no matter what you're considering as a weapon, you will not try anything. Not this time. I will tolerate no more of your violence. You will obey me and you will be quiet, no more of your disobedience. Come along now."

"No."

Alexandra whipped Fanny around and dug her heels into the mare's fat sides. In the next instant, a bolt of thunder rang out, making the earth tremble, making the trees beside the road shudder. Then there was a thick flash of lightning, ripping through the rain and darkness, white and jagged.

It struck a maple tree.

Alex jumped, nearly losing her seat. She twisted about on Fanny's back and watched, so astonished and terrified, she couldn't believe what she was seeing. The lightning struck a thick branch at its base. The branch snapped, sending plumes of smoke into the air, and it slammed downward onto the road, not a foot from Garth's front hooves. The stallion, maddened with fear, screamed, twisted about, and entangled himself in the thick limbs and leaves on the maple branch.

Douglas didn't have a chance. He was thrown, landing at the side of the road. He didn't move.

Alex screamed, loud, shrill, terrified. She was at his side in an instant, kneeling over him, trying to protect him from the slashing dense rain.

He was still. She found finally the pulse in his neck. It was steady, slow. She sat back on her ankles a moment, staring down at him. "Wake up, damn you, Douglas!"

She shook him, then slapped him soundly.

"Wake up! I won't have this! You do not play fairly, not at all. You hold me here because you are helpless. It is not well done of you. No, I can't leave you like this. Wake up!"

He didn't move. His eyes remained closed. Then she saw the blood seeping from behind his left ear. He'd struck a rock when he'd fallen.

Alexandra didn't realize at first that she was rocking back and forth over him, keening deep in her throat, so frightened she thought she'd choke on it.

"Get hold of yourself, Douglas! Don't just lie there." There, it was her voice, and it was strong and she had to do something. Douglas needed her. She looked up. Both horses had bolted, probably back to the Sherbrooke stables. They were alone. It was raining like the very devil. Douglas was unconscious, perhaps dying.

What to do?

She leaned over him again, blocking the rain from his face. If only he'd regain consciousness. What if he didn't? What if he simply remained silent as death until he did indeed die?

She couldn't, wouldn't, accept it. She had to do something.

But there was nothing to do. She couldn't lift him or carry him. She could possibly drag him along the ground, but where to?

She cradled his head in her lap, bent over him, protecting him as best she could. She was cramped and so cold her flesh rippled then grew blessedly numb.

"My God, will you suffocate me, woman?"

She froze, disbelieving the voice she heard, the voice that was filled with irritation and annoyance, the muffled voice coming from her bosom. Slowly she raised her face and looked down at him. His eyes were open.

Her hair straggled about his face, a thick curtain of dripping strands. "Douglas, you're all right?"

"Of course I'm all right. Do you believe me a weakling? My head hurts like the very devil, but I'm just fine." He paused a moment, his nose not two inches from hers. "I preferred having my face buried between your breasts, though."

She could only stare down at him. He wouldn't die. He was too mean, too unreasonable, too outrageous, to die. She smiled as she said, "Both horses have left us. We're stranded. I don't know how far we are from home. It's raining very hard. There is blood behind your left ear. You struck your head on a rock, just a small one, but still a rock and thus hard, thus the blood. You were unconscious for a minute or two. If I help you up, you will simply become soaked." She stopped, not knowing what else to say, staring down at him.

Douglas silently queried his body. Only his head gave reply but it wasn't all that bad, just a steady deep throbbing. "Move," he said to himself.

He sat up, his head lowered for a moment, then he straightened and looked about. "See that narrow path there? We're near my gamekeeper's cottage. His name is Tom O'Malley, and of all my people, he's the one who won't faint with consternation when we arrive on his doorstep past midnight wet and in this piteous state. Come, Alexandra, help me rise, and we'll go there. 'Tis too far to walk back to the hall." It came into his head at that moment that she'd called the hall home. Stupid thought. She shouldn't have said it. It wasn't her home and it probably never would be.

Douglas remained silent until he was upright and realized he was a mite dizzy. Even more than a mite. Irritation was clearly in evidence as he said, "I must lean on you. Are you strong enough to bear some of my weight?"

"Yes, certainly," she said, and hunkered over, bracing herself as she wrapped her arm around his waist. She peered up at him through the thick rain. "I'm ready, Douglas. I won't drop you."

His head hurt. He was cold, he was dizzy. He looked down at the dripping female, scrunched against his side. She was half his size, yet she was trying to keep him upright. He couldn't help himself. He laughed. "A veritable Hercules. I don't damned believe it. This way, Alexandra."

He fell once, bringing her to her knees with him.

"I hope it isn't stinging nettles," she said, her breath coming in short gasps as she pushed off the suspicious foliage. "Are you all right, Douglas? I'm sorry I dropped you but that root did me in."

He wanted to vomit, but he didn't, even though the nausea was great. He remained on his knees for a moment, knew he had to rise, knew he wasn't going to disgrace himself, and so he rose, his face white, his mouth closed, his bile swallowed. "No, it wasn't your fault. I was on my way down when you hit that root. I didn't hurt you, did I?"

"No, no," she said, scrambling to her feet. She was shivering with cold and slapped her hands on her arms.

"That isn't stinging nettles, thank the magnanimous Lord, or we'd be itching right now. Let's hurry. It's not far now."

Tom O'Malley's cottage sat at the end of the narrow path in the middle of a small clearing. It was clearly the home of someone who valued his privacy, a slope-roofed cottage of sturdy oak, but one story and freshly painted, the grounds surrounding it clear of weeds. There were roses and honeysuckle, all well tended, climbing up the sides of the cottage. It looked like a mansion to Alexandra and as dark as a tomb.

"I don't want him to shoot us," Douglas said quietly, and began to lightly pound on the stout door, saying, "Tom. Tom O'Malley." He pounded harder then. "It's Lord Northcliffe! Come, man, let us in."

Alexandra didn't know what to expect, but the very tall, very gaunt-looking man of middle years, fully dressed, quite calm to see his master on his doorstep in the middle of the night, wasn't quite it. He had a very long, very thin nose and it quivered as he said in a low gruff voice, "My lord, aye, but surely 'tis ye. And this be yer new countess? Aye, and certainly she is for Willie at the stables told me about her and how she was comely and a bit slight, and light-handed with a horse. Welcome, milady. I'll build up the fire so that ye may warm yerselves. Nay, it matters not that ye are wet. The floor will dry, and 'tis but wood after all. Come in, come in. Don't tarry in this miserable rain."

"This is Tom O'Malley," Douglas said to Alexandra. "He and his mother arrived at Northcliffe from County Cork some twenty-five years ago, thank the heavens."

"Aye, 'tis me all right, milord, and 'twere twenty-six years before. Ah, 'tis blood on yer face, milord, and ye came to a grief, eh, and struck yer head." He efficiently took Alexandra's place, assisting Douglas to a plain high-backed chair in front of the fireplace. "Just rest yer bones, milord. Milady," he added, turning to Alexandra, who was dripping very close to a beautiful multicolored handwoven cotton rug. She quickly stood aside, exclaiming, "Oh, it's lovely, Mr. O'Malley."

"Aye, milady, me blessed mother made it with her own caring hands, she did, aye, 'twere a wonderful woman she were. Come here now, and warm yerself. 'Tis dry clothing ye be needing now. Nothing fancy, ye understand, but dry."

"That will be wonderful, Mr. O'Malley. His Lordship and I thank you."

She moved swiftly to Douglas, who was sitting in the chair, staring blankly into the fireplace. "Your head still pains you, doesn't it?"

He looked up at her. "Build up the fire, please."

She did as he bid, then wiped her hands on her sodden skirt. He eyed her then said, "Actually I was just trying to credit that I was with you in the middle of the night in my gamekeeper's cottage. It isn't what one would expect. It isn't even on my list of worst nightmares."

Her chin went up and the broom handle down

her back stiffened. "You wouldn't be here if you weren't so stubborn. You wouldn't even be here if you were better able to handle your horse."

As a verbal blow it wasn't bad. Douglas wanted to give as good as she'd just given, but he felt too rotten. He said only, "Make no more sport with me. Hush and move closer to the fire. No, don't look at me as if I'm drawing my last breath. My head hurts just a bit. Ah, Tom, with dry clothes."

Alexandra wouldn't move until Douglas went first into the small bedchamber to change out of his wet clothes. When he emerged, she smiled. He looked wonderful to her in his homespun trousers and handmade white linen shirt. The trousers were very tight on him and she found that she couldn't quite turn away as quickly as undoubtedly a lady should. The shirt laced up the front, but Douglas hadn't bothered lacing the rolled cotton strings all the way to his throat. For several moments, she forgot that she was wet and frowzy and bedraggled.

"Your turn, Alexandra. You look quite pitiful. Tom has no gowns, needless to say. You will be my twin, of sorts."

And thus it was that in ten minutes the lord and lady of Northcliffe Hall were seated on a rough-hewn bench in a gamekeeper's cottage sipping the most delicious tea either had ever drunk and wearing Tom O'Malley's clothes.

Their own clothing was draped over every available surface to dry. The earl said after a moment,

"We thank you, Tom, for your hospitality. If you have extra blankets, Her Ladyship and I will sleep here, on the hearth."

Tom O'Malley stared and paled and gasped. "Nay and niver, milord! Niver! Ask not such a repugnant thing from O'Malley. Me sweet mother would come back from her celestial mansion in heaven and thrash me till me nose bled off me face."

The earl remonstrated. Alexandra watched and listened to both of them. It was amusing and she knew Douglas would lose. Tom was pleading now, saying over and over, "Nay, milord, please don't make me, please. Me dear dead mother, aye, 'tis she looking upon us this minute and she's yelling in me ear, milord."

Douglas gave it up. His head was aching vilely and Alexandra looked ready to fall to the floor she was so exhausted. They adjourned to Tom O'Malley's bedchamber.

"That shirt comes to your knees," Douglas said to Alexandra across the narrow bed. "You might as well keep it on as a nightgown."

"Of course I shall! Did you fear I would pull it off and stand here naked before you again? Or perhaps parade about to provoke some interest in you?"

Douglas shook his head even as he said, "I don't think you're up to much parading." He shrugged, not looking at her. "Besides, you do things I don't expect."

"You needn't worry, my lord, that I will do

anything unexpected now. You will be rid of me as soon as I can manage it. I will never disgust you again in that manner."

"I wasn't disgusted."

Alex snorted, a sound that was loud and quite odd in the small room. Douglas laughed.

"I had planned to wear Tom's shirt until it rotted off me, if necessary."

"I trust such a sacrifice won't be necessary."

"I hope so as well." She nodded as she looked about the small room. It was cleaner than her bedchamber had been at Claybourn Hall, its furnishings sparse but well made and well tended. The cover on the bed was soft and pale blue and beautifully knitted.

She unfastened the belt at her waist, then began unrolling the homespun trousers. There were at least eight rolls, and despite everything, she was giggling by the time she was ready to pull them down. She realized then what she had done and where she was, and froze. "Tom is very tall but so skinny that they nearly fit me everywhere else." She looked over at Douglas as she spoke. He had pulled the shirt over his head. His hands were on the waist buttons of the trousers. He looked at her when he heard the small gasp. He looked annoyed.

"For heaven's sake," he said, and pinched out the single candle. "I have no intention of shocking you the way you shocked me. Do women believe that men can't be embarrassed when they play the seductress? No matter, I don't want an answer from you. Unlike you, all my stripping will be done in the dark. Don't squawk."

When they were both lying on their backs, not two inches separating them, Alexandra said, "Tom didn't seem at all surprised to see us."

"Tom comes from a long line of phlegmatic O'Malleys. He's a good man, though I don't like taking his bed. He's as tall as I am and the damned bed is too short. I shall have to see about a new one for him. It's the least I can do."

Douglas moved, cursed when his elbow bumped her head. "Damnation, woman, your hair is still wet. Do you want to die of a damned chill? Spread it on the pillow to dry." He kept muttering about thoughtless, stupid women under his breath as Alex made a halo of her hair.

"You needn't use your foul language with me."

"Come, lie down and I'll spread the hair away from your head. You haven't done it right."

She could feel his warm breath on her cheek, his long fingers stroking through her hair, pulling out the wet ripples as he fanned it out. "There," he said, sounding bored. "Go to sleep now. I'm tired. You've quite exhausted me with your recklessness."

What to do, Alex asked herself again and again, indeed, the question plagued her until she fell asleep beside her husband in the gamekeeper's bed.

Douglas awoke feeling very hot and very aroused. His member was hard, uncomfortably so, and for an instant, he was disoriented. Never had he felt such intense desire, a desire so urgent, a desire that was pushing him, prodding at him, making him forget who he was, where he was. He realized that Alexandra's cheek was pressed against his bare shoulder, her bare right leg was resting on his bare belly. The linen shirt she wore was up around her waist and he felt every exquisite female inch of her. He wanted to touch her breasts, to feel their texture, their softness. He saw her standing there beside his chair, naked, her arms at her sides, her hands fisted for she was set on her course, and he, well, he had humiliated her thoroughly.

It hadn't been well done of him. But what was he to have done? To have taken what she offered would have admitted that he'd given in and accepted her, that she'd won, that her damned father had won, and all because she'd stripped down to her lovely white skin and let him look at her? She'd offered herself to him. He cursed now but it didn't help. His sex hurt, actually hurt with want. Well, why not? She was very nearly naked now, pressed up against him. Why shouldn't he feel lust? He was a normal man, wasn't he? He gave it up. None of it seemed to matter now. It was dark, they were alone, the rain was lashing heavily against the single windowpane and thudding loudly upon the roof. Everything that was real, everything that was solid, everything that mattered, everything that shrieked for decisions and consequences, was blessedly far away. It could all be ignored for a good long while.

He turned slightly toward her and his hand caressed her breast. She moaned. The low soft sound froze him, then made his heart pound frantically. He wanted to come inside her right this instant. Damn her, he hurt. He cursed again even as his hand cupped her, but only for a moment. He quickly unlaced the front of her shirt. He pulled it off her, shoving the shirt to her waist. Why didn't she wake up? He could barely see her, but he knew her breasts were magnificent. He wanted to touch her now, kiss her now, taste her. He didn't think, didn't consider a single consequence of his actions, merely lowered his head and took her nipple into his mouth. She tasted hot, so incredibly hot, and so sweet he couldn't bear it. He was in a sorry state, and he knew it.

He raised his head a moment, and again she moaned and then moaned again, her head falling to the side. He kissed her throat, as his fingers caressed her breast. He wanted her mouth. He wanted her to groan into his mouth, to fill him with the passion he was rousing in her. When his mouth closed over hers, he was aware again of the immense heat of her. So very hot she was, hot with passion, hot for him. Again she moaned.

He was nearly frantic now, his body surging, his sex swelled against her thigh. Why the hell didn't she wake up? "Let me get this ridiculous shirt off you." She moaned again and he paused, frowning down at her. Surely she should only moan if what he was doing to her made her feel passion.

"Alexandra," he said softly, and lightly tapped his palm against her cheek. Heat.

For a moment he simply didn't want to believe it. She moaned again, twisting away from him. Dear God, she wasn't moaning because she wanted him; she wasn't moaning to seduce him; she was moaning because she was burning with fever.

He felt like an animal; he felt guilty as hell, then he wanted to laugh at himself for his conceit. He shook his head, the seriousness of it washing over him. She was ill. She was very ill. He got hold of himself. His lust died a quick death. He saw then the many men bathed in fevers after battles. So many had died. Too many. But at least he knew what to do. It was still raining hard. There was no way to fetch a doctor. It was up to him. Douglas quickly rose and went into the front room.

"Tom," he said quietly.

"Milord, there be a problem?"

"Aye, Her Ladyship is ill. I need you to make her some herbal tea and I'll bathe her with cold water to bring down the fever. Have you any special potions that would help her?"

Tom had no potions, but he had his dear mother's excellent herbal tea.

When Douglas returned to Alexandra, a lighted candle in his hand, he realized he hadn't even noticed that during his conversation with Tom he'd been quite naked. He shook his head at himself, set the candle down on the small table next to the bed, and quickly pulled on Tom's pants. He touched his palms to her cheeks, then to her shoulders. She was soaked with sweat. He pulled the damp linen shirt off her. Within moments Tom brought a bowl of cold water and a soft cloth.

Douglas straightened her arms and legs. He began methodically to wipe her down, long steady strokes from her face to her toes. When the cold wet cloth returned to her face, she tried to twist away, but he held her, saying quietly, "No, Alexandra. Hold still. You're the one who is now ill. Hold still."

She couldn't understand him, he knew. He wiped her face, holding the cold cloth still for several moments. She turned her face against his palm, trying to burrow into the cloth.

"Yes, you're hot, aren't you? No, I won't stop doing this, I promise. I know it must feel good. I know you're burning up. Trust me in this, at least." The cloth went down her throat to her shoulders. He lifted the cloth then and realized it was hot. The fever was heavy upon her.

He eased her onto her stomach. Again and again he stroked the cloth over her. He tried not to look at her, tried not to assess how he felt as he looked at her, tried not to acknowledge that his sex was swelled even though she was ill and not ready for him, that she probably wouldn't want him even if she wasn't ill.

"Alexandra," he said. "Listen to me now. You're ill but I fully intend that you get well and very quickly. Do you hear me? Stop this foolishness now. Open your eyes and look at me. Damn you, open your eyes!"

She did. She gazed up at him, her eyes clear. "Hello," she said. "Does your head pain you, Douglas?"

"Who gives a damn about my head? How do you feel?"

"I hurt."

"I know you do. Does this feel good?" He wiped the cloth over her breasts and down her belly.

"Oh yes," she said, and closed her eyes.

Douglas continued until Tom knocked on the door with his mother's special tea.

Douglas covered her and propped her up on the pillows. He sat beside her and held her up against his arm. "Wake up again, Alexandra. I want you to drink this tea. It's important that you drink liquids or you'll dry up and blow away. Come now, open your mouth."

She did. She choked on the tea and he slowed it to a trickle. He was patient. She drank the entire cup. Then she moaned again. He laid her back down and began again to stroke the cloth over her body.

At the end of an hour, the fever was down. She soon began to tremble and shudder with cold.

Douglas didn't hesitate. He crawled into bed with her and drew her against him. She sought him out then, trying to burrow inside him, her legs pushing against his, her face under his right arm. He smiled even as he tried to straighten her body. He was soon sweating but he didn't pull away from her; he pulled her closer, trying to cover every inch of her. Odd that she was so hot yet felt so very cold inside. This is very strange, Douglas thought as he leaned his cheek against the top of her head. Her hair, at least, was now dry. He was fully aware that she was his responsibility, fully aware that his hands were stroking up and down her back.

Damnation.

She moaned softly, her nose pressing against his rib, very close to his heart. He felt something altogether strange and unwelcome as her warm breath feathered against his skin.

He came awake when it was dawn, a gray dull dawn with the rain still pounding down, lessening but a little bit. He wouldn't be able to take her back to the hall. A carriage couldn't drive up to Tom's front door and he couldn't risk carrying her back to the road. She was too ill.

He forced more tea down her, cajoling her, threatening her, until the cup was empty. Tom left for the hall to get medicine from Mrs. Peacham and clothing for them both.

Douglas continued to hold her and wipe her with the wet cloth. Her fever rose and fell in cycles, endless cycles that scared him to death.

He was so scared he was praying.

He'd rather expected Mrs. Peacham to return with Tom, for she'd nursed all the Sherbrookes during his lifetime, but she didn't. Only Finkle, his one-time batman and valet, came back with Tom. Finkle, fit and strong, just turned forty, and nearly as short as Alexandra, said without preamble, "The idiot doctor is in bed with a broken leg. I will assist you, my lord. I've brought all sorts of medicines. Her Ladyship will be well in a trice."

Douglas tended her, alternately bullying her into drinking tea or eating Tom's thick gruel, and bathing her. Toward the end of one of the longest days of Douglas's life, he knew she was going to live. He'd forgotten his own headache and was surprised to feel the lump over his left ear where he'd struck the rock when he'd fallen.

He stood over the bed, staring down at her, knowing that the fever had broken, knowing that if only she would try, she would get well.

"Don't you dare give up now," he told her. "I'll thrash you but good if you dare to give up."

She moaned softly and tried to turn on her side. He helped her, then nestled the blankets snugly against her.

"She'll do," Finkle said matter-of-factly from the doorway. "She's got guts worthy of a Sherbrooke."

Douglas walked to the door and quietly closed it after him. He turned to his valet. "Don't give me any of your damned impertinence. She's only a temporary Sherbrooke, only a Sherbrooke through guile and betrayal, and just because she's ill, it doesn't make her my wife by default."

Finkle, in His Lordship's service for eleven years, said, "You aren't thinking clearly, my lord. She will live, thank the good beneficent being who dwells above us, and it is you who have saved her. Once you save a person's life, you cannot discard the saved person like an old boot."

"I can do whatever I wish to the damned deceitful chit. Do you so quickly forget what she and her father and my dear cousin Tony did?"

"Her sister, Lady Melissande, said her ladyship, the temporary one who lies here, was never ill. She said it was most likely a ruse to gain your sympathy, but that she said it was her duty to come and see for herself."

"Oh God," said Douglas, whipping around toward the door, as if expecting Melissande to appear at any instant.

"She's not here, my lord."

"How did you stop her?"

"I told her if Her Ladyship wasn't pretending illness, it was very possible that she could catch the fever herself and that a fever immediately ruined a lady's looks for the rest of her life. I told her a fever always left spots on a lady's face."

Douglas could only stare at his valet. "My God, that was well done of you."

"Lord Rathmore agreed that this was so, that he himself had witnessed such phenomena as nursing spots many times before. He said that it shouldn't deter her, though. He commended her on her selflessness. He nicely inquired if she would like him to drive her here to see her sister, to tend to her herself if she was indeed ill and not playacting. Lady Melissande shrieked. Quite loudly. Lord Rathmore laughed."

"You did well, Finkle, as did my cousin, the bounder. Now, since I must, since there is no one else, I will go back to the chit and see to her. Why didn't Mrs. Peacham come with you?"

"She and Hollis decided it wasn't the right thing to do."

"Ha! Hollis decided that and you know it, damn his interfering hide! Why he wants this chit to remain as the Countess of Northcliffe is beyond me. You'd think he would remember where his loyalties should lie."

Finkle merely looked at his master. "You disappoint me, my lord," he said and left Douglas to himself.

"Well, hell," Douglas said. Within minutes he was under the covers next to Alexandra, knowing even before realizing it that she was cold again. Cold from the inside out.

He supposed it was later that night when she was snuggled against him, both of them naked and warm, that he considered accepting her. It would please her, no doubt about that. It would make her deliriously happy, no doubt about that either. After all, she'd tried to seduce him. She was a lady, a young lady of impeccable breeding and upbringing who had, nevertheless, stripped off her clothes in front of him. Well, he just might keep her. Perhaps she would come to suit him as well as any other young lady. The good

Lord knew that her father would fall on his knees with prayers of thanksgiving to heaven. Everyone would be delighted, except perhaps him. Ah, but she would probably come to suit him as well as any other female.

It was a pity that she wasn't as beautiful as Melissande.

But no young lady on the face of the earth was as beautiful as Melissande.

There was no point in trying to locate another female to match her beauty. On the other hand, he wouldn't have to watch every man who came in sight of Alexandra for signs of complete besottedness. Nor would he have to worry that she would flirt with the men she'd rendered besotted. He frowned at that thought, for Melissande didn't just flirt; she flirted outrageously. She basked in the flow of compliments men rained upon her beautiful head. He wondered then, for the first time, if Tony hated the effect she had on every nondead male between the ages of ten and eighty who saw her. He wondered if some day he would ask his cousin.

He doubted it. He still wanted to kill Tony.

Alexandra cried out softly beside him. Without conscious thought Douglas kissed her forehead and drew her closer.

What to do?

He would think about it. He imagined the relief, the joy on her face were he to tell her that he had decided to keep her.

Why not make her deliriously happy?

CHAPTER 11

It felt really rather good. She was alive, truly, honestly alive.

Alexandra took a deep breath and was relieved that it didn't hurt too much. She felt absurdly weak, so weak in fact that when she spotted the glass of water on the small table beside the bed, she didn't have the strength to get to it, and oh, did she ever want it.

She did manage to turn onto her side and raise her arm toward the glass. She was near to tears of frustration when the bedchamber door opened and Douglas looked in.

"You're awake. How do you feel?"

She stared at the water, saying in a low hoarse voice, "Thirsty. Please, I'm so thirsty."

He was there in but a moment. He sat beside her, brought her head against his shoulder, picked up the glass, and efficiently put it to her lips. "Why didn't you call me? I wasn't all that far away, no more than twelve feet."

She closed her eyes in bliss. The water tasted wonderful. Douglas allowed only a trickle but it was just fine with her. To swallow was a chore.

When she finished nearly half the glass, he set

it down, but continued to hold her. He repeated, "Why didn't you call me? Tom's cottage isn't all that large, you know. I would have heard you."

"I didn't think about it."

"Why not? You haven't been taking care of yourself. I have been taking care of you and I've done a rather good job of it. You do remember that, don't you?"

"What day is it?"

He frowned down at her, but said, "It's Wednesday, early afternoon. You were very ill for only a day and a half. With my good doctoring, you'll be just fine now."

"How is your head?"

"My head is filled with its own importance again."

"Are we still in Tom O'Malley's cottage?"

"Yes, as I said, you should have called me if you needed anything. Finkle has returned to Northcliffe Hall to fetch a carriage. You'll be in your own bed soon."

"I don't have any clothes on."

"I know."

"I don't like it. You're dressed and I'm not."

"Should you like me to bathe you now and help you to dress? It's the old gown you were wearing but at least it's dry."

"I can do it myself."

"Nastiness won't help your recuperation." He held up his hand. "All right, stubbornness, then. I should realize that you're never nasty. No, don't berate me. You're not even stubborn, it's maidenly sensibility that directs your every word. I think I should simply bundle you up in blankets and take you back to the hall that way."

One hour later, the earl's crested carriage pulled up in front of Northcliffe Hall, the two matched grays blowing and snorting in the warm afternoon sunlight. The earl stepped out of the carriage carrying his countess in his arms.

Douglas stopped cold in his tracks when there came loud cheering from his staff. He stared toward Hollis, who was grinning like a wily old fox. He was responsible for this outpouring, of that Douglas had no doubt. He wondered if Hollis had paid the servants to give this wondrous cheerful homecoming. He would tell him a thing or two as soon as he deposited Alexandra in her bed.

She said nothing. He realized that her eyes were closed and that she was limp as a sweaty handkerchief in his arms.

He leaned his head down and whispered, "It's all right. It's natural for you to feel weak. Just a few more minutes and I'll have you tucked up."

"Why are all your people cheering?"

Because Hollis bribed and threatened them to. "They're pleased we're alive and back."

She retreated into silence again. He saw Melissande at the top of the stairs, looking so utterly delectable he swallowed convulsively. Her lovely face was pale, and she was wringing her hands.

Her incredible eyes were brimming with tears of concern, yet she didn't move closer to her sister.

"Alex? Are you all right? Truly?"

Alexandra roused herself and lifted her head from Douglas's shoulder. "Yes, Melissande, I will be just fine now."

"Good," said Tony, coming up to stand beside his wife. "We hear from Finkle that Douglas has been taking very good care of you. He never left your side for a single moment."

Melissande said loudly, "I would have been the one to care for you, Alex, but Tony wouldn't allow it. He didn't want me to endanger myself, but oh, I wanted to. I did pray for you."

"That's right," Tony said. "On her knees every night."

"Thank you," Alexandra said, turning her face against Douglas's shoulder.

"You're not contagious any more, are you?"

"No, Mellie, she isn't contagious. You won't contract any spots."

"Don't call me that horrid name!"

Tony clutched a handful of Melissande's thick glorious black hair and bent his wife back against his arm, reminiscent of Mrs. Bardsleys's finest heroes. He then kissed her and kept kissing her until she was quiescent. He raised his head and grinned down at her, then over at Douglas, who looked fit to kill him.

He said calmly, belying the racing of his heart from kissing his wife, "I have saved you a great deal of vexation and aggravation, Douglas. One of these years you will realize it. Her temperament is not that of a devoted nurse. I have discovered that she needs constant attention to her various needs, and they are many and diverse. Believe me, Douglas."

Melissande gasped and struck her fists against Tony's chest.

He laughed and kissed her again, hard. " 'Twas a compliment, love."

"It didn't sound like one to me," Melissande said, her voice laden with suspicion. "Are you certain?"

"More certain than I am of the color of my stallion's fetlock."

"In that case, I'll forgive you."

"That is handsomely done of you, Mellie. Very handsomely done."

Douglas stomped away in angry silence toward the countess's bedchamber.

"Damned bounder," he said finally under his breath, but not under enough.

"He deals well with her," Alexandra said, wonder in her voice. "It is amazing."

Douglas cursed floridly.

"I can't imagine why my father would think you a good influence on Reginald. He has not heard the foul level of vocabulary you have."

"I see you're feeling much better. I'm relieved because I've gotten behind in my estate work taking care of you. I trust you'll keep to your bed for a while and leave me in peace."

He could feel that broom handle stiffening her back and he regretted his hasty words, but he'd said them and they would remain said. She'd deserved every one of them. She was stiff and starchy and she galled him, shoving him on the defensive, and it both surprised and angered him.

Alexandra said nothing. There was a young maid — Tess was her name, Douglas said — and she would see to her ladyship's needs. "Also," Douglas continued, "Mrs. Peacham will doubtless fill your craw to overflowing with advice and potions and all sorts of invalid dishes. Deal with her as you wish to but know that she means well."

He left her. Alex slept the remainder of the day. Mrs. Peacham herself brought a beautiful silver tray filled with at least a half-dozen selections to tempt a mending patient. "His Lordship said I was to stay with you until you ate enough," Mrs. Peacham announced as she sat herself down in a wing chair next to Alexandra's bed. It seemed to Alexandra that she counted every bite she took.

"Where is His Lordship?"

Mrs. Peacham looked uncomfortable, but for just an instant, then she nodded. "You know, my lady, gentlemen aren't really the thing in a sickroom. They're all thumbs and confusion and contradiction."

"He wasn't at all confused at Tom's cottage. He was a tyrant, but he knew well what he was doing."

"Well, now, that was quite different, wasn't it?"

"Yes, I suppose it was," Alexandra said, and began on another dish, this one of stewed potatoes and peas, that Mrs. Peacham uncovered for her. She spent the evening alone. Neither her husband nor her sister came to see her.

She felt very sorry for herself.

When she slept, it was fitfully. She dreamed, a similar dream to the one she'd had before. A beautiful young lady was standing beside her, motionless, just looking down at her. She looked all floaty and insubstantial, very beautiful but also frightened. It was strange. She wanted to speak but she didn't. Somehow Alexandra knew this. She wanted to warn her about something and Alex knew this as well even though she didn't know how she knew it. The lady came closer to her, bent down until she could touch her face, then she retreated suddenly nearly back to the door. Once she raised her arms in supplication. It was very odd. The dream ebbed and flowed until Alexandra brought herself awake at dawn. Because she'd been locked so tightly into the dream, because it had been so very real, she found herself looking into every corner of her bedchamber. Her room was empty, of course. She realized she needed to relieve herself. She reached for the bell but knew she couldn't wait.

The chamber pot was behind a screen not more than twelve feet from her bed. Just twelve feet. No great distance.

Alex swung her legs over the side of the bed. At least Tess had helped her into one of her nightgowns so she didn't have to worry about the dressing gown that was laid over a chair in the other direction from the chamber pot. She closed her eyes for a moment against the memory of Douglas dealing with her needs while she was quite without a stitch on. He'd looked his fill at her, that was certain, for there had been no one to gainsay him, no one else to see to her. She'd heard whispers that gentlemen were many times victims to their baser natures and that was why a young lady had to take such care with her person. If she did not exercise sufficient caution, why then, it would be her fault if the gentleman suddenly became a ravening beast. She'd been unable to exercise any caution whatsoever and evidently Douglas had been bored with what he'd seen; hadn't he already rejected her?

Well, she'd been ill and helpless then. She wasn't now.

She rose and quickly grabbed the intricately carved bedpost, clutching at a cherub's fat neck. How could she still be so weak?

She took a step, was successful, then took another. Three more shuffling steps and she had to release the cherub. The screen that hid the chamber pot looked to be two villages and a turnpike away still.

She sighed and released the cherub. She stood there, weaving back and forth, then gained her balance. "I will make it," she said over and over, her eyes on that screen. "I will not shame myself and fall into a heap on the floor."

When she weaved against a chair, then grabbed its back for balance, the wretched thing went skidding across the polished floor into the desk, jarring it so that the ink pot went flying, spewing black ink to the floor and onto the exquisite Aubusson carpet just beyond. Two books hit the floor with resounding thuds. Alexandra, so frustrated and furious that she wanted to yell, just stood there, dizzy and weak, wanting to kill.

The person who obligingly came through the adjoining door was a perfect victim. It was Douglas and he was hastily knotting a belt around his dressing gown as he came toward her.

"What is all the commotion? What the hell are you doing out of bed?"

She wished she had a cannon. Or a knife. Even a bow and arrow. "What does it look like I'm doing? I'm taking my morning constitutional. Doesn't everyone do that at dawn?"

"Damnation, you're destroying my home!"

She followed his line of vision to the awful stream of black ink that was quickly soaking into the carpet, raised her chin, and declared, "Yes, I am. I hate Northcliffe Hall and I fully intend to wreck everything before I leave. This is but my opening salvo."

Douglas, realizing that she was about to fall on her face, quickly strode to her and grasped her arms to hold her upright. "What are you doing out of bed?"

She couldn't believe how obtuse he was. "I was going down to the kitchen for some warm milk."

"Absurd! You couldn't even make it halfway across your room."

"Of course I can. I have a meeting with Mrs. Peacham to talk about replacing all the linens. The ones on my bed smell like moth bait."

"Alexandra, I would that you cease this nonsense and —"

"Damn you, don't be so stupid! I must relieve myself!"

"Oh, well that's different."

"Just go away. I hate you. Go away and leave me be."

Douglas frowned down at her. He was still firmly set upon his plan to make her deliriously happy by accepting her as his wife, but she didn't particularly seem in the mood to be the recipient of this proffered bliss. He'd left her alone the previous evening, wanting her to rest, wanting her to regain some strength before he made her the happiest woman on earth. And now here she was acting like a termagant, acting as if he were the devil himself, acting as if she weren't at all pleased to see him. And he was her husband and he'd taken fine care of her.

Unaccountable twit.

He scooped her up in his arms, saying even as she tried to push away from him, "Just shut up and hold still. I will take you to the chamber pot. No, keep your damned mouth shut."

"You will leave."

"Not until you're back in bed."

She subsided because she doubted she could get back to bed without his assistance. She should have rung for Tess. Douglas left her behind the screen. She managed, but it was difficult for her, knowing that he was standing just on the other side of the screen. He was so close and he could hear everything. It left her body nearly paralyzed.

When she emerged, finally, he made no remarks. He picked her up again, continued to remain thankfully silent until he'd tucked her under the covers in her bed.

"There, that wasn't quite such an appalling degradation, was it? You did take rather a long time with the chamber pot, but — Do you think you can sleep again or would you like some laudanum?"

"Go away." She gave him a brooding look, realized that she wasn't behaving well, and said in a voice that was as stiff as her back, "Thank you for helping me. I'm sorry I woke you. I'm sorry I hit that chair and that it bumped the desk and made the ink pot fall and the ink ruin that beautiful carpet. I will replace the carpet. I do have some money of my own."

"Do you now? I find that difficult to believe. Your precious father didn't have a bloody sou. Both you and Melissande left your homes without a dowry. You don't even have an idea of the settlement your father made with Tony, do you? For that matter, you don't even know if I'm going to give you any sort of allowance at all. Hell, if I do give you an allowance, and you graciously replace the carpet, why I'll still be paying for the damned rug after all."

"No you won't. I have thirty pounds with me. I have saved that amount over the past four years."

"Thirty pounds! Ha! That would replace a chamber pot or two, not a carpet of value."

"Perhaps it can be cleaned."

Douglas looked over at the ruined carpet, its exquisite pattern black as soot. "Yes, and perhaps one of Napoleon's ministers will throw a cake in his face."

"Anything is possible."

"You're too young to realize that idiots continue to survive in this world. Go back to sleep. You are absurdly confident and it is annoying."

So much for making her a happy woman, Douglas thought as he marched back into his bedchamber. How could she act so spitefully? What the devil was the matter with her? He'd been the perfect gentleman, the devil, he'd probably saved her life with the fine care he'd given her and what was his reward? She hated him. She told him to leave her alone. She destroyed one of his grandmother's favorite carpets.

Douglas fell asleep with the acrid taste of anger on his tongue.

It was Friday morning. Alexandra ordered Tess to dress her after she'd bathed. She still felt a bit weak, but nothing she couldn't deal with. It was time for her to leave. She was buoyed by righteous resolve and she prayed it would last until she was gone from Northcliffe Hall.

He'd rejected her. He'd treated her as if she were naught but a bothersome gnat, a sexless encumbrance.

She'd destroyed his grandmother's lovely rug.

He'd laughed at her thirty pounds. He had no idea how difficult it had been to accumulate that thirty pounds, penny by penny, hoarding it.

Not only had he rejected her when she'd been fool enough to attempt the disastrous seduction, he'd only cared for her because there'd been no choice.

It was a litany in her mind. It was something she would never forget. She stoked anger and resentment because it was better than the annihilating pain of his disinterest in her, his distaste of her.

She had failed, utterly, to win him over, to show him that she could suit him nicely, that she could and would love him until the day she passed from this earth. What had he meant about giving her an allowance? She quashed that inquiry; he'd not meant anything.

He still wanted Melissande. Everyone knew that he still wanted his cousin's wife. He still spoke of butchering Tony on the field of honor though nothing had come of it yet. Alexandra had heard the servants gossiping about it. Ah, and how they speculated and wondered.

Douglas hadn't come near her again after their one skirmish at dawn. She was glad of it. Her sister had visited twice, both times standing a good ten feet away from her and looking delicately pale in her concern. Alexandra had remembered Tony's kiss during her sister's second visit, and said, "You appear to like having Tony kiss you."

To her surprise, Melissande lowered her head and mumbled, "He is most outrageous sometimes. I cannot always control him. It is difficult to know what to do."

Control, ha! Melissande had met her match. "But you seem to like it."

"You don't know, Alex! You can't imagine what he does to me — to my person!"

"Tell me then."

"So, the earl hasn't bedded you. Tony rather hoped that he had. It would make it all so very legal then and we could leave and go to London."

"No, it wouldn't make it legal at all. Douglas said he could do just as he pleased to me, and our marriage could still be annulled."

"But if you got pregnant —"

"Douglas said that he can easily prevent that."

"Oh," said Melissande, who was now frowning ferociously. "But Tony insisted that —" She broke off, and her glorious eyes were narrowed slits, diminishing her beauty but making her all the more enticing for it.

"But what does Tony do to you?"

Melissande waved an impatient hand. "It isn't proper that I tell you what goes on. Tony is a madman and he insists upon ordering me about and then he does things that he really shouldn't do but the way he does them, well . . . However —" Again, she fell silent, and Alexandra was left wondering if what went on between a husband and wife wasn't to be devoutly wished for. She'd asked no more questions. Melissande had left, somewhat routed, and Alexandra found she was coming to believe that Tony was the perfect mate for her sister. She wondered how Douglas would have treated Melissande were he married to her. She doubted he would ever be nasty to her.

It didn't matter. There was nothing more for her here. She was well; she had no intention of having Douglas recognize that she was well, and allowing him to be one to take her back to her father. She would not allow him to serve her that final indignity.

She didn't deserve it. She deserved a lot of things, for she had been part of his betrayal, but she didn't deserve the kind of humiliation he would dish out. She would dish it up to herself, with no assistance from him. She pictured her father's face in her mind when she arrived at Claybourn Hall, alone, kicked out, soon-to-be-annulled. It was an appalling picture, but it was better than the one with Douglas gloating as he stood beside her, telling her father that she wasn't adequate, that he didn't want her, would never want her. She didn't want to think of what the lost settlement would mean to her father. In any case, there was nothing to do about it. She'd tried.

She waited until she knew that Douglas had ridden out with his estate manager, a man whose name was Tuffs, then made her way confidently downstairs. She paused, hearing Tony speaking to Hollis.

"I wish Ryder hadn't left before we discovered Douglas and Alex were missing. He was trying to help Douglas get his brains unscrambled."

"I agree," said the stately Hollis. "But Master Ryder is gone and there are none to assist His Lordship, save you, my lord. Has His Lordship, ah, ceased yet to demand your guts on a platter?"

"No," Tony said. "Hell, I grow tired of remaining here trying to make Douglas see that Melissande isn't at all the sort of wife who would suit him. Stubborn blighter! Why can't he see beyond her beautiful face to her altogether self-indulgent nature? I think it time I took my wife away, Hollis, to Strawberry Hill."

"I have come to understand that Lady Melissande would prefer London, my lord."

"So she would, but she will prefer differently when she comes to understand what it is I wish her to want."

If Alexandra thought it strange for a peer of the realm to speak with such intimacy to a butler, her brief stay at Northcliffe Hall had taught her differently.

"Perhaps it would be best for you to depart, my lord. Ah, but His Lordship's humors are so uncertain. I am concerned about Her Ladyship."

"I too, Hollis. But her illness at O'Malley's

cottage — I can't help but feel it was a good thing. Douglas seemed affected, and he did care for her intimately. An excellent idea of yours that no one go back with O'Malley to the cottage."

Alexandra backed up a step. She didn't want to hear any more about intimacy or the machinations of Douglas's staff. She wasn't sure that Tony wouldn't try to stop her from leaving. Or Hollis, for that matter. Or Mrs. Peacham. She chewed on her lower lip, trying to figure out what to do.

Then it occurred to her that none of them dared touch her. They could rant and rave, but even Tony, easygoing, and an immense rogue with unlimited loyalty to his cousin, despite his ultimate poaching in Douglas's nuptials, wouldn't dare to lock her in a room, and that is what it would require, for she would not remain willingly.

She was still, and at this moment, the Countess of Northcliffe. She could do whatever she pleased. Only Douglas could stop her and he wouldn't. Still, because she wasn't completely daft, she waited until Tony drove out with Melissande. She'd heard Melissande say to Mrs. Peacham, excitement in her lovely voice, that he was taking her to Rye, a town of wondrous historic importance. "Yes, Mellie," Tony had said fondly, kissing her temple, "Rye was chartered in 1285. Edward the First, you know. It's lovely and I'll kiss you again on the cliff walk."

At one o'clock on Friday afternoon, Lady Alexandra, soon to be the discarded Countess of Northcliffe, armed with one valise and her own thirty pounds, walked firmly out the front door of the hall.

Hollis stood slack-mouthed in the entranceway, his most convincing arguments exhausted in the dust, and with no discernible effect on Her Ladyship.

Mrs. Peacham was twisting her black bombazine skirts.

The earl was riding at the eastern end of the Sherbrooke property, inspecting two tenants' cottages that had suffered badly in the heavy rainstorm.

What to do?

Hollis tried again. "Please, my lady, you must wait. You aren't well enough yet to travel. Please, wait for the earl's return."

"I shall walk if you don't have a carriage fetched this instant, Hollis."

Hollis was very tempted to let her walk. She wouldn't get very far before the earl caught up with her. Damn the boy! Hollis couldn't be certain that he would go after her. He had the first time, but now? Why hadn't he come to grips with anything? He'd been foul-tempered with everyone since his return from O'Malley's cottage. Hollis didn't blame the countess. He put the blame squarely on the earl's shoulders. He deserved to be whipped. "All right, my lady," Hollis said at last, nearly choking on the bitter taste of defeat. He instructed a footman to have a carriage fetched from the stables and he also instructed the footman to have one of the stable lads search out the earl. "Have the lad find him quickly, else I'll have his ears in my mutton stew!"

Ten minutes later Alexandra was settled in one of the earl's carriages, John Coachman instructed to take her home. Her single valise sat on the seat opposite her. She was leaving only with what she'd brought with her.

Life wasn't going at all well.

When John Coachman suddenly pulled up the team at a shout from another carriage, Alexandra poked her head out the window to see what was happening.

She came face to face with an older woman who had the look of the Sherbrookes, a woman who simply stared at her, as gape-mouthed as Hollis had been.

A young face appeared, a quite lovely young girl who said happily, "Why, are you Douglas's new bride? How wonderful, of course you are! I'm Sinjun, his sister. This is marvelous! You are Melis— no, no, you are the other sister! Welcome to the Sherbrooke family."

Alexandra looked skyward. Her luck, which she'd thought was on the rise, she now saw plummeting to earth, and soon her face would be rubbed in the dirt.

The other woman, doubtless Alexandra's soon-to-be-annulled mother-in-law, sniffed with alarming loudness, and said, "I don't understand why you're still here. You shouldn't be out visiting tenants for it is not your responsibility. You are nothing compared to your sister, from all I have been told. You are nothing at all out of the ordinary. My son could never have selected you."

Alexandra felt the clout, but she said calmly, "You are certainly right about that. Your son doesn't want me. I am not visiting the tenants. I am leaving. No, don't say it. I am delighted to give you the pleasure of my departure."

She was on the point of telling John Coachman to continue, when the door to the other carriage opened and the young girl jumped to the ground. "Do let me ride with you!"

Alexandra closed his eyes, ground her teeth until her jaw hurt, and cursed, one of Douglas's colorfully lurid expressions.

The other woman yelled, "Joan, you will come back here this instant! The chit is going away, let her go!"

The girl ignored her, flinging open the carriage door and bounding exuberantly inside. Alexandra was facing her soon-to-be non-sister-in-law.

"Where are we going? Sinjun asked, smiling brilliantly at Alexandra.

CHAPTER 12

Alexandra stared hard at her sister-in-law. "I want you to get out, please. You heard what I said — I am not visiting tenants or anyone else. I'm leaving Northcliffe Hall and I have no intention of returning ever again."

Sinjun gave her the placid look of a nun. "I will go with you, of course. It's all the same to me. Please don't make me get out. I am your sister now by marriage and I'm not a bad person, really, and —"

"I don't assume you're a bad person, but I am leaving your brother, just as your mother obviously wishes, just as your brother wishes, just as, doubtless, the backstairs maids wish. I cannot be responsible for you. Goodness, I don't even know you or you me! You must go about your business. Would you please get out of the carriage?"

Sinjun found this complication profoundly interesting. So this was marriage in the making. It was far more engrossing than any of the Greek plays she'd read by candlelight at midnight in Douglas's library. It was closer to the Restoration plays she'd read by Dryden and Wycherley.

Though she didn't understand all the speeches of the plays, she understood enough to laugh herself silly. She also knew enough not to tell Douglas that she'd read them. She had this feeling he wouldn't be at all amused.

"Why are you leaving Douglas?"

"Please, get out."

Instead, Sinjun waved to the other coachman and the carriage rolled away. Alexandra's mother-in-law was still looking out the window back at her. There was a look of confusion mixed with hopefulness on her face. She didn't attempt to halt the carriage.

"Now there is no choice unless you want me to walk. No, I didn't think you would. You must talk to me."

It was simply too much. Alexandra merely shook her head, opened the door, grabbed her valise, and stepped to the ground. She looked up at the homely appalled face of John Coachman. "Take her home, if you please."

"I can't," the coachman wailed. "His Lordship would feed my innards to the pigs. I can't! Please, my lady, don't ask me to do that. I can't leave you. 'Twould mean my throat being slit, my hide being whipped off my back!"

"I had not believed the earl so very vicious and unfair. It matters not. It is no longer my problem. In truth, I don't care what you do. Remain or return to Northcliffe. I will be the one to leave." She swung away and began walking. The valise was heavier than she'd believed. She would make do. She wouldn't stop and she wouldn't let her shoulders stoop.

Sinjun was soon at her side, humming under her breath as if she hadn't a care in the world, as if they were out for an afternoon stroll with nothing more on their minds than the varieties of butterflies they would see. The carriage was soon following some paces behind them.

"This is absurd," Alexandra said, so frustrated she was nearly shrieking. She whirled about to face Sinjun. "Why are you doing this to me? I haven't ever done anything to you that I know of. As I said, I don't even know you."

Sinjun cocked her head to one side and said simply, "You're my sister. I've never had a sister, only three brothers, and I can tell you it's not at all the same thing. Douglas has obviously upset you. He is sometimes a bit autocratic, perhaps even stern and forbidding. But he means well. He wouldn't strap John Coachman, believe me."

"He means well toward you but I am perfectly nothing to him. Go away now."

"Oh no, I shan't leave you. Douglas would feed my innards to the pigs too. He has very firm ideas about protecting ladies. A bit old-fashioned, but nonetheless, he is the head of the Sherbrooke family and takes his responsibilities very seriously. There are scores of us, you know."

"He doesn't take his marriage seriously. Go away."

"I did hear that he wasn't expecting you, but I paid no attention to that. Tony would never serve him up a pig in a poke, if you know what I mean. I've never seen Melissande but everyone says she is the most glorious creature in southern England, perhaps even in western England as well. But I can see Douglas quickly becoming very morose had Tony married her to him rather than to himself. I don't mean to insult your sister, but Douglas wouldn't deal with a female who knew she was beautiful and expected everyone to recognize her beauty all the time. Tony did the right thing, though I do hope he knows what he's doing. But what I don't understand is why —"

Alexandra stopped her. She said clearly and quite calmly, "Listen to me now. Your brother doesn't want me. He wants my sister. He loves her. Moroseness has nothing to do with anything. He doesn't care that she knows she's beautiful. He is perfectly willing to praise her eyebrows for the next fifty years. He wants to kill Tony. He is bitterly unhappy. I am leaving so that he doesn't take me himself back to my father and drop me on the doorstep of Claybourn Hall like some unwanted package. Would you not do the same thing, Sinjun? Would you not want to escape such humiliation?"

Her sister-in-law had called her Sinjun, and without hesitation. Sinjun smiled. "I am only fifteen so I don't perfectly understand what has happened. But I agree with you. Humiliation is not a good thing. Are you certain Douglas would humiliate you in that way? I cannot see him doing it. He isn't a cruel man."

"He wouldn't be to you."

Sinjun just shook her head. "Douglas took a birch rod to my bottom last year. He thought I deserved it but, of course, I heartily disagreed. I don't even remember what I did. Isn't that odd? Listen now, I cannot leave you alone. I fully intend to go with you. May I call you Alexandra? Perhaps even Alex? It is a man's nickname, just like mine. Do you have any money? We will need money, you know."

Alexandra stared at the young girl with frustrated awe. The Sherbrookes were a family beyond her comprehension and experience. She found herself nodding. She'd heard of tidal waves, but she'd never before imagined that she could experience the effects of one and not be close to the sea.

"Good, because Mother never gives me any money at all, except at Christmas, and even then I must account for every shilling, every penny, even to what I paid for her present. And she always criticizes my choices. Why, last Christmas, I hand-sewed a half-dozen handkerchiefs for Douglas and she said the linen had cost too dear and that my stitches were crooked and they should be tossed away. Of course Douglas didn't throw them away. He said he liked them. He uses them. It was humiliating now that I think on it. Perhaps I can understand just a little bit. I would like to be treated like a reasonable person, not patted on the head like a silly pug."

"Yes," said Alexandra.

Sinjun rubbed her hands together. "I am taller than you and much larger so I doubt I can wear any of the clothes in your valise, but perhaps we can buy me something else to wear on our way to your home. How far must we go? Several days away, I hope. I long for some adventure. Yes, it will be great fun, you'll see. Perhaps we'll even meet some highwaymen. How vastly romantic that will be! Don't you agree?"

It was then that Alexandra began to realize that she'd been firmly trapped and netted and by a guileless fifteen-year-old girl.

"I do so love to walk and enjoy nature," Sinjun continued, taking a skip. "I also know a number of quite interesting stories and that will pass the time. If I bore you, why then, you must tell me and I will be quiet."

Alexandra, overwhelmed, bewildered, and routed could only nod.

"Douglas merely tells me to shut my trap, as does Ryder. Tysen — he plans to be a vicar — he wants to say the same things but he fears the fires of hell if he did say what he truly wanted to. His perceived path of rectitude is sometimes extremely annoying, but Douglas says we must be patient because Tysen is young and not yet thinking clearly. He says his belfry is still filled with nonsense. Tysen also fancies himself in love with a twit who makes me cringe she is so appallingly *good* and priggishly *proper*. Ryder just laughs at Tysen and says she has two names — Melinda Beatrice! — which is nauseating, and she simpers and has no bosom."

Alexandra gave it up. She eyed the sweet-faced very enthusiastic girl beside her. She turned and waved toward John Coachman.

"What are you doing, Alexandra?"

"Going home," she said. "We're going home."

"Oh dear, no adventure then. How disappointing. Perhaps someday in the future you and I can go seashell collecting. That's good sport. Come along then, let me assist you into the carriage."

It wasn't until five more minutes had passed that Alexandra noticed the quite smug grin on Sinjun's face. She stared and winced and shuddered as understanding hit her. The chit had knowingly done her in. Guileless, ha! Alexandra felt a perfect fool. Dear God, what malignant force had set her in the midst of this remarkably horrid family?

Done in by a fifteen-year-old girl who looked as innocent as a nun. It was very lowering, more lowering than falling off a horse and landing on her bottom.

Douglas stood on the bottom step of Northcliffe Hall, his hands on his hips. He watched the carriage pull into a wide arc and come to a halt not six feet from him. John Coachman looked triumphant. Relief flowed from his smile. Douglas was glad he'd sent his mother into the hall with orders that she remain there. Her initial impression of Alexandra hadn't been promising.

He sighed even as he stoked his anger. Tysen stood at his elbow, telling him what Sinjun had done, how forward she'd been and how he should discipline the chit, but Douglas had only smiled, knowing rather that he would thank her.

He knew Sinjun. And he'd been right. She'd brought his errant wife back, and with little waste of time. She should have been born a male; she would have made a masterful general.

When the carriage door opened and Sinjun leapt out, Douglas didn't move. He stared beyond her. Finally, Alexandra emerged, her head down, her shoulders bowed. She looked defeated and that angered him even more.

"I see you came back," he said, cold as a fish on ice.

"Yes," Alexandra said, not looking at him. "I don't want to be, but it appears that I cannot even best the youngest Sherbrooke."

She was trying to hold her valise and that angered him even more. She was still recovering from her illness and yet she'd tried to leave him again — and carrying that damned valise herself!

"The Sherbrookes are competent, for the most part."

"May I leave now, my lord?" As she spoke, she raised her head and looked him squarely in the face. "I want to leave. May I have Your Lordship's august permission?"

"No." Douglas strode to her and pulled the valise from her fingers. "Come along now."

She didn't move. He was aware that every

Sherbrooke servant was an avid watcher to the damnable melodrama they were witnessing, and that he was serving up meaty gossip for many winter nights to come.

He moved closer to her and said very quietly, "I am tired to death of your imprudence. You act without thought, you are reckless, and I will tolerate it no more. You will come with me this instant, and for God's sake, stop acting like I am going to beat you!"

She straightened her shoulders and walked beside him into the hall.

Her mother-in-law stood there, looking ready to breathe fire at her. Alexandra hung back. She didn't want this. She looked at the other young man, and knew him to be Tysen, the youngest brother who was in love with the twit of two names and no bosom. Sinjun was nowhere to be seen, but Alex knew she was watching. No Sherbrooke would pass up such a promising spectacle.

Douglas turned back when she stopped. "What is it now?"

"When are you going to take me back to my father?"

"What the devil does that mean?"

"You know very well that you don't want me to remain here. I simply left to save you valuable time and to spare myself further mortification at your hands. If you would but allow me to leave, you would never have to see me again." She paused and the bitterness crept into her voice.

"I suppose you prefer to take me back, don't you? Will it give you pleasure to further humiliate me? To tell my father that I am sorely deficient and that you want all your money back?"

"Lower your voice, damn you!"

"Why? Your mother wants me here about as much as she would welcome the plague! My words must make her rejoice."

"Be quiet!"

"I will not be quiet! I no longer recognize you as my husband. I will no longer obey you."

"You are in my home! I am master here, no one else. You will do exactly what I tell you to do and that's an end to it! No more of your nonsense, madam."

And Alexandra, mild of manner and of quiet, thoughtful temperament, flew at her husband and struck his chest with her fists.

He let her strike him simply because he was frozen with shock and surprise. Her face was flushed, her eyes dilated. He very gently clasped her wrists and pulled her hands to her sides.

"No more, Alexandra, no more. Now, you and I have some talking to do."

"No," she said.

Douglas was a firm believer in reason and calm. He exercised beneficent control. He also was quite used to being the master in his home, he hadn't been bragging about that for it was the simple truth. He was not a despot nor was he a malignant savage. But his word was the law and his opinions the ones that counted. But this damned woman dared to go against him. It was infuriating and intolerable. He found himself uncertain what to do. In the army, any recalcitrant soldier he faced would simply have been removed and whipped or confined to quarters. But what did a man do when his wife disobeyed him in front of every servant and his mother and his brother and sister? If she struck him?

"No," she said again.

"Let her leave," said the Dowager Countess of Northcliffe. "She wants to go, Douglas, let her."

He bent on her a look she had never before received from him. "Mother, I would that you keep still."

His mother gasped.

Douglas ignored her and turned back to his wife. "If you don't come with me this moment, I will throw you over my shoulder and carry you."

As a threat, it was specific and precise. However, Alexandra didn't think he would want to provide more scenes for the servants' delectation. No, he was far too proud to do something so very indecorous. She turned on her heel and walked toward the front door, head high, the broom handle well in place.

In that instant, Sinjun shrieked, an unearthly sound that brought everyone's attention to her, including Alexandra's.

She was jumping up and down, shouting herself hoarse.

"Damnation, Sinjun," Douglas shouted. "Be quiet!"

"A rat, Douglas, a huge, awful, hairy rat! look, over there! Right next to Alexandra! Oh my God, I can't believe it, it is going to climb her skirt!"

Alexandra grasped her skirts and ran into the nearest room, which was the Gold Salon. She slammed the door, stopped in the middle of the room, quickly realized there had been no rodent, that Sinjun had done it to her again. She'd prevented her from walking out on Douglas, perhaps prevented Douglas from humiliating her further . . . but it was quite possible that Douglas would have simply let her walk out. When the door opened, she didn't turn around. When the door closed and when she heard the sound of a key turning in the lock, she still didn't turn around.

"Your sister is a menace," she said.

"If you are careful, you just might save yourself a good thrashing. If you do, why then, you can thank Sinjun for rescuing you."

Alexandra walked slowly to a sofa and sat down. She folded her hands in her lap and remained completely quiet.

"Would you like a glass of wine? Brandy? Ratafia?"

She shook her head.

He was standing directly in front of her, his arms crossed over his chest.

"How do you feel?"

That surprised her and she looked up. "I am fine, thank you. Certainly well enough to travel back to Claybourn Hall. By myself, without your noble presence."

"I doubt that."

"Well, if I collapsed dead in a ditch, why then, it would result in the same thing, wouldn't it?"

"No, not at all. I wouldn't get my settlement back from your father."

Alexandra stood up. She held out her hand. "Give me the key to that door. I have been a fool to remain here for as long as I have, enduring your insults and your ridicule. I was wrong to believe that you would come to accept me, that you would realize that I would be a quite good wife for you. I was wrong in what I felt about . . . never mind. I have come quickly to despise you, nearly as much as you despise me. I won't stay here for another minute. Give me the bloody key."

Douglas ran his fingers through his hair, and cursed. "I didn't mean that precisely. What I meant to do was talk to you, not fight with you, not insult you or have you insult me. You don't despise me, surely you don't mean that. Nor do I despise you. Never did I have any intention of hauling you back to your father in disgrace."

"I don't believe you."

"Please sit down."

"Give me the key and I will leave."

Douglas closed his hands around her waist and lifted her. He carried her to a chair and sat her down in it. He stood directly in front of her, blocking any escape. "Now you will listen to me.

I don't know how we have come to such a pass. I had thought you more reasonable, more —"

"Submissive? Malleable? Stupid?"

"Damnation, be quiet! None of those things. You're being absurd, you're trying to rile me." He began to pace back and forth in front of her chair. She watched him, not understanding and uncertain whether or not she wanted to.

He came to a halt, bent over, his hands clutching the arms of her chair, his face not three inches from hers. "All right, I will simply tell you what I have decided to do, decided in fact when we were still at Tom O'Malley's cottage."

She looked about as interested as an oak tree.

He straightened, looking down on her from his impressive height. "I have decided to keep you as my wife. I will not have this marriage annulled. Your father can keep the bloody settlement. You will suit me, I suppose, as well as any other female. You were right; you will make me a quite good wife. You carry a good bloodline; you have excellent breeding, as least you should. By keeping you, I won't have to travel to London to find a likely candidate and court her until I am demented with boredom. Tony was right in that, curse his bounder's hide. Of course, you are not all that I could wish for. You must learn to moderate your damnable tongue. I fancy I can assist you in improving your manners and your behavior toward me. So, Alexandra, there is no need for you to leave. There is no reason for you to act unreasonably. You are now my wife — I recognize you as such — you are now the Countess of Northcliffe."

He beamed at her.

Alexandra rose very slowly. He stepped back, still beaming at her, obviously eager for her to throw herself on his manly chest and weep her relief, to bless him for his wondrous nobility, to kiss his hands and vow eternal devotion and servitude.

She turned, very slowly, picked up the spindle-legged marquetry table beside the chair, raised it over her head and brought it down. He stared at her in disbelief, jerked out of the way, and the table crashed down on his shoulder, not his head. The key dropped from his hand and fell to the floor.

She picked it up and raced to the door. Douglas was shaking his head, furious, bewildered, a bit disoriented. He was fast, but not fast enough. She was out of the door in a trice, had slammed it in his face in the very next instant, and even as his hand closed over the doorknob, he heard the key grate in the lock. She'd locked him in.

He stared at the door.

The damned woman had locked him in the Gold Salon. The door was old and beautiful and stout and thick. It would take five men, at least, to knock it open.

Douglas had been a soldier. He was strong, he was wily, he'd lost few fights. Damnation, he even spoke French and Spanish fluently. And yet this female kept catching him off guard. It was beyond too much.

He gave it up and yelled, "Open this damned door! Alexandra, open the door!"

There was pounding on the outside of the door, and a babble of voices, but no sound of a key in the lock.

"Open the door!"

He finally heard Hollis's voice raised above the din, saying firmly, "Just a moment, my lord. Her, ah, Ladyship, has flung the key away, somewhere under the stairs we think, and we are currently searching it out."

"Stop her, Hollis! Don't let her get away!"

"There is no need for you to fret, my lord. Lady Sinjun has, ah, detained her as we speak."

It was simply too much. Douglas stood there like a fool, saying nothing more, simply standing there, helpless, unable to do anything at all. The door opened. He walked out into a press of servants and family. From somewhere Uncle Albert and Aunt Mildred had appeared. Everyone was yelling and jabbering in a cacophony that made his ears ring.

He stared over at his sister, who was sitting astride Alexandra, holding her down, stretching her arms flung over her head on the Italian black and white marble floor.

He shook his head. Northcliffe Hall had gone to seed faster than any army could lose a battle. He threw back his head and laughed.

"My goodness," came a familiar drawling voice from the open front door, "I say, Douglas, what the devil is going on here? Whatever is Sinjun doing sitting on Alex? Where did all these people come from? I believe it is nearly every Sherbrooke from London to Cornwall."

Tony and Melissande stepped into the entrance hall and quickly joined the bedlam.

CHAPTER 13

Given the earlier ruckus, it was an amazingly sedate group of people who were seated around the formal dining table that early afternoon for luncheon. Hollis was at his post, looking as unflappable as a bishop, unobtrusively directing two footmen to serve. Neither Harry nor Barnaby said a word. They appeared to be treading on eggs. Douglas sat at the head of the long mahogany table, and Alexandra, still as a statue, sat on his right, placed there by a gently insistent Hollis. The Dowager Countess of Northcliffe sat at the foot of the table.

Ah, Douglas thought, what a damnable mess.

He took a bit of thin-sliced ham and chewed thoughtfully. His mother had established herself quickly, before Alexandra had come lagging into the dining room. As for Douglas, he hadn't noticed until it was too late. He said nothing. No more upsets, no more scenes, at least for this afternoon. He couldn't begin to imagine what his mother would say when informed she was no longer the mistress of Northcliffe and that chair down the expanse of long table was no longer hers. She was, at the moment, looking rather pleased with herself, and that bothered him. Did she enjoy the immense embarrassment his wife had caused? Did she believe that he would remove Alexandra from Northcliffe? Did she believe she could still remain the mistress here even if Alexandra remained?

Of course, Alexandra seemed oblivious of her duty as mistress, the damned little twit, oblivious of the fact that the dowager was sitting in her, Alexandra's, rightful place. What to do?

He gave her lowered head a look of acute dislike. He'd offered her the earth and the moon and himself as a husband, and she'd flown at him like a damned bat, coshed him with a marquetry table, and locked him in the Gold Salon. She should have been grateful, happy as a grig, she should have thanked him for his generosity of spirit, for his forgiveness, for she'd been as duplicitous as Tony and her father. It really made no sense, particularly given her own behavior. Hadn't she stripped off her clothes and offered herself to him to make him forget about an annulment? On the other hand, perhaps he hadn't treated her all that well. He had rejected her, firmly and rather coldly. But no, that wasn't important any more. He'd saved her, taking excellent care of her when she'd been ill. He shook his head. All that was in the past, both the well done and the miserably done. What was important now was that he'd finally decided to accept her.

His humor at seeing his sister sitting on top

of Alexandra, holding both her arms over her head in the entrance hall had faded quickly. Alexandra had looked furious, her face flushed, but Sinjun was the stronger and she hadn't been able to move. He'd looked at her when the laughter had burst out of him, really looked. Now he didn't think there could be a funny nerve left in his body.

There was only grimness. His wife was still recovering from her illness, yet she wasn't eating enough to keep her left leg alive. He wanted to tell her to eat more because she needed her strength, when in his mind's eye, he saw her wielding that damned table at his head. She'd certainly been strong enough to bring him low. He sighed as he looked over at Melissande, so beautiful she made the room and everyone in it pale into insignificance. He chewed thoughtfully, growing more depressed by the minute.

Finally, Sinjun broke the silence, saying cheerfully, "Well, isn't this pleasant! All of us together, and so many of us. It is very nice to meet you, Melissande. Since we are related, I hope you don't mind me being informal?"

Melissande raised her beautiful face, glanced with little interest at the eager young girl opposite her, and gave her a slight nod, saying, "No, not at all."

Tony said, "Call her Mellie, Sinjun. My dear, Sinjun is my favorite female cousin."

"I am your only female cousin, Tony!"

"Oh no, there are three maiden cousins, all

with protruding teeth, who live with twenty cats, and knit me slippers every Christmas."

"Well, thank you, I guess," Sinjun said. "Mellie. I like that name."

To Alexandra's surprise, her sister actually smiled and said, "To the best of my knowledge Alex has never before been flung to the floor and sat upon. I could but stare. You are very enterprising."

To Alexandra's further surprise, Sinjun, for the first time since Alexandra had met her — what was it, two hours before? — kept her mouth shut and her head lowered after shooting Alexandra a guilty look.

When Aunt Mildred, an older lady of iron-gray hair, thin as a stick, with a pair of very sharp eyes, said in her fulsome voice, "All this is not what I am used to, Douglas," he knew that any calm at the dining table was at an end. He mentally girded his loins for Aunt Mildred's offensive, and he wasn't disappointed.

"Your uncle and I arrive with a message from the Marquess of Dacre, informing you of the imminent visit of his dear daughter, Juliette, who, as you know, is beautiful and sweet-tempered and immensely well dowered, to see this person on the floor and everyone yelling and babbling. Juliette is, incidentally, arriving tomorrow. She, I am certain, has never in her life spent even an instant lying on the floor, particularly with someone sitting on her. You have made a mess of things, Douglas. We discover you're already wed by proxy to *her*. We're told that Tony wed *her* for himself, the girl you had originally wanted to marry, not this one sitting next to you. It is passing strange, Douglas. And all of this without a word to us. It is perhaps an unwelcome omen that you are in danger of Becoming Like Your Grandfather."

Uncle Albert cleared his throat. "Er, Mildred refers to your father's father, Douglas, not your dear mother's father. The other father died on the hunting field, if you will recall, back in seventy-nine."

"All of us have heard of Dicked-in-the-Nob Charles," Tony said. "But didn't the fox turn on his hunter and frighten him so badly that the old earl fell off and broke his neck?"

"Tony, of course not," said Uncle Albert. "The horse wasn't all that frightened. It was a bit of bad luck, that's all. Doubtless Charles was thinking about his chemicals and not really paying attention. And don't be flippant, boy, it don't become you."

Aunt Mildred then turned on her spouse with ruthless speed. "Perhaps a hunting accident is what finally killed him, Albert, but he wasn't right in his brain well before then. His notions of behavior were really most unacceptable — I mean, having three talking parrots with him at all times — and his experiments in the east wing caused the most noxious odors to float throughout the hall, making everyone's eyes water."

Douglas stared, fascinated. They'd all grown

up with stories about their eccentric grandfather. Then he recalled the awful bit of news his aunt had dropped. He groaned silently, then said with ominous calm, "You say, Aunt Mildred, that the Marquess of Dacre's daughter is coming here?"

"Certainly. Your uncle and I invited her. It was time someone took a hand to correct this deplorable situation. You weren't behaving as you should, Douglas. Now, however, what you've done is beyond even what I can repair. You're married to *her* and not to this lovely girl over here who is married to Tony, and now dear Juliette is coming as well. It is quite a pointless tangle. I'm sure I don't know what to do. None of it is my fault. You will have to make arrangements to set everything aright."

And just how, Douglas wondered, was he to do that?

Aunt Mildred sat back and regarded her veal stew in awful gloom.

The Dowager Countess of Northcliffe said in a loud, clear voice, "I agree, Mildred. It is distressing, all of it. However, Douglas isn't to blame. It's Tony and this girl here. Tony took Melissande and left Douglas with this — this —"

"Mother," Douglas said, leaning forward, his voice low and deadly calm, "you will moderate your speech. I am master here and I will be the one to decide what is to be or not to be."

"Ah," said Sinjun, grinning at her brother, "that is the question, isn't it?"

Douglas gave it up. He had no control over

anyone, even his fifteen-year-old sister.

The dowager continued after a moment, just a bit moderated. "Lady Melissande, should you like some more apple tart? It's quite tasty, one of cook's specialties."

Melissande shook her head and asked her husband in a lowered voice, "Who is this Juliette?"

"Ah, my love, Juliette is second only to you in her beauty. But second, I swear it."

"I would like to meet her," said Melissande. "She sounds charming."

Oh Lord, Douglas thought, that was all he needed, two exquisite diamonds glittering around his house making every man in their vicinity hard with lust, and numb in the brain, and incoherent in speech.

"Well," said Aunt Mildred, "there is no way to prevent her arrival unless a highwayman kidnaps her."

"Now that is a thought," Tony said, grinning toward Douglas who was looking at Alexandra. "What do you say, Tysen? You've been very quiet. Would you like to court this Juliette?"

"Oh no," Sinjun said. "Tysen is in love with Melinda Beatrice, but he will get over it soon enough." Then Sinjun made all the motions of praying.

Tysen looked ready to box his sister's ears. He restrained himself, saying with all the seriousness of a hanging judge, "I am shortly returning to Oxford. To complete my divinity studies. This Juliette indeed sounds charming, but

I cannot remain. I am sorry, Tony."

That stopped all conversation.

Douglas looked over at Alexandra.

She had effectively removed herself, he realized. She'd closed down and moved inward. Oh, she was still seated in her chair, but the spark in her was effectively doused. She looked pale and cold and flattened.

Douglas couldn't bear it. He tossed his napkin on his plate and pushed back his chair. "Alexandra, you will accompany me to the library, if you please." Douglas had learned his lesson. Instead of merely walking out of the dining room, assuming she would instantly follow him, he remained standing beside her chair, waiting. She looked up at him and sighed. No more scenes, she thought, knowing that suddenly everyone at the table, Hollis and the two footmen, all of them were holding their breaths, waiting to see what outrageous act she would pull next.

"Certainly, my lord," she said, and allowed Harry to pull back her chair. She even placed her hand on Douglas's proffered forearm.

"Excuse us," Douglas said. "Please continue. Tony, do strive for a little conversation. And don't shred my character any more than has already been done."

"I shall tell an anecdote from our misspent youth," Tony said, his eyes on Alexandra.

"Oh yes, do," Sinjun said. "I remember both Douglas and Ryder were greatly misspent."

The dowager countess said in a penetrating

voice just as Douglas and Alexandra were nearly out of the dining room, "Poor Douglas. Whatever will he do with that one? You were a wicked boy, Tony, to saddle him with the likes of her and keep this beautiful jewel for yourself."

Melissande, to Douglas's surprise, said, "Alexandra is my sister, ma'am. You will not speak of her in a displeasing manner, if you please."

"Hummmph," said the dowager countess.

"Well done, love," Tony said very close to his wife's beautifully perfect small ear.

"Yes," Melissande said, "I rather thought you would approve."

"You are learning," he said slowly. "Perhaps someday it will become a habit with you. You won't have to consider my reaction before you take action."

Alexandra didn't say a word. She walked beside Douglas across the entrance hall, looking inadvertently from the corner of her eye where she'd been ignominiously tripped up by Sinjun and straddled on the marble floor.

She felt stripped and exposed and completely alone. She felt defeated. It was a relief to be away from all those dreadful people, but now she was with Douglas, the only person in the world who could truly crush her.

Douglas led her to the library, shut and locked the door. This time, he offered her the key. "To save me from possible further physical attack," he said. "Although I see no furnishings in here you could use for another attack. Even you could not lift that wing chair. As for that hassock, don't be deceived by its lack of mass. It weighs more than you do."

She shook her head, moved quickly away from him, and stood behind a sofa, a dark brown leather affair that suited him immensely well.

He wished she would say something, but she didn't. He tossed the key to the desktop.

He drew a deep breath and fastened her with his major's eye. "All right, Alexandra, the time has finally come for us to get a few things straightened out."

She looked at him, no clue to her thoughts or feelings showing on her face.

He frowned. "You have made me a laughingstock. I am not particularly pleased about that. However, what's done is done. I am even willing to say that I did play something of a part in what happened, that I am somewhat to blame. Have you anything to say for yourself?"

"Your family made me a laughingstock. I am not particularly pleased about that. What's done shouldn't have happened, but it did. I'd further say that you played the largest part available. That's what I have to say."

"You're right, to a point. It wasn't well done of them. I won't let it happen like that in future. Now we will get back to you and your behavior."

She stared at him, mute.

"Were I you, I wouldn't say anything either. An apology would sound suspect since your behavior has been that of a bedlamite, of a thoughtless, feckless hoyden unworthy of the title of countess." Douglas came to a grinding halt. The diatribe was merited, indeed it was, but it wouldn't gain him anything, not after the rounds of fire in the dining room. Aye, given the likely penchant of her current temper, she just might try to hurl the sofa at his head. He moderated his voice. "But, as I said, what's done is done." He gave her a smarmy smile. "We must look to the future now."

"What future?"

"That is what I wish to discuss."

"I cannot see much hope for a future. Your mother is distressed that you are married to me. It is also obvious that she would dote on Melissande as a daughter-in-law. But since Melissande is out of the running, there is still this Juliette person, who, although second to Melissande in beauty, still rates quite highly in terms of comeliness. As for me, I appear to be off the other end of the scale. Your mother would never accept me. I don't fancy having to endure humiliation from you and then endure nastiness from her."

And Douglas said without thought, "I imagine my mother looks at Melissande and sees no challenge to her authority. You, however, are made of sterner stuff and couldn't be counted on to spend all your time on your clothing and planning for parties and balls. No, you would likely want to oversee the management of household affairs yourself." He stopped, both surprised and appalled at what had come out of his mouth.

She saw that he was chagrined and said, "Be careful, my lord, else I might take that as a compliment, regardless of your intentions."

"I didn't mean it," he said. "Melissande could most certainly be counted on to do her duty."

Alexandra could have told him that Melissande would be shown a torn sheet and look bewildered.

Instead, she said, "Melissande also enjoys watercolors. She's really quite talented. Whilst I am fully able to oversee darning sheets, she leaves such mundane tasks to those who haven't her talent."

Douglas didn't know what to say to that.

"However, I can sing. I am not Madame Belle Orzinski but I have been told that my voice is quite nice. Also, flowers and plants of all kind respond to me. The Northcliffe gardens are in horrible condition."

He said very quietly, his dark eyes glittering, "Are you trying to convince me that you would make me a good wife, Alexandra? You're trotting out your other sterling qualities?" He was pleased when she paled, obviously unaware of what she'd said until he'd pointed it out.

"No," she said. "I don't want to be your wife any more. I want to go home. You cannot force me to remain here, my lord."

"I can most certainly force you to do whatever I wish. It would behoove you not to forget that."

Instead of hurling curses at him, Alexandra drew a deep calming breath. She was moderate in her behavior and thinking, she was in control, she was mild-tempered and now she would prove it, both to herself and to him. She would not attack him. "You said you wished to speak to me. About what?"

That was well done, he thought, pleased. "There is a rip beneath your right arm. Either from hurling the marquetry table at me or having Sinjun sit on you and jerk your arms over your head."

"If I wheedle, will you buy me a new gown?"

"Probably."

"I don't want anything from you! You would throw it up to me endlessly whenever I chanced to displease you, which would be every other minute."

"A pity, because you've got me and all my bad habits. You've also got all my cursed relatives who have the sensitivities of goats, and a good two dozen meddlesome servants that come with me. No, don't hurl invectives at me. Your calm is refreshing, albeit unusual. Now, I told you that I wouldn't annul the marriage. I told you I accepted you as my wife. I have not changed my mind. Now, have you anything to say?"

"You are perverse."

"No more than you are."

He had a point there. She sat down, stretched and raised her arms to lie on the sofa back. She crossed her legs and dangled one foot. She looked amused. "So, I understand you now. You are doing this to avoid a scandal."

"No, but that's a good point. There would be a scandal, probably a vastly annoying one. But that isn't the reason. I think, once you have recovered your more temperate humors, that we can deal reasonably well together."

He was giving her what she'd wanted for the past three years, what she'd wanted so desperately that she'd even tried to seduce him. She'd taken off all her clothes and offered herself to him. And he'd turned her down and insulted her. Now she was dressed in a gown with a rip under the right arm and he was offering not to annul her. She couldn't quite grasp it. On the other hand, what real choice did she have? Wasn't this precisely what she wanted more than anything else?

She looked up at him then and said, "All right."

Douglas smiled. Something loosened inside him. He hadn't realized he was so very tense, hadn't realized he was so very apprehensive about what she would say.

"You look very different when you smile."

"I suppose you haven't seen much humor from me."

"No. I suppose you haven't observed much placid behavior from me either."

"No."

She blurted out, "What do you intend to do now?"

He cocked his head to one side. "What do you mean? Do you wish to go riding? Since Sinjun is here, you must ask her if you can ride Fanny.

I will buy you another mount. Perhaps you can go with me. There is a stud over at Branderleigh Farm that sells mares with fine bloodlines."

"No, about this Juliette."

"Ah, a diamond of the second water."

"Yes! Currently being imported for your perusal. I can't bear it, Douglas!" Alexandra jumped to her feet and began pacing. "And I can't bear more comparisons, truly. This Juliette — goodness, named after a Shakespeare play! — will arrive and all your relatives will look from her to Melissande and then to me and they'll show their displeasure at what has happened. They'll be verbal in their displeasure. I can't bear it, Douglas."

"No, it wouldn't be pleasant for either of us. Let me think about it. Since I now know you won't be bagging it out of here, why then, I can set my brain to solving this particular problem. All right?"

She nodded numbly.

"You won't try to leave again, will you?"

"No. I doubt I could outsmart your sister."

"Will you prove it by giving me your thirty pounds?"

"No, never."

"So you don't trust me. All right, it seems that I'll just have to trust you first. Are you still hungry? You didn't eat much. Would you rather lie down and rest? I can ensure that you aren't disturbed."

"Yes," she said, desperation clear in her voice. "Yes, I should like that."

He gave her a long look, but said nothing.

CHAPTER 14

It was eleven o'clock at night. Alexandra was sitting up in her bed, bolstered up by three thick pillows, staring at the dying embers in the fireplace. The room was in shadow, the only light coming from a branch of five candles at her right elbow.

Would he come to her tonight?

Molière's play *The Misanthrope* lay facedown on her lap. She had just read the line "Women like me are not for such as you." And now she couldn't get it out of her mind. It read itself over and over. Poor Douglas, not only had he lost the first diamond, but the second diamond as well. She wondered what gem she could aspire to be. Perhaps a topaz, she thought, aye, a topaz, only semiprecious, not worth much, but still pleasant to look at. A solid sort of stone, surely, steady and to be counted upon. She picked up the play and turned a page, trying to force herself to read.

Would he come to her tonight?

A shadow fell across the white page of the book and Alexandra started. Douglas stood next to her bed and he was wearing a dressing gown of thick brocade, a rich blue with gold thread interwoven.

His feet were bare. She looked up the length of him, met his dark night eyes, and said, "What are you doing here?"

He just smiled down at her and took the book from her hands. "Ah, *The Misanthrope.* And in English, unfortunately. You don't read French? It is much more amusing in French, you know."

"Perhaps," she said, "but I know the play well and like it more than well, even in English."

He flipped over several pages, then read, " 'Nothing but trickery prospers nowadays . . .' What think you of that, Alexandra?"

Ah, yes, her trickery, Tony's trickery. Douglas would never let it go, never. Her voice was dull as she said, "I think it is unkind of you to select that particular passage when there are so many other lines from which to choose."

"I was thinking of my sister, actually, and all her machinations. I was hearing her yowling at the top of her lungs about that huge hairy rat climbing up your skirt. I was seeing her laughing as she held you down on the floor. I missed you at the dinner table."

"I can't imagine why."

"It was rather boring, truth be told. Since you — the target — were no longer in their midst, all my relatives ate more than they should have and spoke of the weather. However, I did have to partner Aunt Mildred in whist. Do you play?"

"Yes."

"Then you will partner me next time. You cannot continue to hide in here, you know. Do you play as well as your sister?"

"Yes."

Douglas looked thoughtful. "I don't think now that it is that her play is so subtle. It is that she is so beautiful that one forgets the cards one holds and the strategies one has concocted."

"Your strategies will remain intact with me."

"Possibly. I really must insist, Alexandra. As mistress of Northcliffe Hall, it is your responsibility to see to my family and to my guests."

She looked up at him, her expression giving nothing away, and said, " 'I'm clever, handsome, gracefully polite; My waist is small, my teeth are strong and white.' "

Douglas laughed. "Now that's a line from the play I remember well. But you needn't trot out those particular qualities, my dear, for they are there for all to see. Shall we put Molière back on his shelf? Good." He then turned to look into the fireplace. "Didn't you expect to see me tonight?"

"I wasn't certain."

"Did you want me to come to you?"

At that moment she looked about as happy as she would welcoming the plague into her house. "I don't know. I'm very concerned about all this."

"About all what? What I'm going to teach you?"

"Yes."

"How very odd. I didn't expect one morsel of concern from the woman who came into my bedchamber not long ago and stripped off her nightgown and came to stand between my legs.

Indeed, I hurried in here because I thought you just might repeat your performance. The husband is supposed to be the one to come to his bride on their wedding night, not the other way around. And this is our wedding night. Would you have trotted into my bedchamber, ready to do your worst to me? Truly, Alexandra, I didn't believe you had a modest bone in your very lovely body. Concern? Are you afraid that I shall beat you?"

"No, I was afraid that you would look at me again and not want me."

Douglas's mouth snapped shut. Dear God, he wished she had more guile. This honesty of hers was appalling, and he wished she would learn to keep it behind her teeth. "Well, I am your husband. This is the last time I will tell you that I have accepted this marriage. And now this marriage must be consummated if it is to be a real marriage."

She felt a frisson of both anticipation and fear. He did not sound particularly pleased to be in her bedchamber. He sounded as if this would be a chore for him.

"I am never certain what you will do. You are unpredictable. But I don't think you really wish to be in here, with me."

He waved his hand. "I am perfectly capable of enjoying myself with you. From this night on I won't be unpredictable when it comes to bedding you. You realize that I must be here, don't you? Do you understand about consummation, Alexandra? You do understand what we will do?"

He was still standing beside her, tall and broad, looking down at her from his commanding height. "Do you?"

"I know that you admire my bosom. You told me that. I assume that you weren't lying."

" 'Bosom' is a woman's word. What you have, Alexandra, is breasts. Full white breasts, large enough to overflow a man's hands. Yes, I like your breasts. They are most pleasing. They will be plentiful enough, certainly, to suckle my son. And until my son arrives, why then, they will suckle me."

"Suckle you? You are not a babe."

His mouth thinned a bit. "I will have to show you. Now, do you understand what is going to happen? I ask, Alexandra, because you are a virgin, and I have no particular wish to shock you or disgust you."

"Why would you do that? You make me angry, Douglas, but you've never disgusted me, save in your unregulated speech upon occasion."

"You might find my body disgusting. I am dark and hairy and large. I have heard that young ladies of quality occasionally are repulsed by the male body."

"Oh no."

"Surely this is a strange conversation," he said, frowning toward the fireplace. "Let us finish it. Consummation, Alexandra?"

"I know a little bit. I asked Melissande, but she —" She stopped when Douglas suddenly sucked in his breath. She felt a shaft of pain, deep and raw. He had thought of Melissande making love with Tony and it distressed him. But what could she expect?

"What did she tell you?"

He was trying to downplay his reaction, she would give him that. "She didn't tell me much of anything. She said it wasn't proper but then she got all flushed and stammered and I was left not knowing what to think."

Douglas pulled a loose gold thread from his sleeve. "It is common knowledge that Tony is an excellent lover."

"Common amongst whom?"

"At first amongst ladies, but then they talk to her lovers and husbands, and the gentlemen learn who amongst them enjoys success."

"So the more excellent the lover the more women the lover enjoys? It doesn't matter if he is married or not? Or if she is married or not?"

Douglas frowned. It was the accepted way of things, but he couldn't quite bring himself to tell her so. He said only, "I suppose so."

"What is an excellent lover? A man who is kind? A man who is very gentle? A man who kisses very well?"

"All those things and much more."

"It would seem to me that those things and much more would require practice and a good deal of experience."

"They do. Tony has years of both."

"And you?"

"I, too."

"And Ryder?"

Douglas laughed. "Ah, my younger brother was probably born an excellent lover. He has but to show himself and the ladies, as well as the females who aren't ladies, swoon and flirt and simper. However, he tends to forget himself in his own pleasure."

"What do you mean?"

"Never mind. Later. Perhaps when you know a bit more about things than you do now."

"Is it common knowledge you are an excellent lover?"

"I trust so. I have never been a selfish pig and I am careful to see to a woman's pleasure."

"You don't make it sound very enjoyable for yourself if you are being so careful about everything."

"Nature has dictated that sex is very enjoyable for a man, no matter the circumstance. It is to keep the race going, you understand. Pleasure is not necessary for a woman since she is only the recipient of a man's seed, and thus doesn't have to play an active role. She was deprived by Nature. It is a pity, but a man, if he's an excellent lover, will overcome Nature's oversight. I do enjoy overcoming."

"Even if you don't particularly care for the woman?"

"I don't generally have sex with women I don't care for. Except on rare occasion."

Well, she had asked and he'd told her the truth, a bit baldly perhaps, but it was the truth nonetheless.

"Yes," he continued, "for a woman, more care is required if she is to —" He broke off, then added, "I enjoy watching a woman find her release." He stopped at the look of pain in her eyes, intense pain and hurt. What the devil had he said? Perhaps it was just a maiden's fear. She didn't understand, but she would before this night was over.

Then she closed her eyes. "Then I shall forever be compared to all the beautiful women you've known and watched and enjoyed. And because I am ignorant and not a diamond, I probably will never find out what this release is all about, and you will be displeased with me. And then I will always lose and you will always feel sorry that you are wedded to me."

"But you just quoted to me that you are graceful with a narrow waist and white teeth. Ah, and handsome." He paused a moment, then said very quietly, "As to release, I will give you such pleasure that you will shriek with the joy of it. As for the rest of what you said, it's drivel."

"I don't know, Douglas. Perhaps when you begin this business, you will be sorry that I am the recipient of your excellent technique. You will feel as though you are wasting your excellence on such as me."

"I doubt that, for I have seen you and touched you and cared for you and your body pleases me, Alexandra. Very much. I am a man and not a boy. You may trust that I will take good care of you, that I will do what is just right at just the right moment to give you pleasure."

"It sounds very cold-blooded to me."

He only shrugged. It was, upon occasion, but he didn't intend to tell her that. "Do you know that this is all in all a very strange conversation to be having on one's wedding night? And that's what this is, Alexandra. Now, shall we?"

"No," she said. "I don't think so. Douglas, wait. Did you really want to come to me tonight?"

"Damn you, Alexandra, it's enough that I am here! It goes with me accepting you as my wife. No, don't look at me as if I will kill you." He grasped her arms and pulled her off the bed. "Sit down now," he said, then proceeded to push her down upon the counterpane. Her feet didn't touch the floor. They were bare, narrow, nice toes. Her nightgown was virginal; she looked about sixteen. But she hadn't braided her hair and it was really quite lovely, that deep red color, the waves thick and full, falling down her back. She'd brushed it and that must mean that she'd expected him to come to her. It was something, at least. Douglas took a step back from her and began to unfasten the belt around his waist.

"Oh dear, what are you doing?"

"I'm going to show you what a man looks like," he said and tossed the belt to the floor. Very slowly, he shrugged one shoulder and then the other out of the dressing gown. It fell to the floor and he kicked it away from him. Then, still looking at her directly in her eyes, he straightened, his arms at his sides, and stood there naked.

"Oh goodness," she said, her eyes immediately on his groin.

"I am not at all like you," Douglas said. He was watching her closely and he saw her eyes widen and glaze a bit. "With you looking at me with such interest, I tend to become quite enthusiastic. My brain has nothing to do with it."

"Oh goodness," she said again.

Still he stood there, letting her look her fill at him. Finally, to his relief, she nodded, as if coming to a decision. He hadn't the foggiest notion of what his next step would have been had she continued to look at him as if he were going to kill her.

"Your nightgown is in the way. Let's get rid of it."

He didn't wait, but pulled her to her feet to stand in front of him. He leaned down, grasped the hem of her nightgown and pulled it over her head. "Now," he said, "we are in the same boat, so to speak."

"You're very dark and hairy and big."

"Yes, and you're very white-skinned with no hair at all except between your thighs. Lovely, that."

"Oh goodness."

"Touch me, Alexandra. I would appreciate it very much."

"Where?"

"Anywhere that pleases you so long as it's between my chest and my thighs."

She pressed the open palms of both hands against his chest. Black hair crinkled against her flesh. She felt the thud of his heart, slow and steady. Slowly, very slowly, her hands came down.

He sucked in his breath. His sex grew thicker. His hands fisted at his sides, but he forced himself to stand still, to let her keep the control. He would be frightening her soon enough. When her hands were against his belly, his sex was throbbing and he prayed now that she wouldn't touch him.

"You're very big, Douglas."

He smiled painfully. "That's true, but you will learn that a man is made to give a woman pleasure. It is his role, that, and spilling his seed inside the woman."

"I can't believe this will work."

Then before he could think of anything to say, her fingertips lightly touched him. He jerked and moaned.

"Did I hurt you?"

"Yes and it was wonderful. Don't touch my sex again, Alexandra, else I might embarrass myself." Douglas couldn't believe it. He was the man Ryder accused of being a cold fish, the man who would control himself with an angel, and it was true. He'd never had to fight for control in his life. Yet she was touching him and it was making him crazy. He'd been without a woman for too long, that was it. But he hadn't, not really.

"But you are so —"

"So what?" he said between gritted teeth. Her hands were hovering over him, her face lowered, and she was looking closely at him, and he suddenly saw her on her knees in front of him, and she was going to take him into her mouth. He could practically feel the warmth of her breath on his sex. To have her take him into her mouth — the thought made him tremble and shake, and in that moment, he simply couldn't bear it any more. He couldn't call up a bit of cold-bloodedness. It was insanity and it had him. He jerked her close and pressed her hard against him.

"I want you," he said against her mouth. "Part your lips, now, now, yes, that's it," and his warm breath was inside her mouth and his large hands were stroking wildly down her back and cupping under her buttocks. Then he was groaning into her mouth, his tongue touching hers, and he was pressing her upward against him and he was hard and hot and his hands were on her bare legs now, feverishly stroking upward, and his fingertips pushed against her buttocks and touched her. She flinched and in that instant, he realized she was scared. She was stiff as a board.

Douglas got hold of himself. Too quickly, he was going much too quickly. It wasn't at all like him. He was careful, slow, very deliberate, yet here he was, acting like a wild man. He, the excellent lover, was scaring the devil out of her. Ah, but he wanted to part her woman's flesh and he wanted to thrust into her this very second, this instant, deep into her, and hard, but he'd told her he wasn't a pig. Damn, he'd even bragged about how good he was to a woman. He had to gain control. She was a virgin and he wasn't. He was an experienced man, he knew how things were to be done. This grabbing and pawing and panting wasn't a sign of excellence. He drew a deep breath. He set her away from him and took a step back. He grabbed up his dressing gown and shrugged into it. He wouldn't spill his seed too quickly and leave her to wonder how he could ever believe himself a matchless bedmate.

"I'm sorry," he said, his voice raw and low. "I frightened you. I'm sorry." Then he laughed at himself. "You won't believe this, Alexandra," he said, grasping her arms and stroking them, up and down and up and down because he had to touch her, just have contact with her. "Never, please believe me, never have I felt so frantic before, so damned urgent. It's true and it shocks me that I could lose my control. I don't like it a bit. It isn't at all like me. You're just a woman, truth be told, like any other woman, despite the fact that you're my wife. I'm not lying to you, Alexandra. No, don't look at me as if I'm a monster. I am not rejecting you, never that. That other time I was a fool and I want to make it up to you tonight. I don't want to hurt you, to frighten you. God, your breasts are lovely."

He was breathing hard, as if he'd just run to Northcliffe's north field and back. His sex was thrusting outward still. Alexandra pressed her palm against his heart. Fast pounding. He wanted her.

And she'd acted like a stupid ninny, freezing

up on him. "Please, Douglas, I'm sorry I'm afraid. I won't act like a virgin again."

He laughed and it hurt. "You are a virgin." Yet he marveled at her unquestioned acceptance. She still looked wary, but also she was eager and he was more than eager to teach her.

"Come here."

She took the three steps until she was standing directly in front of him.

"As you can see, I still want you very much. As I told you, I can't control my reaction. Do you want to stay here or come with me into my bedchamber?"

"I want to go with you."

Without another word, Douglas picked her up and held her tightly against him. Her breath was warm on his cheek and then she kissed him, a light kiss, one with her lips closed, a virgin's kiss, an innocent kiss a girl would give her uncle, and it pleased him and drove him mad with lust. He dropped her to her feet and took her hand, dragging her into his bedchamber. Once there, he turned to face her and pulled her up against him. She kissed him again, this time on his ear and then she lightly bit his earlobe.

He ran the last few feet to his bed. He was breathing hard, and it was going to be touch and go. "Now, listen to me," he said, forcing himself not to touch her, just to look down at her, sprawled in the middle of his bed. "I don't want you to touch me or kiss me again. I don't know what the matter with me is, but I can't take it,

Alexandra. Do you understand?"

Even as he spoke the words, he remembered again Ryder telling him he was a cold fish. Cold, ha!

Her eyes were large with astonishment as she stared up at him.

"I know you don't understand, dammit, just tell me that you do, all right?"

"I understand, Douglas," she said, and reached up to clasp her arms around his neck, drawing him down. He fell atop her, his mouth was on hers, and he was kissing her again and again, whispering for her to part her lips, and when she did, he groaned into her mouth, and didn't stop. "Alexandra." He said her name over and over, and he didn't want to stop kissing her, not until he had no more breath, not until he was dead, and then he'd stop, maybe. He managed to jerk off his dressing gown, but the touch of her flesh against his sent him over the edge. He was on top of her, hard against her belly and he wanted to fit himself between her legs. He reared back and pushed her legs wide apart. He fell on her again and his sex was pushing against her and he thought he would die if he couldn't come into her this instant, this very moment in time. He held on, but his tongue was wild in her mouth, deepening, his tongue touching hers, and the heat of her made his heart pound and speed up faster and faster. He raised his head and stared down at her. "I don't believe this," he said, and kissed her again. Her arms were around his back, her fingers digging into his shoulders, and she was moving beneath him and he jerked back to look down at her body, open for him, his for the taking, and he saw that she was pale, her face as white as her smooth belly, and he looked at her sprawled legs and felt himself tense and tremble, and he couldn't believe it. He sat back on his heels between her legs and stared down at her. "You are incredible," he said and his hands cupped her breasts, kneading them, and then he was leaning down, suckling her nipple and Alexandra, shocked, terrified until this moment, yelled.

Her back arched up, and at her response, Douglas went mad. His hands were all over her, everywhere he could reach, and he was pleased she was small and that his hands spanned her belly and at the same time his fingers were delving through the dark red hair that covered her woman's mound and she was wet and he was so relieved, so maddened with lust, that he simply couldn't wait to soothe her, to prepare her. He lifted her off the bed and brought her to his mouth.

Alexandra had no time for shock at this act. His tongue was hot and wet and all she could think of was, "Oh my God, something is going to happen to me!" And then it did, quickly, and she was screaming with the pounding and the scalding heat between her thighs and his mouth deepened and a finger gently came into her and she lurched up, her hands fisting in his hair and she shuddered and cried out and his words burned into her as she spun outside herself, yet deep into herself, and he was there, and he was saying, "Yes, come to me, Alexandra, come, come . . . yes. You're mine now and that is a woman's release . . . come."

The powerful burning and clenching eased and in the next instant, his fingers were stroking her there, parting her, and then he was easing inside her and she wanted to tell him to stop because it hurt and she knew it couldn't work for he was large and he would tear her, but his fingers were on her slick flesh again, probing and caressing, and she was sobbing with the power of it as he came more deeply inside her.

"Alexandra, look at me!"

She stared up at him. His face was taut, there was sweat on his brow, he looked to be in pain, and he groaned, his powerful back arching, and he lunged forward, and she screamed for the pain was deep inside her, tearing, rending, and there was raw pain and more pain. He came down over her, balancing himself on his elbows, but he couldn't stop himself. He was panting now, and he looked both incredulous and beyond reason, and he was pumping deep within her, hard and fast, and faster still, and the pleasure was forgotten and she was crying.

Then he froze over her. She was surprised that he was utterly still. She looked up at his face and saw the look of astonishment and intense satisfaction written there. Then he moaned long and deep, and his dark eyes were vague and wild and she felt the wetness of him at her womb. And it went on and on and she was slick now and the pain had lessened.

Just as suddenly, he was lying on her, breathing painfully hard, crushing her into the mattress, and it was over and she was wondering what had happened and what more would happen. After some minutes, Douglas raised himself on his elbows. He looked down at her face. He stared at her for a very long time. He frowned.

He said finally, his voice harsh and angry, "My God, I don't believe this. It shouldn't have happened. It never has happened before. It wasn't what I wanted, expected. Damnation!"

He pulled away from her, aware of her flesh quivering as he pulled out of her. He rolled off the bed and stood there for a moment, staring at her. "Go to sleep," he said, and to her astonishment, he turned and left her, going into the countess's bedchamber, jerking the door closed behind him.

CHAPTER 15

The scream brought Alexandra bolting up in bed. It was loud, piercing, and it was coming from the countess's bedchamber, the bedchamber she wasn't in. She jumped out of Douglas's bed, realized she was quite naked, and grabbed the counterpane, wrapped it around her as she dashed to the adjoining door and flung it open.

There was a maid, Dora by name, fifteen and foolish and thin, and she was shrieking, her hands covering her face, and she was staring at the bed through her fingers.

Douglas was sitting up in bed, staring in some confusion down at his naked chest, now covered with hot chocolate. The white sheet came only to his belly.

Alexandra skidded to a halt, staring.

Douglas raised his head and yelled at the maid, "For God's sake, you silly wench, shut up!"

Dora clamped her jaws together. She began to wring her hands. Alexandra quickly came into the room, and Dora, seeing the mistress she'd expected instead of His Lordship who was amazingly naked, said, "Oh, my lady! Oh dear! 'Tis His Lordship and I thought it was you and I gently shook your — his — shoulder and he came up and he doesn't have any clothes on and it scared me so that I spilled the chocolate all over him and I burned him. Oh, my lady!"

Alexandra looked at Douglas. There was chocolate matting the thick hair on his chest and staining the white covers. His hair was tousled, his jaws dark with whiskers, and he looked so beautiful to her that she couldn't understand why Dora had been shrieking. If she had discovered him thus, she would have leapt into the bed with him and kissed him until she was breathless.

She said to the maid, "It's all right, Dora. You may leave now. Fetch some warm water and washcloths and towels. Hurry now, His Lordship can't be all that comfortable with the chocolate on his chest."

Alexandra turned to her husband. "Are you all right? Did the chocolate burn you?"

He looked vastly irritated. "Dammit, no, but she startled the devil out of me, the hysterical little —"

"You probably scared her more, being in my bed."

She managed to hold herself quiet until Dora let herself out of the bedchamber. Then she laughed and laughed, so hard that tears pooled in her eyes. She hugged her stomach, bending over, still laughing.

"Damnation! Be quiet!"

"Yes, my lord," she said and laughed some more. Finally, Alexandra wiped her eyes on the edge of the counterpane, and looked at her husband.

Douglas, pulled from a deep sleep, doused with hot chocolate, and then shrieked at, shoved away the covers and rose from the bed. He was quite naked and Alexandra became quite still at the sight of him.

He didn't look at all like he had the night before.

"Good Lord, woman, stop staring at me!" It was then that Douglas looked down at himself. He drew in his breath. There was blood on his member.

He looked at the shrouded woman with long tousled dark red hair who was standing there like a half-wit staring at him, the woman he'd taken the previous night, that former virgin woman who was also his wife, and said, his voice deep and gruff, "Did I hurt you?"

She stared at him, unconsciously clutching the counterpane more closely. "Yes."

"Do you still hurt?"

She was terribly embarrassed, standing here with him perfectly naked, asking her questions that made the roots of her hair turn even redder. "A little bit. No, not really. Some, it's strange."

He walked past her into his own bedchamber, grabbed up his dressing gown and shrugged into it. He looked back at her, and said, "Come here."

Alexandra, her head cocked to the side in question, walked slowly to him. Without warning, he lifted her and laid her onto her back on the bed. He began unrolling the counterpane.

"Stop! Oh dear, what are you doing? Douglas!" She was swatting at him, but it did no good. Soon she was lying naked and he was looking down at her. "Part your legs."

She twisted away from him, but he grabbed her ankles and flipped her back. "Dammit, hold still, woman!"

"No, this is horrid! Stop it, Douglas! I might not be a virgin now, but this is still very embarrassing."

He came down on top of her. "Be quiet. I saw blood on my member, your blood, your virgin's blood, and I need to see if you're all right. Did you bleed much? I forgot to warn you. Were you frightened? Blessed hell, I'm sorry."

She stared up at him. "I don't know."

"What do you mean you don't know?"

"I feel sticky but I didn't look at myself. It was dark and you had left me."

"It's not dark now. Hold still, Alexandra." He rolled off her and shoved her thighs apart. "Damn," he said, "it's you who need the water Dora is bringing. You're a mess."

She was so humiliated, so utterly mortified, that she just lay there, her eyes tightly closed. She felt his big warm hands on her thighs, touching her, knew he was looking at her and it was a bright morning, sun flooding through the windows. She wanted, quite simply, to open her eyes and discover that she was ten years old again, waiting for her nanny to come fetch her for breakfast, and none of this was happening.

She felt the mattress shift and knew he was standing beside the bed now, staring down at her. "Don't move. I'll bring the water and bathe you."

She heard the master bedchamber door open, and she did move, faster than she'd thought possible. She buried herself in the sheets.

"My lord?"

It was Finkle, Douglas's valet.

"Go away!"

"My lady? Is that you, all muffled? Oh dear. Excuse me, oh dear."

"Finkle, is that you?"

"Oh my lord, forgive me, but I thought it was you but it wasn't, it was her —"

"No matter. I do understand, believe me. Go away and bring bathwater. Next time, knock. Her Ladyship still isn't certain which bed is hers. She has problems with direction, you know, and I have assured her that I quite understand."

When the door closed, Douglas looked down at the shrouded figure on his bed. It was his turn to laugh, which he did. She burrowed more deeply. Finally, he said, amusement filling his voice, "You can come out now. Finkle is quite gone. Can you imagine how I felt?"

"This is worse. Men don't seem to care who sees what. They have no modesty."

"This conclusion, I gather, is from your vast well of experience? Never mind. Get used to me seeing you, whenever and wherever I please. As for poor Finkle, with all those 'oh dears,' you and my valet could sing a duet. Come along, there's warm water in your room."

She came along, the counterpane trailing after her like a very long bridal veil.

She dug in her heels in the doorway. "I will bathe myself, Douglas."

"Nonsense, I need to see that you're all right. I am the one responsible for wounding you, though that is not the appropriate thing to say about the rending of your maidenhead, but no matter. I did it and I will tend you."

"You will go away. I cannot allow this. It is too embarrassing."

Douglas frowned. "Do you so soon forget what I did to you last night, madam? Do you so soon forget how you squealed with pleasure? Believe me, I was looking at you then. Now it's different, but just a bit. Be quiet."

"No." She fidgeted. "It was dark last night. You said the blood is natural?"

He heard the fear in her voice, and softened his own. "Yes. I should have warned you, but I didn't." He frowned, remembering how he'd felt so utterly stripped of everything comfortable, everything known and accepted at the power of his release, so completely unfamiliar to himself, an alien feeling he hated, that he'd reeled away from her and from the scene of his fall.

"Go away, Douglas."

Douglas picked up the bowl of warm water and set it on the tabletop next to the bed. He laid the washcloths next to the water. Then he turned to her. Alexandra tried to run but the counterpane tripped her up and she fell into his arms. He picked her up and dumped her onto the bed. He unrolled her, then said, "I am tired of playing Caesar to your Cleopatra, though you continue to unroll well. I am weary of telling you to be quiet and to hold still. I don't wish to tell you again."

She lay there, her head turned away, her eyes tightly closed, as he pushed her legs apart and bathed off the blood and his seed.

Douglas felt calm and in control even when his fingers touched her flesh and she quivered. He remembered he'd felt just as calm, just as in control when he'd tended her during her illness. No savage lust for him then and none for him now. It was finished, thank God. He was back to normal. When he decided to take her again, it would be accomplished with reason and logic and a modicum of involvement. No abandon, no frenzy. She would not disturb him again to the point that he lost himself entirely. He took one final swipe, then tossed the cloth aside. He turned back to tell her to get up when he looked down at her and discovered that he couldn't seem to look away from her. His calm fled from one short breath to the next. His task was done and so was his control. His vaunted control was a valueless memory. Now he couldn't stop looking at her, his fingers twitching at the closeness of her body. Her flesh was soft and pink and warm and he found that he'd begun to tremble. No, he wouldn't tremble at the sight of a naked woman. He never had before. His fingers dug slightly into her inner thighs. He wanted to stroke her, and he wanted to caress her with his fingertips and his mouth. And her breasts, he wanted to cup her breasts, to fill his hands with her breasts, he wanted to suckle her, to rub his cheek against the soft flesh and hear her heartbeat against his face.

He sucked in his breath. It was worse than it had been the previous night, this crippling lust, this alien urgency that turned him into a wild man, a man he didn't recognize, a man the logical side of him could not approve of. He felt blood pounding in his head, felt his muscles, his sex, tighten and throb. His sex was hard and he was filled with such desire for her that he was shaking with it. He tried to find a shred of reason in his brain, but there wasn't any, not even a thread. "Damnation," he said, and fell on top of her, parting her legs wider as he came between them.

"Lift your hips," he said, then lifted them with his big hands. He was panting now, close to shattering, so close to releasing his seed, and he couldn't understand it, couldn't begin to explain it, and then, suddenly, he thrust into her.

Alexandra cried out in surprise.

Douglas froze over her, but for just an instant. She was hot and very small, and he could feel her flesh accommodating to him; she was accepting him smoothly, so there must have been some desire in her for him as well. There was no force, only the soft acceptance of her, and he could feel every movement she made and it was exquisite and he felt everything he understood spinning away from him and he arched his back and thrust deeper and deeper still. She was crying and it was those small broken sobs that brought him a semblance of reason. He was pressed against her womb, so deep, yet it wasn't enough for he wanted his tongue in her mouth, wanted to have her breasts heaving and pressing against his chest.

"Alexandra." She opened her eyes. "Please, hold very still. Am I hurting you?"

"Not really hurt, it's just that I don't know what will happen and it is frightening."

"I promise the next time it will be very slow. I swear it to you, but not this time. Please, don't move. If you move I will go insane. Do you understand?"

She looked at him, at sea.

"Just say you understand."

"I understand."

"Good. Don't move. I don't know what's wrong with me. It is beyond my experience. This isn't acceptable to me or —" He felt her muscles clench around him and he groaned and tensed and heaved. He cursed and his eyes closed. He pushed deep then withdrew only to thrust forward, his hands digging into her hips as he lifted her higher.

He yelled when his climax hit him, yelled like a madman, yelled like he'd never yelled before in his life. Then he was flat on top of her and he was kissing her, wanting to consume her, tasting her tears, tasting the warmth of her mouth and still he was moving inside her, and he simply couldn't believe it, couldn't comprehend it and it just wouldn't stop.

When finally he calmed, he stilled above her. He'd done it again. He'd lost himself again and forgotten who he was and what he was. And it was this woman who had brought him to this ludicrous pass and he wouldn't accept it. He frowned. She was crying, her face pale, her hair tousled around her face.

"I'm sorry," he said, and pulled out of her. "Next time, I swear it will be slow and you won't be afraid. I'm sorry."

He stood there, stiff, his chest still heaving, looking at her sprawled legs. "I'm sorry," he said again, "but I can't —"

He turned quickly, his dressing gown flapping open, only to be brought up sharply by a very angry voice. "If you run away again, Douglas Sherbrooke, I swear I will leave Northcliffe Hall and travel to London and tell everyone that you are a pig and not an excellent lover. I will tell all the ladies that you have no control at all, that you're a raving lunatic, that you can't think of anything except yourself. Oh yes, and you're very hairy and you sweat a lot!"

"Damn you, it's your fault! If you weren't so —"

"So what? So extravagantly beautiful? So utterly perfect?"

"Well, no, you're not, not really, it's just that

. . . it has to be your fault. No woman has ever before made me into such a fool, such an uncontrolled imbecile, and God knows you're not your sister so —"

"No, I'm not my bloody sister, I'm just me and you barely even can bring yourself to look at me!"

"That's been soundly disproved. All I have to do look at you and go mad — Well, maybe not your face, but the rest of you and that's still you. You must be a witch. You've brought me low. It must be those breasts of yours. But there are your thighs and belly and . . . What have you done to me?"

"I have done nothing as yet, but I tell you that I am considering taking a sharp knife to your miserable throat!"

"Don't you dare threaten me! Well, blessed hell! The good Lord knows I was much better off before you thrust yourself into my life! At least I knew who I was and why I did what I did."

At least this time, she thought, staring at the newly slammed adjoining door, he had retreated to his own room and not to hers.

She pulled her legs together. She was very sore, deep inside, and her thigh muscles ached and pulled. She was also no longer a virgin. If she hadn't recalled the incredible pleasure of the previous night, she surely would have cursed him now for being an animal. As it was, Alexandra sighed and pulled herself out of the rumpled counterpane. She was a mess, he'd been right about that.

She gave the bell cord a jerk.

It was close to an hour later when Alexandra emerged from her bedchamber to see Douglas standing there, leaning against the opposite wall between two Sherbrooke paintings, his arms folded across his chest.

"You took long enough," he said and pushed off the wall. "I trust you're ready for your breakfast."

"Why not? Perhaps your mother will have put some rat poison in my scrambled eggs."

"I will eat off your plate, just as I slept in your bed. I will be your royal taster. Incidentally, that gown isn't at all what is acceptable for the Countess of Northcliffe."

"Give me a moment, and I will contrive a wheedle."

"No, you don't have to. Since I accepted you, why then, I must also clothe you appropriately. I particularly don't like the way all your gowns flatten down your breasts. Also, it can't be particularly healthful. Not that I want them on display when we select new gowns, but a bit more hint of cleavage would be nice. I won't have to be dependent entirely on my imagination to —"

"What are you doing here?"

He grinned down at her as he offered her his arm. "I thought you just might bolt. You were all but spitting fire at me, lying there on your back with your legs sprawled. I can't allow you to go to London and tell all the ladies how I have behaved." He gave her a bigger grin. "Not, of course, that they would believe you. They wouldn't. They would snigger at you. They would think you a jealous woman and a liar."

She wouldn't look at him. "I will leave for London as soon as I am certain your sister is nowhere around. I shall convince them."

"You won't leave."

"Stop grinding your teeth, it will do you no good. I will do whatever I want to do."

He said very quietly, "You could be with child."

That brought her face around and she gaped up at him. "Oh no, that can't be possible. You can't be that efficient. No, it isn't reasonable and you're making that up just to make me toe the line. Can it?"

"Certainly it's very possible." He placed the flat of his hand on her stomach, splaying his fingers. "I did spill my seed inside you twice. Don't tell me they were both such forgettable experiences that you'd already dismissed them?"

"How could I? The first time you hurt me and the second time you were a mauling savage."

Douglas frowned and removed his hand. "Yes, well, I didn't mean to. And you're lying about the first time. You squealed like a —"

"Be quiet! If that is supposed to pass for an apology, let me tell you, my lord, that it is sorely lacking. At least you didn't blame me again."

He gave her a brooding look. "I would be the

same man if you weren't here, so what am I to do?"

"I believe I shall go sharpen a knife."

Douglas was grinning when he looked up to see his cousin approaching from the other end of the corridor. "Ah, if it isn't Tony, you traitorous sod. I would that you stay out of my sight. Where's your wife?"

Tony gave them a sleepy, quite sated smile. "Still asleep, doubtless dreaming of me."

Douglas's grin dissolved into a growl and Alexandra, so furious with him that she couldn't help herself, struck him hard in his belly with her fist.

He sucked in his breath, but smiled over the pain. "It's Tony you're supposed to attack, not me, not your husband, who made you scream with pleasure last night."

"Ah," Tony said, eyeing Alexandra's furiously embarrassed face. "About time, Douglas."

Alexandra couldn't cope with this outrageous man at her side. Had he no modesty, no discretion?

"I suppose it is also my fault that you speak so disgracefully, my lord? Just be quiet, and you too, Tony."

"A wife isn't a bad thing," Tony said, falling into step beside Alexandra. "Always there, beside you, ready to be kissed and stroked and fondled."

"A wife isn't a pet."

"Oh no, she's much more than a pet. What

do you say, Douglas?"

It seemed to Alexandra that Douglas was concentrating on the stairs, not listening to Tony. He was probably thinking of Melissande, the clod. He was frowning and said abruptly, "Are Uncle Albert and Aunt Mildred still here?"

Tony yawned and scratched his elbow. "I suppose so. It's your house. You're the bloody host. You should know who is residing under your roof."

"You're here and God knows I don't want you to be."

As a complaint, it lacked heat, and Tony was pleased. He said easily, "Now, now, cousin, I would have thought all would be forgiven this morning. After all, at last you took Alexandra the way a man takes his bride and from the looks of her and the looks of you, I'd say —"

"Don't say it, Tony!"

"Sorry, Alex, you're right. Now, Douglas, I fancy that I will take Melissande to Strawberry Hill on Friday. Does that please you?"

"That's three more days of your damned company!"

"And my sister's," Alexandra said. "You should be pleased with half the bargain. You can sit about and brood and sigh and look melancholy."

"I would be pleased if you would contrive to hold your tongue, madam."

"I've never seen Douglas brood over any woman, Alex. Surely he would have more pride."

"Hello! Good morning, Alexandra! Goodness, you

look pale. Didn't you sleep well? Is Douglas picking at you again? Good morning, gentlemen."

Alexandra looked at her enthusiastic young sister-in-law, who looked healthy and vigorous and repellently fit, and sighed.

"Hello, Sinjun."

"Good morning, brat," Tony said.

Douglas grunted at his sister.

"Is your mother in the breakfast room?" Alexandra asked.

"Oh no, it's far too early for Mother. She won't rise until nearly noon. Come along, Alexandra, there's no reason for you to dally. Only Aunt Mildred is there. She eats a lot, you know, so she won't say much. Odd, isn't it, and she's so thin."

Alexandra sighed again.

"Mother has the disposition of a lemon in the morning. Aunt Mildred is more like a prune." Sinjun frowned, then remarked to her brother, "It is difficult to imagine a prune eating a lot."

"You're abominable, you know that, Sinjun?"

"You aren't in a particularly excellent temper this morning, Douglas. Has Tony been twitting you again? Don't pay him any mind. I am so glad you're home and you're married to Alex. Shall we go riding after breakfast?"

"Why not?" said Alexandra. "I wish to mark the closest road to London."

Aunt Mildred was indeed occupied with two scones that dripped honey and butter. She gave

Alexandra a look from beneath lowered brows but said nothing.

Alexandra felt Douglas's hand on her elbow, pulling her to a halt. She paused, looking up at him. "It's time you sat where you're supposed to."

She looked at the countess's chair and actually shuddered. "But it isn't necessary and —"

"And nothing. Be quiet and obey me. It will be a new experience for you. Here, sit down."

"You look very fine in that chair," Sinjun said. "Mother will gnash her teeth, but it is only right, you know, that Douglas's wife take precedence. You are the mistress here now. And, according to Douglas, a Sherbrooke must always do his or her duty and be responsible."

"A pity my cousin didn't heed any of the famous Sherbrooke maxims, the perfidious cur."

Aunt Mildred said to the table at large, "She is too small for that chair."

Douglas smiled down the expanse of table to his wife. "Should you like to sit on a pillow?"

Sinjun said, "Actually, Aunt, this chair is quite the right size for Alex. I must say that Mother overflowed it a bit. It is the chair in the formal dining room that must needs be cushioned for Alex."

"You're right, Sinjun," Tony said.

"No one requires your opinion, Anthony," Aunt Mildred said. "You have behaved abominably. Really! Marrying two girls and handing over the wrong one to Douglas."

"The scones are delicious," Sinjun said, and

offered one to her aunt.

"Don't, I pray, say that to my wife, Aunt," Tony said. "Why, she lives to breathe the very air I breathe, she pines if I am gone from her for even a veritable instant, she —"

"I believe we should buy Alex a mare today, Douglas," Sinjun said, waving another scone in Tony's direction. "Now, you can't thrash Tony at the breakfast table. Oh, Douglas, I saw Tom O'Malley and he told me all about your and Alex's visit and how you took excellent care of Alex and how you sent him a new bed the very next day. He said it was heaven, it surely was, the first bed he'd ever owned that was longer than he was. Ah, here's Hollis. His Lordship is in need of coffee, Hollis."

"I see that he is indeed in need," Hollis agreed and poured coffee from a delicate silver pot. "Would Your Ladyship care for some coffee?"

Alex jumped. *Ladyship!* She looked into Hollis's kind face. "Some tea, if you please, Hollis. I haven't gotten the taste for coffee."

"I believe, young lady, that you are seated in my chair!"

"Oh dear," Sinjun said, "we're in the suds now and it isn't even close to noon."

The Dowager Countess of Northcliffe presented an impressive portrait of outrage. "Be quiet this instant, Joan, else you will spend the rest of the year in your bedchamber. I can see how you encourage her. Now, as for you, you will remove yourself."

CHAPTER 16

A sudden thick silence swallowed every sound in the breakfast room.

Alex looked toward Douglas. He was sitting perfectly still, his fork in his right hand, suspended still as a stone in the silence. He gave her a slight nod. So, he was leaving it to her. He was not going to intervene. She swallowed, then turned to face her mother-in-law.

She said mildly, "You know, my name isn't 'young lady,' it's Alexandra. To be more precise, it's Lady Alexandra. I'm the daughter of a duke. It is strange, is it not, that if we were at Carlton House, I would take precedence over you. Even though I have taken a step down, nuptially speaking, I still would take precedence. However, you are now my relative, you are much older than I and thus I owe you respect. I have never understood why age demanded more respect, but it seems to be the way of things. Now, should you like to call me Alexandra or Lady Northcliffe?"

The Dowager Countess of Northcliffe wasn't a twig to be snapped in a stiff breeze, yet she saw the steel in the girl seated in her chair —

her chair — and was forced to reassess her position. Her son wasn't saying a word. He wasn't defending her, his own dear mother. The dowager drew in a deep breath, but she was forestalled by Hollis, who said very quietly, "My lady, cook has prepared a special nutty bun for you this morning, topped with frosted almonds and cinnamon. It is delightful, truly, and she is waiting breathlessly for your opinion. Here, my lady, do sit here in this lovely chair that gives such a fine view onto the eastern lawn. You can see that the peacocks are strutting this morning. I have always thought it the best-placed chair at the table."

The dowager wasn't certain what to do. It was her sham daughter-in-law who decided her. Alexandra said quickly, clapping her hands in excitement, "Oh, I should very much like to see the peacocks, Hollis. Are their tails fully fanned? How wonderful! Ma'am, would you mind if I sat there this morning so that I can look at them? I had remarked before that the placement of that chair was marvelous."

The dowager said, all three chins elevated, "No, I wish to watch them this morning. They are amusing. Well, Hollis, I am waiting to be seated. I am waiting for my nutty bun."

Douglas was impressed, very impressed. He looked toward Alexandra, but her head was down. That impressed him as well. No crowing from her, no gloating at this small but quite significant victory. She'd managed, with Hollis's help, not to turn the breakfast room into a battleground. He said then, "After breakfast, Alexandra and I are going to Branderleigh Farm to buy her a mare. Sinjun, would you care to accompany us?"

Sinjun had a mouthful of kippers and could only nod. It was Melissande who said gaily from the doorway, "Oh, how delightful! Tony, shouldn't you also like to buy me a mare? I should like a white mare, pure white, I think, with a long thick white mane."

She looked so exquisitely beautiful that Douglas's fork remained for several moments poised an inch from his mouth. Her morning gown was of a soft pale blue, plain, truth be told, but nothing more was required. Her hair had a blue ribbon threaded through the thick fat black curls. She looked fragile, delicate, immensely provocative.

"And a new riding habit, Melissande?" Sinjun said. "Pure white with perhaps a bright green feather in your hat? Oh, how lovely you would look. And seated on a lovely saddle atop a white mare, ah, you would look like a fairy princess."

"White makes her look sallow," Tony said matter-of-factly as he stirred the eggs on his plate. "It was with great relief I realized she wasn't required to wear any more white once she was married to me."

"Sallow! I am never sallow! Doesn't that mean that I would look a nasty sort of yellow? No, it is absurd. I am never, never sallow."

"Are you not, Mellie? In this instance, your mirror isn't telling you the truth. You must learn to trust your husband. I have exquisite taste, you know. Why, I was planning to toss away all your girlish nightwear. No more white. I was thinking of bright blues and greens — all silk and satin, of course — and slippers to match. What do you think, my love?"

Melissande was in something of a bind. "I am not ever yellow," she said, "but I should much enjoy new things."

"I thought you would. After we have visited Strawberry Hill for as long as I wish, why then, we will go to London and you will flail young male hearts with your incomparable beauty and your silks and satins."

"But I want to go to London now, Tony!"

"Should you like a scone, my dear?" asked the Dowager Countess of Northcliffe.

Douglas was looking at Melissande. He was also frowning, Sinjun saw. She smiled into her teacup.

"You must show everyone your lovely watercolors, Mellie," Tony said, watching his bride delicately tear apart a scone with beautiful slender fingers. "Douglas, she has done several of Northcliffe. I think you will be very impressed."

Melissande dropped her scone and smiled brilliantly at her husband, leaning toward him, her eyes sparkling. "Do you really like them, Tony? Truly? It is difficult, you know, what with the ever-changing light, particularly near the maple copse. Shall I try to paint the peacocks that everyone wishes to watch?"

"I don't know," he said, looking at her thoughtfully. "Perhaps you can begin by painting the mare I shall buy you. Not a white mare, please, Mellie, perhaps a bay with white stockings. I don't wish you to be trite."

"Trite! I am never — what precisely do you mean?"

"I mean that you would lack originality. You would be humdrum, run-of-the-mill."

Melissande frowned over this, then gave her husband a very beautiful smile. "Well then, my lord. You shall select a mare for me that is original."

"Yes, I shall. You will contrive to trust me in the future to always do what is best for you."

Melissande nodded slowly.

Sinjun shot Alexandra a wicked look.

The Dowager Countess of Northcliffe said in a very carrying voice to Aunt Mildred, "After breakfast, I wish to speak to you about Lady Juliette's arrival. We must have a small soirée for her, don't you think? Her importance calls for recognition and now that Douglas isn't here to wed her, why then —"

Oh dear, Alexandra thought, staring at Douglas, who looked now ready to spit on his fond mother. She forestalled him, saying quickly, "I should like to meet all the neighbors as well. A party for this Juliette would be just the thing, I think, for all of us to get acquainted."

"The party will be to introduce my wife," Douglas said, his voice as stern and cold as a judge's. "Lady Juliette, as our guest for as few a number of days as we can politely manage, will naturally be invited. Under no circumstance, Mother, will you intimate that it is a gathering in her honor. Do you understand me?"

"The peacocks have folded their tails," said the Dowager Countess of Northcliffe, and rose from the table. Her departure from the breakfast room was majestic.

Tony very nearly choked on his coffee.

Lady Juliette arrived not an hour later, just ten minutes before they would have escaped to Branderleigh Farm.

Sinjun moaned behind Alexandra. Alexandra would have moaned but she was older and a wife and so she straightened her back and drew a deep breath.

"The broom handle is back, I see," Douglas said, as he came to stand beside her at the top of the wide stairs that led to the gravel drive in front of Northcliffe Hall.

"What are you talking about?"

He waved a hand in dismissal and stared at the young woman who was being gently assisted from the ducal carriage by a footman in yellow and white livery. Another footman placed the steps beneath her dainty feet. A sour-faced maid followed her from the carriage, hugging a huge jewelry box to her meager bosom.

"Lady Juliette, daughter of the Marquess of Dacre," the footman called out.

"Do we curtsy?" Sinjun said behind her teeth. "Perhaps request a boon?"

"Be quiet," said Douglas.

The dowager countess was fulsome in her welcome. It was soon apparent that Lady Juliette was not only immensely beautiful, she was also immensely filled with her own importance. She also looked immensely pleased to be at Northcliffe Hall, until she saw Melissande. She was staring at the unexpected and unwelcome vision as the dowager was saying, "And, my dear Juliette, our Douglas here has gotten himself wedded. Such a surprise, but you will understand that —"

Lady Juliette stared blank-faced at the dowager. "He has married? Without seeing me?"

"Yes," said the dowager.

Lady Juliette wanted to leave immediately. She felt humiliated. The wretched earl had married, without even seeing her, Juliette, the most beautiful young lady in three counties. She was closer now to Melissande and her vision was at its sharpest. She went perfectly still. In a spate of inner honesty, Juliette had to admit that this Melissande, the earl's new wife, was possibly the most beautiful young lady in nearly all of England. Inner honesty led instantly to hostility and bone-deep hatred. He'd found and wed a lady more beautiful than she. It wasn't to be borne. He was a cad. He deserved to be skewered on the end of her father's sword.

"Where did Douglas meet you?" she asked, staring Melissande straight in the eye.

"Why he met me some three years ago when he was back in England because he'd been wounded in some battle. I don't recall now which one it was."

"Oh, then you married because of a family agreement? There was a prior entanglement?"

Melissande tilted her lovely head to the side in question. "No, we married because we were vastly suited to each other."

"But that is impossible!"

Douglas and Tony both stepped forward at the same time. Tony said easily, "I fear, my dear Lady Juliette, that you have come to a hasty conclusion. Melissande is my wife. Alexandra, her sister, is Douglas's countess."

There was another moment of heavy silence, then a babble of voices. Douglas finally said loudly, "Everyone hush! Now, Lady Juliette, allow me to introduce you to my wife, Alexandra."

Juliette looked at Alexandra upon the introduction and felt a good deal better. She said with a trilling laugh, "Oh dear, how very charming, my lord. You appear to have found yourself a wife in too short a time. This must have been the result of some old family agreement. Sometimes it is wise to take one's time. But it is still delightful to visit Northcliffe."

"Yes," Sinjun said in a voice loud enough for her to hear, "it is true, isn't it, what Tony said. Juliette is pretty but indeed a distant second to Melissande."

Douglas wanted to box his sister's ears.

Alexandra knew with chilling certainty that this houseguest would not add to any air of festivity.

She smiled when she heard Melissande say to Tony as they were turning to walk back into the hall, "Isn't it the oddest thing! Why, she doesn't like me and yet she doesn't even know me. Tony, I know well enough that I am beautiful, but you know, beautiful perhaps isn't the most important thing . . . well, even if it is, there are other things, such as a person's character, that should be considered, isn't that right?"

Tony kissed his wife in the full sight of anyone who happened to be looking. "You are wonderful and your character, in the not too distant future, should come to rival your beauty."

Sinjun said to Alexandra, "Good. Douglas didn't hear that. Tony is careful, you know, how he doles out the praise and the spurs. He's doing just excellently."

"Does nothing escape you?"

Sinjun looked startled. "Certainly, but this is important, Alex, very important. Douglas must be assisted to see everyone very clearly." She giggled, just like a little girl. "That Juliette is clearly a twit. I wonder if she is stupid as well as conceited? Douglas would like to box her ears even more than mine."

"Don't count on it," Alexandra said. "He is most appreciative of beautiful women."

Sinjun gave her a severe look. "Now it's you who act the twit. Don't talk such nonsense. Do you think we'll be able to leave Juliette to my mother and Aunt Mildred and go to Branderleigh Farm?"

"I sincerely hope so."

They weren't able to escape. For two interminable hours, Alexandra listened to a recounting of each of Juliette's conquests from her London Season. She turned finally to Melissande, who was examining one of Tony's fingers. "I understand that you are beyond having a Season now, Lady Rathmore. You were fortunate to find a husband after so many unsuccessful endeavors."

"Yes, 'tis true," Tony said in a mournful voice. "Just look at her. So hagged, so ancient, so long in the tooth. It was difficult for me to pull her off the shelf, she was set so far back and so very high up. It required all my resolution to bring myself to the sticking point. Even now I try to convince her to wear a pillow sheet over her head, to spare sensibilities, don't you know. Aye, I wed her because I felt pity for her. I suppose that every other man on earth must also feel pity for her for they look at her from thirty feet away and become fools and addle-brained."

To Alexandra's surprise, she saw Melissande bite Tony's finger, then lightly rub her cheek against his palm. Then she looked at Douglas, who looked the perfect picture of a polite nobleman, standing with his shoulders against the mantel, his arms crossed over his chest. He was staring from Juliette to Melissande to Alexandra. There was no expression on his face, at least none that she could read. Comparisons in this instance brought on severe depression. It was time to do something, not just sit here like a stupid log.

She rose, smiled, and extended her hand to Juliette. "If you will forgive me I must see to our dinner. If there is anything you need, don't hesitate to ask. Welcome to Northcliffe."

She left the room, aware that her mother-in-law's face was brick red with annoyance. She'd lied; she didn't try to find Mrs. Peacham. She knew well enough that the dinner cook would present would make even a skinny ascetic eat until he groaned.

She went to the gardens where all the Greek statues were displayed. The grounds were in abysmal shape. She would have to speak to Douglas. She needed his permission to direct the Northcliffe gardeners, the lazy clods. There was a particularly beautiful rosebush that was being choked to death with weeds. Alexandra didn't hesitate, for her gown was old and quite unappetizing, as Douglas had told her. She dropped to her knees and began weeding. Soon, she was humming. Soon after that, she felt calm and even-keeled. She forgot Juliette; she even managed to forget her mother-in-law.

It began to drizzle lightly. The earth softened even more and she dug and plucked and smoothed down and lovingly tended. She was unaware of the trickle of water that fell off the end of her nose.

Finally, the rosebush was free. It seemed to

glow in front of her eyes. The blooms were redder, larger, the leaves greener and more lush.

She sat back on her heels and smiled.

"My God."

She turned, still smiling, to see Douglas standing over her, eyes narrowed, his hands on his hips.

"Hello. Isn't it beautiful? And so much happier now, so much more healthy."

Douglas looked at the damned rosebush and saw that it was true. Then he looked at his filthy wife, her hair wilted with rain over her forehead, and forgot the rosebush. "Come along, it's time for you to dress for dinner."

"How did you find me?" she asked as she got to her feet and swiped her dirt-blackened hands on her already ruined gown.

"Melissande. She said that while she painted you made things grow. I have half a score of gardeners. There is no need for you to become quite so dirty."

She gave him a severe look that made him smile. "These gardeners are taking advantage of you, my lord. These beautiful gardens haven't been touched in far too long a time. It is appalling."

"I shall speak to Danvers about it."

"He's the head gardener?"

"No, he's my steward. He isn't here at the moment. His father is ill and he is visiting his ailing father in Couthmouth."

"It is the head gardener who is the one responsible, my lord."

"Fine, you may speak with Strathe whenever

it pleases you. Tell him you have my permission. Come along now, you must do something about yourself."

"There is not much that can be done."

Douglas frowned. "I have wondered every time I see your sister why it is that she is always so superbly garbed and you are not."

"I would have had new gowns had I had a Season. Instead, Tony married me to you and thus there was no Season and no new gowns. Do not believe Melissande to be spoiled and pampered. Most of her gowns are from her last Season."

"I see," he said and Alexandra wondered just what it was that he saw.

Dinner that evening with two diamonds in the same room, eating at the same table, was a trial. Juliette spoke of Lord Melberry who was smitten with her and gave Melissande a superior smile. Melissande shrugged and said he'd bored her with his interminable talk of his succession houses. After all, commenting on the fatness of grapes paled after ten minutes.

Juliette told of turning down Lord Downley's proposal and how wounded he had been. Melissande laughed and said that Lord Downley had proposed to every woman who claimed to have more than a thousand pounds dowry. On and on it went.

At last Alexandra was able to rise and motion for the ladies to leave the dining room. She didn't notice that her mother-in-law gave her a very annoyed look. She immediately went to the pianoforte and sat down. She played some French ballads, trying to ignore the verbal flotsam around her.

"My parents are very fond of me," Juliette announced. "They gave me a beautiful name. Lord Blaystock told me they must have known I would be so beautiful." She turned very gray eyes toward Alexandra, who began to play a bit more vigorously. She raised her voice. "Your parents must not have wished for what they got with you. Your name is manly, don't you agree, my lady?"

"Which lady?" Sinjun inquired. "There are so many here."

"You are very young to still be allowed amongst the adults, are you not? I refer, of course, to Alex. Why it is a man's nickname, to be sure."

"I have a good friend whose horse is named Juliette."

"Joan! Hush and apologize to Lady Juliette!"

"Yes, Mother. Excuse me, Lady Juliette. But it is a very nice horse, a mare actually, and she has the softest nose and the roundest belly and her tail, it is lush and thick, and twitches whenever there are flies or stallions around."

Douglas overheard the last and he laughed, he couldn't help it. His sister was the best weapon he'd ever had in his arsenal and he'd never before realized her wondrous capabilities. He was pleased that he had allowed her to remain downstairs this evening.

"Joan! Douglas, speak to your sister."

"Hello, Sinjun. Pour me a cup of tea, if you please. Alexandra, continue your playing. You are quite accomplished. It pleases me."

Tony went to sit beside his wife.

The dowager, seeing the evening spiraling downward, announced that whist was to be enjoyed. Douglas, grinning, asked Alexandra to be his partner.

Their opponents were Tony and Juliette.

Douglas wondered if his wife played as skillfully as she'd hinted. He wasn't left long in doubt. She didn't count all that well, but she played with verve and imagination, with a strategy remarkably similar to his own. That annoyed him as well as pleased him and he wondered, but just for an instant, how well Melissande would play if she wore a bag over her head. He and Alexandra won most hands. Tony groaned good-naturedly even when Juliette trumped a good lead or whined about a valueless hand.

Douglas had to hold his cards in front of his mouth so that no one would remark the unholy grin that overtook him when Alex did Juliette in, and the twit didn't have the brains to keep quiet. Oh no, she squawked. She threw down her remaining cards, rose and actually stomped her foot.

"However could you have known that I held the king of spades? Why, it is impossible. Why would you lead the ace, a bad lead surely? It is luck, all of it. Or it is that mirror I have been remarking."

That was quite beyond the line. Douglas rose himself and said in a very cold voice, "I believe you are fatigued, Lady Juliette. Surely such unmeasured words could not come from a well-rested mouth."

Juliette sucked in her breath and held her tongue, a difficult proposition in any circumstance, and allowed a very solicitous Uncle Albert to lead her out of the drawing room.

"She is beautiful," Sinjun said dispassionately, "but she is so very stupid. A pity."

"Why a pity, brat?" Tony asked, grinning over at her.

"Some poor gentleman will wed her, all enthralled with her beauty, and then wake up to find he's married to a stupid woman who hasn't any kindness."

Melissande came to stand beside her husband. Her hand rested lightly on his shoulder and his hand came up unconsciously to pat hers. "I pity you for playing against Alex. She is a killer. Papa taught her. Reginald tried to teach her to cheat, but she never did that particularly well. She always turned red whenever she tried."

"She needs to learn to count better," Douglas said.

"I venture to say that you will be responsible for teaching her many new things, cousin," Tony said, and rose, bowing to Alexandra, then saying his good-nights to the remaining company.

Alexandra actually sighed once she and Douglas were mounting the stairs.

"It was a long evening, I'll grant you that."

"Yes," she said, her voice suddenly clipped. Oh dear, would he insist upon coming to her again? Her step lagged.

Douglas stopped in the middle of the long corridor, took her shoulders in his hands and said very clearly, "Let me make this perfectly clear to you so you don't have to sigh again. You only have one choice. Do you wish to be in my bed or shall I be in yours?"

And even then, he took the choice from her. He lightly shoved her into his bedchamber, then closed and locked the door. He stood there watching her, his look brooding in the sluggish firelight.

"I will not frighten you tonight. I will be calm and subtle. I will control your pleasure just as I will control my own. I am an experienced man, a man of the world. I will be as tranquil and placid in my movements as that fire. Do you understand?"

She stared from him to the fire and back again.

"Say you understand, dammit."

"I understand." Then, she held out her arms to him, an unplanned gesture, and in the next instant, he'd lifted her and was carrying her to his bed. He came down over her and his hands were wild on her gown, pulling and jerking and ripping it to shreds. "It doesn't matter, dammit!" Then there were no words for he wouldn't stop kissing her. When he bared her breasts, his eyes blazed and he moaned even as he nuzzled her with his mouth, even as he suckled her. He was trembling, lurching over her, trying to cover her with his mouth and hands, all of her, even as he was jerking away her clothes and his.

And when she was naked beneath him, he had to rise to get off his trousers. He wasn't very graceful; he was frantic and ripped his britches. Then he was naked, splendidly naked. His body glowed in the firelight and she said, "You are so beautiful, Douglas."

"Oh no, no," he said, but he didn't fall on her this time. He pulled her legs apart and came down between them and lifted her to his mouth. "I won't allow you to hold back from me this time. No, I won't allow it. Do you like that, Alexandra? Dear Lord, you're hot. Yes, you're trembling. Please, tell me what you're feeling."

She moaned and dug her fingers in his hair, pressing him closer and closer still and she felt his warm breath on her flesh and it was too much. She screamed, her back bowing off the bed.

Douglas felt her nails digging into his shoulder, felt the frantic clenching of her muscles, and he was drawn into her pleasure, deep and deeper still. He didn't wait for her to calm. He thrust into her, lifting her as he rose. "Wrap your legs around my waist," he said once, then again, for she was oblivious, held in pleasure and surprise.

Her arms were around his neck and her mouth found his and as he came sharply up into her, his hands big and warm on her buttocks, she kissed him again and again, moaning softly, wringing all semblance of control from him.

He carried her to the large carpet in front of the hearth and just as he knew he would soon be lost, he also knew that he wouldn't be able to stand with the force of it, he lowered her to her back and came so deeply inside her he touched her womb.

When he came to his release, Alexandra was beyond anything in her experience. He heaved in her arms and she stroked him, feeling powerful and warm and she said without thinking, "I love you, Douglas. I've loved you forever."

He groaned, then fell to the side, drawing her against him. She felt the heat of the dying fire against her back and legs. She felt the strength of his arms around her waist. She felt the warmth of his breath against her temple.

But she felt cold in the next moment, for she realized what she'd said to him. She realized that he had remained quiet. She realized the power she'd given him. She felt his seed, wet on her thighs, and tried to move.

"No," he said, his voice low and slurred. "No." He scooped her up in his arms and carried her to his bed. "No," he said again as he pushed her between the covers. "I want my seed to stay inside you." He came in with her then, and covered them, holding her close. In the next moment, he was sleeping, his breath deep and rhythmic.

There was nothing like a young fool, she thought, and gave it up, nestling her face against his chest, feeling the hair tickle her nose. At least he hadn't tried to run from the room. She kissed his collarbone, letting her tongue glide downward to the small male nipples. She licked him and he sighed, deeply asleep, his arms tightening around her back, and she watched her breasts pressing against his chest, and she knew there was no going back now. She slept.

CHAPTER 17

"What are you doing?"

Douglas turned to see Alexandra standing in the doorway. "I'm seeing exactly how bad this situation really is."

"But you're going through my clothes!"

"How will I know what you need if I don't? Curse that meddling twit of a sister of mine, but she was saying that if she was to attend that damned soirée, she must have a new gown. Then the chit shook her head and said no, she couldn't. Mind you, she spoke in the most mournful sainted voice you can imagine. Yes, she milked it wonderfully, saying it wouldn't be right, not since you didn't have anything new to wear. Then she had the gall to look at me as though I were abusing you. I, who assured you that you could wheedle me!"

"Just stop it, Douglas! I don't need or want any new gowns, it's ridiculous, and Sinjun should be smacked."

"The girl was right in this instance. Come on, Alexandra, be reasonable, if you please."

"All right, perhaps I do need a new ball gown, but I have my own money, Douglas, I don't want you to —"

"What? That infamous thirty pounds again? My dear girl, that wouldn't purchase the bodice for a flat-chested girl. Merciful heavens, the amount of groats alone to cover your upper works will empty my pockets. No, don't squawk. Be quiet. My mind is made up. I've arranged for a seamstress from Rye to arrive later this morning. She will take your measurements and then I will select a proper gown for you for the little soirée next Wednesday. From the looks of the remainder of these gowns, I will need to take you to Madame Jordan in London." Douglas snapped the door to the armoire closed. He pulled it open again, and began pawing through her slippers. "Ah, as I thought. You need coverings from your toes to the top of your head."

"Douglas," she said, desperation in her voice, "I don't need for you to buy me things, truly. All that talk about wheedling, it was silly jesting, nothing more. Sinjun was just meddling, as you said. You're right about the ball gown and I thank you, but no more, please. I don't think —"

"Be quiet."

"No, I won't be quiet! I am not one of your retainers you can order about. Listen to me, I don't wish to be beholden on you, I don't —"

"Ah, so you would rather shame me wearing your damned rags. Blessed hell, woman! I will not be called niggardly; I will not allow people to think I keep you on a skinny string. I imagine the gossip about us is confused enough without adding the fact that my wife looks like a dowd."

"But you don't particularly care what people think," she said slowly, eyeing him. "I'm not a dowd. I only resemble a dowd if I have the misfortune to stand beside Melissande. In truth, my gowns just aren't quite up to snuff."

"Well, the chances are you will be standing next to her, so we must do something. I have also decided that I will have your breasts kept well covered, no matter the cost. Not flattened down or bound or anything like that, but camouflaged just a bit, giving only a hint of your endowments. Perhaps even a hint is too much. I will have to give this more thought. There are too many gentlemen who would ogle you and make you uncomfortable. Further, I won't accept any argument from you. Don't you realize that if you allow your gowns to be at all low-cut, gentlemen will be able to see you all the way down to your toes?"

"That's absurd!"

"No. You're not all that tall, and the result is that most gentlemen would have the advantage of staring down at you. I will not have your breasts on display for all those bounders to salivate over, so you can just stop arguing with me."

"But I'm not arguing with you!"

"Ah, what would you call it? You're shouting your head off, yelling like a bloody fishwife."

"All right! Take me to London, take me to see this Madame Jordan, spend all your groats on my back!"

"Ha! Don't you mean your front?"

"Oh goodness. Douglas, please."

He grinned then.

"Blessed hell, you're as evil as Sinjun, damn you!"

"Not entirely. I see you've appropriated one of the favored Sherbrooke curses. I've tried to curb my tongue around you but you've learned it nonetheless. From whom, I won't demand to know. We will leave for London after the soirée, all right? No, don't argue with me. You've already agreed and I hold you to it. Also, by then, that traitorous sod will have left with Melissande."

"And there's no reason for you to remain here if she isn't."

"Your syntax is nothing short of spectacular and you don't know what you're talking about. Now, if you continue to stand there, thrusting your breasts toward me, I will rip off that gown and then you will be late to meet with the seamstress."

He left her standing in the middle of her bedchamber, staring at nothing in particular, saying toward the armoire, "He is a strange man."

If Alexandra fancied Douglas would relent and allow her to be alone with Mrs. Plack, the seamstress from Rye, she was soon to see her grievous error. Sinjun lounged on a chaise longue and Douglas very calmly sat in the wing chair, crossed his legs at the ankles and folded his arms over his chest and said, "Pray begin, Mrs. Plack."

She wanted to order both of them out of her bedchamber but she knew from short but powerful experience that when Douglas had made up his mind, he couldn't be budged. She stood stiff as a stone while Mrs. Plack measured her. She raised her arms, stretched her full height; then she tried to slump just a bit so her breasts would not poke out so much, which made Douglas say sharply, "No, straighten your back!"

She did. Then she was allowed to remain while Douglas perused fashion plates until he found a gown that pleased him. "Except," he said, stroking his jaw, "remove that flounce at the hemline. It's too much. Ah, yes, the smooth lines and the raised waist will make her appear taller. Oh, and hoist up the neckline at least an inch."

"But, my lord, it will make Her Ladyship look provincial! This is the latest fashion from Paris!"

"An inch," His Lordship said again. "Raise it an inch."

"May I see?" Alexandra asked sweetly.

"Certainly," Douglas said and took her arm, drawing her to his side. "Do you agree that this will become you vastly?"

She stared down at the gown and swallowed. It was exquisite. "What color did you have in mind?"

"A soft pomona green with a dark green overskirt."

"I do not wish to look provincial."

Mrs. Plack heaved a sigh of relief. "Good. I shall leave the neckline where it is then."

"No," said Douglas. "I want her to be admired but I don't want her to be stared at."

Alexandra grinned up at him, saying nothing. She looked at his mouth and her eyes darkened. She loved his mouth, the feel of his mouth on her own; she saw his hands clench. She loved the strength of his hands, the frenzy of his mouth and his hands when he touched her, when he turned wild and savage and uncivilized, when she became the most important thing in the world to him.

"Stop it," he said beneath his breath.

"Hi ho," Sinjun said, yawning hugely. "I think you have chosen wisely, brother. Now, don't you think we can go buy Alexandra that mare?"

"You will remain and be measured for your own gown, Sinjun. I've selected it and Mother has given her approval. No, don't try to thank me —"

"I was going to take you to task for being so high-handed! I should like to choose my own gown."

"No, you're too young, too green. Don't argue with me. Alexandra and I will see you later. Thank you, Mrs. Plack. Don't forget, an inch."

"You were high-handed, you know," Alexandra said to her husband as they walked toward the stables.

He brushed a fly from his buckskin thigh. "You need it as does my impertinent sister." He kept walking, speaking quietly now, not looking at her as he said, "On your return to the Hall, I will take you back to that charming stream. I have decided that it is bedchambers with those big beds that make me lose my rationality and my perspective. Yes, it is the place rather than you that is responsible for turning me into a man with absolutely no finesse or *savoir-faire.*

"We will go to the stream and I will remain myself. I will take off your clothes, lay you down on your back and touch you and kiss your breasts and fondle you between your legs, and I will smile and talk to you while I caress you. Perhaps we will discuss the situation in Naples, from both Napoleon's and the Royalists' points of view. And I will wax brilliant because I am concentrating on my words and not on your body. My control will be uplifting, my experience will be at my brain's command. Then, when I decide that I wish to continue with you, why, I will do so, and I will go slowly and do all the things to you I haven't taken the time to do up to now. Well, more time, in any case, and you will scream and bellow until you are hoarse. And you will be very pleased that I am gentleman enough to have figured all this out."

He turned then to look down at her. She looked both amazed and incredulous and her face was hectic with color. He laughed. "You will be able to scream as loudly as you wish. There will be no one around save a few ducks and birds. Yes, I enjoy hearing you cry out in the middle of the day with the sun on your face and me pressing you into the warmth of the earth."

She poked him in his belly and he just laughed some more. She wanted to tell him that he could be as savage as he wished, but she hesitated, and then he said, "You will enjoy me even more when I return to being an excellent lover." She wondered how that could possibly be true.

At Branderleigh Farm they found a three-year-old mare of Barb descent whose sire was Pander of Foxhall Stud. She was spirited, soft-mouthed, long in the back, and black as midnight with a white star on her nose. She tried to bite Alexandra on her shoulder, Alexandra jerked away in time, and the mare then butted her chin with her nose. It was love at first sight.

"That's what I will call her," Alexandra said, skipping in delight next to Douglas after he had finalized the sale with a Mr. Crimpton. The new mare was tied to the back of the gig.

"Midnight? Blackie?"

"Oh no, that would be trite, and you know how much we must avoid that accusation!"

He handed her up into the gig then walked around to climb up into his seat. He click-clicked the horse forward. "Well?" he asked again some moments later.

"Her name is Colleen."

"There is no Irish blood in her."

"I know. She is an original."

He grinned. He realized he felt marvelous. He clicked the horse faster. He wanted to get to the stream and prove that he was the most controlled of lovers. He marshaled quite logical arguments for Napoleon's invasion of Naples while he drove. He was scarce aware that she was seated next to him. It was splendid. He was himself again.

He helped her down from the gig, and just that — the mere closing his hands around her waist to lift her down — sent his hands to her breasts and his mouth to hers and he kissed her and touched her, and was gone. He ripped her chemise to shreds. It was hard and fast and when he finally managed to raise himself off Alexandra, his heart still pounding so hard he could hear it, he said numbly, "I truly can't stand this, truly I can't. Blessed hell, it is too much for a man to suffer. There, you have even wrung the Sherbrooke curse out of me and I have tried hard not to use profanity in front of you. I've failed. Jesus, I'm nothing but a rutting stoat, a stupid man with no sense and fewer brains."

As for Alexandra, she doubted she would be able to move. He'd taken her quickly, as usual, and he'd been so deep inside her after he'd brought her to pleasure, making her scream as she lurched up, shafts of sunlight splashing through the oak branches onto her face. Her new mare had whinnied in response. Douglas had panted and heaved and said things to her that she guessed were very sexual, but she hadn't understood all of them. It was odd of her, but she rather wanted to ask him to translate so she could say them to him and understand what she was saying.

"Yes," he said, "far too much for me to bear." Then he leaned down and kissed her. She parted her lips for him and it began again. “Damnation!” he howled to the pure sweet air, then kissed her again and he was hard inside her and pushing more and more deeply only to withdraw, to find her with his fingers and his mouth and it went on and on as she spun out of control and yet turned inward, to him, to burrow inside his passion. She didn’t want him to be civilized; she didn’t want him to do anything differently. She wanted him to be a pig.

She told him again that she loved him between kisses on his jaw, his shoulder, his throat, her hands feverish on his chest and downward on his belly. Her fingertips touched his sex and he shuddered.

“No, not again.” He gently pushed her down onto her back. He stared down at her, his eyes hard. “No you don’t,” he said. “Heed me well, Alexandra. A woman says she loves a man because she has to justify her own passion to herself. If she is abandoned, if she finds great pleasure, why then, it must be love, not lust. You, particularly, are young and romantic; it is very important that you try to wrap your bodily pleasures in more inspiring packaging. It is the way your female brain functions, bolstered by all those trashy novels you have doubtless swooned over, but you will get over it if you will just be reasonable.”

“You absurd clod!” Alexandra sent her fist hard into his jaw. He was balanced on his elbow and the surprise of her blow sent him over onto his back.

"You stupid boor! You mindless rutting stoat!"

"Well, the last of it is true, I already laid claim to that."

"Go to the devil!"

She was up and jerking on her clothing, panting and heaving, so furious with him that she was trembling.

"Alexandra, be reasonable. Stop it."

She didn't. If anything she jerked so hard a button went flying.

He came up on his elbows, lying stretched out, naked and sweating and feeling very relaxed. He was even grinning at her. "Alexandra, why become so distraught at the simple truth? Love is a poet's nonsensical plaything and if he can bend one silly word to rhyme with another, why all the better. It is as insubstantial as a dream, as meaningless as the rain that flows through your fingers. Don't use it as a crutch or as an excuse to enjoy me and yourself, you don't need it. You and I do well together in bed. You respond fully to me, even though I seem to have this rutting-stoat disease with you. Don't feel you have to cover it up with romantic nonsense."

She was dressed now, though her stockings and boots were still on the ground. Her hands on her hips, she said very slowly, very calmly, "I knew I shouldn't have told you. I knew that you don't feel at all the same way about me and I was afraid it would give you power over me. I was quite wrong. You care so little for me that power doesn't even come into it. I didn't realize you would mock my words and my feelings, that you would make sport at what I feel. Your cynicism is pathetic, Douglas. If it makes you feel any better, if it makes you feel as if your beliefs are justified, well, I don't love you at this moment. I should like to cosh you with a hammer at this moment. I would like to kick you on your backside. Instead, I think I will punish you in another way." She picked up his boots and his trousers and ran with them toward the stream. She stopped and threw them as hard and as far as she could.

Douglas bounded up to grab for his clothes, but he was too late. "Blessed hell!" He jumped into the stream to grab his boots and trousers and Alexandra untied the horse, bounded into the gig, and was off in the next moment. His shirt and jacket lay beside her on the plank seat.

She heard him yelling at her and just click-clicked the horse faster. He couldn't catch her, not in his bare feet, and he could whistle to the horses all he wanted, they wouldn't pay him any heed. Alexandra smiled. The cynical bounder. Retribution tasted very sweet.

Thirty minutes later, Douglas passed the yew bush that flew his shirt like a white flag of surrender. He'd wondered where his shirt had gone to. She'd taken it, damn her eyes. He was hot, sweating, and wished he had her neck between his hands, just for an instant, just long enough for him to squeeze and make her face turn blue.

Damned twit. Lust, good full-powered bone-deep lust, and like every other female in the history of the world, she had to make it into something more grand, more elevated than it really was. Doubtless if he encouraged her, she would begin to wax eloquent about a spiritual joining, a mating of their very souls. It wasn't to be borne.

His shirt stuck to his sweaty back. The afternoon sun was grueling. Another quarter of a mile and he spotted his coat flying from the lower branch of a maple tree.

When he finally stomped up the wide front steps of Northcliffe Hall, he was ready to kill.

Hollis greeted him, looking as bland as a bowl of broth. "Ah, Your Lordship is back from your nature walk. Her Ladyship told us how you lauded the lovely tulip trees that were bowed so gracefully over the stream; she said you strained your neck to see to the top of the poplar trees alongside the trails. She said you were humming with the lovely song thrushes and smelling the lilac flowers. She said you then wished to commune with the fishes and thus swam in the stream. She said how very kind you were to allow her to continue back here since she had the headache. You look a bit hot, my lord. Should you like a lemonade, perhaps?"

Douglas knew that Hollis was lying and he knew that Hollis knew that he knew. Why did everyone insist upon protecting her? What about him? He'd been the one to have to leap into the stream and pull his boots from bottom silt. He'd been the one to trudge three miles back to the Hall. Lemonade?

"Where is Her Ladyship?"

"Why, she is communing with the nature that's confined here at Northcliffe, my lord. She is in the gardens."

"I thought you said she had a bloody headache."

"I fancy she cured that."

"Just so," Douglas said. The thought of her sitting at her ease on a chaise longue, cool and sweat-free, would have sent him into a rage. Douglas drew himself up. He shook his head at himself. All of this, it was ridiculous.

A month ago he'd been a free man.

Two weeks ago and he'd thought himself married to the most beautiful woman in England.

And now he was shackled to a twit he'd never seen before and who tortured him. She also turned him into a wild man. She tortured him very well.

In the east gardens, Tony leaned negligently against the skinny trunk of a larch, his eyes on his sister-in-law. She was filthy, sweat darkening her hair, her hands were black with dirt. She was murdering a weed, her movements jerky, and she was muttering to herself.

"I think things march along just fine," he said.

Alexandra paused and raised her face to Tony's. "Nothing is marching anywhere, Tony. He doesn't like me, truly."

"You mistake the matter, my dear. He's accepted you as his wife. Too, I've seen him look at you. I've seen him look violent with need and replete with pleasure."

"He hates that. Until today, he blamed me for his loss of control whenever he touched me. Just two hours ago, he decided to blame the bedchambers and the beds. He planned to discuss philosophy or war or something whilst he loved me." She sighed. "When that failed, he . . . well, now he is probably intent on finding me and wringing my neck."

"What you did to him was splendid, Alex. I wish I could have seen him dash naked into the stream to save his pants and boots. As I recall there are many rocks to trip the naked foot."

"I know it isn't proper to speak like this, Tony, but I have no one else. I was a fool. I told him that I loved him. I couldn't help it, it just came out of my mouth. He told me that all I feel, that all he feels is just lust. He said that love is nonsense and that the notion of a spiritual joining makes him physically ill."

"He really said that?"

"Not exactly. I am simply making the words fit his feelings more precisely. Actually what he said was worse — more insulting, more cynical."

"But now he is your husband and I swear to you, Alex, where a man finds pleasure, other pleasures usually follow, if the man and woman are at all reasonable. You love Douglas. Half the battle is won. More than half, for he goes crazy whenever he touches you. You will see. The soirée is tomorrow night. Melissande and I will leave the next day. You won't have to worry about my lovely witch any longer. Besides, I do believe that Douglas is already beginning to wonder how he would have dealt with her."

"I can't believe she allows you to call her Mellie."

"I dislike the name immensely. Mellie, bah! It sounds like an overweight girl with spots on her face. However, it is important that she bend to me completely. If I wish to call her pug, why then, she must accept it since it comes from me, her husband, her master."

Alexandra could but stare at him. "You are terrifying, Tony."

He grinned down at her. "No, not really. As much as I love your sister, I will not allow her to have the upper hand. Ah, I believe I see your errant husband striding this way. Normally a man will pause — just a moment, you understand — to look at the Greek statues, but not Douglas. He looks fit to kill. This should be interesting. Should you like me to draw him off?"

"No, he would challenge you to a duel or assault you right here." She shook her head. "Then I should have to attack you again, Tony."

"Very true. Ah, we are saved. Here is Melissande, carrying her watercolors. Now she is pausing to look at the statues and not with an eye to painting them either, I vow. She and Douglas are now met up and speaking. He must control his bile. He must be charming, no matter he wants to kill you. Yes, he appears to have stopped gnashing his teeth. You know, Alex, I have an idea, a thoroughly reprehensible idea."

She looked at him and understood and quickly said, "Oh no, Tony. It wouldn't work, it wouldn't —"

Douglas and Melissande came around a thick yew bush to see Tony on his knees in front of Alexandra, his arms around her, kissing her hair.

Douglas froze.

Melissande jerked back as if she'd been struck. She threw her watercolors to the ground, and yelling like a banshee, ran to the couple, grabbed Tony's hair and yanked with all her might. He fell onto his back, grinned up at her, only Melissande wasn't looking at him, but at her sister.

"You miserable husband stealer!" she yelled and threw herself on Alexandra, knocking her over backward. "How dare you, Alex! You have a husband, and you have the nerve to try to take mine!" She yanked at Alexandra's hair.

"Stop it! For God's sake —"

Douglas grabbed Melissande and picked her up, shoving her toward Tony, who caught her and held her arms to her sides. "I'll make her bald, I'll make her two inches shorter!"

"Hush, Mellie, hush now."

Melissande turned on her husband and yelled not an inch from his nose, "Don't call me that horrid name! What were you doing, kissing her hair? I have a beautiful hair, if you want to kiss hair, you will kiss mine! You faithless lout, I'll pull out all her hair and then you'll — Don't you dare try to kiss me now, you miserable clod!"

Douglas heard the yelling behind him, but he didn't move. He dropped to his haunches in front of his wife. She was shaking her head, as if to see if it were still on her shoulders. She was filthy, her face streaked with dirt, her eyes watering.

"Are you all right?"

"No, my scalp is on fire. I hadn't realized Melissande was so strong."

"It serves you right."

"Yes, quite probably, it does."

"I fancy it didn't occur to Tony that she would attack you. It's obvious his plan wasn't at all well thought through."

She looked up at him and saw that he knew exactly what had happened. "No, I imagine he was surprised. But pleased at the same time."

"Yes. Come along now, you're a mess, a greater one than I am. I won't bathe with you or we'll remain messes."

They rose and turned to see Tony kissing his wife very passionately.

Douglas said mildly, "Yes, Tony proved something, didn't he? Something he hadn't counted on. Now he is greatly pleased with himself."

Tony made love to his wife there next to a Greek statue and it was as violent and urgent a performance as his cousin would have given. Melissande actually didn't give a single thought to her lovely gown or to grass stains or to possible interlopers coming along. She lost her reason, all of it, and it was quite delicious. When she told him she loved him and she would kill any woman who tried to take him away from her, he grinned like a blissful fool and said with a good deal of satisfaction in his voice, "I believe that I love you as well. Your fierceness pleases me, as does your jealousy. Yes, you please me, very much."

As for Douglas: He sat brooding in his copper bathtub, his valet standing over him, wringing his hands, bemoaning the ruined boots and trousers.

CHAPTER 18

Tysen Sherbrooke stood tall and proud as a rooster, his eyes reverent as he said to Alexandra, "I would like to present Melinda Beatrice Hardesty. My sister-in-law, Lady Alexandra."

So this was the flat-chested simpering pious young woman Sinjun detested. Alex smiled at her. "I am charmed, Miss Hardesty. Tysen has told us all so much about you. I hope you will enjoy yourself this evening."

Melinda Beatrice, who knew her own worth, was nevertheless a bit shy with a countess, even though she appeared to be not a month older than Alex was. She gave her a graceful curtsy and said in her prim voice, "Thank you, ma'am."

"I trust you and Tysen will enjoy the dancing."

"Mr. Sherbrooke has asked my mama if I may dance with him. She has refused, naturally, for I'm not out yet."

"A pity," Alex said. "Perhaps you can play cards instead."

"Oh no, ma'am. Why, that wouldn't be at all proper and my mama would be most upset. Mama says that only wastrels play cards."

"Well," Alexandra said, shooting the love-slain Tysen a harassed look, "perhaps you and Mr. Sherbrooke can take a turn in the gardens. It's warm tonight so your dear mama surely can't object and there are so many adults just feet away to protect your reputation."

"Yes, I should like that," said Miss Hardesty. "If Mama won't object."

"What a twit," Douglas remarked as he watched his brother lead Miss Hardesty away. "I do hope Tysen will outgrow her. He goes back to Oxford soon, thank God." He looked back to his wife, whose bodice had been raised only a half-inch and frowned. He'd overheard Sinjun laughing about it. He'd said nothing, however, for when Alexandra had come earlier into the drawing room, looking toward him like a hopeful puppy, he was too busy thinking how lovely she looked to say anything. The green made her skin as creamy and white as her belly, and her hair, thick and redder than sin, was piled artfully atop her head, with several glossy tendrils trailing over her shoulder. He looked down at the expanse of rich white flesh and felt himself begin to shake. "Let's dance, otherwise I might be tempted to thrust my hand down your bosom."

"All right."

"All right what?"

She gave him a siren's smile. "Whichever you choose, Douglas."

He struggled with himself. As for Alexandra, she tried to keep down the bubble of laughter.

As he continued to struggle, she stared with no little pride and relief over the ballroom that was gaily festooned with hanging blue, white, and gold crepe. Potted plants and thick bouquets were in every corner and on every tabletop, their scent fragrant in the warm evening air. There were at least fifteen couples dancing and another thirty standing or seated about the perimeter of the dance floor. Every invitation had been accepted except for Sir James Evertson, who'd had the bad manners to die just that morning. Everything was perfect and she had helped organize all of it. There was plentiful food and the champagne punch had been pronounced fit even for the pickiest matrons by Aunt Mildred. For the first time, Alexandra truly felt like the mistress of Northcliffe Hall. It was a heady feeling and she loved it. Her mother-in-law had harumphed a bit at some of her orders, but hadn't gainsaid her, at least to her face. Yes, she'd proved she could deal with her mother-in-law, at least in this.

She sought out Melissande, who looked like a princess, dancing with a young man who looked ready to collapse at her feet and pant.

Douglas, having finished his struggle, said finally, sounding just a bit shocked, "Are you trying to tease me, Alexandra?"

She smiled up at her husband. "What were we speaking about? You took so long to reply. Oh yes, it is your choice, Douglas. You insist that all I feel for you is lust. Well, then, since you're older than I, and far more experienced,

I expect you're right. I accept that now. You're staring down at my bosom and it is only lust you feel. Now I am staring at your mouth and you must know that I want to kiss you, to feel you with my hands, all of you, especially over your belly and down to touch you, you're so hot and alive and smooth. All of it is lust. After all, you told me to be reasonable and that you are a man with vast experience in everything, so yes, lust it is." She gave him a wicked smile and held out her hand. "Dance, my lord?"

He wanted to smack her.

He was breathing hard. He was seeing her white hands stroking down his chest, her fingers splayed on his belly, her fingers curling around him, caressing him, and his muscles spasmed. "I'm going to the cardroom," he said and left her with a sharp nod.

Alexandra smiled. Let him taste his own turnips, she thought. Just let him believe that she felt nothing for him except his precious lust.

Lady Juliette seemed to enjoy herself, Alexandra saw. She'd established herself and her own court far away from Melissande. She laughed rather a lot and loudly, but Alexandra didn't care. The chit would leave on the morrow.

When Hollis whispered in Alexandra's ear that the dinner buffet was ready to be served, she was startled at how quickly the time had passed. It was Tony who led her into dinner and Douglas who escorted Melissande. Juliette was on the besotted arm of a local squire who had been complaining at great length about his gout until he had seen Juliette.

"Douglas is still in a snit," Alexandra said to Tony as she forked down a bite of delicious salmon patty. "And all because I finally agreed with him about my feelings, rather my lack of them."

"Just lust, hm?"

"Yes. He puffed up like a haughty cardinal and took himself off to the cardroom. His mother isn't pleased with him. She blames me for his defection, of course. I am tempted to tell her exactly why he defected. I vow it would make her look at Douglas in a different light."

"And you as well, hussy."

Alex laughed. "True, but the look on her face would be worth it, almost."

"Are you pregnant yet?"

She dropped her fork. "Goodness. I have no idea. Oh dear, Tony, I hadn't thought about it. *Pregnant*. Why ever would you ask me that?"

"I heard the dowager speaking of it to Aunt Mildred. She just hopes you will do your duty before the year is out since that is the only reason Douglas was willing to marry in the first place. The precious heir, you know."

She gave him a stark look. "I suppose if I do not produce the precious heir within a year, Douglas will toss me out on my ear and try to breed with another female?"

"You make it sound like livestock on a farm. And no, Douglas will keep on trying manfully, I doubt not." Tony fiddled with a slice of bread, saying finally, "I know this is difficult for you to believe, but it's true. I've never in my adult life seen Douglas lose his control. In battle he was a cold-blooded bastard, never faltering, never losing sight of his goals, never forgetting a detail that would make a possible difference in an outcome. He was good, Alex, very good; he never lost his head. His men worshiped him because they knew they could trust him. He would never let them down.

"I have seen him so angry that another man would have exploded with the pressure, but not Douglas. Obviously I haven't observed him in bed with women in the past, but men being men, we do discuss things, and always, in the past, it's been something of a game to him. He enjoys having a woman lose her head over what he's doing to her; he enjoys controlling, setting the pace, deciding when and what will be done. You have shocked him to his Sherbrooke toes. He is reeling. I find it quite amusing. Also, Alex, I think your approach this evening was a master stroke. Ah, I wish I could stay and witness his downfall."

"Downfall. I don't like the sound of that."

"His upfall, then, his acceptance that he is very fond of his wife both in and out of bed and that it isn't at all a bad thing to be utterly mad about your wife."

"Do you know, if anyone overheard us, they would ship us off to that horrible Botany Bay. I have never even thought in terms of what we now speak about openly." She grinned. "As for Douglas, he knows no reticence, no shame —"

Tony grabbed her hand and kissed it, laughing. He looked over at Douglas to see his cousin frowning at him, murder in his dark eyes. As for Melissande, there was not only murder in her beautiful eyes, there was also dismemberment, if Tony didn't miss his guess. He was excessively pleased. He would never in his life forget their lovemaking in the garden. He rather hoped Melissande was pregnant. She certainly deserved to be.

"Ah, it is a pity to miss any of the drama."

Alexandra laughed. "You keep that up and you won't be alive for the rest of the drama."

The evening ended at two o'clock in the morning. Alexandra was still too excited to be tired, but the lavender feather on her mother-in-law's turban was listing sharply to port; Aunt Mildred was no longer tapping her toes to the beat of the music; Uncle Albert was snoring softly against a potted palm. Douglas emerged from the cardroom, five hundred pounds richer, to take his place beside his wife as their guests departed.

"You were a success," he said, "but I still don't like your breasts sticking out like that."

"I think you were a success yourself, Douglas, particularly with those black knee britches of yours molding your thighs and well, the rest of you. I imagine all the ladies remarked on your male endowments."

She turned immediately to speak to Sir Thomas Hardesty and his wife, complimenting them on their lovely daughter, Melinda Beatrice, winking at a hovering Tysen whilst she did so. To her surprise Sir Thomas held her hand overlong and there was a definite loose look about his mouth. Douglas was stiff as a poker until they took their leave. "That damned old lecher. How dare he ogle you like that!"

"It wasn't really ogling," Tysen said. "He is short-sighted, that's all."

"You are becoming more of a fool by the day and it is excessively irritating. I should have sent you with Ryder. He would have beat the naïveté out of you."

"Well," Alexandra said after Tysen had given his brother an uncertain look and taken himself off, "Lady Hardesty was, I believe, ogling you a bit too."

"You will pay for your quite inappropriate observations, Alexandra."

She gave him a sunny smile. "Why don't you call me Alex?"

Melissande and Tony came over and Douglas looked at the two sisters standing side by side. One was so achingly beautiful that it made a man's tongue stick to the roof of his mouth just to look at her; and the other . . . Good Lord, just hearing her laugh made him hard and sweaty, and made him think about her lying naked beneath him. She didn't look at all dowdy standing next to Melissande. He wanted to kiss the tip of her shiny nose.

Douglas couldn't wait to let his hands dive into

her bodice and pull it away from her breasts. He followed her into her bedchamber, dismissed her maid, and did just that. When his hands were cupping her breasts, he sighed with pleasure, closing his eyes. Then, suddenly, he felt her hands on his legs, moving up and toward his groin. He froze. Then her hands were molding him and he wanted to yell with the pleasure of it.

"Ah," she said into his mouth as he kissed her, "I love lust, don't you, Douglas?"

"Blessed hell," he said and had her stripped within a minute. She gave no thought to the beautiful ball gown that had cost him at least one hundred pounds. She was too busy undressing him, stroking him, caressing him, staring at him as she touched him.

Again, there was no time, no overture, no prelude. He was on top of her, panting, his big body shaking, and she arched up against him and he came into her. She was ready for him, always ready, and the power of him made her cry out and lurch upward. She grabbed his head and brought his mouth down to hers and she kissed him, biting his lower lip, her hands wild on his shoulders and back even as she pushed upward against him, bringing him deeper.

For one single instant, Douglas managed to regain his sanity, and in that instant, she climaxed, and he watched her eyes go vague and soft and he kissed her mouth, taking the gasping cries into his. But it was just for an instant, one small instant, then he was raging over her again, beyond himself, surging into her, and it wouldn't stop. He felt her hands on his buttocks and that sent him over the edge. "Alexandra," he said, then collapsed on top of her.

They were lying half off the bed. He was very heavy but she didn't care. She wondered if it would always be like this — this fierce wild love-making, always so fast, so hard and deep. She knew she wouldn't mind a bit; she was always with him, just as frenzied, just as urgent. Douglas would accept nothing else. She said, when she was able to draw a complete breath, "Am I pregnant, do you think?"

"Yes," he said without hesitation. "I made you pregnant the first time I took you."

"Well, then, if you are right, I will be proved worthy. That's what everyone wanted, isn't it? A Sherbrooke heir?"

"Yes. As I recall, you volunteered to produce the heir."

"Yes," she said readily, "I'll give you half a dozen heirs if you wish. I should like to have a little boy who looks just like you, Douglas."

He didn't like the way her words made him feel. He grunted and said, "I am tired. You've worn me to a bone. Go to sleep."

"If you could control your lust, perhaps you would have more energy to talk to me."

"Go to sleep, damn you."

She did, a smile on her lips.

When Alexandra awoke the next morning, she was in her own bed but Douglas wasn't. She sat up, missing him, for it was his habit to awaken her with kisses, with his hands between her thighs, touching her, making her ready for him even before she was fully awake. She was alone. She didn't like it one bit.

I made you pregnant the first time I took you.

No, no, he couldn't know that, could he? She'd had no monthly flow since Douglas had taken her, that was true, but she was very unpredictable and thus she simply didn't know.

She rose and quickly bathed and dressed. Tony and Melissande were leaving today as were both Uncle Albert and Aunt Mildred. And Lady Juliette, thank the good Lord.

It was nearly two o'clock in the afternoon when the first of their guests, Lady Juliette, departed, berating her maid even as she said her good-byes to her host and hostess.

The dowager was frowning. "That girl was a severe disappointment, Mildred. I shouldn't have liked it if Douglas had wedded her."

"The girl is a shrew," Aunt Mildred said.

"She is divine, nonetheless," Uncle Albert said. "She is young and full of high spirits, that is all."

"She is a spoiled bitch and will only get worse as she ages," said his fond wife.

As for Tony, he had hugged Alexandra, whispering in her ear, "I am proud of you. Don't change. Keep going as you are now doing. All will be well."

As for Melissande, she gave her sister a long

look and said, "I don't mind that you're a countess and I'm a viscountess. I do mind that you might want Tony. You will never have him, Alex, so you may forget it."

Alexandra looked at her exquisitely beautiful sister and wanted to giggle at the absurdity of it. "I promise I won't ever try to steal him from you again."

"See that you don't! You wanted Douglas Sherbrooke and you got him. If you have decided you don't want him now, it is too bad. You will just have to make do with him because Tony is mine."

"I shall try," Alexandra said in a humble voice.

Douglas, who'd overheard most of this, had a difficult time keeping his aplomb. He managed to say in a somewhat mellow voice to Tony, "We will see you in London?"

"Perhaps. If you would, Douglas, try to prepare everyone for my wife. It might prevent duels and I would appreciate it."

"She's already been there for a Season. They're all prepared."

"No, there is a difference this time. She is more . . . sympathetic now, more sensitive, and thus more vulnerable. Prepare them, Douglas. She's now a human goddess. You've seen her wrinkle her brow."

"All right, I'll tell everyone that you've trained her."

"Don't forget the discipline, my dear fellow."

Douglas laughed and punched his cousin in his

arm. There was humor toward his cousin now, not the outraged bitterness of even the previous week. Alexandra felt a flood of hope. She was also relieved that Melissande hadn't heard this exchange. She would have broken Tony's arm.

They stood on the wide front steps of Northcliffe Hall until the last of the carriages bowled down the drive.

"Well," said the Dowager Countess of Northcliffe, "we are a small group again and will doubtless be downcast."

"Not I," said Douglas, looking down at his wife.

"Oh dear," said Sinjun, "stop looking at her like that, Douglas. I had hoped you would like to go for a ride."

"Not I," said Douglas again. "At least for a while."

"Well, I never!" said Douglas's fond mama, as she watched him grab his wife's hand and race into the hall.

Douglas heard Aunt Mildred say, "Now, Lydia, we all want an heir. Douglas is just doing his duty. He is a good boy."

He pulled her up the stairs to his bedchamber. He made love to her twice, quick and hard both times, and not once did he think about an heir. He stared down at her when he'd finished, breathing hard, his heart still pounding fast, but said nothing. He shook his head, dressed, and then immediately left her to go riding.

Alexandra stared up at the ceiling, not moving

for fifteen minutes before she finally rose to pull herself together. As she bathed and dressed, she thought of the stunned look on his face when she said into his mouth just at the moment of his release, "Ah, Douglas, I lust for you so very much."

He'd snarled at her.

Douglas didn't come to her that night. Alexandra suspected he was brooding about lust and such in the library, at least she hoped so. She fell asleep in her own bedchamber. It was in the middle of the night when the darkness was heavy and thick when she awoke completely and very suddenly. She didn't move, not understanding. She simply knew she wasn't alone.

Then she saw her. The young woman she'd seen before, all white and floaty, her hair lustrous down her back, so blond it was nearly white, framing an exquisite face. She looked so sad and her hands were held out toward Alexandra.

"Who are you?"

Goodness, was that her voice, all thin and wispy with fear?

The figure didn't move, just stood there not three feet from the bed, her body shimmering as if she weren't really standing on the floor but rather hovering over it, her arms held out to Alexandra.

"What do you want? Why are you here?"

Again, the figure remained just as it was.

"I know you're called the Virgin Bride because

your new husband was killed before you could become his wife. But I am not a virgin. My husband didn't die. Why are you here?"

Then the figure made a soft deep sound and Alexandra nearly leapt off the bed in fright.

Suddenly, everything was as clear as if the figure had spoken. Alexandra knew why she was here. "You want to warn me, don't you?"

The figure shifted subtly, deepening the lights and shadows.

"You're worried that something will happen to me?"

The figure shimmered softly and Alexandra suddenly wasn't certain whether or not it was her, no, not her . . . or was it? She was losing her mind, she was guessing a ghost's intentions. It was madness.

"What the hell is going on here? Alexandra, who are you talking to?"

The figure shuddered, gave off a soft glittering light, then simply faded into the wainscoting.

Douglas came through the connecting door. He was quite naked.

"It's all right. I was just entertaining my lover. But now you've chased him off."

She didn't realize her voice was shaking, that she sounded as if she were about to be shoved off a precipice, but Douglas did. He came across the room and looked down at her for just an instant before coming into bed with her. He drew her tightly against him, felt the shudders of her body, and simply held her. "It's all right, it was just a nightmare, nothing more, just a nightmare."

"Oh my," she said finally, her face buried into his shoulder. "It wasn't a dream or a nightmare, I swear it to you. Goodness, Douglas, I not only saw her but I also spoke to her. I started thinking I understood her."

"It was a dream," he said firmly. "That damned ghost is a collective figment. You dreamed her up because I wasn't here to love you until you were exhausted."

"You've seen her, haven't you?"

"Naturally not. I am not a silly twit of an empty-headed female."

"You have seen her, don't lie to me, Douglas! When? What was the circumstance?"

He kissed her temple and hugged her more tightly to him, pressing her face into his shoulder. When she spoke again, her warm breath fanned his flesh. "I told her that I wasn't a virgin and that you weren't dead; I asked her why she was here. She was warning me but I'm not sure it's me who's in danger . . . maybe it isn't, but then you came in and she left."

"Yes, I can just imagine it. She floated away, her shroud wafting romantically around her."

"I want to know when you saw her."

Douglas kissed her temple again, but his thoughts were on that night when Alexandra had run away from him yet he'd heard her crying in here and he'd come in and seen her . . . not Alexandra, but her, that damned ghost. He shook his head. "No," he said. "No."

He stiffened then. "My God, do you realize that I'm not attacking you? I haven't got you on your back? We've actually spoken together for at least three minutes, and we're here naked and —" She turned up her face then, and he felt her warm breath on his mouth and he kissed her.

"Well, damn," he said, and swept his hands down her back until they were cupping her buttocks and he was turning to face her, his sex hard and thick against her belly. Her arms were tight around his neck and she was kissing him wildly. It was difficult but he managed to get off her nightgown.

He was breathing hard and fast and when he knew that it was going to be closer than he'd thought, he lifted her leg and came into her. She gasped with the surprise and pleasure of it, and then she did more than gasp because his hands and his fingers were caressing her woman's flesh as his mouth was hot on her breast.

"Douglas," she said, and climaxed with a choking cry.

He pushed her onto her back to come more deeply into her and when she lifted her hips to draw him deeper, he cried out, tensing over her before pounding into her, his seed spewing inside her.

"Oh Douglas," she whispered against his neck. "She did sort of float."

"Blessed hell. She wasn't here, it was a silly

dream. You were susceptible because you hadn't had me — like a tonic — before you fell asleep. You won't see that damned ghost any more tonight. Now be quiet." He pulled her on top of him, arranging the blankets over them as he did so. "All you'll think about is me. You understand?"

"Yes," she said, kissing his throat, his ear, his shoulder. "Just you and the wonderful lust you give me. Isn't it nice that we're leaving for London in the morning? Perhaps that's what she was trying to tell me. There were so many more men for me to lust upon."

"You are as amusing as a boil on a backside."

She laughed and kissed the spot behind his ear.

Douglas stared grim-faced into the darkness even as his hands stroked down her back and molded around her hips. He finally fell asleep with her breath against his neck, her breasts pressed against his chest, her heartbeat soft and steady against his.

The Sherbrooke town house was a three-story mansion on the corner of Putnam Place. It had been built sixty years before to grand expectations of an Earl of Northcliffe with more groats than good taste. Still, the Greek columns were inspiring to some — those in their cups, Douglas would say with a snort — and the interior with all its niches for statuary were filled now mostly with flowers and books, the abundant Greek statuary exiled to the attic. It was the same earl, Douglas told Alexandra, who had filled the Northcliffe gardens to overflowing with Greek statues. "So I have pleased myself," Douglas said, as he pointed to exquisite crimson brocade drapes that were drawn in the large central drawing room. "I expect that my heirs just might think I'm short in the upper works and do something else."

He frowned then, saying, "Perhaps you will wish to make alterations. I did nothing to the countess's rooms."

"All right," Alexandra said, still so dazed and overwhelmed by their actually being in London, a city of grace and wealth and poverty and excitement — and the smells — that she would have agreed to anything he said. He had pointed out everything to her and she'd gawked through the carriage window. Douglas grinned down at her. "A bit overwhelming, isn't it?"

She nodded, touching her fingertips lightly to a lovely Spanish table.

"You will grow accustomed soon enough. As for the house, Mrs. Goodgame will show you everything. Burgess, our plump London butler, is as efficient as Hollis. You can trust him. We will remain in London for two weeks, enough time for you to be fitted for new gowns and bonnets and the like and to meet society. Do you wish to rest now or can we visit Madame Jordan?"

Madame Jordan was genuinely French, born and raised in Rennes. She had six shop assistants, an impressive establishment in the heart of Piccadilly, and a doting eye for the Earl of Northcliffe. Alexandra stood there, an unimportant member of Douglas's entourage, listening to Madame and her husband discussing what was to be done with her. She was measured and clucked over. When she was to the point of screaming at Douglas that she wasn't invisible and she did have good taste, Madame suddenly splayed her fingers over Alexandra's bosom and went off with a salvo of rapid, intense French. Ah, Alexandra thought, grinning at Douglas, whose face was closed and hard, she wants my bosom to be fashionable. "I agree with Madame," she said loudly, and Douglas turned on her, a wonderful target for his ire. "Be quiet, Alexandra, or you will go sit in the carriage! This has nothing to do with you!"

"Ha! You want me to look like a nun and Madame disagrees, as do I. Give in, Douglas, and stop being strange about it. I am a woman like every other woman on the face of this earth, and all women are built just like me. No one will care, no one. If you insist that I be covered to my chin, why everyone will wonder if I have some sort of horrible deformity!"

"I agree with the countess," said Madame Jordan in perfect English. "Come, my lord, you are too possessive of your bride. It isn't at all fashionable to wear your heart on your sleeve."

"I'm not," Douglas roared, slamming his fist on the glossy painting of a woman at least seven feet tall draped in willowy garments, as wispy and insubstantial as the ghost's had been. "It's just that she's too innocent and doesn't realize what men want and —" He ground to a stop. He was furious and felt impotent. He was outnumbered and outgunned and he knew it. Both women were regarding him with tolerant scorn. He had reason on his side, surely he did, only he sounded ridiculous. "Blessed hell! Do as you wish!" And he stomped out, saying over his shoulder, "I will await you in the carriage. Lower every bloody neckline to your bloody waist, I don't care!"

"Ah, I love a passionate man, don't you?" said Madame Jordan fondly, smiling after the earl.

"Oh yes," Alexandra agreed. "Your English is superb, Madame."

Madame nodded, not one whit affected by the contretemps. "I also speak German and Italian and a bit of Russian. I have a Russian count who is my lover, you know? He is probably as wild and possessive a lover as your husband, a wild man and he keeps my heart racing."

That sounded wonderful to Alexandra.

Before the afternoon was over, Alexandra was so weary she could scarce stand. She was also the proud owner of six new gowns, two riding habits, nightgowns, chemises. Goodness, the list went on and on. Douglas regained a proper mood after they left Madame Jordan's. Then he bought her bonnets and shoes and handkerchiefs and stockings and reticules, even an umbrella.

He was still a fount of energy when at last he handed her into the carriage. He shoved a stack of boxes away on the seat. Alexandra was so tired she didn't care if she was in London or in the Hebrides. Her head fell against his shoulder and he squeezed her against him, dropping a kiss on top of her head.

"It has been a long day. You did well. I was proud of you. For the most part anyway. I still am displeased by your necklines."

Alexandra wasn't about to touch that topic again. She chewed her bottom lip, then burst out, "You know everything about clothes. You and Madame Jordan were obviously well acquainted. Have you bought clothing for many women?"

CHAPTER 19

Douglas looked at her thoughtfully, then shrugged. "It's really none of a wife's affair what a husband does, but I see no harm in educating you. Yes, it's something all females appreciate. I realized when I was no more than a very charming lad of nineteen years that I should gain expertise in the area of fashion and so I did. If a man wishes to maintain a constant supply of women, why then, he must adapt himself to their little vagaries."

"It sounds rather cold-blooded to me."

"Aren't you the least bit grateful for my generosity today? Six new gowns . . . two new riding habits. In addition, I even allowed you and Madame to have your own way. Won't you reward me suitably?"

It was very strange, she thought, and rather predictable that men always seemed to remember things differently. Alexandra sighed. "I am perfectly willing, but you never give me the chance to reward you, Douglas. You are all over me before I have a chance to do anything, and thus it is I who get all the rewards, and I never buy you anything."

"That is an interesting way of looking at it. Most women and men would consider you an oddity, that or a woman of immense guile." He frowned at her, as if uncertain of something, then said, "You still have the thirty pounds?"

"Yes. You mean, to have a constant supply of men I need to adapt myself to their little vagaries?"

"It doesn't work that way. Men are always in constant supply. Men are excessively easy to attach. Men won't ever simper or play the tease or make excuses."

"Come, Douglas, I may not have much experience, but what experience I have convinces me that the goose and gander apply here. The thirty pounds won't go very far. It wouldn't do for the mythical men to feel slighted, no matter how eager they are. Perhaps I could purchase several dozen of a single item and give them out as I go along. What do you think?"

"I think you're pushing me and it isn't wise. I think you need to be beaten. I think your humor needs silence and reflection. You are being impertinent and I won't allow it. Be quiet, Alexandra."

"Perhaps watch fobs," she said in an idle voice against his shoulder. "And I could have my initials engraved next to theirs on each one. Personalized, you know."

He said calmly, his voice controlled and cold, "If you provide me quickly with an heir, all the money I have spent on you will have been worth it."

Oh dear, she thought. She had pushed him and his retaliation was swift and rather brutal.

"If you tell me you don't mean that, I will be quiet and forget about the watch fobs and the humor."

"I won't tell you anything. Now, London is thin of company this time of year. However, there are still adequate amusements. The Ranleaghs' ball is tonight and it will suffice for your debut. You will wear the ball gown you wore at Northcliffe Hall. I have asked Mrs. Goodgame to assist you."

That evening, just after eleven o'clock, at the Ranleaghs' magnificent mansion on Carlisle Street, Alexandra came face to face with a woman who obviously knew Douglas well and wanted him still.

She was eavesdropping and she felt only a dollop of guilt. But in matter of fact, she was far more furious than guilty. They were speaking French and she couldn't understand a bloody word.

The woman was too pretty for her own good, slight, very feminine with her large eyes, in her mid-twenties, Alexandra thought, and her white hand was on Douglas's sleeve. She was standing very close to him, and leaning even closer, her breath doubtless warm on his cheek, the way Alexandra's was when she was kissing his face. Her voice was low and vibrant with feeling. Douglas was patting her hand, speaking very quietly, his French as smooth and fluent as could be.

Why had her father insisted she learn Italian?

It was worthless. Ah, the woman looked so serious, so intent, so interested in Douglas. Who was she? Had Douglas bought her clothes? Was she offering him a reward?

Douglas turned at that moment and Alexandra pulled back behind a curtain that gave into a small alcove. A couple were there, passionately kissing, and Alexandra blurted out, "Oh, do excuse me!" She fled.

Since she had met nearly fifty people and remembered no one's name, she was quite alone. She saw Lady Ranleagh but that good lady was in close conversation with a bewigged gentleman who looked very important and somewhat drunk.

Since she had no choice, Alexandra stood on the edge of the dance floor, watching the couples dance a charming minuet. They performed flawlessly; they were all beautiful and rich and sophisticated and she felt like an interloper, a provincial with her gown a half-inch too high. At any moment, they would turn and point at her and yell, "She doesn't belong here! Get her out!"

"Dare I believe you are a lost lamb in search of an amiable shepherd?"

That was an interesting approach, Alexandra thought as she turned to look at the gentleman who'd spoken it. He was tall, and well built, his linen immaculate, and very fair-haired. He was probably not more than twenty-five years old, but his eyes, a very dark blue, were so filled with unhappy wisdom and weary cynicism that he gave the impression of being older. He was handsome, she'd give him that, and he did indeed look dazzling in his evening wear, but that glint of too much knowledge in his eyes was disconcerting. And now he was offering to be her amiable shepherd?

"I'm not at all lost, sir, but it is kind of you to inquire."

"You are Melissande's little sister, aren't you? One of the ladies pointed you out to me."

"Yes. You know my sister?"

"Oh yes. She is most charming, a glorious creature. Is it true that she married Tony Parrish, Lord Rathmore?"

Alexandra nodded. "It was love at first sight. They will be coming to London soon."

"I fancy Teresa Carleton won't be overpleased to hear who snapped him up. Ah, you don't know, do you? Tony was engaged to her, then suddenly, the engagement was no more. He didn't say a word, just left London. Teresa let it about that she didn't want him for a husband for he was proving to be unfashionably priggish in his notions. Ah, forgive me, my dear. I am Hetherington, you know."

"No, I didn't know. It is a pleasure to meet you, sir. What this lady said about Tony — if you are acquainted with him, you must know it is a clanker. Tony, priggish? It is too absurd. You know my husband, Douglas Sherbrooke?"

"So that is true as well. All know Sherbrooke, or North, as many of his army friends call him.

He is a man not easily dismissed. I shouldn't like him for an enemy. And no one really believed Teresa. No, Tony is no prig."

"He is a great deal of fun and he and my sister deal well together. They are much in love."

He shrugged, staring at her intently. "What I find odd is you, my dear. You married to Douglas Sherbrooke. You appear warm and quite joyous, really, whilst your husband is a cold man, hard and severe, truth be told."

"My husband cold? Are we speaking of the same man, sir? *Cold?* It is too funny," and Alexandra laughed.

"Beecham, a surprise to see you." Douglas neatly inserted himself between the man and Alexandra. She said, frowning at her husband, "I thought he was Heatherington."

Douglas was infuriated with the young man who was nevertheless a seasoned roué. The dog had the gall to flirt with his wife. He said, "It is Lord Beecham."

"Heatherington is my family name," he said, giving her an intimate look. "I congratulate you, Northcliffe. She is charming. Very different from her sister. An original, I should say. I see that a quadrille is forming itself and I am promised to Miss Danvers, who fancies herself the soul of charm and discretion. I doubt she is worth your time, Northcliffe."

"No, she isn't," Douglas said.

Heatherington managed a shadow of a grin. "I doubt she's worth my time either."

"Keep away from that man," he added to Alexandra as he stared after Baron Beecham, who was making languid progress toward Miss Danvers. "He's known to have a woman's skirts over her head before he even has learned her last name."

"He is so young."

"He is but two years my junior. But you're right. His is a strange past. Keep away from him."

"He must have excellent fashion sense and a deep purse to have such success at such a tender age."

"It isn't funny, Alexandra. I don't like the way he was looking at you. Keep away from him."

"Very well, I shall, if you will keep away from that French hussy who had her hand on your sleeve and was practically speaking into your mouth."

"What French —" He frowned ferociously down at her. "Don't gesticulate so wildly. I can see every white inch of you to your waist. I will have that damned bodice raised before you wear that gown again."

"You will not distract me, Douglas! Who was that wretched hussy?"

He stared at her, surprise and satisfaction in his eyes, eyes that had grown darker if that were possible. "Good God, you're jealous."

She was, and it was humiliating that he had caught her at it. "If I knew anyone, I would walk away from you and go conduct a well-bred conversation with that person. But if I walk away, I will be alone and that isn't a good thing."

"Her name is no concern of yours. She is simply someone I know, nothing more."

"What was she telling you?"

He lied, but it wasn't clean and neat. "That her grandmother was ill."

"Bosh," Alexandra said.

"Very well. I went to France to rescue her and sent Tony to Claybourn Hall. The result wasn't quite what either of us had intended."

"Ah, so that is that Janine person you told me about. She's that bloody woman who offered herself to you."

"Your memory is beyond frightening. I won't say another word. I beg you to dismiss what I said that day. It makes no mind now. Stick to your own affairs, Alexandra."

"Come along then and dance with me since I don't wish to force you to more confidences, though the ones you gave me were meager indeed."

He danced with her, then took her into dinner, then introduced her to young matrons he hoped she would like. And he kept a wary eye open for Georges Cadoudal. Damnation, the last enemy he wanted on this earth was that maniac, Georges.

Why the hell wasn't the man in France where he was supposed to be? Maybe he was, maybe Janine was just hysterical. And that's who he'd been speaking to, Janine Daudet, the woman he'd rescued in France.

"I wish to meet Teresa Carleton."

"So, Beecham told you about her, did he? He enjoys making mischief. I wouldn't be at all surprised if he himself slept with the lady in question."

"Did she break off the engagement with Tony?"

"She didn't. He discovered she was bedding a friend of his. He nearly collapsed from shock and outrage. He came to Northcliffe to regain his mental balance and I looked upon him as my savior. He then went to Claybourn Hall and married my wife."

"Do you think, perhaps, Douglas, that you could rephrase that just a bit?"

"Why? It's the truth. Just because you pop out of the bottle doesn't change the facts."

She sighed. "You're right, of course. However, if you will change your words just a bit, I will reward you when we return home, if you don't reward me first, which you always do. You don't give me a chance, Douglas."

"Perhaps in fifty years I will."

That sounded like a fine commitment to Alexandra and she gave him a brilliant smile. Douglas, on the other hand, rethought his words, and wanted to kick himself. He cursed, drank too much brandy, then brightened. Too much liquor and it just might slow him down a bit. He was fuzzyheaded in the carriage. He was whistling vacantly on the way upstairs. Yes, maybe the brandy would work.

It didn't, but it had been worth a try. When finally he pulled out of her and rolled over onto his back, he crossed his arms over his head and concentrated on calming his breathing. "You will kill me," he said finally. "A man cannot continue like this. It isn't natural. It isn't healthy."

"What about me?"

He lowered an arm and placed his hand over her breast. Her heart was galloping. He grinned. "We'll be buried side by side in the Northcliffe family cemetery."

"I don't like the sound of that."

"You must give me an heir first."

"I thought ladies were supposed to feel ill when they were pregnant."

"Most do, so I've heard."

"I feel wonderful."

"When was your last monthly flow?"

It was dark and they had just made love and were now lying side by side on the large bed, naked and sated, but still it was embarrassing.

When her silence dragged out beyond his patience, Douglas said, "You haven't bled since we were married, have you?"

She shook her head and he felt the movement.

He lightly laid his palm on her belly. "You're very flat." He extended his fingers to her pelvic bones. "You're small, but not too small, I hope, to hold my child. But it is true that I am a big man, Alexandra. My mother complains bitterly even now that I nearly killed her with my size at birth. No, I don't think you're large enough.

I will have a physician come and examine you."

"You will do no such thing!"

"Well, fancy that, she can talk," Douglas said.

"Douglas, listen to me." She came up onto her elbow and her hair fell onto his chest. "I am a woman and it is women who have babies. I won't allow any man other than you to touch me. Do you understand?"

"Who will deliver our child?"

"A midwife. My mother was delivered by a midwife. She doesn't care for men either."

He laughed at that, then skimmed his palm over her belly, down to cup her. He pressed her again onto her back. His hand was large and very warm. His fingers caressed and stroked her. She sucked in her breath. "You don't care for me, Alexandra? I am a man."

"I know you're a man, Douglas. What I don't understand is why anyone would believe you a cold man. Why, just look at what you are doing, and how warm your voice is. Cold! Ha!"

"Who told you that?"

"That young man you said was bad. Heatherington."

"Ah. He was perhaps seeing if you were unhappy with me, thus his comment."

"Why would he care whether or not I was happy? Ah, Douglas, that is very nice."

His fingers stopped but the warmth of his flesh was still there, settled against her flesh, and she shifted slightly. "You will make me forget what I was saying, Douglas, if you continue doing that."

"Accustom yourself for I will touch you whenever and however I please. Now, heed me well, Alexandra. I am a cold man, you could say, if you spoke starkly. By that I mean that I am a man who endeavors not to be overly fooled by artifice or guile. I am a man who lives by logic and reason and not by —" He broke off, his fingers moving over her again, and then he cursed even as he kissed her, rolling over onto her and sliding into her. It was as it always was: fast and hard and deep and she fell into the pleasure of it, crying out and holding him, burrowing into him, wanting him more than she could imagine and the feelings were deeper than he was inside her, so deep she couldn't remember how it had been before he had been with her. But she didn't whisper the words to him. She moaned when she found her release, biting into his shoulder with the power of it. And Douglas, he simply took her pleasure into himself and gave her his own, holding her tightly to him after his release and into sleep.

Alexandra came into the drawing room to see a slight, balding, middle-aged gentleman standing in front of the bow windows, rocking back and forth on his heels, staring at his watch, not across the street at the beautiful park. When he saw her he quickly put the watch back into his vest pocket and gave her a slight bow. She said, her head cocked to one side in question, "Our butler told me there was a gentleman to see me. It is odd since I don't know many gentlemen yet in London. For a moment I thought it must be Beecham, but no, I vow he would not be so indiscreet. It would not be his style. Who are you, sir?"

"I?" He stared at her, unblinking. "I? Surely, His Lordship said I was coming. Surely you must know who I am."

His astonishment at her ignorance was genuine and she smiled. "No, Burgess merely said there was a gentleman in here. Are you perhaps a playwright or an actor who seeks patronage? Perhaps a vicar who needs a living? If that is so, I regret to tell you that His Lordship's young brother will doubtless —"

"No! I am Dr. John Mortimer! I am a physician! I am one of the premier physicians in all of London! His Lordship asked me to visit you. As you know, he is concerned that you will bear his heir and that you are perhaps too small to complete the task successfully. He wished me to ascertain if this is true."

She stared at him, disbelieving. Douglas, curse his black eyes and hair, had been called out earlier in the morning and had not returned. So, he'd arranged for this man to come. Well, at least he hadn't yet returned, so that meant she wouldn't have to argue with him in front of Dr. Mortimer.

"Dr. Mortimer," she said, still smiling, but it was difficult, "I fear you have come for nothing. My husband worries overly. Besides, if I am already with child, then there is nothing to be done if I am too small, is that not true?"

Dr. Mortimer, a man who knew his own worth, which was great, and a man unused to a lady speaking so forwardly, a lady who treated him with such presumption, drew himself up and smiled kindly down at her. She was embarrassed, that was it. It was the only explanation for her odd behavior, though she didn't seem to be at all. Still, he chose his avuncular voice, one that always soothed nervous ladies, chuckled slightly at her foray into wit, and said, "My dear Lady Northcliffe, ladies, no matter their beliefs or what they think they believe — undoubtedly provided with good intent by their older female relations — don't have the ability to discern what is or is not appropriate for them. It is why they have husbands, you know. I am here to examine you, my lady, as requested by your husband. I will then tell your husband what is best for you when you conceive his heir. His concern for your size is laudable. As a physician, I take all factors into consideration and then guide you into the proper steps during the months until the child is born. Now, my lady —"

Alexandra couldn't quite believe that this pretentious, thoroughly irritating man, physician or no, had walked into her drawing room and was treating her like a half-wit stray. But it was Douglas she wanted to cosh, not this specimen.

She smiled sweetly. "Would you like a cup of tea, sir?"

He smiled back at her, showing teeth. "No,

thank you, my lady." He fanned his hands in a gesture of spurious modesty. "My time isn't always my own, you know. Why, in an hour, I must be off to see Lady Abercrombie. She is a cousin to the queen, you know, and I am her private physician. It was difficult for me to come and see you this quickly, but your husband is well-known to me and I decided to oblige him in this. Now, my lady, it is time for us to go upstairs to your bedchamber. If you would like to have your maid present, that is certainly fine."

"Sir, we will not continue anywhere. I am sorry that you made this wasted trip. As I said, my husband worries overly." With that, Alexandra walked to the bell cord and gave it a healthy jerk. Her heart was pounding, she knew her face was flushed. Oddly, she still wasn't particularly angry at this condescending little man, for he was what he was. Ah, but Douglas, he was another matter entirely.

"My lady, really —"

She raised her hand to cut him off. "No, sir, please don't apologize. Do go along to Lady Abercrombie, the queen's cousin, who doubtless is on her toes in anticipation of your coming, and as a result her heart is beating much too quickly for her good health awaiting you."

"I wasn't going to apologize! Your husband pleaded with me to come here and —"

"I beg your pardon, sir, but my husband wouldn't plead with the king himself. It's obvious you don't know him well at all. Ah, Burgess, please see the good doctor out. He is in quite a hurry. He must see the queen, you know."

"No, no, it is Lady Abercrombie, the queen's cousin. Surely you can't wish me to leave!"

"I am certain the queen would swoon to see you as well, Dr. Mortimer. Now, good sir, if you would excuse me —"

Burgess was in an unenviable quandary. The earl had informed him of the physician's impending visit. He knew the countess hadn't been informed and that had bothered him. Knowing her just briefly, he still knew she wouldn't be pleased with what His Lordship had done. And now Her Ladyship was evidently booting out the good doctor. Burgess knew his duty. He also knew what was good for him. He drew himself up to his full five feet four inches and said calmly, "Dr. Mortimer, if you could come this way if you please."

"Good-bye, sir. How very amiable of you to call." Mortimer wanted to be insulted; however, he was more confused by what had passed. He didn't understand how the young lady, countess or not, had managed to rout him, and thus allowed himself to be led out without a word by a butler who looked more like an ostler, bald, round of belly, needing only a large apron about his middle. He was also very short, not at all what Mortimer would have deemed proper in an earl's household. He stood for a moment on the front steps, staring back at the front door of the town house.

Douglas had hurried as quickly as he could to be here when the physician arrived. He imagined that Alexandra wouldn't be too pleased to see the man, but he was concerned and he'd wanted the physician to see her immediately. He wanted the man's word that she would be all right. The fact that he had no idea whether or not she was indeed pregnant didn't matter. If she wasn't now, she would be sooner or later. No, he was worried and he wanted his worries allayed by a man who should know what was what and Mortimer had been recommended by his own physician who'd tended him three years before when he'd been wounded.

Thus, when he saw the physician, standing outside his town house, staring foolishly back at the closed door, his greeting stilled in his mouth, and he frowned. Oh God, something was wrong. She was too small, he knew it; she was with child now and she would die and it would be all his fault. His voice was hoarse and urgent, but he didn't question it, saying, "Dr. Mortimer. Is my wife all right?"

"Oh, my lord! Your wife? She offered me tea, you know. Your wife is fine. She is not at all what I expected. She isn't as I am used to seeing in a lady. She is young, perhaps that is at the root of it. Most strange. I must go now, my lord. Ah, your wife, yes, my lord, your wife. I wish you all the best, my lord. Good luck. I dare say you will need it."

Mortimer continued in that vein as he walked quickly down the steps and into his waiting carriage.

Douglas stood, his hand on the front doorknob, staring after the doctor. He appeared vague; he appeared to ramble; he appeared not at all the way he'd appeared early that morning when Douglas had called upon him. Still, he would have said something if Alexandra wasn't all right. Wouldn't he?

He found her in the drawing room, standing by the bowed front windows, holding back the heavy draperies, staring out at the street and the park just beyond.

She looked over her shoulder at him when he came into the room but didn't say anything. She gave her attention back to the park across the street.

"I saw Dr. Mortimer on the front steps."

She didn't respond.

"He seemed a bit strange. He said you were fine, at least I think he did. He must have been very early."

She continued not to respond. That broom handle was stiff up her back.

"Look, Alexandra, I wanted to be certain you would be all right. Surely you aren't angry because I was worried about you. I know he is a man, but only men are physicians, and thus there was really no choice. I tried to hurry, to be back here when he came, but I was unable to. I would have been with you if I could have. Come, it wasn't all that horrible, was it?"

"Oh no, it wasn't horrible at all."

"Then why are you standing there ignoring me?

Treating me as if I didn't exist? It isn't what I am used to from my wife. Don't you remember? You love me."

"Oh, surely not, Douglas. It is lust, nothing more. You convinced me of that. As for your precious doctor, why I hope the pompous fool falls into a ditch and succumbs to water in his mouth."

Douglas raked his fingers through his hair. "I'm sorry if he didn't treat you as I would have. No, no, I take that back. That is a truly appalling thought. Didn't you like him? Wasn't he gentle enough with you? Did he embarrass you more than he should have?"

She turned to face him now, her expression remote. "I told you last night I wouldn't be examined by any man —"

"Other than me."

As a jesting gambit, it didn't succeed. "That's correct. Your memory serves you well when it is your own ends you wish to serve. I was polite to him, Douglas, but we did not leave this drawing room —"

"You let him examine you here? Where, on the sofa? No? Then on that large wing chair over there? My God, that wasn't well done of you, Alexandra. It was indelicate of you and not at all wise. Why, Mrs. Goodgame could have come in. Burgess could have come in with the tea tray. A maid could have come in to dust, for God's sake. I would have expected you to demand that your modesty be preserved, that at least three female maids be present to keep careful watch. No, that wasn't —"

"He didn't touch me. I told you last night I wouldn't allow it. Did you disbelieve me?"

"You are my damned wife! You weren't at first, but then after I decided that you were, it became your obligation to oblige me — no, that sounds ridiculous. It became your damned duty! It is your damned duty! I want you examined. I don't want another man touching you, but he isn't really what you would call a man; he's a doctor, a sort of male eunuch, and he's paid to touch you and to know what it is he's touching. Dammit, Alexandra, what did you do to him?"

"Oh yes, your superior Dr. Mortimer is a man, Douglas! He spouted all your precious male nonsense. He treated me as if I were a child, a stupid child at that. Besides, how can he possibly know what he's doing? He isn't a woman; he isn't built like a woman. How can he know how a woman works and when something isn't working right?"

"I won't argue with you about this, Alexandra. I will ask him to come back. If you wish it, I will remain with you and keep an eye on him, if that is what concerns you. That is what I wished to do today. Now, enough. Would you like to go riding to Richmond? We could take a picnic. I wouldn't be able to attack you — to reward you, that is — there would be too many people about. What do you say?"

She could only stare at him. "Douglas, don't you realize what you did?"

"You are irritating me, Alexandra."

"You went against my wishes. You didn't even consult me. I will not tolerate that sort of thing, Douglas."

He turned red and actually yelled at her, "Damn you, you are my wife. Can't you understand that if I get you with child, you could die? I don't want to kill you!"

"Why?" Her voice was now soft as butter, and Douglas heard the change and wanted to kick himself.

"Don't try your bloody guile on me, madam. Go change into your riding habit. You have fifteen minutes. If you are late, I shall lose you in the maze."

It was a start, Alexandra thought, as she climbed the stairs. It was a very promising start.

However, not half an hour later, she wanted to kick him. Her promising start had fallen into ashes.

CHAPTER 20

"Douglas, who called you away so early this morning?" Her question was one of random curiosity. However, Douglas stiffened alarmingly in the saddle. The stallion he kept in London, Prince by name, a huge roan gelding, didn't like the stiffening and danced sideways. Alexandra's mare, a foul-tempered chestnut, decided it was her rider's fault that the stallion was upset, whipped her head around, and bit her boot. She yelped in surprise.

Douglas said sharply, "I told you she wasn't like your mare at home. Pay attention, Alexandra."

She frowned at the back of his head. They were cantering sedately in Rotten Row. Douglas had decided they didn't have time to go to Richmond maze. It was too early by far for all the fashionable to be in attendance, which pleased Alexandra. It was a pleasant early afternoon, a light breeze ruffling the loose curls around her face. She said again, this time more than random interest in her voice, "Who wanted you so badly this morning? No one in your family is ill? Everyone is all right?"

"My family is now your family. Contrive to remember that, please. Also, it is none of your business where I go or what I do. A wife shouldn't meddle in her husband's affairs. Pay attention to your mount and —"

"Douglas," she said in what she believed a most reasonable tone of voice, "you are sulking because I didn't take that wretched doctor up to my bedchamber. I will continue not to take him anywhere, and unless you want to create a god-awful scene, you won't force me to. Now, what was all the urgency? I am your wife. Please tell me what is happening."

He remained mulish and silent and her imagination flowed into dramatic channels. "It isn't anything to do with an invasion, is it? Oh dear, the ministry doesn't want you back in the army, do they? You won't go, will you? Please consider well, Douglas. There is so much at Northcliffe Hall that requires your constant attention. So I don't think —"

"Be quiet! It has nothing to do with that, dammit! It has to do with a brilliant madman named Georges Cadoudal."

"Who is he?"

How had she managed to get him to spit out the name, he wondered, staring between his horse's ears. "It is none of your affair. Be quiet. Leave me alone. I won't tell you anything more."

"All right," she said. Georges Cadoudal. He was French and Douglas spoke French as if he'd been nursed on it at his mother's breast. She remembered the intensity of that French woman — that hussy he'd rescued, Janine — the previous night at the Ranleaghs' ball and said, "Is he involved somehow with that bawd who was trying to seduce you last night?"

Douglas simply stared at her. She couldn't know. It was just a guess and he was a fool. The last thing he wanted to do was worry her, to scare her. The absolute last thing he wanted was for her to pry into the absurd business. He dug his heels into Prince's sides and the stallion shot forward.

Alexandra wished she had a rock; she would surely throw it at the back of his head. But more than that, she was worried. How to find out who this Georges Cadoudal was and how it affected Douglas? She remembered the note brought to him by his valet, Finkle, who had come to London with them. Perhaps the note was still about somewhere. She resolved to find it. He'd said that his was now her family as well. Very well. She was his wife; it was time he realized that having a wife meant an end to his own counsels. She could be of help to him; he had to learn that.

She found the note. Finkle had deposited it carefully with His Lordship's other missives on his massive desk in the library. Alexandra frowned as she read it. It was from a Lord Avery. The scrawl, which was large and black, simply informed Douglas that this Georges Cadoudal was, it appeared, not in Paris where he was supposed to be, but rather back in England. Lord Avery was worried; he needed to speak with Douglas immediately.

Alexandra scrupulously refolded the letter, placing it back into the pile, giving no visual hint it had been moved. Douglas came unexpectedly into the room just as she finished. She flushed to the top of her forehead and quickly pushed away from the desk.

"Good day, my lord," she said and gave him an airy wave.

He was frowning; he blocked her escape. "What are you doing in here, Alexandra?"

She sent her chin upward. "Isn't this my house as well? Are there some rooms that I'm not allowed to visit? If that is so, it is only fair that you tell me where I am not to go and I will, naturally, obey you."

Douglas looked toward his desk, his frown still in place. "Your efforts to distract me have never worked. And, you have never obeyed me. Now, what is on my desk that was of such interest to you?"

As he took a step forward, she tried to duck around him. He caught her wrist in his hand. She felt his thumb gently caress the soft flesh and knew that if he continued, she would be on her back on the floor, or perhaps the sofa, and she would enjoy herself most thoroughly.

It was as if Douglas realized the same thing. He dropped her wrist. "Don't move," he said, "or I will see to it that you pay for your interest in my affairs." She wondered if he knew what he would do were she to duck out of the room. She decided the threat wasn't specific enough and was out of the room in an instant.

Douglas let her go. He'd find her quickly enough; he went to his desk and thumbed through the papers. When he found the note from Lord Avery, he cursed. Damn Finkle, why did he have to be so fastidious? Well, she knew very little more now than she had before. Still, he was worried. Georges Cadoudal wasn't predictable. From experience, Douglas knew that once Georges got a particular idea in his brain, he couldn't be budged from it. It was both an asset and a terrible drawback. Like now.

Douglas cursed. What to do?

His course of action was decided that very evening. He took Alexandra to a small soirée at the home of Lord and Lady Marchpane, a delightful older couple who were very fond of Douglas for he'd looked after their grandson in the army. They greeted him and Alexandra warmly.

As for Alexandra, she was wary, though Douglas had said naught to her of retribution or punishment. He'd appeared rather preoccupied, even when she'd presented herself in a new gown whose neckline wasn't all that high. He'd merely nodded at her and that had been that. She watched him from the corner of her eye. She would have preferred to have remained at the town house, with him. Perhaps she should apologize for her nosiness. She touched her fingertips to his sleeve. He looked down at her, saying nothing, his face expressionless.

"I'm sorry, Douglas."

"For what specifically?"

"For prying, but you made me so angry, not telling me what is happening. I am your wife, you know. I can be of assistance to you if you would but allow me."

His look was, if nothing, more remote. "I accept your apology though it is sparse as a gorse heath. As for the other, I cannot help but be aware that you are my wife. You are with me every blessed moment. I doubt I could relieve myself without you demanding where it is I went to and what it is I did. Ah, here is Teddy Summerton. He dances well. I will give you over to him. No, don't argue with me. You will do as I bid you. Do you understand me?"

"I understand," she said.

And she dutifully danced the next country dance with Teddy Summerton, a very nice young gentleman with a pallid complexion and large ears who appeared to worship her husband. When the dance was over, Douglas was nowhere to be seen.

Alexandra wondered if he were once again with that French hussy. She wandered slowly around the perimeter of the ballroom; some of the people recognized her and nodded. She nodded back, smiling. Where was Douglas?

It was a warm evening, the air heavy with impending rain. Alexandra went onto the balcony and leaned over the stone balustrade to peer down into the gardens below. There were lanterns hung at romantic intervals, but still there were many shadows, many dark places, and she felt a gnawing of fear.

She called out softly, "Douglas?"

There was no response. She thought she heard a rustle in the bushes to her left but couldn't be certain. She called his name again, then quickly skipped down the deep-set stone steps to the garden. Again she called his name. Then she fell silent. She quickly walked along one of the narrow stone paths, her ears on full alert. Nothing. Then, suddenly, she heard a man's deep voice that sounded like a low hissing, but she didn't understand what he was saying. Damnation, it was French he was speaking. She wanted to scream with vexation until she heard Douglas reply, in French, and he sounded both cold and remarkably angry.

Suddenly there came the unmistakable sounds of a scuffle. She didn't wait but ran full-tilt toward the fray. She ran into the bushes to see two men attacking Douglas. She watched with astonishment when he whirled about on the balls of his feet and struck one of the men hard in his belly with his fist, then as he turned, faster than the wind, his elbow struck the other man in his throat. It was all done so quickly she just stood there, frozen like a rabbit. The one man, rubbing his throat, yelled something in French at Douglas; in the next instant, both he and his henchman had melted into the shadows.

Douglas stood there motionless, rubbing the

knuckles of his left hand, staring off into the darkness. She ran to him then, her hand on his arms, his shoulders, finally to cup his face. "Are you all right? You were so fine, Douglas. You moved so quickly. I couldn't believe it. You didn't need my help at all. Are you all right? Can you not speak? Please, Douglas, speak to me." As she spoke, her hands continued to caress him, to feel him and still he stood motionless, his breathing deep and steady.

Finally, he raised his arms, grasped her hands in his, and lowered his face to within an inch of hers. "What the hell are you doing out here?"

Her hands stilled, but she didn't flinch away from him. "I was worried about you. I couldn't find you. I thought perhaps you would need me."

"Need you? Good Lord, madam, spare me your assistance! Now, we're leaving."

"But who were those men? Why did they attack you? I heard all of you arguing but I couldn't understand. It was in French, blast it. Why —"

He shook her, saying nothing, and dragged her back along the path to the town house. He was terrified for her, for the last thing Georges Cadoudal had shouted at him was a threat against her. Just as he'd destroyed Janine, he, Georges, would destroy Douglas's new wife.

He said nothing in the carriage, until she asked, "I've never seen anyone hit another like that. You didn't fight Tony like that."

"I wanted to thrash Tony, not kill him."

"Where did you learn to fight like that?"

He turned to look at her in the dim light of the carriage. He smiled just a bit, remembering. "I was in Portugal and I got to know some members in this gang of bandits in Oporto who were the foulest, meanest, dirtiest fighters I've ever seen in my life. They taught me and I managed to live through it."

"Oh. Who were those men who tried to hurt you?"

He took her left hand in his and held it firm.

"Listen to me, Alexandra. You are to go nowhere without me, do you understand? Don't look at me like that, just trust me. Tell me you understand."

"Yes, I understand."

"Of course you don't, but it doesn't matter. The day after tomorrow, we are returning to Northcliffe."

"Why?"

"You will do as I tell you and ask no more questions."

She decided to let the matter rest. She knew him well enough to recognize that once he'd shut off the valve to his meager supply of information, it wouldn't again be opened. He was the most stubborn man she'd ever known. She leaned back her head against the soft leather squabs, closed her eyes, and began to snore.

She thought he chuckled, but she couldn't be certain. She now had a plan; not much of one, but at least it was a start; it was something.

The following day at just after eleven o'clock in the morning, Douglas returned to the town house. His meeting with Lord Avery had been short and to the point. Yes, Georges Cadoudal was here in London, not in Paris, where he should be with all the English government's groats and apparently he was out for blood, Douglas's blood.

Douglas sighed, handed Burgess his cane, and asked, "Where is Her Ladyship?"

Burgess looked pained but brave. "She is with a person, my lord."

"A person, you say? Is this person male?"

"Yes, my lord. It is a French male person."

He immediately thought of Georges Cadoudal and paled. But no, Georges wouldn't come here. Damn her eyes. Was she trying to spy on him by bribing some Frenchman she'd picked up off the street? "I see. And just where is she with this French male person?"

"In the morning room, my lord."

"Why did you not inquire the mission of this French male person, Burgess?"

"Her Ladyship said it was none of my affair. Her tone and words were very much in your fashion, my lord."

"It has never made you shut your mouth before!"

"Her Ladyship also asked me about my nephew who has a putrid throat, my lord. You have never shown such solicitude, thus, I favored her with my silence."

"Damn you. I didn't know you had a nephew!"

"No, my lord."

Douglas, still more intrigued than otherwise, walked quickly down the corridor toward the back of the house. The morning room gave onto the enclosed garden. It was light and airy, a delightful room. He hadn't been in here often. Sinjun had told him it was a room for the ladies and for him to stay away. He didn't knock on the door, just opened it quietly. He saw a long-faced young gentleman dressed in frayed black, sitting across from Alexandra. He was silent. She was saying slowly, *"Je vais à Paris demain. Je vais prendre mon mari avec moi."*

The young man exploded with evident pleasure. *"Excellent, madame! Et maintenant —"*

Douglas said abruptly from the doorway, "I am not going with you to Paris tomorrow, Alexandra. Nor is there anything excellent about such a suggestion."

Under his fascinated eye, she flushed to the roots of her red hair, sputtered several times, then said to the French male person opposite her, *"Je crois que c'est ici mon mari."*

"You only *think* I'm your husband?" Douglas nodded to the Frenchman, who was now on his feet, staring at him nervously, fiddling with his watch fob. A watch fob!

"What is he doing here, Alexandra?"

She was on her feet too and she was running lightly toward him, giving him a fat smile. "Ah, he is just a very nice young gentleman I met

. . . well, yes, I met him at Gunthers' and I asked him to visit here and we could, well, we could talk about things."

"Things French?"

"I suppose you could say that."

"Are you paying him?"

"Well, yes."

"He is spying for you? Do you expect him to follow me and eavesdrop on my conversations and report back to you?"

She stared at him. "You really believe I would do that, Douglas?"

"No," he said shortly. "No, I don't, at least not in the usual run of things. But I do believe you would do anything you could think of to help me even when I don't require it or want it or need it and would, in fact, beat you if you tried it."

She cocked her head to one side. "You are saying several things there, Douglas, and I'm not at all certain —"

"Dammit, woman, who is this fellow and what is he doing here?"

Her chin went into the air. "Very well. His name is Monsieur Lessage and he is giving me French lessons."

"What?"

"You heard me. If you would now leave, Douglas, we are not yet through."

Douglas cursed in French with such sophisticated fluency that the young Frenchman was moved to give him a very toothy approving smile. He said something quickly to Douglas, and Douglas said something even more quickly back to him. Then the two men proceeded to speak in that accursed language, excluding her, making her feel like an outsider.

"Douglas," she said in a very loud voice, "Monsieur Lessage is my teacher. You are interrupting us. *S'il vous plaît,* please leave."

Douglas said something to Monsieur and the man grinned.

"I apologize, Alexandra, but Monsieur just remembered that he has another lesson to give, very shortly, and all the way on the other side of London." Douglas shook the man's hand, and money went from her husband's hand into the Frenchman's.

Alexandra wanted to hit him. She wished she could curse him in the fluent French he used so effortlessly. No, all she wanted was just one French curse word, just one. Her hands were fisted at her sides. She waited for the door to close, then bounded to her feet. "How dare you! He was my teacher, he was not at your beck and command! Ah, I would like to tell you in French just how angry I am!"

"Want to curse me out, hm?"

"Yes. *Oui!*"

"Merde."

"What?"

"You may say *merde.* It means . . . never mind, it's a curse and it will relieve your spleen. Trust me."

"Merde!"

He winced, then grinned at her. "Feel better?" She said nothing, and he continued, "Why did you want to learn French?"

"To find out what that hussy said to you and why that man, Georges whatever, wanted to kill you last night!"

"Ah, so I was right. You are picturing yourself as Saint Georgina." He walked to the floor-to-ceiling glass doors that gave directly into the garden. He opened the door and breathed in the fresh morning air. "Alexandra, you were planning to rescue me again? This time with schoolgirl French?"

"If you won't tell me what is wrong, why, I must do something! It is my nature, I can't help it. I wish you wouldn't regard it as interference."

"A pity," he said, not turning to look at her. "Yes, a pity that you aren't more like your sister, a lady, I fancy, who is perfectly willing to wait to see what her husband wishes of her before hurling herself like a hoyden into one mess after another. Messes, I add, that have nothing to do with you."

"I wish you would be more clear in your condemnation, Douglas."

"In what way am I not perfectly clear?"

"That you love Melissande, still?"

He turned then to face her, this wife of his, and he saw the hurt in her eyes. It bothered him. He hadn't made love to her the previous night. He'd wanted to, Lord, that was nothing new, he always wanted her, but he had to teach her that she couldn't have him whenever she wished to, that he would decide when and where and how, and he'd had to show her his displeasure. Well, he'd done that and now he wanted her like the very devil. Her morning gown wasn't all that alluring, for God's sake, just a soft yellow muslin, yet he wanted to rip that very feminine row of lace from the neckline and bare her breasts. He wanted her breasts in his hands, he wanted to caress and kiss the soft flesh on the underside of her breasts. He wanted to press his face against her heart.

He sighed, and kept his back to her for he'd become hard, painfully so, just thinking about her damned breasts. He didn't like it at all.

And he said, to his own surprise, "No, I don't love Melissande. I never loved her but I wanted her. I suppose she was something of a dream to me, not a real woman, just this exquisite phantom that made my nights less lonely. No, I don't love her. I fear Tony was right about that, the damned sod."

"Tony loves her."

"Yes, he does."

And she wanted desperately to ask him if perhaps he couldn't bring himself to love her, just a little bit. But she remained silent. She did say, "I am as I am, Douglas. I cannot bear to think of you in danger. I cannot believe that you would prefer me to sit drinking tea when a villain comes up to plant a knife in your back."

"Perhaps if that were the case, you could yell at the top of your lungs for some assistance from a man."

"And if there were none of your precious specimens about?"

"Cease your games with me, Alexandra. I don't want you doing things I haven't approved. I want to know where you are, what you're doing. I do not want or require your interference in my affairs."

"You want a bloodless wife."

"Bloodless? Ha, do you so soon forget your screams and moans when I take you?" He shut his mouth for his sex was very painful now, his britches stretched.

He gave her a long brooding look. She was too close. "I wish you to remain here, in the house. Do not go out. Oversee our preparations to leave, early in the morning. Is that enough for you to do?"

She rose, her hands fisted at her sides. He simply wouldn't give over, she thought. She wondered in that bleak moment if he would ever give over. Perhaps not. She gave him a smile, ah, but it hurt to make her mouth move like that, but she did it, then just nodded to him, and left the room.

She walked up the wide stairway, not turning when she heard Mrs. Goodgame call to her. She walked to her bedchamber, walked inside, and locked the door. She stood for a very long time in the middle of the room, then slowly, she went down onto her knees. She wrapped her arms about herself and cried.

She was deep in her misery and didn't hear the adjoining door quietly open. Douglas, an order forming in his mouth, let the order die. He stared and felt a shifting hollow feeling in his belly. He hadn't really scolded her, for God's sake, nothing to bring on this misery. He couldn't bear it. He walked quickly to her, lifted her into his arms, and carried her to her bed. He came down on top of her, his mouth on hers, and he tasted her tears and sought to make her forget the tears, the pain, forget all but the pleasure he would give her. He jerked up her gown, shredded her stockings and flung away her slippers.

He unfastened his britches and came into her and she was soft and willing, quite ready for him, and it amazed him, this awareness of him that was deep in her, this yielding that was his even when he had hurt her. "Alexandra," he said into her mouth and thrust hard and harder still.

She opened her eyes even as she pushed upward against him to draw him deeper.

"I seems I must take you every day, for our health, you understand, otherwise we will grow quickly old and mean and testy. Do you understand? Tell me you understand."

"I understand," she said, and pulled his face down to hers. She was hungry for him, always this hunger, and she kissed him, her tongue in his mouth, taking the lead, and it both surprised him and made him instantly wild.

"Ah, don't," he said, but it was too late. Always too late with her and he surged into her and over her, panting and heaving, his eyes closed against the intensity of the feelings coursing through him, and that pressure, always building, and then, quite suddenly, he jerked out of her. Her eyes flew open but he only shook his head. He lifted her hips in his large hands and brought her to his mouth.

Alexandra screamed.

Then she groaned, softly, beyond herself, and it went on and on and he forced her to ease then he built the sensations again. He was controlling her this time but there was nothing she could do about it. She cried out, her head thrashing on the bed until finally, he left her and came inside her once more and he arched his back and yelled her name at his release.

When it was over, when he could find a breath, Douglas came up on his elbows over her, and said into her dazed face, "Don't you cry again. I don't like it. There is no reason for you to cry. I came to you, did I not? Did I not give you great pleasure?"

"Yes," she said. "Yes, you did."

He was still deep inside her. It was time for lunch. Absurd, the middle of the day and he was growing hard again. He forced himself to pull out of her.

"No more crying," he said and rose to stand over her. He straightened his britches.

"Why can't you trust me, Douglas?"

"You speak nonsense."

"Did I not try to save you from Tony?"

"That has naught to do with anything."

She managed to come up to a sitting position, pulling down her gown. She was wet with him and with herself, she supposed; she still felt the pull of the languorous feelings, the draining pleasure. She looked at her feet, bare, hanging over the side of the bed, not reaching the floor. "Very well, Douglas, I will do as you wish. I will not pry into anything. If you get into trouble, I shall be sorry for it, but I will do nothing. That is what you wish, is it not?"

He frowned. No, it wasn't, but it had been what he'd said.

"I wish you to arrange yourself. I am hungry. It is time for luncheon." He left her then, going into his own bedchamber, closing the adjoining door behind him. She sat there, staring after him.

"Merde," she said.

CHAPTER 21

Douglas came awake suddenly. He didn't know what had awakened him, but one instant he was deep in a dream, in a heavy skirmish near Pena, the French drawing closer and closer to his flank, and the next, he was staring into the darkness, breathing fast. He shook his head and automatically turned to reach for Alexandra.

His hand landed on smooth sheets. Foolishly, he ran his hands over her pillow and on the blankets bunched up at the foot of the bed. She wasn't there. She was gone. He felt panic surge, raw and painful in his belly. Dear God, Georges Cadoudal had taken her.

No, that was absurd. Georges couldn't have gotten into the house, up here into the bedchamber, and taken her, all without waking him. No, it was impossible.

Douglas was still wrapping the belt around his dark blue velvet dressing gown when he walked quickly downstairs, his feet bare and soundless on the heavy carpet. Where the devil could she have gone?

He quietly looked into the two salons, the breakfast room, the huge formal dining room.

He paused in the wide entrance hall, frowning. Then, he walked quickly back toward the library. He stopped, seeing the flicker of light coming from beneath the door.

Very quietly, he turned the knob and looked in.

Alexandra was sitting at his desk, a candle at her left elbow, an open book in front of her. She was concentrating fiercely, her forehead furrowed.

He was on the point of charging in and demanding what the devil she was doing when he heard her say quite clearly, "So that is what *merde* means. Well, well, it is certainly bad enough and Douglas was right. It would relieve a person's spleen splendidly and very quickly." She said the word several times, then added aloud, "Of course it won't do much good in the long run. Come on, my girl, let's get to it."

He had a difficult time to keep the laughter in his throat, but he managed, for now she had begun repeating aloud in poor but understandable French, "I won't go. *Je ne vais pas.* He won't go. *Il ne va pas.* They won't go. *Ils ne vont pas.*"

He stared. What the devil?

She was trying to teach herself French. All because she wanted to help him if she could.

Douglas simply stood there, staring at his wife, slowly shaking his head, grappling with what he saw and what was happening to him. Something deep and sweet began to fill him, something he hadn't felt before in his life, something new and wondrous and rich, something he'd never expected simply because he hadn't realized there was something to be felt and he hadn't known . . . hadn't known that he was lacking.

He continued to stare at her. She was sitting there in her white nightgown with its collar to her chin, her dark red hair in a braid that fell over her right shoulder. She was using her hands as she repeated the words in French. The candlelight flickered over her face, making her eyes luminous, breaking shadows on her cheeks and hair. She continued speaking, repeating endlessly the same phrases, over and over.

He could understand the French. If he really tried.

"I am helping him. *Je l'aide.* Ah, what is this?" She fell silent, then said very softly, "I love him. *Je l'aime.* I love Douglas. *J'aime Douglas.* I love my husband. *J'aime mon mari.*"

He stood there, letting the feelings expand and overflow in him, and then he smiled, a gentle smile that he could feel inside himself, and even that smile warmed him, made him feel incredibly lucky and that smile of his was his acceptance of her, of what she was to him and of what he knew he would always feel for her, his wife.

Very quietly he closed the door and walked thoughtfully back upstairs. He lay awake, reveling in the newness of his feelings, waiting.

When she eased into the bed beside him an hour later, he pretended sleep. For ten minutes. Then he turned to her and took her into his arms and began kissing her.

Alexandra gave a start of surprise, then returned his kisses with enthusiasm, as always. But there was no frenzy, no wild urgency this time. When he came into her, it was tender and gentle and slow, something he'd never been able to accomplish with her before, and he continued to kiss her, teasing her with his tongue, nipping at her lower lip, stroking her as he gave himself over to her. And it was good and she sighed in soft pleasure when it was done; she was bound to him now. She would be bound to him forever.

And when he knew she was asleep, he kissed her temple and said very quietly against her warm cheek, *"Je t'aime aussi."*

Seven hours later, at the breakfast table, Douglas slammed his fist so hard his plate jumped and a slice of bacon slid off onto the white tablecloth.

"I said no, Alexandra. If Sinjun asked you to fetch her a book at Hookams, it is just too bad. I haven't the time to accompany you and you will go nowhere without me with you. Do you understand?"

She was silent.

"Tell me you understand."

"I understand."

"Good. Now; see to our packing. I'm sorry we can't leave this morning, but there is business I must attend to. I will return later." And just as he was at the door, he froze, hearing her say *"Merde!"*

He pretended not to hear her and was gone. Alexandra stared at her eggs and wondered why one could rhapsodize so stupidly in the middle of the night and imagine that it would last beyond a man's passion.

She remained busy the remainder of the morning although, truth be told, Mrs. Goodgame had little use for a mistress who was clearly distracted and really didn't care if her gowns were packed carefully in tissue paper or simply thrown into the trunk.

Douglas didn't return for luncheon. Alexandra was near to screaming with vexation and with fear for him. Why couldn't she make him promise that he would go nowhere without her in attendance? She tried to study her French but she was so angry with him that she spent most of the time searching for more curse words.

"You have the fidgets, my lady," Mrs. Goodgame finally told her, her voice weary with aggravation. "Why don't you take a nice ride in the carriage? There is nothing needing your attention here, I assure you."

So Douglas hadn't told his staff that his wife was to be a prisoner. Her mouth thinned. She would go fetch Sinjun her novel and Douglas be damned. However, just to be on the safe side, she removed a small pistol from Douglas's desk in the library that she'd come across the night before when she was resting from her French lesson, and slipped it into her reticule. She had no idea if it were primed. Just looking at it scared her; she prayed if she had to use it, the person she was using it on would be equally frightened just seeing it. She asked one of the footmen to accompany her, sitting next to John Coachman. What more could Douglas ask? She had two armed guards and a pistol.

Burgess did know that Her Ladyship was to remain indoors but he wasn't at his post when Alexandra slipped out, James the footman in tow.

The carriage bowled up Piccadilly, past Hyde Park corner to St. Edward's Street. John Coachman remained with the carriage and James accompanied Alexandra into Hookams. It was a drafty place, floor-to-ceiling shelves crammed full with books. It was dusty with little space between the aisles, but nonetheless, it had been pronounced a meeting place by the ton and thus the aisles were crammed with chatting gentlemen and ladies. Near the front of the shop, maids and footmen waited to relieve their mistresses and masters of their parcels. Alexandra left James to eye a pretty maid and allowed a harried clerk to lead her to where Sinjun's novel was. Ah, yes, there, on the third shelf. She reached for *The Mysterious Count* then froze when a man's voice hissed low into her right ear.

"Ah, the little pigeon leaves the nest, eh?"

It wasn't Heatherington, she thought. No, he'd been the sheep and the shepherd. She sighed and said, not looking back at the man, "Your approach is not to my liking, sir. It lacks originality. It lacks grace and charm. It lacks wit. You should hire someone to instruct you. I do like your affectation of a French accent though, but it really doesn't fit all that well with your excellent English. You don't reverse your words, you know?"

"Damn you, I do not mean to charm you! I speak three languages fluently!"

"Well, then, what is your purpose?" She turned as she spoke and stared up at a gaunt, very tall man, dark-haired, eyes blacker than Douglas's, garbed in gentleman's morning wear. She knew suddenly that this was Georges Cadoudal. Oh dear, this man's accent was quite legitimate.

"My purpose? Well, I will tell you. I have a very small and very deadly pistol here in my right hand and it is pointed at your breast. I suggest, madame, that you come with me, and keep that charming smile on your face. Consider me your lover and we shall deal together famously, eh? Let's go."

Alexandra saw the intent in his eyes, the cold hardness, the determination. *"Je ne vais pas!"* she shouted at the top of her lungs. She smashed *The Mysterious Count* in his face, hoping she'd at least broken his long nose. Then when he raised his arm to strike her, she screamed, *"Merde! Merde! Je vais à Paris demain avec mon mari! Aidez-moi!"*

He struck her against the side of her head, cursing all the while, whilst the patrons of Hookams stared in frozen shock.

"James, help! *Aidez-moi!*"

"Damn you," Georges Cadoudal hissed in her

face, and then in the next instant, he was gone. James was at her side, shocked to his toes, knowing that he'd failed the mistress, but it had been so unexpected, the attack by the unknown villain.

"Are you all right, my lady? Oh dear, please tell me you're all right."

Alexandra shook her head to clear it. The blow had made her eyes blur and cross. "Yes, I'm all right." Then she looked at the novel she was holding and straightened out its ruffled pages. "I coshed him in the nose, James. Did you hear my French?"

"*Merde,* my lady?"

This time it was Heatherington, the man Douglas had told her would toss up a woman's skirts even before he knew her name, and he was smiling down at her, not the sardonic smile of a practiced roué, but a genuine smile. Oddly, there was a good deal of warmth in that smile. "Ah yes, I heard your magnificent French. Who is the poor soul who dared to agitate you?"

"He is gone," Alexandra said. She looked as proud as a little peahen. "My French scared him off."

Heatherington gave her a long look, then he laughed, a sound that was rusty because he hadn't laughed, really laughed in a very long time. It didn't go with the image he so carefully cultivated for himself. He laughed louder, shaking his head. *"Merde,"* he said. *"Merde,"* he said again, then turned away and left the bookstore.

Alexandra stared after him for a moment, then

paid for her novel, ignoring all the whispering ladies and gentlemen staring at her. James walked very close to her until he handed her up into the carriage. They were at the Sherbrooke town house in twenty minutes. As James walked up the front steps just behind her, she stopped and said urgently, her fingers plucking at his coat sleeve, "Please, James, I don't wish His Lordship to know about the small, ah, contretemps, all right? It was nothing, nothing at all. The man was doubtless confused as to who I was, but nothing more."

James wasn't at all certain she was right. He was worried and rightfully so, for the first person he saw in the entrance hall was His Lordship and he looked fit to kill. In fact, he looked filled with anticipation to kill.

James had never before heard a man roar, but he did now. His Lordship straightened to his full height, and yelled at the top of his lungs at his wife who only came to his shoulder, "Where the hell did you go? How dare you disobey me! My God, Alexandra, you've pushed me too far this time! Bloody hell, it is too much, much too much!"

James retreated, bumping into Burgess, who glided into the fray without a tremor of agitation showing on his face.

"My lady, welcome back. Ah, I can see that James here stayed closely with you, as did John Coachman. His Lordship was worried, naturally, even though —"

"Damnation, Burgess! Be quiet! Believe me, she doesn't need your protection or interference." Douglas grabbed her arm and pulled her into the salon. He kicked the door shut with the heel of his boot.

"Trying to defend you, damn his traitor's eyes," Douglas said, shaking her now, his fingers digging into her upper arms. She said nothing, merely looked up at him. The shock of Georges Cadoudal's sudden appearance at Hookams had passed during the carriage ride home. Now, she was more calm than not in the face of Douglas's fury.

"I purchased Sinjun's novel," she said when he'd momentarily run out of bile.

"Damn Sinjun's bloody novel!"

"Douglas, your language is deteriorating. Please calm down. Nothing happened, really . . ."

He shook her again. "And now you compound your disobedience with a lie. How dare you, Alexandra? How dare you lie to me?"

No, she thought, it was impossible that he knew anything of what had happened at the bookshop.

"I ran into Heatherington," he said, seeing more deceit would come from her mouth.

"Oh," she said, then gave him a very tentative smile. Heatherington hadn't known a thing, not really. "It was just a man who didn't know what was proper —"

"It was Georges Cadoudal and he would have taken you."

"How did you know?"

"The good Lord save me from stupid females.

Alexandra, you were screeching French loud enough for all of London to hear. I saw another gentleman you haven't even met and he told me about your *merde* at the top of your lungs. Everyone knows and I doubt not that I will receive a good dozen visits from people to tell me of my wife's exceedingly odd behavior."

"I said other things too, Douglas."

"Yes, I know. You're going to Paris with your husband tomorrow."

"And I screamed for help too in French."

"And another thing," he began, really warming up to his theme now, then stopped cold, for she'd pulled a small pistol from her reticule.

"I also took this. I'm not stupid, Douglas. That man couldn't have harmed me. I didn't leave the house without thought and preparation. I was bored, Douglas, please understand. I was bored and I wanted to do something. All went just fine. He tried but he failed. I also hit him on the head with Sinjun's novel. He didn't have a chance."

Douglas could but stare down at her. She looked so proud of herself, the little twit. She was completely convinced she was in the right of it. She was innocent and guileless. She had no more chance than a chicken against a man like Cadoudal. He took the pistol from her, his muscles spasming at the thought of having that damned thing turned back on her, and then walked very tall and straight and very quietly from the room. He didn't say another word.

Alexandra looked at the closed door. "He is trying very hard to control himself," she said to no one in particular.

He wasn't at home for dinner. He didn't come to her that night.

They left London at eight-thirty the following morning. Summer fog hung low and thick throughout the city, clinging like a dismal chilled blanket until they were well onto the road south.

Douglas sat silently beside his wife. She, curse her nonchalance, was reading Sinjun's novel. *The Mysterious Count.* What bloody drivel. Then he remembered Sinjun telling him about his Greek plays, and shuddered. This was probably filled with heroines swooning rather than taking off their clothes. "Why do you read that nonsense?" he asked, thoroughly irritated.

Alexandra looked up and smiled at him. "You don't wish to speak civilly to me, the scenery is nothing out of the ordinary, and I don't wish to nap. Have you a better suggestion than reading? Perhaps you have a volume of moral sermons that would elevate my thoughts?"

"I'll speak to you," he said, his voice on the edge of testy.

"Ah, that is very nice of you, Douglas."

He searched her words and tone for irony but couldn't detect any. He sighed. "Very well. I was worried about you. You must give me leave to worry, particularly when there is danger I know exists and it could touch you. All right, I apologize for leaving you alone, but you should have obeyed me."

"That is kind of you. I do appreciate your concern. I should appreciate it even more if you would explain the nature of the danger to me."

"I don't wish to. I wish you to trust me. Don't you understand the need to trust me? Tell me you understand."

She looked at his austere profile and said, "Yes, Douglas, I understand." She returned to her novel.

Douglas brooded in solitary silence for nearly an hour. Then he called out the window of the carriage for John Coachman to stop. They were deep in the country. There were no people about, no dwellings, no cows, nothing of any particular interest, just trees, blackberry bushes, and hedge rows.

Alexandra looked up, alarm in her eyes.

"No, it's just that I imagine you would like to stretch a bit, perhaps relieve yourself, in the woods yon."

She did wish to relieve herself, but she imagined that it was Douglas who had the need as well and thus the reason for their stopping.

He helped her down, clasping his hands around her waist, swinging her to him, hugging her close for a brief moment, then setting her on her feet. "Go to the maple copse. Be brief and call if you need me. French isn't necessary, but if you would like to, I shall be listening."

Alexandra smiled at him, saying nothing, and

gave him a small wave as she walked into the midst of the maple trees. It was silent in the wood, the maple leaves thick and heavy, blocking out the sunlight. She was quickly done and was on the point of returning to Douglas, when, quick as a flash, a hand went over her mouth and she was jerked back violently against a man's body.

"This time I've got you," the man said, and she recognized Georges Cadoudal's voice. "This time I'm going to keep you." She had neither Douglas's pistol nor James the footman nor John Coachman. But she had Douglas if only she could free herself for just a moment, for just a brief instant.

She bit his hand and his grip relieved for just a moment. A scream was ready to burst from her mouth when she heard the whoosh then felt something very hard strike her right temple. She went down like a stone.

Douglas was pacing. It had been a good ten minutes since she'd walked into the maple wood. Was she ill? He fretted, then cursed, then walked swiftly toward the wood, calling, "Alexandra! Come along now! Alexandra!"

Silence.

He shouted, *"Aidez-moi! Je veux aller à Paris demain avec ma femme!"* Even as he shouted that he wanted to go to Paris on the morrow with his wife, he felt his muscles tensing, felt his mouth go dry with fear.

There was more silence, deep, deep silence.

He ran into the woods. She was gone. He looked

closely, finally seeing where two people had stood. There'd been no struggle. There hadn't been a sound. Georges had taken her and he'd either killed her or knocked her unconscious. No, if he'd killed her, he would have left her here. Douglas continued his search. He quickly found where a horse had stood, tethered to a yew bush. He saw the horse's tracks going out of the woods, saw that the hooves were deeper because the animal was now carrying two people.

He had no horse. There was only the carriage. He couldn't follow. It was another hour before the carriage bowled into Terkton-on-Byne and he was able to obtain a horse that wasn't so old and feeble it swayed and groaned when it moved.

He was furious and he was scared. He was back at the maple wood in half an hour and he was tracking the other horse within another ten minutes.

He prayed it wouldn't rain but the building gray clouds overhead didn't look promising. Cadoudal was heading due south, toward Eastbourne, directly on the coast. Was he intending to take her to France? Douglas's blood ran cold.

It began to rain two hours later. Douglas cursed, but it didn't help. The tracks quickly disappeared, but he had this feeling that Georges, the brilliant strategist, wasn't going to have an easy time of it with Alexandra. She wouldn't swoon; she'd try her best to get away from him and that frightened him more than soothed him. Cadoudal wasn't used to having anyone go against him; he was unpredictable; he could be vicious. Douglas plowed forward toward Eastbourne.

Just before he reached the town, soaked to his skin and trembling with cold, he knew that it would be next to impossible to find Cadoudal by himself. He would need much more than luck; he would need help. He needed many men to scour the inns and the docks and check into all the ships' passages.

He was tired, exhausted really, and knew that there was simply nothing more he could do. Yet he still rode into Eastbourne and stopped at three inns. None recognized his descriptions, that or they'd been paid by Georges to lie. Defeated, he mounted his horse, more exhausted than he was, and rode the fifteen miles to Northcliffe Hall.

Hollis took one look at His Lordship and called immediately for his valet. Douglas was bundled off to his bedchamber and put into a warm dressing gown. Hollis then deemed it appropriate for him to receive family, beginning with himself.

He said, "John Coachman told us what happened. I've sent out word and there are thirty men ready to do your bidding. You have but to give me instructions."

Douglas stared at his butler and wanted to fling his arms around the man. He said instead, his voice slow and slurred with fatigue, "Georges Cadoudal has her, Hollis, and I fear that he has already taken her to France. I did track him nearly to Eastbourne but it began to rain. I had no luck at the local inns."

Hollis patted his shoulder as if he were a lad of ten again. "No trouble, my lord. You will provide me with a description of this Cadoudal and I shall give it to all the men. They can be off within the hour. As for you, you will rest before you leave this chamber."

Douglas wanted to resist but he was so weary he merely nodded.

"I will bring you food and some nice brandy. Your brain will commence to work again very soon."

So it was that twenty-two men fanned out toward Eastbourne within thirty minutes, such an efficient general was Hollis.

He said to Douglas, "I also sent word to Lord Rathmore. I expect him shortly. His Lordship has never let you down before, you know."

Douglas grunted and sipped at the stomach-warming brandy. He'd eaten his fill, the fire in the fireplace was warm and soothing. He leaned back in his chair and closed his eyes. He slept deeply for an hour undisturbed, awoke and was greatly refreshed.

He opened his eyes to see Sinjun standing by his chair. For an instant he didn't remember and said, "Hello, brat. Where is Alexandra?"

The truth slammed through him and Sinjun watched as he paled.

"I'm sorry, Douglas. Despite what Mother says, I will accompany you to search for her. Shall I notify Tysen?"

"No, leave him be at Oxford." Douglas rose

and stretched. "I don't believe this," he said to no one in particular.

"It's late, Douglas. Too late really for you to set out again. 'Tis nearly midnight."

"There are twenty-two men out searching, Sinjun. I must join them." He paused and gently cupped her face in his palm. "I thank you for wishing to come, yet I must ask you to remain here and run things. You know Mother . . . well, I want to be assured that all will be in readiness for Alexandra's return."

Douglas rode from Northcliffe Hall toward Eastbourne. It had stopped raining, thank the benevolent Lord, and there was a half-moon to light the way. He met McCallum, his head stable lad, at the Drowning Duck Inn on the docks in Eastbourne.

"Ah, Your Lordship needs a pint. Sit down and I will tell you what we've learned. I've made this inn a headquarters and each thirty minutes a group of fellows come to report their progress to me. That's right, drink your ale and sit down. Now just listen, my lord."

At two o'clock in the morning, five men trooped into the taproom to report that Cadoudal and Her Ladyship had taken a packet to Calais. Unfortunately they couldn't follow because of the contrary tides and the storm that was now blowing in. There was nothing they could do until the weather cleared and the tide changed.

Douglas told McCallum to send the men home. He arrived back at Northcliffe Hall at four o'clock in the morning.

He found himself going into Alexandra's bedchamber. He lay down on her bed in the darkness, staring up at the ceiling, exhausted but wide awake. He remembered every harsh word he'd ever said to her. He remembered the hurt in her eyes when he'd spoken of Melissande and how she would have acted the lady and done as her husband told her.

He felt pain wash through him, deep aching pain and an emptiness that was at once unusual yet not unexpected, not now, now that he'd finally come to realize that he couldn't live without his wife.

He heard her speaking French, saw her sitting at his desk, looking so very young, her voice clear and precise, her accent atrocious. He smiled even as the pain ebbed and flowed deep inside him.

He would find her; he had to. He couldn't now imagine facing a life without her.

The following day the storm had become a gale. No one was going anywhere. Rain splattered the windowpanes, and thunder shook the earth. Tree branches on the poplars were pressed nearly to the ground by the force of the wind. Douglas prayed that Georges had gotten Alexandra to France safely. He laughed harshly even as he prayed for that.

As for his mother, Lady Lydia sensed that the upstart wife who had been unknown to her son before she'd thrust herself into their lives had shifted in his regard. She wasn't stupid; she kept such thoughts as let the twit stay gone behind her teeth. As for Sinjun, she tried to keep her brother occupied.

It was no good. The storm raged outside and Douglas raged inside. Even Hollis was looking thin about the mouth. The entire household was tense, silent.

That night Douglas slept in Alexandra's room. He slept deeply simply because Hollis had slipped laudanum in his wine. He dreamed of Alexandra and she was standing there at the stables, laughing, patting her mare's nose all the while, telling Douglas that she loved him, loved him, loved him . . .

And then he was awake and Alexandra was standing there beside the bed, speaking to him.

CHAPTER 22

He stared then blinked rapidly. It wasn't so very dark in the bedchamber and that was surely strange for it had been black as pitch when he'd gone to bed. But no, there she was, standing next to the bed, and he could see her clearly, too clearly really, and she was smiling gently down at him, saying, "She is all right." But she hadn't really said anything, had she? Yet he'd heard those words clearly in his mind.

It wasn't Alexandra. He reached out his hand and she stepped back very quickly, yet she hardly seemed to move, but he knew that he'd touched her sleeve, though he'd felt nothing, just the still air.

He felt a deep strangling fear, fear of the unknown, fear of ghosts and goblins and evil monsters that lived in cupboards and came out at night to bedevil little boys.

"No," Douglas said. "No, you're not bloody real. I'm worried sick and my mind has dished you up to torment me, nothing more, nothing, damn you!"

Her hair was long and straight and so light a blond that it was white, and the gown was billowing gently around her yet the air was still and heavy with the weight of the storm. He had, of course, seen her before, rather his mind had produced her before with a goodly amount of fanfare. She'd come to him that long-ago night when Alexandra had tried to escape him. She would have succeeded in escaping him had his mind not brought *her* to him.

Suddenly, without warning, Douglas saw Alexandra in his mind's eye. She was in a small room lying on a narrow cot. Her gown was wrinkled and torn. Her hair was straggling around her face. She was pale but he saw no fear. Her wrists and ankles were tied with rope. She was awake and he could practically see her thinking, plotting madly for a way to escape, and that made him smile. She had guts. Then he saw just as clearly the small cottage where she was and the village. It was Etaples.

Georges Cadoudal had a sense of irony.

He said aloud, his voice low and slightly blurred, "This isn't possible. You're not real. But how . . ."

"The storm will be gone early in the morning." The words swirled and eddied in his mind. She was leaving, gently and slowly she backed away and she was smiling at him and nodding slightly, moving backward, always moving, more like floating, and then she was simply gone.

Douglas refused to accept it. He leapt from the bed and he ran in the direction she'd gone. Nothing. He lit the candle beside the bed and held it up. The room was empty except for him. He was breathing fast, his heart pounding hard with the shock of it, the fear of it.

"You wretched piece of nothing, come back here! Coward! You ridiculous mind phantom!"

There was no sound save the rain beating steadily against the windows and the occasional branch slashing and raking against the glass.

He stood there for a very long time, naked and shivering and wondering. He had a headache.

At dawn the rain had slowed to a drizzle. At seven o'clock, the clouds parted and the sun came out.

Douglas came downstairs, fully dressed, and strode into the breakfast room. He drew up short. Tony Parrish was seated at the breakfast table drinking coffee and eating his way through eggs and bacon and kippers and scones.

He looked up and smiled at his cousin. "Sit down and eat. Then we'll leave. We'll find her, Douglas, don't worry."

"I know," Douglas said and joined him.

Tony waited until Douglas had eaten steadily for several minutes. "What do you mean you know?"

To tell the truth? Ah, no, not the truth, but it would be a treat to watch Tony's face change until he was regarding him like a Bedlamite. He just smiled, saying, "Georges Cadoudal took her to Etaples. We'll leave in just a few more minutes. We'll make the tide and be in France, with luck, in eight hours. Then we'll hire mounts and be in Etaples in the early morning."

"How do you know where she is, Douglas? Did Cadoudal leave a ransom note?"

"Yes," Douglas said and took a bite of toast. "Yes, it was a note. I would have left sooner but the storm prevented it. Is Melissande with you?"

"Yes, she's sleeping."

"Ah."

"While you're eating, tell me about this Cadoudal fellow and why he took Alexandra."

Douglas told him the truth, there was no reason now not to. He didn't tell him of Cadoudal's plan nor his million guineas from the English government to bring Napoleon down, sow insurrection in Paris, and put Louis XVI's brother, the Comte d'Artois, on the throne. But he told him of Janine Daudet and how the woman had told her lover Georges Cadoudal, that he, Douglas, was the father of her child. She'd been too afraid to tell him that it had been General Belesain or one of the men he'd given her to who had impregnated her. And then she couldn't take it back. She hadn't known that Georges would seek retribution until it was too late.

"The woman's mad!" Tony said. "Why should she serve you such a turn, Douglas? Good God, you saved her!"

Douglas toyed with a limp slice of bacon, memory ebbing and flowing in his mind. "It's quite simple, really, from her point of view. I rejected her."

"I don't understand any of this. What the devil

are you talking about?"

But Douglas had pushed back his chair and stood. "I will tell you on the way to Eastbourne."

The air was crisp and cool and a slight breeze blew in their faces. Garth was full of energy and spirits and Douglas had his hands full controlling him. Both men carried pistols and knives. They both wore tall boots and buckskins and capes.

Douglas said finally to Tony, "She believed I didn't want to take her to bed because she'd been turned into a whore by General Belesain. It wasn't true, of course. As for the general, it's quite possible he used her as his own private whore, for visitors, for friends, whoever. He gave her to me for my enjoyment, no reason to believe that he hadn't given her to other men before I arrived. In any case, she was furious and hurt because I wouldn't bed her and she dished me up when she realized she was pregnant."

Tony shook his head. He cursed. Then he frowned, musing aloud, "I wonder why Cadoudal sent you a note. If he wanted retribution why wouldn't he simply take Alexandra and say nothing? He wants money?"

"No. He wants something else."

Tony started to ask what it was the man wanted, saw the closed look on Douglas's face, and held his counsel.

They arrived in Eastbourne in good time. Douglas had hired a weathered but worthy sloop. Their captain cursed the air blue. The crew didn't seem to mind, just went efficiently about their business. They were on their way within two hours. The tide was strong and swift.

They arrived in Calais seven and a half hours later.

She'd fought and struggled when he'd held her in front of him on his horse. He'd struck her with his pistol to keep her quiet. He'd struck her hard so that when she finally came to herself again, she had a deep pounding headache that made her want to retch. She was lying propped up against an oak tree. Since her hands were bound, she determined not to retch. She would be strong; she would control her body. She had scarce time to gather her wits when he was there, beside her, and he was forcing liquid down her throat. Before she lost consciousness she knew she smelled the sea.

She realized once she'd awakened that he'd drugged her. But how long ago? Where had he brought her now? She had no idea where she was, in a small house somewhere, since she was lying on a bed, securely bound, feeling dirty, hungry, and quite thirsty, but where?

She was alone. Any guards he'd left were outside the single door. Her thoughts were muzzy and she closed her eyes to try to regain clarity.

"So, you're awake. I'd hoped I hadn't killed you. I have never been any good guessing at amounts of laudanum. Of course," he added quickly, "I am good at everything else."

She opened her eyes. He was standing beside

the bed, looking down at her. How had he come into the room so quietly? He looked tired, his flesh drawn more tightly over his cheekbones, his eyes more heavily lidded. His black hair was long and needed some soap and water. His clothing was that of an English gentleman, of good quality, but wrinkled and soiled. His expression was chilling. Still, oddly enough, she wasn't afraid, at least not at that moment, for Douglas was safe.

"I'm glad you didn't kill me too. I didn't hear you. You must have cat's feet."

He started, then shrugged. "Yes, I have many talents, and revenge is one that I take very seriously. I have perfected it to a fine art. I am a genius. It is unfortunate that you will never know of my fame, for I am also discreet. I leave nothing to chance, nothing to find, nothing to lead your damned husband to me. Your husband won't find you so you may quash your silly hopes that he will."

Still the fear simply wasn't upon her even though she was flat on her back, lying on a bed, bound. "I will tell you the truth, monsieur. I want only that my husband be safe. He is all that is important to me."

Georges laughed, a mean laugh that made his eyes look as black as satan's. "How very affecting! What a romantic child you are. Well, I imagine that this childish devotion of yours gratifies Lord Northcliffe at the moment. I also imagine that you are pleasing enough to his eye and young enough to give him passing pleasure. Men of his stamp aren't ever satisfied though, even with a little virgin with hero worship in her eyes. He would have played you false, probably by the end of summer."

Alexandra frowned at him. Because she loved her husband he believed her to feel hero worship for him? She wanted to inform him that she wasn't such a silly twit, but she said instead, "You are thinking of Janine."

Again, Georges Cadoudal started. "How do you know of Janine? Did he actually have the arrogance to tell you what he did to her? Did he boast about it? To you? His wife?"

"He told me that he rescued her in France and brought her to England."

"Ha! I trust Douglas Sherbrooke as much as I can trust any ruthless Englishman. He betrayed me. He raped her. That animal who was holding her prisoner gave her to Douglas because he'd won a card game, and he raped her repeatedly, hurting her, ripping her. Then he demanded her cooperation for she is strong, my Janine, and not easily subdued. It was his price for bringing her to safety in England, to me."

"Oh no, Douglas would never do that. He is a gentleman, a man of honor. You are wrong. This Janine lied to you. I wish I knew why she lied, but I don't speak French so I couldn't understand what she was saying to Douglas. I did ask him but he told me it was none of my business."

Georges Cadoudal had planned to ravish this

little pullet, then send her back pregnant to Douglas. He didn't doubt his own virility for a moment. It would not take long. It would be an eye for an eye and then he would continue with his plan to kidnap Napoleon. But she wasn't at all what he expected. He shook his head, remembering how she'd reacted in that damned bookshop, screeching like a banshee in her absurd French. She'd even struck him in the nose with that book of hers. His nose hadn't been broken, but he hadn't liked the humiliation of it nor the pain. He looked at her now, brooding. Why wasn't she crying? Why wasn't she pleading with him to spare her, begging him not to hurt her?

"Just what do you mean you heard her speaking to Douglas?"

"It was at the Ranleaghs' ball. I saw her clutching at Douglas's sleeve. She looked as if she were trying to seduce him. I tried to listen, to eavesdrop if you will, but as I told you, I don't speak French. It was so provoking. I tried to get Douglas to tell me, but he wouldn't. He has too much honor to break a promise. I am very thirsty. May I have some water?"

He did as she wished, simply because she took him so utterly off guard. After he'd unbound her hands, watched her rub feeling back into them, he handed her the mug. He realized what he had done, but it was too late to jerk the mug of water from her hands. It was proof that he'd temporarily lost his control and his dignity and hadn't even realized it until it was too late. She finished it quickly, taking great gulps, so thirsty that water dribbled down her chin. She wiped it away with the back of her hand, then closed her eyes in bliss.

He stared at her and heard himself say, "Do you want more?"

"Yes, please. You are kind."

"Damn you, I'm not kind!" He stomped out of the door, slammed it behind him, and she heard the key grate in the lock. Alexandra would swear that she heard him cursing under his breath. She'd swear she heard at least one *merde.* At least Douglas had evidently taught her one of the most useful of French curses.

The moment she was alone again, the fear, stark and ugly, struck her full force. Lord, what had she done? She'd spoken to him as she would to a vicar, all trusting and confiding. She was a fool. He was probably now plotting how to torture her, to make her pay for what he believed Douglas had done to this Janine woman, the wretched lying hussy. Why had Janine lied like that about Douglas to her lover? After all, he had rescued her. To make him jealous? Surely that was going too far.

Alexandra lay back, closing her eyes, wishing that Douglas had spoken frankly to her so she could use the truth now with Georges Cadoudal. It was another minute before she realized that he had left her hands unbound. She couldn't believe it. She raised her hands and just looked at them.

New energy pounded through her. Alexandra untied the rope about her ankles. She stood and promptly fell back onto the bed. Several minutes of rubbing her ankles, of trying to stand and falling and trying yet again.

And when she could finally walk, she ran on light feet to the door. She knew it was locked but she tried it nonetheless. She turned back to the single window. It was narrow, maybe too narrow for her shoulders and her hips.

She could but try.

Douglas and Tony rode from Calais toward Etaples. The day was warm, the sun bright overhead. It was market day and the roads were filled with open wagons and drays and laden-down donkeys and farmers walking with their produce in bags slung over their shoulders. It would also be market day in Etaples. Perhaps it could be useful if they were forced to escape. Market days always were chaotic. Too, there were all the French soldiers, all the French carpenters and artisans and laborers and ship builders. Cadoudal was mad to have brought her here. It was beyond dangerous. It was foolhardy and it was precisely something that Georges would do. It was like laughing in the devil's face; it was like twitching his forked tail.

Tony said, riding close, "Did this Cadoudal fellow give you precise instructions, Douglas? You appear to know exactly where to go."

"Yes," Douglas said, looking between his

horse's ears, "I know exactly where to go."

"I really don't understand this. What does he want from you?"

Douglas only shook his head. He couldn't get that damned insubstantial ghostly dream out of his mind. And it had been naught but a dream. He realized now that he'd been thinking so deeply, his thoughts so concentrated, about where Cadoudal had taken her, that he himself had come up with the likely solution. For some unknown reason, his mind had insisted upon giving further credence to his own deductions by providing him with a prescient ghost.

Yes, everything fit. Everything, once he knew Cadoudal had taken her to France. Everything, except the absurd ghost, the ridiculous Virgin Bride.

Even the house where he was holding her. It was the grandmother's farmhouse, and Douglas had seen the place. It was ideal for Cadoudal's purposes. Yes, everything fit.

Why the devil would a ghost give a damn about what happened to Alexandra?

He dismissed it; he needed to plan, to decide upon their best strategy. He realized that Tony had asked him another question, one he couldn't answer, one he didn't want to attempt to answer.

It was another hour to Etaples and then another ten minutes to the farmhouse.

Alexandra managed to twist enough to get her shoulders through the dirty open window. Her hips were more of a problem but she finally popped through, falling four feet to land on her face on the muddy ground. She lay there a moment, breathing hard, then lifted her head to get her bearings.

There was a small garden just beyond, filled with weeds and a few surviving vegetables. She was at the back of the farmhouse. There was a stable, dilapidated, with very old shingles hanging off the roof at odd angles. She heard chickens squawking. There was a goat eating what looked to be an old boot not ten feet from her. He chewed and looked at her with complete indifference.

She didn't hear any voices. There was no sign of life.

How long did she have before Georges Cadoudal returned?

That galvanized her. She kept low, skirting the vegetable patch, running toward the straggly stand of trees some thirty feet beyond. She was panting, a stitch in her side, when she slid behind one of the trees, falling to her knees, and peering back toward the farmhouse. She saw nothing except that goat, still chewing on the boot.

Now, where was she? She looked at the sun, hot now in the midday, and gathered her wits together. She wanted to go north to the English Channel. But where the devil was she? Surely not too far away from the sea because she hadn't been unconscious for all that long. Had she?

She realized after five minutes of running that the trees were going to give out. There was nothing northward save an endless stretch of meadow, not even any low bushes, nothing to protect her, to hide her.

She couldn't remain here. It was now or never. She rose and began to run northward.

The sun beat down. She was bareheaded and soon she was light-headed from the heat and from hunger. Her breathing was rough and getting rougher. She was so tired she couldn't imagine being more so, but she forced herself to keep running, even walking quickly as the stitch in her side forced her to hobble like an old woman.

When she heard the horse's hooves pounding behind her, when she felt the earth shaking from the horse's hooves, she wanted to scream with fury, but instead, she just kept running.

She heard his voice and it was loud and mean. "You perfidious female!"

In the next moment, he scooped her up about her waist, bringing her against him and the horse's side.

Alexandra twisted around and struck at his face. She clipped his jaw solidly and knew a flare of success, but he jerked back and her next blow did nothing but glance off his cheek. He shook her like a bundle of rags and threw her facedown over the saddle. His hands were on her back to prevent her from lurching up. "Hold still, damn you!"

Alexandra felt bile rise in her throat. She tasted failure and she tasted fear and her own nausea. She was going to throw up. She tried desperately to control herself, but in the end, she couldn't.

She vomited on the saddle, on his buckskins, on the horse.

The stallion went berserk at her uncontrollable jerking, the horrible retching noises. He reared violently, jerking the reins from Cadoudal's hands, flinging them both onto the ground. Alexandra came up immediately, her arms around herself, jerking and shuddering with dry heaves. Finally, the dreadful cramps stopped and she remained still, on her hands and knees, her head lowered, trying to control her breathing.

Finally she looked over and saw Cadoudal on his side looking at her.

She said, "I'm sorry. I tried to stop it but I couldn't. Is the horse all right?"

He could only stare at her and wonder if he hadn't struck his head when he landed on the ground. He shook his head now as if to verify that his brains were still inside his skull. His horse was grazing some yards away, looking quite unperturbed by all the ruckus.

"The horse looks to be fine, no thanks to you."

Her belly cramped again and she moaned softly, jerking once again with the dry heaves.

She was panting when she said, "I'm glad you didn't feed me. That would have been awful."

"Why are you ill? I didn't hurt you, dammit!"

"I don't know."

Georges Cadoudal rose and dusted himself off. He leaned down, clasped her beneath her arms, and drew her upright. He frowned at her. "You're a frowzy mess. You look like hell. I can't abide a woman who looks like you do."

Alexandra's eyes narrowed. "And you look like a man who's not been outside a brandy bottle in two nights. Ha! Telling me I looked awful!"

Georges Cadoudal laughed.

"Come along. I'm taking you back to the farmhouse."

She had no choice but to follow him. When they reached the horse, the animal slewed its head around and gave her a ruminating look. "I can't," she said, pulling back. "I'll throw up again."

She turned to look up at him. "You wouldn't be so cruel, would you? To make me get on that horse again?"

"I won't throw you across the horse on your stomach. That's what made you sick. If you promise to behave yourself, to just sit in front of me, we'll go slowly."

"All right."

It took only a few moments to return to the farmhouse. Alexandra had felt as if she'd run at least one hundred miles if not more. The stitch in her side was only now easing. With a horse, it took only a few minutes. It wasn't fair.

He dismounted first then lifted her down. "Go into the farmhouse. Drink some water. Sit down. If you so much as show your nose out the door or any of the windows, you will be very sorry."

Had it been one of Douglas's threats, Alexandra wouldn't have paid any attention. However, Georges Cadoudal was an unknown. He was cruel and ruthless and he'd shown himself to be quite determined. It was possible that he planned to kill her. Of course he had given her water to drink. It didn't quite fit together.

She went into the farmhouse, drank a little water, and sat down on one of the rickety chairs.

When he stepped through the door, kicking it closed behind him, she merely looked at him. He had washed his buckskins and the sick odor was no longer clinging to him.

She said, "Are you going to kill me?"

"No."

"What are you going to do to me?"

He eyed her.

"Will you ransom me? Oh, no!" Her face, already pale, was now paper white. And he knew what she was thinking. He would send the Earl of Northcliffe a note and he would come and Georges would kill him. He had never before in his life seen such naked pain. He wouldn't let it touch him. He had seen more death in his lifetime than this tender pullet would in a dozen lifetimes. He'd brought about more deaths than an English regiment.

She rushed into speech. "No, Douglas won't come to me, he won't, I swear it to you. He is in love with my sister, Melissande. He had to keep me, his cousin married me to him by proxy. It was all a horrible mistake. Douglas wants me gone, truly. Please, monsieur. Please, he won't care."

"I don't suppose you can cook? I'll just bet you are one of those utterly useless English ladies who never soiled her hands in her life."

"I am not useless! I am a fine gardener, though." She paused, then continued slowly, "I really can't cook anything that would look toothsome. I am sorry but in truth, I'm not at all hungry."

He grunted, then turned toward the small kitchen set back in the far corner of the room. He said over his shoulder, "Don't move."

She didn't. She sat there staring at the door, at him in the small alcove, at the thick layer of dust on every surface in the room.

"Where are we?" she called out.

"Be quiet."

"I know we're in France."

"How do you know that?"

She hadn't been completely certain, and she was pleased to have her conclusion so easily verified. She had remembered smelling the sea; then deep inside her, she remembered the rocking of a boat.

Some minutes later, he came into the room carrying two plates. One held slices of thick bread, the other a stew of sorts, reeking of garlic. Alexandra nearly gagged.

He said only, "Eat a piece of bread. It will probably settle your guts."

She chewed on the bread, trying to avoid looking at him downing the noxious stew.

The few bites stayed down. She looked toward the small crock of butter but was afraid to smear any on the bread. Georges continued to spoon down the stew.

When she couldn't bear it any longer, she said, "What are you going to do to me?"

He raised his head and simply looked at her. "I'm going to strip off your clothes first and I'm going to bathe you. Then I'm going to rape you as your husband did to my Janine. I will keep you with me until you are pregnant. Then I will send you back to Douglas."

She stared at him. Men were unaccountable. "But," she said, cocking her head to one side, "that doesn't make any sense, does it?"

He flung his spoon against the wall, rising from his chair, and leaning toward her, his palms flat on the rough wooden surface. "You will cease your unexpected prattle! I don't like it. It annoys me. Do you understand me?"

"No, I don't. It seems vastly stupid and just plain dishonorable and ungentlemanly to even consider doing such a thing. To force me? To keep me a prisoner and humiliate me like that? No, it isn't reasonable. Besides, Douglas says it can take a long time to create a babe. Will you keep me with you here for the next five years?"

He growled in fury, in frustration. "Damn you, beg me not to do it!"

She stared at him.

"Ah, be quiet!"

She was still quiet.

He said, "I am going to fetch you some bath-water now. I want you sweet-smelling when I take you."

She couldn't allow him to do that. She knew she wouldn't allow him to do that. The only problem was how to stop him. He was the stronger; he had hit upon this revenge and she realized that he was a man, who, once committed to a goal, couldn't be easily swerved from his set course. The thought of five years in her company didn't even seem to deter him.

What to do?

The main street of Etaples was crammed with stalls with people hawking everything from potatoes to blackberries. Tony and Douglas dismounted, leading their horses, pressing always forward.

Douglas cursed. They should have skirted Etaples but no, he'd thought he'd take a good look around in case they needed to hide here. How could he have forgotten the utter confusion and madness of market day?

It took twenty minutes and by the end of it, Tony was chewing on an apple and Douglas was eating a carrot.

"Well, we did need to eat," Tony said.

Douglas cursed again.

"Not long now. Er, Douglas, you're certain she will be here at this farmhouse?"

"She will be there."

Douglas dismounted and purchased apples from a farmer. He threw one to Tony. "Eat your fill, cousin."

They continued on their way.

—

"You will take off those clothes or I will rip them off you."

She didn't disbelieve him, but neither could she imagine simply stripping down to her skin in front of him. He wasn't Douglas. No one was Douglas.

The tub of water was behind her, steam rising because he'd heated the water. It had taken a good half-hour but she hadn't managed to come up with a plan to escape him.

"Your face is filthy."

"I landed on my nose when I wriggled out of that window."

"Take off your damned clothes."

She was mute; she just shook her head.

He actually sighed. He looked unhappy. He looked uncertain. Then, he was on her and she fought him, indeed she fought him, kicking his shin and making him grunt in pain, but in but a few minutes she was naked and trembling, her clothing shredded and strewn on the floor around her.

"There." He lifted her under her arms and set her down into the tub of water. He handed her a cloth and a bar of soap. "Bathe. Do a good job of it."

He seemed completely disinterested in her. She was so relieved, so surprised, she said nothing, merely stared at him. After all, hadn't her mother assured her that once men saw a female form, they went berserk? Douglas had, but it had required several viewings before he had succumbed. Perhaps it took men time to get used to her before their animal urges consumed them. She prayed it would take Georges Cadoudal much, much longer. A decade perhaps.

"Wash your hair as well. It looks hellish. I don't like red hair on a woman."

Good, she thought and said, "All right."

He looked at her, that brooding look that raised more questions in her mind than answered them, then left her, cursing under his breath.

Alexandra bathed.

Unfortunately she was so exhausted, she fell asleep. She awoke with a start when Georges Cadoudal said from above her, "Damn you, the water's nearly cold. You fell asleep? That isn't normal, by God. You should be scheming something, you should be terrified of me, you should be screaming, piercing screams for help. Are you finished?"

She shook her head and pressed herself deeper into the water.

He frowned down at her as one would to a child. He grabbed the wet cloth, soaped it thoroughly, flattened it against her face, and rubbed vigorously.

She tried to yell but only got soap in her mouth for her efforts. Then she felt his hands on her breasts and froze.

CHAPTER 23

"Lo and behold," Georges said, staring down at her breasts. He shook his head even as she was trying to shrink away from his hands, but yet he was scowling. It was as if he were forcing himself to look at her. "You are well endowed. It is amazing. I should have remarked these breasts of yours before. I am disturbed that I didn't, but I am too tired, too concerned with all my future plans, and you have been naught but a vexing burden, but still —" He shook his head, frowning at himself.

Then he appeared to get himself well in hand. He rose and tossed her the cloth.

"Finish bathing and don't go to sleep again or it will be the worse for you."

She did, quickly. It was as if he had been watching her even though she knew he was in the other room, for the moment she stepped out of the tub, he was there, and he tossed her a thin ragged towel. She quickly wrapped it around her.

"Your hair," he said, and tossed her the other towel. "Did I tell you I didn't like red hair on a woman?"

"Yes, you were most specific. Could you leave please, monsieur?"

"No. I must look my fill at you. It will excite me, or it should, and allow me to get this over with quickly."

"I would prefer that you wouldn't."

He shrugged, an elaborate Gallic shrug that meant nothing and everything and she knew exactly what it meant.

She managed to get the towel firmly wrapped around herself, then took the other towel, more a rag really, to her hair.

He said, "Come into the other room. I've lit a fire. It is summer yet it is cold. I thought the fire would heat my blood as well as the room. I must try; it was my vow to myself."

She followed him into the outer room, her eyes on the front door.

"Even if you managed to escape me," he said dispassionately, "I can't imagine you running down the road wearing only a towel, your feet bare."

"You're right," she said and walked to stand in front of the fireplace. It was warm and it felt wonderful. She stood there, rubbing her hair, rubbing and rubbing until it hurt, wanting to put him off.

"Enough," he said finally, but he didn't sound or look like a man who wanted to ravish her. He sounded tired and angry and distracted.

She turned slowly and stared at him. He stared back, not yet moving. He opened his mouth, then closed it. He said something then in French and thrashed his fingers through his hair. "Well," he said finally in English, "damn you. Why you? Douglas should have to pay, curse his foul hide, but I cannot, I —"

She wanted to defend her husband, but what came out of her mouth was a sharp cry of pain. She pressed her hands to her belly. The cramp hardened and twisted and made her stagger against a chair. She was panting when it released her, only to cry out when it struck again.

"What the devil is wrong with you? You can't be ill. I don't like it."

Her face was white, her mouth twisted with pain. "You shouldn't have any more cramps, it's ridiculous! You're not on the horse. You ate only the bread I gave you. Stop it, do you hear me? I told you I don't like this."

The cramp eased and she felt hot sticky liquid between her legs. She looked down to see rivulets of blood running down her legs. She raised her head to look at him.

"What is wrong with me? What is happening?" Then she cried out, falling to her knees to the floor. Tears were hot on her face; the blood was hot on her legs. The pain was building and building.

She fell back, drawing her legs up, hugging her belly, crying, trying to control the pain, but it was sharper and harder and she couldn't do anything save lie there.

Georges was on the floor beside her. He tugged

the towel open and saw the blood on her thighs, the deep red streaks on the white towel. He swallowed. He didn't know what to do.

The door flew open to the farmhouse and Douglas came through, pistol in hand. "Get off her, you damned bastard! I'll kill you, you filthy sod!"

Tony was right behind Douglas. He saw Alexandra's white body, saw Cadoudal over her and felt himself raw with fury. Had the bastard already raped her? Oh God, she was bleeding, so much blood, too much blood. Had he brutalized her?

Georges Cadoudal whipped about, saw Douglas, and relief and hope flooded his face. But he had no time to say anything, for Douglas lunged across the room, jerked him away from Alexandra, and slammed his fist into his face. Georges yelled. Douglas struck him again, pummeling his ribs. Georges didn't fight back; he only tried to protect himself.

"Douglas, hold!"

Douglas hit him again before Tony's voice got through to him.

"Douglas, stop it now! Alexandra, she's hurt!"

Douglas reared up, his right fist hovering over Georges's nose, still straddling him, but looking at his wife. She was sprawled on her back and she was panting with pain and there was blood, so much blood.

His fist lowered and Georges quickly said, "No, no, don't strike me again. I can't remain defensive too much longer. I am a man, and cannot continue to allow this. Ah, but thank God it's you, Douglas. Quickly, quickly! She is having a miscarriage. Dammit, I don't know what to do. I don't want her to die. Ah, *mon Dieu!* Help me!"

"She's *what?*" Douglas's fist was not six inches from Georges's face.

Alexandra moaned and tried to draw her legs up.

"Look at her, Douglas. I didn't rape her. I swear I wouldn't have raped her in any case. Look, damn you! She is losing a child!"

Douglas took in the truth of the situation in that moment. He roared into action, rolled off Georges in an instant, and was on his knees beside his wife. "Georges, heat water and get clean clothes, immediately! Tony, go into the other room and fetch the mattress off the bed. We'll keep her here in front of the fire."

Both men were instantly in action although Georges did stagger a bit. Both were grateful to have something to do, anything.

Douglas was at his wife's side. She was moaning, her head thrashing back and forth as the cramps seized her. When they eased, she lay there panting, her eyes closed, gulping down deep breaths.

"Alexandra," he said, taking her face between his hands. "Alexandra."

She opened her eyes and stared up at him. To his astonishment, she smiled up at him. "I knew you would come. Please help me, Douglas. It hurts so very badly. Please make it stop."

"I'll help you, love." He picked her up in his

arms and gently laid her onto the mattress Tony had laid close to the hearth.

"Now, listen to me. You're losing a babe. You are not so very far along so this will be over quickly, I promise you. Just hold on, love. Now, I'm going to press these cloths against you to get this bleeding stopped. No, don't fight the pain. That's right, hold my hand, squeeze as hard as you want to, that's right."

He felt a shot of pain go up his arm, her grip was so hard.

He prayed it would be over soon. He knew little to nothing about miscarriage, a subject never spoken about in a gentleman's presence.

Suddenly, her body stiffened, her back arching off the mattress, and she yelled. He felt the hot blood coming from her and it soaked through the cloth and onto his hand.

She looked up at him, her eyes dumb, then her head lolled back. She was unconscious.

Douglas kept the pressure against her.

"Here is the hot water," Georges Cadoudal said. "God, is she all right, Douglas?"

"She'll be all right. I'll strangle her if she isn't."

Georges looked oddly at him. "She told me you wouldn't come after her. She told me you loved her sister. She knew you wouldn't care what I did to her."

"She's sometimes quite wrong," Douglas said, not looking at Georges, not looking away from her face.

"I thought as much. She's unusual." He sighed, running his hands through his hair. "I couldn't have raped her, dammit. I'm telling you the truth. Damn, I could kill a hundred men without blinking an eye, but this one . . . I'm sorry I stole her, Douglas. It was wrong of me. You didn't rape Janine, did you?"

"No."

"The little one here was certain you hadn't. You're a man of honor, you see."

Douglas merely smiled.

Tony brought a blanket and covered her. He laid his palm on her brow. She was cool to the touch.

Georges Cadoudal turned away. To Douglas's astonishment, he looked as if he were in pain. He said, as if in confession to a priest, "I brought this on her."

Douglas looked at him, his mouth tight. "Tell me what happened."

"She escaped me. I'd given her water to drink and had forgotten to tie her hands again. She disconcerted me. I don't know how she did it but she managed to wriggle through that narrow window in the bedchamber. She landed on her face in the mud outside. She ran, she really did, ran and ran, but I chased her down. I threw her over my horse's back. She vomited."

Tony said, "I have been told that a miscarriage is a very natural thing. If a man's seed isn't meant to remain planted in a woman's womb, her body will expel it. It just happens sometimes."

"No, if I hadn't kidnapped her, it wouldn't have happened."

"That's right," Douglas said, not looking up from his wife's pale face. "I plan to beat the living hell out of you for that."

"For God's sake, Douglas," Tony said, "no one will ever know if he's to blame or not. You've already thrashed him. What's happened can't be changed. She will be all right and you will have your heir. Besides, if Cadoudal really is to blame for it, he will go to hell and the devil will punish him throughout eternity."

"I doubt the devil will have time to punish Georges for this particular infraction. There are too many others." Douglas paused, then added, "Another thing, Tony, I don't give a damn about any precious heir." Douglas stared silently toward Georges. "If she dies, I will kill you. Then the devil can have his go at you."

"I accept that you would have to try," Georges said and shrugged. His left eye was already nearly closed from the blow Douglas had given him.

Tony said nothing. Georges moved over to the dirty front window of the farmhouse. Several moments passed in silence. Then Georges cursed and cursed again. Tony and Douglas looked up. Georges jerked open the front door.

Janine Daudet stood there, dusty and disheveled and alone, a pistol in her hand.

She grabbed Georges, shook him, yelling at him all the while in French. "Tell me you didn't ravish her, tell me —" Her voice dropped into stunned silence. "Douglas, you are here?"

"Yes."

"Who is that man?"

"He is my cousin, Lord Rathmore."

"Ah, the woman, your wife. What is wrong with her? All that blood . . . oh God, Georges, you didn't murder her?"

"No," Douglas said calmly. "She miscarried."

Tony watched the woman keen softly to herself, watched Georges Cadoudal gather her into his arms and attempt to soothe her. He gently removed the pistol from her hand and slipped it into his pocket. The woman was saying over and over, "It is all my fault, my fault, my fault."

"Enough of this caterwauling!" Douglas yelled. "Be quiet, Janine. It is certainly your fault that Alexandra is here, scared out of her mind I'll wager, because Georges threatened to rape her, as revenge for what I supposedly did to you."

"Ha," said Georges. "She wasn't scared, Douglas. She has steel, that one, all the way up her backbone. And she talks like no woman I have ever known in my life. She made me feel like a naughty schoolboy who should have a switch taken to his backside." But he knew he'd frightened her and he was sorry for it, but he simply couldn't bring himself to admit it aloud because that would make it real and that would make the guilt weigh so heavily upon him that he didn't think he could stand it. He didn't understand it. He'd killed with no remorse in the past and he would do whatever necessary in the future to bring the Bourbons back to the French throne. But this one particular woman was different.

"What are you doing here, Janine?"

She raised her head at Douglas's voice. "I had to come when I realized what Georges had done. I had to stop it. I knew I had to tell him the truth."

"And what is the truth, *chérie?*"

Janine pulled away from him, her eyes on her dusty riding boots. "He raped me — no, no, not Douglas — the general. Many times and he made me do humiliating things to him and to other men and he watched many times when he gave me to other men, and always, always, Georges, he threatened to kill my grandmother if I refused to obey him. The child I carry won't know his father for I don't know. Oh God!"

There was utter silence except for her low sobs.

"Why did you blame Lord Northcliffe?" Georges said. Tony started at the austere formality of his tone and his words.

"He was kind to me."

"A noble reason, surely!"

"It was close enough," Douglas said smoothly. "She feared you wouldn't want her if you knew what General Belesain had done to her. I was a better father for her child than any of those bastards."

Georges hissed through his front teeth, "All those bloody men should die."

"Quite possibly," Douglas agreed.

Tony said after a moment of tense silence, "All this is quite interesting, but isn't the scoundrel responsible for all this misery enjoying himself at this moment? All these bloody unknown men will remain unknown. Why don't we go teach this Belesain fellow a lesson he won't ever forget? Why shouldn't he be the one to pay for all this misery?"

Georges Cadoudal didn't often smile. He was merciless in achieving the ends for the causes he believed in. He couldn't afford softness and all lightness and humor had fled from his life many years before when he'd watched his mother and father and two sisters murdered by Robespierre. He was a man committed; a man committed didn't smile.

He smiled more widely.

"Jesus," he said. "How should I kill him? There are many methods, you know. Many, indeed. I have quite a range, a lot of choice. Shall it be slow? Shall we make him scream and plead and beg to know the final moment of his miserable life? Shall I use the garrote?" He rubbed his hands together, his eyes alight, his mind racing with plans and strategies.

Douglas said, "You forget that he is surrounded by more soldiers than I could count. He lives in a fortress. He has guards accompany him everywhere. He also knows me by sight and you and Janine."

They brooded in silence.

Tony said, "He's never seen me before."

"Oh no," Douglas said. "This isn't your fight, Tony."

"I don't know about that, it —"

Alexandra moaned softly; she opened her eyes to see Douglas over her, smiling gently. She felt his hand pressed against her. "Am I going to live, Douglas?"

He leaned down and lightly kissed her mouth. He said very quietly, "Oh yes. I have missed your impertinent tongue, madam. I have missed your pathetic flights of French. Most of all I have missed holding you against me."

She was crying; she didn't want to but the tears fell and trickled down the sides of her face. He wiped them away with his fingers. "Hush, love, I don't want you to make yourself ill. Hush. Now, just hold still. Are you warm enough?"

She nodded, gulping.

"I will continue the pressure for some more minutes. Then I'll bathe you and make you more comfortable."

"I lost our child. I lost your heir, Douglas, and that is all you wanted from a wife, from me. I did promise to be a brood mare but I've failed. I am so very sorry, but —"

"You will be quiet. It happened and that is that. I want you to be all right. You are what is important. Do you understand me? I'm not lying. It's the truth."

He hated the pain in her eyes, the pain of her loss, the pain of what she believed to be an irreparable loss to him. He would convince her otherwise. And eventually she would believe him. He started to say something but saw that she was no longer crying. Her eyes had narrowed. It was remarkable how she could be crying pathetically one moment and looking mean as hell the next. "What is that French hussy doing here? Did she follow you again, Douglas? I won't have it, I tell you! Tell me what to say to her, please."

"All right. Say, '*Je suis la femme de Douglas and je l'aime. Il est à moi.*' "

She looked at him suspiciously.

"You are telling her that you are my wife and that you love me. You are telling her that I belong to you."

"Say it again."

He did, slowly.

Alexandra opened her mouth and shouted the words to Janine Daudet.

There was stunned silence, then Georges said thoughtfully, "I prefer your rendition of *merde,* I think. It brought the entire Hookams bookshop your English aristocracy love so well to a standstill."

Douglas smiled, something he wouldn't have thought possible. As for Alexandra, she was still thin-lipped as she looked at Janine Daudet. "Tell her, Douglas, tell her that if she ever again lies about you, I will make her very sorry."

Douglas didn't hesitate. He spoke rapid French to Janine. She stared from him to Alexandra, then nodded slowly.

Georges was rubbing his jaw as he said to Douglas, "Thankfully you didn't break it."

"You deserve that I thrash you within an inch of your life. However, I agree with Tony. I want to see Belesain pay for his crimes."

"Your eye is quite black," Janine said. "Did she do this to you?"

"No, but it doesn't sound odd to think that she would be quite capable of blacking both my eyes."

It was one o'clock in the morning. There was no moon. Dark clouds hid the few stars that would have shed light on the three men as they ran, bent low, from the shelter of one tree to the next.

There were no lights coming from the mayor's charming house in Etaples. There were four guards patrolling the perimeter. They were bored and tired and they spoke in low voices, trying to keep themselves awake.

The three men were on their haunches not fifteen yards from the guards. Douglas said low, "Tony, take down the one on the right. You take the one at the far corner over there, Georges."

"But that leaves two of them," Tony said.

"Don't worry, they're mine," Douglas said and he rubbed his hands together. He saw that Georges would disagree and quickly said, "No, I am a better fighter in the dark. Obey me in this. Once we're away from France, you can kill entire battalions, Georges."

Georges didn't like it. He was always the one in control, the commander of any and all raids. But he owed Douglas; he also respected his abilities, and thus held his tongue. Further, it hurt to talk because Douglas had hit him so hard in the jaw. Also it was difficult to see clearly. His right eye was now only a tiny slit.

They waited in absolute silence until the four guards were at their farthest points, then they scattered, hunkered down, appearing just shadows in the night.

Douglas planned to take the two remaining guards when they came together. He couldn't wait. He was grinning in the darkness. The dried mud on his face itched but he ignored it. The three of them were dark shadows on this particular night. He watched Tony make his way toward the guard. He remained relaxed. He grunted in satisfaction when Tony brought the man down, his forearm pressed hard into his throat, the only noise the man was making was a soft gurgling sound. As for Georges, he grabbed his guard, twisting his arms behind him and arching his back. He didn't kill him but Douglas knew he wanted to. He was relieved that Georges was sticking to their agreement.

Douglas readied himself. The guards were drawing closer. One was speaking and Douglas heard him say, "Ho, where's Jacques?"

"Probably relieving himself. He drank too much of that cheap wine."

They were nearly together. Douglas was silent

and fast. He was on them before they saw him. He grinned and said in his flawless French, "Good evening, gentlemen!" He sent his right elbow into one man's belly and his left fist went into the other man's throat. He twirled on the balls of his feet, and slammed his foot into one guard's chin while his other hand struck the other guard dead center in his chest. Both fell like stones. Douglas quickly dragged the two men into the bushes and straightened. He gave a soft hooting sound and Georges and Tony were beside him in an instant.

"Well done," Tony whispered. "Remind me not to enrage you ever again, cousin."

Douglas grunted. They quickly tied the men and stuffed gags into their mouths. Douglas then led the way to the side of the house to the salon where he and General Belesain had played the card game so long before. The window was locked. Douglas gently broke it, tapping it lightly with the palm of his hand.

Tony made a cup with his hands and hefted Douglas up. He slithered through the window, dropping lightly onto the carpeted floor. In moments, Tony and Georges were with him.

Silently they made their way up the wide front stairs, shadows against the wall, low and swift.

There was one guard outside General Belesain's bedchamber. He was sprawled against the wall, sound asleep, his pistol on his lap.

Douglas tapped him with the butt of his own pistol over his right temple. He slumped over and lay on his side against the wall.

"Now," Douglas said. Very quietly he turned the knob to the bedchamber door. The door made no sound. Slowly, slowly, he pressed the door inward. It was perfectly silent. He stepped inside.

He looked toward the bed but couldn't make out the general's body. He took another step forward then froze.

"Ah, that's right," the general said low, not an inch from his ear. His pistol was pointed in the middle of Douglas's back.

"Who are you, eh? A thief breaking into this house? A fool, more like. I will see in a moment. You see, I heard you, for I have the insomnia, you know? I heard you; I hear everything."

Douglas didn't move. He didn't hear any noise from Tony or Georges in the hallway not two feet away.

A candlelight flickered and he was momentarily blinded when Belesain thrust it directly in front of his face.

"You," Belesain said and he was shocked. "I don't believe this, it makes no sense. Why are you here?"

Douglas said nothing.

"Ah, it matters not for you will die in any case. There is no reason not to kill you now, save for one small fact you must tell me. There are four guards. I cannot believe that you disabled all of them."

"He didn't," said Tony, and slammed the door into Belesain's arm. The pistol went flying. Douglas turned on his heel and smashed his fist into Belesain's stomach.

The man was wearing only a white nightshirt and presented a perfect target in the dark room.

Georges came through the door and grabbed Douglas's arm. "Now it is my turn," he said and struck the general hard on the jaw. He went down on his hands and knees and remained there, panting hard, moaning softly.

"He has gotten fatter since last I saw him," Douglas said.

"He could be skinny as a post and still be a pig," Georges said, and spit on the general. "Attend me, old man. I am Georges Cadoudal and I am here for retribution. You abused my Janine. You not only kept her prisoner, you raped her and let other men rape her as well."

"Cadoudal," General Belesain said dumbly, looking up. "God, it is you."

"Yes."

Tony looked dispassionately down at the general whose face had turned whiter than his nightshirt in his fear of Georges. "It is your decision, Georges. What do you wish to do with him?"

Douglas frowned. He prayed Georges wouldn't forget his promise not to kill the man. But he wasn't going to count on it. The rage on Georges's face bespoke pain and fury so deep it couldn't be easily assuaged.

The general said, "Your Janine, Cadoudal? I tell you she wasn't your woman. I had no need to ravish her. I offered her favors, jewels, money, and the like and she willingly came to me, willingly came to all the men who came to her room. They all paid her and she —"

Georges kicked him hard in the ribs, knocking him onto his side.

"That wasn't excessively wise of you, General," Douglas said. "I should say that it was rather stupid. Let's get it over with, Georges."

Tony saw that Georges was smiling in the candlelight. It was a terrifying smile.

"You know what they do to pigs, Douglas?"

The general didn't move.

"No," Douglas said, "but I imagine I am quickly to learn."

The general shrieked and tried to scramble away on his hands and knees.

"Hold, old man, or I'll put a bullet through your left calf."

The general stopped. He was panting hard; he was afraid. He'd been stupid to insult Janine. Now he said quickly, "I know you are an ardent Royalist. I know you want Napoleon exiled or assassinated. I can help you. I have information that will aid you. I can —"

Georges interrupted him easily. "Oh no you don't, General. You have nothing for me. I know you, you see. You are a fat bureaucrat who has no talent, but some power unfortunately. You are malignant; you are a parasite. It is true I hate Napoleon but I also hate fools like you who bleed those around them and torture them for their own enjoyment. Now enough. My friends and I don't wish to remain here."

Amongst the three of them, they dragged the general downstairs and out of the mayor's charming house.

They returned to the farmhouse by five o'clock that morning to find Alexandra sitting up, wrapped in a blanket, sipping on a cup of very strong coffee. Across from her, on the floor, sat Janine, her hands and feet securely bound, looking furious. She was cursing loudly, yelling to Georges when he walked through the door. All three men stopped short and stared.

"How could you do this?" Georges asked Alexandra, who looked quite fit, given that she'd looked white as death but hours before.

"I tricked her," Alexandra said. She took another delicate sip of her coffee. "I told her I didn't feel well and when she came to help me — unwillingly, Douglas — I hit her and then I tied her up. She deserves it for what she did to you, Douglas. Tell me you understand."

He couldn't help it. He was laughing. "I understand."

Janine was shrieking now in French.

"She's been doing that since I got her tied up, but you see, since I don't speak French, I cannot understand her. I have no idea what she's saying. Douglas, is she insulting me?"

Douglas grinned at his wife. "She probably started with you. Now she's insulting your grandchildren."

"Actually," Georges said, eyeing his mistress,

"she is now quite fluently attacking your antecedents and all your former pets."

"I say," Tony said, "that we should untie her. She looks quite uncomfortable. What do you say, Alexandra? Do you feel you've punished her enough?"

Alexandra took another long drink of her coffee. "All right," she said at last. "I don't wish to stomp her into the ground, well, I do, but I'm not up to doing it right now, but I wish her to know that I am mean, that I will not tolerate such wretched behavior toward my husband. She will never try to hurt Douglas again. Never."

Douglas turned and said something very rapid in French to Georges. He and Tony both laughed.

"What did you say?" Alexandra asked, her voice filled with suspicion.

"I said," Douglas said very slowly, smiling at his wife, "that once you are fluent in French, I will unleash you on Napoleon himself. Georges agrees that the Corsican upstart wouldn't stand a chance against you."

"I'm not sure," she said, frowning, her voice filled with worry, "you see, I don't think I'm feeling all that well right now at this particular moment. How long will it take me to learn that bloody language?" She paused, her eyes widening on Douglas's face. "Oh dear," she said.

She fainted. The coffee mug fell to the floor. Janine stopped cursing. Both Tony and Douglas were at her side in an instant.

"It shouldn't take her more than three months

to spout French like a trooper," Tony said, as he gently laid two fingers against the steady pulse in her throat. "Stop shaking, Douglas, she'll be fine. It's the excitement, that's all."

CHAPTER 24

The three men and Janine Daudet arrived at precisely six o'clock the following morning at the massive shipbuilding field that would shortly brim with workers, soldiers, sailors, cooks, prostitutes, hawkers of every item conceivable. They hid themselves and waited.

They remained hidden when the cry went up that General Belesain's headquarters had been breached. Guards were wounded and tied up and the general was gone.

There was some discussion as the men moved forward through the wide gates. Then there was utter silence.

At first there weren't more than fifty men and women; their ranks swelled to several hundred, all silent and staring. Then there was a giggle, a shout of laughter. More and more people arrived. The laughter grew. So did the general's curses and his threats, which ranged from cutting off arms and legs to pulling out tongues to flaying off the hide from every man and woman present. The onlookers paid no attention.

A man shouted, "Good Gawd, it's a pig, a big fat general sort of pig!"

A woman yelled, "Look at that little thing of his! Naught but a tiny sausage!"

"Aye, and that belly, bloated with all our local food he's sent his men to steal, the selfish pig!"

"A pig! A pig! Look at the pig!"

Georges looked at Douglas and then to Tony. They didn't have to take care and be silent. The noise was now deafening. They laughed and slapped each other on the back. Janine Daudet was so pleased she even hugged Tony.

General Belesain was standing on a four-foot-high wooden crate. He was tied securely to a pole, his arms pulled back so far that his back was arched, making his fat belly stick out obscenely. He was quite naked. Pig ears that Georges had stolen from a local butcher were tied on his head, a pig's snout tied around his face, poking out over his nose. The rest of him was fat and pink, no embellishments needed.

His men tried to get to him to free him but the crowd held them back. They weren't through with their fun.

Douglas finally motioned for them to leave. Janine said to Georges in some amazement, "You're laughing. I can't believe it. You never laugh."

He turned sober immediately. "I didn't mean to. It isn't well done of me."

Tony said, "A man should laugh; it gives him back his bearings; it makes him realize how absurd life can be."

Douglas said nothing. He wanted only to see his wife. She'd wanted so much to come but he hadn't allowed it. She was too weak. She argued but he held firm. Now he wished he'd carried her here. She would have enjoyed herself immensely.

Now, he thought, he had to get them out of France and back home to England.

Three days later, Douglas, carrying Alexandra in his arms, followed by Tony, strode into Northcliffe Hall.

There was as much bedlam as there'd been the morning of General Belesain's unveiling, only this bedlam was joyous and welcoming. Douglas looked up to see Melissande coming down the wide staircase, looking more beautiful than a flesh-and-blood woman should look, breathstoppingly beautiful actually, but he found that he just smiled toward her. She was looking for Tony, and when she found him, she picked up her skirts to her knees, and ran full-tilt until she could jump into his arms. She screamed at the top of her lungs, "You're safe, damn you! I was so worried, so —" She said no more for Tony was kissing her soundly.

Douglas still smiled.

He looked at his wife and saw that there were tears in her eyes. He was jolted into immediate fear. "You are ill? What is wrong? You have pain?"

She shook her head and wiped her eyes with the heel of her hand.

"Alexandra, we will be attacked by fifty servants, Sinjun, and my mother in under two minutes. Speak to me."

"She's just so beautiful."

"Who? Oh, Melissande. Yes, she is. Who cares?"

She stiffened in his arms.

He started a smile. "Why, you're still jealous."

"No, damn you!"

"Ah yes, you are, you silly chit. Answer me this, Alex. Can Melissande speak French?"

"No, she's horrible at languages, her accent even more atrocious than mine, but she paints so well."

"So, she couldn't have tried to save me like you did."

"That has less than nothing to do with naught."

Douglas merely continued his teasing grin. "I wonder how one would say that in French. Listen well, Alex —"

"You called me Alex!"

"Yes, certainly. If you prefer sweetheart, you will doubtless hear that as well. And stubborn and cherished and willful and wonderful. Now, listen to me. I think your sister is beautiful. Nothing new in that. But she isn't you. No, it doesn't matter now. What matters, to Tony, is that she is improving by veritable leaps and bounds under his tender tutelage. As Tony told me yesterday, one day soon her character just might begin to approach her beauty."

"Really, Douglas?"

"Really what?"

"Cherished?"

He kissed her. He heard laughter and slowly raised his head. There was Sinjun grinning at him like a fool. His mother stood behind her, her mouth pursed.

His mother called out, "Where have you been, Douglas? What is going on here? I demand to know now. Why are you carrying her?"

"Soon, Mother. As for the little one here, she has been ill."

"She looks quite well to me. Why is she wrapped in a blanket?"

"Because," Douglas said, walking toward his mother. "Because she's quite naked beneath."

"Douglas! You know that's not true." She was wearing one of Janine Daudet's gowns actually, a quite ugly gown really. Doubtless Janine's revenge for the coshing Alexandra had given her. Her feet, however, were quite bare and stuck out from the blanket. Douglas hadn't wanted to slow to buy her shoes. She hadn't argued. It was quite pleasant to be carried by her husband.

"Yes, but if she thinks you're naked, I'll get to escape with you all that much more quickly."

"What happened?" Sinjun asked.

"We will cover all that later." Douglas turned and raised his voice, saying, "We are all alive and well and home to stay. Thank all of you for being concerned."

The servants cheered. Hollis stood proudly, his

arms crossed over his chest. Alexandra felt herself swelling with relief. Perhaps everything would be all right. Perhaps even her mother-in-law would come about. Perhaps Douglas really did cherish her. Perhaps.

Douglas carried her to his bedchamber. He kissed her, then eased her down to sit on the edge of the bed, pulling the blanket off her. "Mother doubtless believes you are a loose woman, that you must have burned your clothes to compromise me. I will tell her that I am already thoroughly compromised, that you have seduced me endlessly and I am used to it, that I can't do without your charms or your company. There was nothing more for you to do."

She was staring up at him, not moving, just sitting there, her legs dangling over the side of the bed, wearing Janine's gown that was too long and bagged around her.

She moistened her lips.

"Do you cherish me, Douglas? Perhaps just a little bit?"

"Perhaps," he said.

He walked, smiling to himself, into her adjoining bedchamber, soon to return with a nightgown. "Come, let's get you into this. You need to rest now."

He pulled the gown over her head, found himself staring at her breasts, then swallowed and quickly pulled the fine linen nightgown over her head, smoothing it down her body. "There." He put her between the covers, then sat down beside her and arranged her hair on the pillow even as he said thoughtfully, "Our marriage hasn't been so very smooth thus far. Do you think perhaps that you could moderate your actions? Perhaps think a bit before you hare off to do something outrageous? Like running away from me and becoming ill? Like getting yourself kidnapped and taken to a foreign country? Like trying to save me when you are really the one in jeopardy?"

She stared up at him, perfectly still as he continued to artfully arrange her hair on the pillow.

"I don't know," she said finally. "You are very important to me, Douglas."

He liked the sound of that. He leaned down and kissed the tip of her nose. "I have decided that if I keep you in bed for, say, three hours a day — not to mention the nights of course — you just might be too busy focusing on me or too busy recovering from lovemaking to bring gray hairs to my head."

"And would you also be too busy recovering from our lovemaking?"

"Never too busy to cease thinking about the next time I would haul you off to bed and have my way with you. You already occupy a great deal of my poor brain."

He frowned then as she remained silent. "Not just haul you off to bed to make love to you. I fancy also I'll haul you off to the stable, to the floor in the library on that soft rug in front of the fireplace. Perhaps also in the breakfast room with the morning sun streaming in on us and then on the formal dining table. You could clutch that ghastly epergne while I made you scream —"

She laughed and poked his arm.

"Tell me you love me, Alexandra."

"I love you, Douglas."

"Do you agree that a man needs to hear that every day of his life?"

"I am in full agreement."

"Good. Now, wife, I want you to rest. I will see to the family, censor our tale just a bit unless Sinjun has already pried all the facts from Tony, and store up all the recent gossip to tell you later on."

He kissed her mouth. He'd intended only a light, sweet kiss, but her arms went around his shoulders and she held him to her and parted her lips.

"You came after me," she said into his mouth. "You were worried about me."

"Naturally," he said, kissing her nose, her lips, her chin, his breath warm against her skin. "You are my wife, I love you, I will even go so far as to say that cherishing has a good deal to do with it. Are you satisfied now?"

"Do you know that a wife must needs hear that every day of her life?"

"I'm not surprised. No, not at all." He kissed her again, tucked the covers about her shoulders, and left her alone to rest.

Two weeks later in the late afternoon, Douglas

came into their bedchamber. Alexandra looked up from her mending, smiling automatically. Good Lord, she loved him so very much.

"What do you have there?" she asked, trying not to look so besotted.

He was frowning. "I had to know," he said more to himself than to her. "I just had to know so I went looking in Sinjun's bedchamber." He spread out on her lap the items he'd found in the back of Sinjun's armoire.

Alexandra gasped. "It's a wig! Goodness, it looks like the Virgin Bride's hair! And that gauzy gown! Douglas, you can't mean it, no, surely not, I —"

"Can't believe that Sinjun was our ghost? Evidently so. Yes, she most certainly was. Here's the proof."

But Alexandra was thinking furiously, trying to remember when she'd first seen the ghost. She remembered quickly enough. Sinjun had been in London. She wasn't wrong. She started to tell Douglas when she saw that he was staring fixedly at the east windows. He was somewhat white about the mouth. He looked tense and stiff, his back and shoulders rigid. She said nothing.

Finally, he said firmly, turning back to her, "It was Sinjun all along. Just my little sister playing at being a ghost because she wanted to stir things up, wanted to have some fun at our expense."

Alexandra was shaking her head. She opened her mouth but Douglas raised his hand.

"Yes, it was just Sinjun, nothing more, nothing extraordinary, nothing ghostly. A real live human being, not a willowy phantom, not a creature who speaks but really doesn't but you hear it in your mind. No, nothing like that. It's true. It's very important that it's true. It will remain true. Tell me you understand this, Alexandra."

"I understand."

He kissed her, stood straight again, and said as he stared at the wig and the gown, "I have decided not to say anything about it to Sinjun. I don't wish to hear her denials, her protestations, I wish to let the entire subject alone. No, don't argue with me. My mind is made up. Do you understand?"

"I understand."

"Unlike my vaunted ancestors, I will never write about that accursed Virgin Bride, no matter the fact that she was of great assistance — in my mind, of course, nowhere else, naturally, and not really there as something substantial or nearly substantial. Since I will burn Sinjun's props, there will be no more appearances by that ghostly young lady. Never again. No one will have a word to say in nonsensical diaries in future years. That's the way it must be. I will accept nothing to the contrary. Do you understand, Alexandra?"

"I understand."

"Good," he said, kissed her again, and left her to look after him. She smiled as she shook her head, and returned to her mending.

The employees of G.K. HALL hope you have enjoyed this Large Print book. All our Large Print titles are designed for easy reading, and all our books are made to last. Other G.K. Hall Large Print books are available at your library, through selected bookstores, or directly from us. For more information about current and upcoming titles, please call or mail your name and address to: